When RIGHT is WRONG

A Novel by E. Milton Klohn

Beaver's Pond Press, Inc.
Edina, Minnesota

WHEN RIGHT IS WRONG © copyright 2006 by E. Milton Klohn.
All rights reserved. No part of this book may be reproduced in any form whatsoever, by photography or xerography or by any other means, by broadcast or transmission, by translation into any kind of language, nor by recording electronically or otherwise, without permission in writing from the author, except by a reviewer, who may quote brief passages in critical articles or reviews.

ISBN 13: 978-1-59298-143-4
ISBN 10: 1-59298-143-7

Library of Congress Catalog Number: 2006922710

Printed in the United States of America

First Printing: April 2006

10 09 08 07 06   5 4 3 2 1

Beaver's Pond Press, Inc.

7104 Ohms Lane, Suite 216
Edina, MN 55439
(952) 829-8818
www.beaverspondpress.com

To order, visit www.BookHouseFulfillment.com
or call 1-800-901-3480. Reseller discounts available.

For Sherwood (Woody) Jensen
A man for all seasons...a great friend.
You left us far too soon!

ACKNOWLEDGEMENTS

Every first-time author needs a push to finally put those pent-up words to paper. Mine was given by attorney and author David Lebedoff. I asked wanna-be writer's questions and his kind and thoughtful answers fired the starting gun for this book.

I also want to thank the readers that encouraged me throughout the writing. If I have omitted anyone, please be assured that your comments contributed to the completion of this novel. Connie Barry, Joan Grzywinski, Glen and LaVonne Johnson, Joan Kennedy, Vint Lewis, Bill Lofquist, Wally McCarthy, Neal & Dee Peterson, Bill Rosacker, Stan Knepp for his contributions on aviation, and especially Lori Charpentier, who read and gave good counsel on each chapter as it was written. Editor Glenn Seaberg and final editor, Catherine Friend, who literally cut to the chaff, and to my wife, Dorothy, who listened patiently to my incessant talk about the book.

The 'Army' portion of the book was based upon my experiences as a sergeant in the signal company of an infantry division many years ago. Please excuse any lack of similarity with today's Army.

Other than public figures, and a few oblique references to some favorite objects, streets or people, the characters and events are fictitious and any resemblance to actual persons, living or dead, is purely coincidental.

1991–92

PART ONE

**February 12th, 1991,
Field Intelligence Unit,
Saudi Arabia, 1300 hours...**

Sand...as far as the eye could see, and as close as his fingertips. Small rivulets of sweat trickled down Adam Packard's chest, leaving clean pathways on his otherwise sand-encrusted skin. The sweltering communications tent resounded to the strains of "Bonaparte's Retreat" from an antique 45RPM record player. He wiped his brow with a gritty handkerchief and studied the computer screen before him. The air war was in full swing against Saddam Hussein's Iraqi Army in Kuwait. General Schwartzkoff's plan was developing as a huge multinational force gathered to complete the mission on the ground.

Adam's thoughts were interrupted by a shout from an inner office of the tent. "Packard, get your ass in here," said a lieutenant-colonel slouched in his chair, shirt soaked from the desert heat. "General Rayburn is looking for an officer to take on a highly classified assignment. The specifications fit you to a 'T'. Any problems with my putting you up for the job?"

First Lieutenant Adam Packard seated himself without snapping a salute, military courtesy being practiced in this highly technical command about as much as on M.A.S.H. "What's the job, Colonel? He must have given you some specs since you apparently think I can handle it."

"No details, all he wants is a cunning, strong, combat-trained soldier who can outthink, outfight or, if necessary, outrun any bad guys. Oh, and incidentally, one with the brain of Thomas A. Edison."

"Well, if that's all he wants, no problem," Adam replied. "But how will you get along without all of those marvelous attributes in this snappy outfit?"

"That's the funny part. With all the crap I give you, I really will miss your talents, not to mention your smart-ass personality." Suddenly dead serious, the colonel continued, "A higher calling awaits and you really are the only man I know with all the qualifications."

The next day at 0700 hours, orders came down transferring *Captain* Adam James Packard from the intelligence unit to division headquarters as a special aide to Major General Arthur Rayburn. Adam spent the balance of the day dividing his former duties between two officers and a non-com. The going-away party in his honor kicked off at 1800 and lasted until the wee hours. He awoke with a splitting headache and a taste in his mouth that rivaled camel dung. He downed four aspirin, shaved, showered and, feeling slightly more human, crammed his belongings into his duffel bag. After donning freshly pressed desert fatigues with shiny new captain's bars on the collar, he met the general's driver at 0830 for the journey to his new assignment.

Ninety minutes later, he was escorted directly from the car to division headquarters. The vast difference between the lax informality of the field and this rigid, polished atmosphere stunned him into asking for the latrine. After splashing cold water on his face and running a comb through his hair, he looked a bit more like an officer and a gentleman. When ushered into the spacious office of General Rayburn, Adam was surprised to see a tall officer standing like a coiled snake, relaxed, but ready to strike in an instant. The two stars on his collar proved his rank, but he was the youngest looking, most fit general officer Adam had ever seen.

"Welcome, Captain. I understand we've given you the bum's rush this morning. Can I get you some coffee?"

"Yes, sir, that would be most welcome." As he accepted the coffee, Adam wondered why Rayburn was meeting with him alone. It was customary in such meetings to have at least one or more field grade officers in attendance.

"I'll get right to the point, Captain. You were chosen from virtually all of the officers in General Schwartzkoff's command. The mission is more in the province of the CIA than Army intelligence, but since this is an Army matter, we want to address it internally. Although I cannot give you many details, I assure you that this will be a difficult and dangerous task. If you accept, and are successful, you will find the Army will be *most* appreciative." The general rose and paced the floor. "This information is highly classified and must not be revealed to anyone, should you refuse the assignment. The mission relates to an Army unit that we believe is operating outside the jurisdiction of Army regulations *and* the law. This unit contains officers and extremely well-trained, highly competent soldiers from enlisted through general officer rank. Once you accept and have been briefed, there is no backing out. Your promotion to captain stands, regardless of your decision." General Rayburn sat across from Adam, leaned forward and asked, "Are you prepared to accept this assignment with the limited information I've given you?"

Adam sat back in his chair and thought about the promotion. Was this a suicide mission with survivor's benefits? He hesitated for a moment and then said, "Sir, I appreciate the promotion and your confidence in my ability, but could you give me any other information, such as who I would report to?"

"Yes, you would report to me and one other officer who will oversee all phases of the mission. This officer will maintain primary contact with you, however, I will be in-the-loop at all times."

Adam considered the vague nature of the assignment and the uncertainty of his future, but felt an excitement about the challenge and was assured by the commanding presence of the general officer before him. After a moment's pause Adam gave an answer he would ponder over many times. He would later wonder what his life would have been if he had simply said, "No."

II

February 15th, 1991, Division Headquarters, Saudi Arabia, 0730 hours...

Adam was again ushered into General Rayburn's office. The general said, "Captain, I'd like you to meet Major Belinda Jackson. She is the other officer I mentioned yesterday. Major Jackson is a psychologist, a Ranger and has substantial CIA training. She will be your primary contact on the mission."

Adam returned the firm handshake offered by a tall, broad-shouldered woman whose femininity was not camouflaged by her well-tailored uniform. Her dark auburn hair, pulled back severely, and her glasses gave her a very professional demeanor. Her lack of makeup added, rather than detracted, from her natural beauty. She greeted Adam in a self-assured manner with a rich, melodious voice. "A pleasure to meet you, Captain Packard. I spent a great deal of time reviewing records before yours popped out at me. Your record and background are ideal for our purpose."

Adam decided this was one of the most interesting women he had ever met. He couldn't help visualizing 'contact' with this contact. The general pushed aside the small talk as he sat them down, perched himself on the edge of his desk, and began a story of almost unbelievable intrigue.

"To understand the background of this problem, we must examine some Army history. Not since the Revolutionary War had the U.S. Army operated the way it did in Vietnam. The CIA operated a number of 'hit squads' with their own agendas. They also teamed up with special forces units from all the services for clandestine activities. Some secret Army units had still another set of agendas. These operations, outside of normal procedures and regulations, created a new, dangerous mind-set in a number of young, otherwise dedicated officers and enlisted men.

"After the war, a number of such veterans and/or their protégés were assigned to the same unit and were later influenced by a group of civilians.

"You are aware of the ultra-conservatives who question the government's right to tax or regulate their lives in any way. Most of these people are poorly educated, poorly organized and as such, present little threat to society."

When a buzzer sounded on Rayburn's phone, he rose and pressed a button. "Yes, that's right, good. Send the documents in when they arrive. Thank you."

He turned back. "That was news of additional information on the people I'm talking about. Now, back to the story. The people we are concerned with are well educated, well organized and they have very substantial financial backing for their activities. These wealthy, far-right private citizens have entered into a conspiracy with an Army high-tech unit. We do not know how many members of this unit are involved. The unit is part of a command led by a highly decorated brigadier general who is an outspoken right-winger. Whether he personally leads this action, or is simply a minor participant, is not clear. The Provost Marshal and the CID have conducted a quiet investigation into the rumors surrounding the unit, but cannot find enough solid evidence to take action. They have taken a position of 'keep an eye on them,' which is not enough. This group is far too clever to be caught by casual observation. We have reason to believe this unit has some highly technical equipment that may need to be enhanced or repaired. This may present an opportunity for us to invade their fortress with a force of one…you."

Major Jackson shifted her body toward Adam as she added, "We learned of their 'problem' when they initiated a search for someone with your unique technical credentials. We want to fill that order with a person who could become part of their operation and bring it down from within. We will transfer you into this unit with some propaganda built into your record regarding your hatred of anything even *smelling* like a liberal point of view."

Adam's attention wavered between her words and the mystical effect she seemed to have on him. He forced himself to shake off the distraction and concentrate on her story.

"It will be your job to get on the right side of these people and bring them to justice. You will be given full support from the general and myself throughout the assignment. The names of the unit and suspected participants will be given to you along with the skinny on your new background, ASAP." She reached into her briefcase, withdrew a large manila envelope and handed it to Adam. "Please provide the information requested in this envelope and personally hand it to the general before noon today."

Adam was excused from the office and returned to the BOQ to work on his task. The packet contained two envelopes. One was a summary of a Provost Marshal report from Fort Monmouth. The second was marked URGENT and contained the information requested. The document requested that Adam provide a list of family members, friends or anyone that a smart investigator would likely question about the political leanings of Adam Packard. Puzzled and concerned about this invasion of privacy, Adam's first thought was to tell Major Jackson where she could put her request. His immediate second thought was, 'If I'm committed to this, I'm going to have to do it their way.'

He handed the completed package to the general at 1030 hours. He spent the rest of the day digesting the summary from the Provost Marshal's office, written by a Lieutenant Mack Rogers.

Adam was ordered back to General Rayburn's office at 1630 hours. When he reported, he found Major Jackson alone, seated at the general's desk. She invited him to sit across from her and review a packet of letters. They were addressed to the people Adam had identified that morning. The letters explained that Adam was involved in a classified assignment and that should anyone inquire about Adam's political beliefs, they should respond that he had always been extremely conservative...even *far* right-wing. They went on to say that he was a man of action whom nobody pushed around. The letters concluded by stressing that any queries must be answered in exact accordance with this request.

Major Jackson said, "You may think this is overkill, but the people we are dealing with are extremely clever and thorough. We cannot afford a mistake. Your life could depend on it. Please sign the letters, Captain."

Adam gazed into the major's gold-flecked, hazel eyes, then noticed a few freckles sprinkled across her nose. He let out an involuntary sigh before turning his attention to and signing the letters. She then gave him a dossier with all of his records and asked him to review the information and comment. The first page detailed his individual statistics and background. Adam James Packard, born April 14th, 1964, height 6'1" – weight 188 lbs, graduate of Edina (MN) High School 1982, Bachelor of Electrical Engineering, Summa Cum Laude, University of Minnesota, 1986, Masters Degree in Electronics, MIT, Boston, MA, 1988.

The next page was his military record. Appointed second lieutenant November 1986 from ROTC, active duty, January 1988. Attended Ranger school, Fort Benning, GA, graduated November 1988. Special Weapons Development Section, December 1988–January 1990, Intelligence school, graduated September 1990, assigned to 87th Airborne, Communications Battalion. Promoted to first lieutenant February 1989. Assigned Saudi Arabia, January 1991.

There were no surprises until Adam turned to the third sheet. The confidential performance appraisals shocked him. His last three fitness reports had praised his general performance highly, but his overall rating had been reduced to barely average because of radical and outspoken political beliefs. His promotion to captain had been based on performance only…at the request of his old C.O., not General Rayburn.

Adam looked up from the papers, tongue-tied for a moment as he met her eyes, then he recovered. "One must have influence on high to be able to change a soldier's military record…but after reviewing the PM report, I see the need for it. I have one question. How sure are you that we can pull this off?"

The major replied, "*We* are counting on *you* to pull it off. I'm confident I can provide the necessary support, but no one will be there to hold your hand at every turn in the road. Do you understand that?"

Adam let her comment sink in, finally saying, "Yes, I'm afraid I do. The word *undercover* implies pretty clearly that I'm on my own."

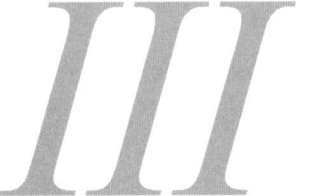

*February 16th, 1991,
Bachelor Officers Quarters,
Saudi Arabia, 0700 hours...*

The phone call was expected. Adam had shaved, showered and dressed in clean fatigues. He picked up the receiver.

"Captain Packard? This is Major Jackson. Are you ready for some honing of your skills and to be introduced to clandestine operations?"

"Major, I cannot express the anticipation I feel regarding my exposure to the world of spooks. When do we start?"

"Enough sarcasm, Captain. This is serious business and I need a serious attitude from my pupil, if that's possible. Please be outside the BOQ at 0730."

"I will be available...and serious at 0730, Major," Adam replied, his sarcasm carefully concealed.

The major arrived in a staff car driven by a young corporal. He joined her in the back seat and was immediately struck by her perfume. He searched his memory, but could not identify the very faint aroma. They drove nearly a mile through the wind-swept desert before turning in to an isolated building with no windows and no sign or identification. The driver left as Major Jackson unlocked the building's heavy steel door. She flipped the light switch as they entered and pointed to a room several doors down a long sterile hallway. The room was about twenty feet square with extensive audio-visual equipment and racks of clothing and makeup stations. Adam was given a full day's training in makeup and matching physical characteristics. The posture and walk were tuned to the age and condition of each character for which he was made-up. The only break was a granola bar and coffee at noon.

At 1700 hours, the major announced, "That should be enough for today. Our driver will arrive momentarily and we will begin again at 0730 tomorrow."

Major Jackson had little to say on the ride back and Adam assumed that she was either bored with the task, or him. She left him with a short, "Goodnight, Captain," and drove off. His interest in her was growing and he wondered what it would take to melt this iceberg.

They repeated the routine for the next two days, moving from make-up to weapons, marksmanship to surveillance. On the fourth day, he was surprised to learn that the training for that day was hand-to-hand combat. Since there were just the two of them throughout this exercise, he couldn't believe this 130-pound woman could possibly handle his 60-pound weight advantage. Add his extensive hand-to-hand Ranger training, and he rather looked forward to having physical contact with this unusual woman.

She proved to be a worthy opponent. While her strength was less than his, she made up for it with speed and cunning. She taught him a number of new tricks and although she said little, it was obvious that she was impressed with how quickly he learned the complex moves. During the entire day, the close physical contact sent bolts of electricity through Adam's body, but to his dismay, it seemed to have no effect on her. At the end of the day, the major announced, "This completes your indoctrination. I have a packet of information which you will take back to the BOQ and commit to memory. When you are through, the information must be returned to me. Nothing will accompany you outside of your memory. Your orders for transfer will be cut tomorrow and we will have a final meeting with General Rayburn before you ship out. Any questions?"

Although Adam felt little confidence in his ability to *get to* this woman, he ventured, "This has been an extraordinary training session, Major. Could we discuss this project…over a drink?"

Jackson replied coolly, "I'm sorry, but it would be inappropriate for us to be seen together at or near this base, or in uniform."

"Somehow, this comes as no great surprise," said Adam, in a icier tone than he intended. "But how will we maintain contact throughout the mission—telephone, or Dick Tracy watch radio?"

"That will be worked out, Captain, but contact will always be made outside of any military installation and out of uniform."

As they drove back to his BOQ, Adam thought 'out of uniform' was just the way he'd prefer to make contact with the icy Major Jackson. This seemed unlikely however, as he received the same formal dismissal that had followed each day of training, "Goodnight, Captain." He was puzzled by her attitude. In spite of her outward lack of interest, he felt a strong sexual tension building between them. She kept such a tight cap on her emotions that his normally accurate intuition was clueless. Her high cheek-boned beauty, combined with an easy grace, was somehow both feminine and military. He imagined her voice could be sultry if she ever chose to express her feelings. He wondered why he was so attracted to a woman who seemingly had no time for him. This was by no means the normal relationship for Adam Packard. Although he had never been sexually promiscuous, he had always attracted the opposite sex with his looks, brains, and open, honest approach to life. Women were torn between wanting to 'mother' him and wanting him in their bed.

Despite many opportunities offered to him, he had always been particular about his relationships. This was a new experience. He found himself totally unprepared to deal with this complex, intriguing woman.

February 21st, 1991,
Division Headquarters,
Saudi Arabia, 0730 hours...

Major General Arthur Rayburn had graduated from West Point and served two tours in Viet Nam as a Ranger officer. He received the Distinguished Service Cross and the Purple Heart for shrapnel wounds in both legs. He returned home in 1969 to his wife, Melanie, and two children. After attending intelligence school he was reassigned to the 43rd Ranger division, which he now commanded. He was the current chairman of an eight-man, multi-branch intelligence committee composed of two each from the Army, Navy and Air Force, one Marine and a CIA Deputy Director. All were of general officer rank and had extensive intelligence experience.

The general shook hands with Adam and asked him to join Major Jackson and himself at a round table. The major acknowledged Adam with a reasonably friendly, "Good morning, Captain."

"How did the training go, Captain?" the general asked with a smile.

"It was outstanding, sir. I don't believe I've ever experienced a week of such concentrated training. The major is a hard taskmaster and I sincerely hope I passed muster in her eyes." Adam looked at Jackson directly as he said this, hoping for a positive response.

Adam thought he saw a slight reddening in her cheeks as the major replied, "Your performance was more than satisfactory, Captain." Turning to the general, she said, "From the training experience, I believe we picked the right man for this job, sir. Providing his mental toughness matches his physical and intellectual prowess, I believe he is fully capable of handling the assignment."

The general had a knowing smile on his face as he said, "Captain Packard, knowing the major as I do, you've just received a compliment. I personally believe you have *all* the tools to complete this task. Your orders have been cut transferring you to Fort Monmouth, NJ. After we complete the briefing, you will be granted seven days leave before reporting to Monmouth."

Adam was given a four-hour briefing on how to gain the confidence of the suspected perpetrators within his new unit and how to contact both the major and the general.

Before dismissing him, Rayburn confided, "The information that interrupted our earlier meeting had to do with the Right Brigade. Although I am uncertain if *every* member has been identified, several industrialists are definitely involved. The leader is the widow of a powerful conservative senator, JoAnn Cleveland. Two others that seem to hold commanding positions are Gordon Foote, Globe Electronics and Richard Thomas, Texacana Oil Co. They and the others have contributed millions to insure the election of conservative candidates...some within the law and some highly suspect. This huge war chest represents both a boon to their cause and a danger to anyone who opposes them. You must be constantly aware that these people are smart, well-financed and ruthless. Oh, and, incidentally," Rayburn smiled, "the tie between the Right Brigade and the Army is none other than JoAnn Cleveland's *son*, Major Jeffrey Randolph."

The general stood and concluded "I know there are going to be many difficult hurdles to surmount in this assignment, but you have my word that Major Jackson and myself will give you the support you need." He shook Adam's hand as he said with sincerity, "Good luck and good hunting."

Adam flew to Minneapolis the next morning. When he reached the gate, George Packard greeted his son with, "Welcome home, Captain! You now technically outrank me, but statistics show that a shave-tail in the Marines outranks a major in the Army."

"Oh, and where might one find such statistics?" queried Adam.

"In the Marine Handbook, of course. As I guide students in the pursuit of absolute truth, I often compare this 'military bible' to the works of Schopenhauer and James."

Adam rolled his eyes and thus began a full week of friendly banter with his father, a professor of philosophy, his mother, a health club owner, and his sister. Each nightly family discussion was a scintillating reward after a full day of heavy exercise and weapons practice.

At the end of the week, he said his goodbyes to the family and boarded a Northwest 727 to Newark International Airport. His smile belied the queasy feeling that was slowly building within him.

February 28th, 1991, 44th Signal Headquarters, Fort Monmouth, NJ, 1045 hours...

Upon arrival, Adam was met by a first lieutenant who identified himself as his driver. Tall, lean and tough was the only way to describe Jeb Carter. His soft Southern accent was a sharp contrast to his angular body and jutting chin. Black eyes that could bore through a steel plate shone over a thin hooked nose. The entire package was wrapped in an exceedingly strict military bearing.

Coming to ramrod attention and snapping a crisp salute, he greeted Adam with a hint of a grin. "Welcome to the 44th, Captain, the best outfit in this man's Army."

"Thank you, Lieutenant, I've heard interesting things about the 44th and if it lives up to half of its advanced billing, it's right down my alley." After picking up his luggage, they walked to the Humvee and Adam began officially working undercover, on the most dangerous job of his life.

Carter drove directly to battalion headquarters and the two officers were ushered into the office of Major Jeffrey Randolph.

"Welcome, Captain Packard," said Randolph with a broad grin and a firm handshake. "The challenges and opportunities are unlimited in this outfit and we look forward to a man like you making a real mark. Lieutenant Carter will show you your quarters and after you've had a chance to stow your gear, we'll give you a treat...chow at our officer's mess."

The differences between Carter and the major were immediately apparent. Height was their only commonality. Randolph was a tanned, well-built man with sandy hair and a winning smile. His steely blue-gray eyes alone betrayed the ruthlessness that lay beneath an otherwise handsome exterior.

Adam saw little difference in the physical appearance of the officer's mess, but when the food arrived, he understood the major's comment about a treat. The gourmet luncheon was served in an elegant manner unlike any officer's mess he had seen. After finishing the scallops with a terrific wine sauce, he said, "Surely this is the Sunday special, Major. This cannot be an example of your everyday meal in this outfit."

"You'll have to get used to culinary delights such as this at virtually every meal," laughed Randolph. "The drawback is that we insist on extraordinary physical conditioning to offset the calories one can gather in this high temple of grub."

"That's right," enjoined Carter with a valiant attempt at friendly banter, "Ever'thing has its price. You up to some hard-ass training, Captain?"

"Absolutely, Lieutenant," said Adam, recognizing the innuendo in Carter's voice and demeanor. "In fact, I relish any challenge…to the mind or body."

Randolph was pleased with the way Packard picked up the gauntlet thrown down by Carter, but he wanted to maintain a friendly atmosphere at this point. He would gradually add fuel to the fire that would test the mettle of Adam Packard. He said lightly, "All in due time. Right now, the important thing is to get you settled in. I suggest you unpack and familiarize yourself with the area. Lieutenant Carter will be happy to show you around and provide any information or supplies you may need. If you'd care to meet us at the officer's club for a drink before dinner, we'd be delighted to have you. Otherwise, please report to my office at 0830 hours and I'll brief you on your assignment."

"Thank you for your hospitable welcome, Major," replied Adam. "I'd like very much to have a drink with you. What time?"

"1700 hours," said Randolph. "See you there."

Although Adam was an excellent drinker with practically a 'hollow leg,' he decided to keep that fact from his new comrades-in-arms. As he dressed for the first social encounter at Fort Monmouth, his thoughts turned to the lonely road ahead. He would have to spend months or possibly years building relationships with men that he would ultimately betray. Lieutenant Carter was clearly an enemy and in Major Randolph, he sensed a calculating, ruthless character under that warm façade. He knew, instinctively, he must never relax his guard in the major's presence. Then there was the cold shoulder he'd received from the elusive Major Jackson. As the only lifeboat in a cold sea of antagonism, she'd have to warm up her act or he faced a bleak future. He let out a deep sigh of resignation, donned his cap and left the BOQ.

He arrived at the officer's club just before the appointed time, but neither Randolph nor Carter was there. At the nearly empty bar, he gazed casually at the wide selection of premium liquor that graced the back bar. When the bartender asked about his 'poison,' he replied, "Do you happen to know what Major Randolph drinks?"

"Sure," said a red-nosed, ample-bellied corporal, "His favorite single malt is the 12 year-old Glenlivit."

"I'll have one on the rocks to see if I agree with his taste."

"Yessir, comin' right up."

Adam tasted the drink and turned to the bartender. "This is damn good scotch. If you remember, you can serve this every time I come in."

"No problem, Capt'n, they gimme me this job because I got a great memory and I know when to keep my trap shut. What we say here stays between me and you. How 'bout another?"

"Not just yet, this is sippin' whisky."

"You said it," said the bartender with a smile. Watching the door through the mirror behind the bar, Adam saw Major Randolph enter.

Randolph said, "Sorry to be late, Packard, but the phone always rings as you head out the door. I suppose you've met our stalwart poison peddler here?"

"Indeed I have, sir, and I must say he knows how to pour a drink."

"Perhaps you'd exhibit your prowess by building one for me," Randolph said. "I believe you know the drill?"

"Yessir, Major, ah'm on it."

With drinks in hand, Randolph escorted Adam to an isolated table at the rear of the club. "Captain, I want to apologize for Lieutenant Carter. He's a good man, but lacks significant social graces. When someone coined the phrase 'officer and gentleman,' I'm afraid they didn't have Jeb Carter in mind. I say this because I want you to understand him for the tough soldier he is. Even though you outrank him, he will be your physical instructor in our training regimen. I have a strong conviction about preparedness and in spite of the fact that we are primarily a technical unit, I want all of our men to be combat-ready at the highest level. Do you have any problem with that?"

"None whatsoever, Major," said Adam, looking Randolph straight in the eye. "I totally agree with your position. I have found that a high level of physical fitness is mandatory for ultimate mental capacity. My mother is a fitness guru and I've been brought up under that philosophy. As far as Carter is concerned, I will enjoy the competition."

"Good, now about your assignment here. As you know, Fort Monmouth is primarily the center for development and training for the signal corps. We work to improve both the equipment and training for signal companies throughout the Army. In addition, we have responsibility for some portions of weapons development, particularly relating to electronic range-finders, sighting and so forth. Our section does not do any basic research or development of equipment, but we test it under field conditions and modify or enhance it to gain maximum effectiveness. We have fine technicians, but we need an officer with a higher level of technical expertise to oversee the review of new and existing equipment. At the same time that you're undergoing physical indoctrination, you will begin reviewing the basic equipment provided to us and the modifications made thereon. You will then report your findings with either a stamp of approval or a suggestion for further modification. We don't expect you to invent a new communication or weapons system for the Army, just make sure they're the best we can possibly make them."

"That's quite an order, Major," said Adam, impressed by Randolph's seemingly sincere attitude, "but as I said before, I relish a challenge. The program you have outlined sounds intriguing. I can't wait to begin."

"Will tomorrow morning be soon enough?" laughed Randolph, signaling the bartender with two fingers. "I'm interested in what makes my men tick and I want them to understand where I'm coming from. Tell me about yourself."

"I grew up in Minnesota, the Twin Cities. My dad was a Marine officer in Vietnam. As I mentioned, my mother is into physical fitness and I have one sister. After getting an EE degree at the U of M, I went to MIT for a graduate degree and entered the Army through ROTC. I'm sure you know what's transpired since I joined the military."

"Pretty much. Did you play any sports? What turns you on?"

"I played football and ran track in high school. Wide receiver, 100 and 220 yard dashes in track. I didn't go out for any varsity sports in college. I enjoy a good drink, a good meal, good music and a good woman. I like sports and the good life in general. What *really* turns me on is working out tough problems."

"You sound like my kind of man," said Randolph as he accepted the drinks from the bartender and held up his glass in a toast.

Adam clinked his glass as he asked, "How did you happen to choose an Army career?"

"My stepfather was a retired Army engineering officer and I wanted to be an Army engineer from the time I was a little boy. I got into electrical engineering at the Point and have been in and around it ever since. This is the best duty of my career. I must add that I have absolutely no quarrel with appreciating the good life. Like myself, I believe you will find every opportunity to fulfill *all* your ambitions here at Fort Monmouth."

Adam thought long and hard about Randolph's words as he lay on his bed. In spite of his reservations about the man, the major had seemed forthright and friendly as he outlined Adam's role. He also had hinted at rewards above-and-beyond normal military compensation. Comparing him with Jeb Carter, he seemed well-bred, a gentleman, but Adam wouldn't let his manner fool him. If Randolph had any idea what Adam was doing here, Adam would be a dead man. As he drifted off, he quieted his fears by thinking about tomorrow's training and he vowed to kick some ass!

VI

March 7th, 1991, BOQ, 44th Signal, Fort Monmouth, NJ, 1730 hours...

As Adam was peeling off his camouflage fatigues, his phone rang. He picked it up on the second ring. "Packard." The voice on the other end was familiar, the tone was not.

"Would this by any chance be the *Adam* Packard I met in Minneapolis last year?" said a sweet voice that mimicked a southern belle.

"Well, I'm afraid you'll have to be a bit more specific. I have met more than one beautiful woman in Minneapolis. Did you happen to drop your name when we met?"

"I sure did, honey, and that's not all I dropped. My hair is blond and we met at the Radisson. Do you remember dancing to 'As Time Goes By' on the rooftop?"

"Do I ever," breathed Adam in his sexiest voice, "Nice to hear from you, 'Lola.' Where are you and how in the world did you find me here?"

"I'm in Newark; I flew in this afternoon for a conference tomorrow and Saturday. I called your folks for your number. Do you think those old Army people would let you off tomorrow night? I'm free from 5:00 p.m. until the conference reconvenes on Saturday morning. I might even skip that if somebody made it worth my while. What do you say, lover boy?"

"I can't think of anything I'd rather do than to make it worth your while. Where are you staying?"

"At the Hilton Newark Gateway on Raymond Boulevard, room 316," she said seductively. "What time do you think you can make it?"

"Depends on traffic, but I should check in about 6:30 or so. Is that too late?"

"You're worth waiting for, honey. Just get here as soon as you can." He heard a click as she hung up the phone. He sat there dumbfounded. He'd love to follow up on Major Jackson's warm invitation. Unfortunately, he suspected that when he arrived, the sexy babe on the phone would be replaced by the cold career soldier he knew so well.

At 6:15 p.m. the next evening, Adam picked up the house phone in the Hilton lobby and asked for room 316. The greeting he received was still Lola. She asked him to come up to the room and he was surprised at how much he anticipated meeting her again. He knocked and when she opened the door, he couldn't believe his eyes. Before him stood a statuesque blond in a form-fitting dress with cleavage that he had only imagined. All he could say was "Wow!"

She took his hand and led him into the room. He hardly saw anything of the room, his eyes fixed on the sexy woman that was Lola, with no trace of Belinda. She said, "Come in, Adam," in the same seductive voice as she closed the door behind him. "Can I fix a tired dogface a drink?"

"After I recover from a severe case of shock," replied Adam, meaning every word. "How about a scotch?"

"Coming right up," said Belinda Jackson in her normal voice, but still friendlier than he expected. She withdrew two Black Labels from the mini-bar and as she mixed the drinks, said, "Before I ask for your report, I should explain the role I am playing and the reason for it. As far as the outside world is concerned, you and I are going to continue a torrid affair that began in Minneapolis last year. In order to make this authentic, I will be very affectionate when we're in public. That is strictly an act, played for that special audience, and will not carry forward to times when we're alone. We must be extraordinarily cautious because of intelligence we have received since our last contact. It seems that a very resourceful rogue agent of the CIA is involved with this group. His name is Sean Ball and although he left the agency, we have reason to believe he has maintained contacts there. He is a very dangerous adversary. For cover, I have established a business relationship in New Jersey that will give me an excuse to visit on a regular basis. We will 'do the town' when I visit."

"It sounds like the 'public' part of the program is going to be far more interesting than the 'private' part," said Adam with a grin.

"Cool it," she said, all business. "The public part will occupy most of our waking hours. The only hitch is that you will have to share the hotel room with me when I'm in town. That comes under the private part where I resume the role as your superior officer. You will reverse your lover-boy role and once again become an officer and a gentleman."

"Since I assume the role of officer and gentleman requires that I sleep on the couch, cold showers will be in order after I portray the lover boy outside of the room all evening. Seriously, Major, I will play the role you've outlined to the best of my thespian ability."

"Good," said Belinda. "Now tell me everything that's happened since you arrived at Fort Monmouth."

Adam told of his meetings with Carter and Randolph and the impressions he gained. He also told of his entry into equipment assessment and the fact that he had not seen anything unusual in the way of equipment. She asked about the physical training he had mentioned.

He began with, "From the first meeting, I had the impression that Jeb Carter had it in for me. I'm not sure if it was personal or that he felt I was invading his territory. In any event, we had quite a week in the field. I want to thank you for some of the tricks you taught me in the desert. When we got into hand-to-hand, even though he was very good, my extra tricks did him in every time. I think if he'd had a weapon in his hand, he'd have killed me. Toward the end, I let him win a few points to cool his anger. I played the tough guy and still acted a little friendly, but he wasn't buying. I really have to watch my back with this guy. Randolph got involved in part of the aerobic training and some shooting. He's good too, but I beat him by just enough to keep him trying, and not get sore about it. I met the non-coms involved, but didn't spend enough time to form any opinions, except that they're a tough bunch."

"When you were doing hand-to-hand with Carter, did you use your special martial arts skills?" asked Belinda.

"Only a few." Adam was very serious as he said, "Although he displayed a few lethal moves, I had the opportunity to kill him a number of times."

"I'm glad you're keeping something back. You never know when you may have to take on several at one time and you always want them to underestimate your abilities. How long do you think they'll pursue the testing, on a physical basis that is?"

Adam replied, "I think that will slow down…soon, although Carter may try something at any time. If he could arrange a serious or fatal 'accident' without pointing any blame toward him, I think he'd do it. This will be more likely after I have accomplished the primary goal they've set for me."

"Randolph's apparent opinion of Carter could play into our hands. If Carter tried something after you've gotten your nose under the tent, your dealing with him could be a final test. I don't think Randolph would have a problem if you were forced to take drastic steps with Carter, but the non-coms involved might have a different idea. In any event, you have to be very, very careful. What about the technical part of your assignment? Have you suggested any ways to improve the equipment you've tested?"

"Just a few minor things so far. The equipment they've shown me to date is pretty basic, well-tested stuff. I expect them to gradually work me up to the newer, high-tech equipment at the same time they're assessing my loyalty."

Belinda stood and once more Adam was startled by her beauty and sensuality. She asked, "Are you hungry? I suppose we should make a public appearance in case anybody's looking. Just remember, my exaggerated show of affection is just an act."

"Yes, to both the question and the statement. However, it would be easier for me if you dressed down just a bit. You're impressing more than the outside audience with that look."

"I'm dressed to establish your image. You are playing a hard-ass who's expected to be hot. We don't want you dating some virgin that looks like your high school sweetheart," she said as she picked up a light coat that matched her dress.

As Adam held her coat, her perfume invaded his senses and he had to force himself to refrain from embracing her. It was the same scent she wore in Saudi Arabia, but not subtle this time. He asked, as they left the room, "Is that, by any chance, Estée's 'Pleasures Intense' you're wearing?"

She turned and gave him a dazzling smile. "Right on the nose, baby."

They walked across the street to Don Pepe's and ordered a bottle of Spanish Red to go with a dinner right out of Madrid. As advertised, 'Lola' had her hands on some part of Adam throughout the meal. When they finished and the check was presented, Adam said, "What about a little nightclubbing, babe, maybe find a dance band?"

With the waiter standing by the booth, she said in a throaty whisper, "Honey, we don't need to go out on the town for entertainment, let's just go to the room and see if anything interesting happens."

"You got it, love." Adam said as he signed the credit card slip and slipped out of the booth. "Let's go." They left the restaurant holding hands and continued all the way through the lobby to the elevators at the Hilton. Inside the room, Belinda said, "Now, if you'll excuse me, I'm going to change into something more comfortable." When she returned, he was not surprised to see her dressed in sweats, with little makeup, somewhat matted auburn hair and glasses. All the glamour was gone, but the beauty was still very apparent to Adam. They discussed her return from Saudi Arabia and her 'arranged' job to justify her trips to Newark. After an hour, she said she was turning in and bade Adam a pleasant good night. He pulled out the sofa bed and began a night of fitful sleep, always thinking of the woman sleeping just a room away. If she continued to frustrate him to this extent, this could be the hardest part of the assignment.

VII

March 28th, 1991,
44th Signal, Fort
Monmouth, NJ,
0930 hours...

The physical training regimen gradually eased in the second week, now reduced to Adam's running and weight training on his own. He was glad he was able to complete the competition with Carter without forcing a showdown.

Major Randolph's friendly demeanor, however, had turned stern and demanding. He insisted on a level of detail in Adam's daily reports that was beyond normal Army reporting procedure. This attitude was largely reversed the day Adam drove up with a nearly new Porsche 911. The car was part of the strategy to paint Adam as a guy in the fast lane needing outside income to fund a champagne lifestyle. The major still held Adam's feet to the fire regarding his research, but adopted more the attitude of a mentor who was bringing a bright student along. There were no specific promises made, but hints at opportunities abounded.

Two things swayed Randolph from careful mentor to cautious collaborator. First was the formal post reception and dance honoring Fort Commandant General Thomas Maxwell. Adam and Belinda made quite an impression.

Adam had met Belinda in Newark on the previous Saturday morning. A pleasant lunch led to a thorough reporting session that afternoon. After their conversation, Belinda excused herself to dress for the dance. When Adam viewed the result, she, once again, literally astounded him. Her beautiful hazel eyes were now blue via contacts and her blond hair was very stylish compared to the sexy wig she had worn previously. The dress really did it. The light blue formal flattered her sumptuous body in a perfect blend of elegant style and restrained sensuality. The 'easy' woman she had portrayed at their first meeting was transformed into a classic beauty that would be accepted in any level of society. The color of the dress also complimented Adam's finely tailored dress blue uniform with the captain's bars woven in gold on civil war style epaulets. To call them a handsome couple was the understatement of the year. They met Major Randolph upon arrival and after greeting Belinda with a very appreciative eye, he insisted that they meet the general and his guest, JoAnn Cleveland. When they were presented, both hosts eyed them carefully, the general carefully noting Belinda's beauty and JoAnn with a warm smile and lingering handshake with Adam. When JoAnn turned to Belinda, her smile hid any sign of female jealousy and was rather one of admiration. She said, "My, you two are certainly the most attractive couple at the ball. Tell me, Captain, where did you find this captivating creature?"

Adam smiled his best smile and said, "You are most kind, dear lady. I found her right in my backyard…Minneapolis. Lola currently has significant business in Newark and that has, once again, allowed me the pleasure of her charming company." He bowed to Belinda as he completed his oratory.

She gave a slight curtsy in acknowledgement as she turned to JoAnn. "We appreciate your kind words, Mrs. Cleveland, but I must say that you and the general are the most striking couple I have seen… here or elsewhere." To Maxwell she said, "General, you certainly run a class organization. I'm most impressed with the people honoring you at this splendid ball. Congratulations."

Bowing to Belinda, Maxwell said, "It seems we have formed a mutual admiration society. Perhaps you would do us the honor of changing partners during the dance?"

"We'd be delighted, sir, although Mrs. Cleveland may find me a poor substitute for your expertise," said Adam with a guileless smile.

"I seriously doubt that, Captain, but you will find JoAnn an outstanding dance partner." Looking at JoAnn, Maxwell continued, "My dear, I fear you will sacrifice little by dancing with the handsome captain…as long as you don't begrudge me the pleasure of dancing with his charming partner."

With a broad smile, JoAnn responded, "Of course not, Tom, I'm even laying odds that the captain is far more capable than his modesty allows, and I look forward to a place on his dance card." With that the general turned to greet the next guests in line and the contrived 'old South' conversation came to an end.

When the general tapped Adam on the shoulder during a Rumba, he turned and JoAnn slid effortlessly into his arms. His mother's insistence on training him in everything from ballet through modern dance was required for his entry into serious martial arts. With the obvious dancing skills of his older, but most attractive partner, they were soon the envy of the floor. The other dancers gradually fell away and the general and Belinda were the only other dancers remaining. The assembled guests greeted them with enthusiastic applause as the two elegant couples left the dance floor. As they returned to the general's table JoAnn said, "I'm always looking for interesting guests to entertain at my home in Arlington and I would be pleased if you and Lola would honor me with your presence. Perhaps sometime soon?"

"Thank you, Mrs. Cleveland," replied Adam, "We'd be delighted. I'm available any time and I'm sure Lola can give you fairly firm dates for her trips to New Jersey."

"I'll check with you to see when we can arrange something." She smiled as she gave him her hand. "It's been a genuine pleasure, Captain. I look forward to seeing you again...soon."

As they drove back to Newark, Belinda said, "You really did a job on old JoAnn, ace. I just hope she didn't evoke any jealousy on the part of Maxwell."

"Hey, he was too busy mooning over you to notice what little JoAnn was up to, but do I sense a hint of jealousy on Lola's part?"

"In your dreams, boy. I must admit I enjoyed spending the evening on your arm, but, remember, the lovey-dovey act is still just an act."

Adam spent another fitful night with the proximity of Belinda, once again working his hormones into a frenzy. At breakfast, she recalled the events of the evening in a surprisingly friendly manner. Adam was encouraged to downplay the somewhat sarcastic tone he had adopted as a defense mechanism. He took an active interest in what Belinda was saying while carefully masking any signs of coming on to her. As the day wore on, they became more comfortable with one another and Adam's frustrations began to lessen.

By the time he dropped her off at the airport, his courage had risen to the point of trying for a kiss goodbye; after all, they were in public, and he was just acting. He parked the Porsche and removed her bag from the tiny trunk. When he met her at the curb, he put down the bag and took her in his arms. She stiffened at first and then put her arms around him, pressed her body to his and gave him a warm lingering kiss. "See you soon, honey," she said, smiling as she picked up her bag and headed for the terminal. Adam stood transfixed for several minutes. Finally, he came to and managed to get in the car and drive back to Fort Monmouth. He was still feeling giddy when he approached the gate and it wasn't until he pulled into his parking area that he finally returned to the harsh reality of his dangerous mission.

The second breakthrough with Major Randolph occurred the next morning when Adam made an unusual proposal to his commanding officer. He had entered the office at 0800 hours and placed his briefcase on the major's desk. "I believe I have a significant business opportunity to discuss it with you, sir."

"Well that's certainly an unusual proposition from one Army officer to another, but you have piqued my curiosity, Captain. Please go on."

"When I was examining the XP-33 laser multiplier, the thought occurred to me that the basic technology could be applied to a security system that would virtually defy tampering. When the usurper attempted to enter the code with any bypass device, the laser would shut it down and sound the alarm. Only properly programmed cards or remote devices would bypass this protection. Now there is no connection between the Army equipment and this concept other than the basic laser technology. I have no doubt that such a device would qualify for a patent and be commercially viable."

"That's interesting, Packard. I am impressed not only with your ability to translate a basic technology to an entirely different application, but with your entrepreneurial spirit. You are exactly the kind of man we have needed in this outfit for a long time. I will think on your proposition and get back to you, Captain…Good work."

Adam reflected on not just their conversation, but the enthusiastic reception it evoked in Randolph. The major had taken the bait, hook, line and sinker.

VIII

*April 13th, 1991,
Arlington, VA, 6:30 p.m....*

JoAnn Cleveland took Belinda's hand in both of hers as she welcomed her and Adam to her sumptuous home. She led them through the expansive hallway to a sitting room larger than some ballrooms. A magnificent grand piano graced one corner and several conversation areas contained a well-chosen assortment of conservative contemporary and antique furniture. JoAnn guided them to a seating area centered on a huge stone fireplace with a roaring fire. She referred to them with glowing remarks as she introduced them to Gordon and Alyce Foote and Richard and Cynthia Thomas. Foote was a huge man who dwarfed his diminutive, dark-haired wife, while Richard Thomas was smaller than his tall, voluptuous spouse. Drinks were ordered and JoAnn said, "I'm sorry that all of my guests have not arrived, but we will punish their tardiness by starting the festivities without them." As she said this, the drinks were delivered followed by an elegant array of hors d'oeuvres. JoAnn was dressed in an orchid creation that perfectly displayed her figure and complimented her jet-black coiffure and peaches-and-cream complexion. Her every motion was feminine and graceful, but with an unmistakable air of authority. In spite of Belinda's youthful beauty, enhanced by a stunning green dress, JoAnn retained the center of attention.

She began the conversation with, "Adam, Gordon is CEO of Globe Electronics and I'm sure you two have a lot of technical expertise in common. Richard owns Texacana Oil and he also knows his way around the world of science. I'm going to take the ladies on a short tour of my new décor while you do your men-talk." With that she escorted the ladies to unknown destinations within her spacious home. Richard Thomas asked Adam about his background and Adam explained his education and Army assignments. Of his current project, he said, "I'm fascinated with my role as an investigator and 'wanna be' enhancer of some of the Army's most complex communication and weapons systems."

"Just how do you go about this analysis?" boomed Gordon Foote with genuine interest.

"In analyzing the efficiency of any system or weapon, one must first know the purpose, then what level of performance is expected and finally, the various technologies the designers have employed to achieve that performance level. It's my job to study the system from the ground up to see if I can determine ways to—and this is in order of importance—make it more efficient, make it more simple, thereby avoiding malfunction and/or excessive maintenance, and finally, make it less expensive to produce."

"Sounds like quite an order to me," said Richard Thomas. "Have you actually accomplished any of these lofty goals?"

"Not to any significant extent and this is for two reasons. First, I have more or less started at the bottom of the totem pole. By this I mean, the initial projects I have undertaken have been on older, simpler equipment that has been tested in the field and gone through many reappraisals. What I have accomplished is to establish a methodology to get to the meat of the issue with minimum wasted time and effort I expect some viable results as we move on to newer, more complex equipment."

"Interesting," mused Foote. "I'll bet you will stumble across a number of commercial applications for some of the technology you will be studying. Think that's a possibility?"

Adam thought this comment could relate to his conversation with Randolph, but felt that he should play dumb until the connection was clear. He replied, "It's quite possible, but it would be pure speculation to anticipate anything of substantial value in that regard."

"Well, it certainly wouldn't hurt to keep your eyes peeled for any opportunity that pops up," Foote said with a smile. "Meanwhile we should probably have another pull on the pump while we wait for the girls to return. I saw JoAnn hit this button and the waiter popped out like a racehorse coming out of the starting gate." With that, he pressed the button and, as predicted, the waiter arrived at once.

The ladies reappeared with several additions to the party. Jeffrey Randolph greeted the three men with smiling familiarity and JoAnn stepped forward and introduced Sean Ball to Adam as a former member of the CIA and now a private contractor specializing in all phases of security. She told Ball about Adam's work with Jeffrey and the high expectations they had for him. As Adam exchanged a firm handshake with Ball, he looked squarely in his dark eyes and said, "A pleasure meeting you, Sean. Major Randolph speaks very highly of your talents." He saw a slight change in Ball's eyes and recognized the animal magnetism that would attract any female and guarantee danger to any adversary.

Ball slashed a sardonic smile. "I'm sure Jeffrey exaggerates, Captain, but I guess you and I will have an opportunity to get to know each other better as time goes by."

JoAnn interrupted the exchange as she introduced a comely woman as Anita Warwick. She said nothing of Ms. Warwick's background, but Adam would soon learn of her talents.

When they adjourned to the large, lavish dining room, JoAnn personally escorted each guest to their appointed place at the table. Belinda was seated between Sean Ball and Jeffrey Randolph, and Adam had Anita Warwick and the hostess on his flanks. Just moments after they were seated, Ball turned to Belinda and said in a low voice, "I'm surprised that Ms. Cleveland would risk inviting a rare beauty such as you. She normally plays the 'Belle of the Ball' role, and I would be careful that she doesn't cut you off at the knees."

"Thank you for the compliment and warning, but regarding Ms. Cleveland, I've not seen that side of her in our brief acquaintance. She mentioned that you had been with the CIA. Did you leave recently?"

"It's been a while. I worked for the agency for over ten years. I escaped to the private sector about eight years ago. Why do you ask?"

"Just curious, the mystery of the spy thing has always fascinated me. I've read Ludlum and Follett since I was a teenager and always envied the danger and adventure that you people encounter."

Ball laughed. "Yeah. The real world of agents is not as romantic as books peddle it to be. If they recorded a day-by-day account of the average CIA agent, it would only sell as a cure for insomnia. I get more excited working for a complex woman like JoAnn than I did as a field agent."

"That's interesting," said Belinda, "Why does she require the security services of an expert of your caliber?"

"Security means more than just personal or property protection. My company provides many services to JoAnn and her associates. I'd blab more, but as a reader of spy thrillers, you know the cost of loose lips. We make a habit of keeping a zipper on it."

Meanwhile, across the table Adam was searching his memory for the identity of his dinner partner. The name Anita Warwick was vaguely familiar and since she could be famous, he was careful not to display his ignorance by asking her profession. He made the mistake of thinking he was on safe ground with, "Perhaps you are used to surroundings such as these, but I'm somewhat overwhelmed."

Anita tilted her head as she smiled. "My home is not in this league, but in my work I'm frequently exposed to similar opulence. Since you are so modest about your lodgings, may I assume that you live on an Army base?"

"You may. I was recently transferred to Fort Monmouth and I work under Major Randolph. I have been so busy since the transfer that I've had no time to think about improving my habitat by moving off post."

"May I ask what you do for the Army? Are you a shooting soldier or a technical wizard?"

It was Adam's turn to smile. "Mostly technical, but we do keep our hand in as infantrymen. I'm an electrical engineer and work primarily with communications equipment. You mentioned your work and I must apologize for my ignorance. Your name is very familiar, but I cannot for the life of me recall what you're famous for."

She laughed. "I thought you were either teasing or fishing when you opened with that line about JoAnn's mansion. I'm afraid my fame is limited and I'm flattered that my name is even vaguely familiar to you. My livelihood is my voice, I'm a singer. I do a little opera, but primarily musical theater and recording. I will sing for my supper here tonight…well, for a little more than my supper. I do this for a few select people and JoAnn is one of my favorites. She's an amazing woman, don't you agree?"

"Without question," Adam agreed. "She is obviously a very powerful woman, brimming with wit, glamour and grace. Both Lola and I are impressed with her and feel lucky to be on her guest list this evening."

"Don't sell yourself short, Adam. You and Lola are the kind of super-attractive people that JoAnn likes in her entourage. If you play your cards right, you'll be back."

At that moment, JoAnn called for attention with a tap on her wineglass. "Thank you all for coming this evening. I'm particularly honored to welcome Adam and Lola and our lovely songbird, Anita. When we finish our dessert and cognac, we will adjourn to the drawing room for an entertainment treat. Meanwhile I propose a toast to all of you for the special places you have in my heart."

The dinner guests raised their wineglasses and Gordon Foote said, "I should like to toast our lovely and gracious hostess. May your reign as 'Queen of the Potomac' be long-lived and ever-fruitful."

Following dessert and outstanding piano and vocal renditions of show tunes by Anita, the party began to break up. As Adam rose, JoAnn put her hand on his arm. "I would appreciate it if you and Lola could stay for a bit after the others leave. I'd like to have a word with you."

"Of course," replied Adam. He went over to Lola and said in a low voice, "JoAnn has asked us to stay for a bit, to talk. Watch her body language and if she seems to want a private conversation with me, you know what to do."

"Thank you for your confidence in my ability to interpret her intentions. I will be a good little girl and disappear if it seems appropriate," said Belinda, her glare matching her sarcasm.

Adam smiled. "Well, well, aren't we thin-skinned this evening? I'm fully aware of your mental abilities and hope you can forgive a poor foot soldier who is obviously ill-trained in psychological warfare."

When JoAnn joined them, she began with, "I'm so happy you two could be with us this evening. Your presence brightened the party considerably. Now I'd like to ask you a favor. I would like you to meet a senator that is somewhat of a problem. He is a liberal Republican who serves on the Senate Armed Services Committee. The problem is that he is unwilling to commit appropriate resources to sophisticated weaponry for the armed forces. The fact that he has a scientific background compounds the problem. As a Ph.D. in physics, he believes he is a master of all technologies. He is relatively young, divorced, and has an eye for the ladies. That's where you come in, Lola. With your beauty and charm, you could attract the moth to the flame, and the flame, in this case, would be Adam. Before you meet him, Adam, you will be well briefed on the issues and hopefully, with your technical expertise, you won't be beat up the way lobbyists have been, trying to talk some sense into him. Also, as a line officer who is not known to have a political agenda, you would be a perfect source for an ongoing relationship with the senator. There would be ample rewards for both of you for taking on this project. Are you interested?"

Adam looked at Belinda with a questioning eye. After receiving a smile for a reply, he said, "I certainly would enjoy the challenge. How do you feel about it, honey?"

"As long as I could fit it into my schedule, I'd enjoy helping to lead a big-brain senator down the primrose path. My interest, however, would depend upon just how far down that path I'm expected to lead him," Belinda said, looking JoAnn straight in the eye.

"Oh, nothing like that, dear. You simply need to show enough interest in him for Adam to receive a meaningful introduction. I'll orchestrate it from there. Shall we say we have a bargain?"

"Absolutely," said Adam as he extended his hand to JoAnn with a smile. "I'll have Lola send you her schedule so you can arrange a meeting. I'm sure Major Randolph will allow me time off for the grand purpose of enhancing the funding of Army projects."

JoAnn took his hand and laughed. "That, Adam, is the least of our problems. I'm certain you will be allowed all the time you require, not only for meetings, but preparation time as well." She turned to Belinda and offered her hand as she said in a serious tone, "I have played this role before, my dear, and I will give you all the information you need before you meet the senator."

As she watched Adam and Lola descend the stairs, arm in arm, a melancholy mood swept over JoAnn. Her thoughts returned to that day, long ago, that began with such glorious anticipation.

She recalled stepping from her bath. She appraised her body in the full-length mirror. Breasts of ample size with little sag. Hips full, but not excessive. Butt holding up nicely. Long shapely legs. Altogether a most desirable woman. As she rubbed cream sensuously over her body, she thought of her husband. He would return from a week overseas in a few short hours. How had she found such a perfect match? A wonderful lover and her equal in ambition and intellect, all wrapped in a handsome package. She felt a familiar wetness between her legs…just thinking of him.

Upon his return, they had dressed and when they entered the ballroom, were the most admired couple in the room. After dinner he received tremendous applause as he stepped to the podium to deliver the keynote speech. She remembered his eloquence so well…and then it happened. A shot rang out and her beloved husband, Senator John Cleveland, slumped to the floor. She held him to her breast as the life ebbed from his body. When she recovered from the initial shock, she made a vow. The vow to avenge his death…a vow that had become the passion of her life.

She brushed a tear from her eye as her thoughts returned to the present. "Yes, I'm sure of it, Adam and Lola will become serious players in the plan, *my* grand plan."

*April 13th, 1991,
Arlington, VA, 9:50 p.m....*

As they waited for the Porsche to be brought up, Adam relayed his suspicions to Belinda, "Our parking attendant looked a little too professional to be parking cars. I may be paranoid, but just in case, let's play 'Adam and Lola' until I can go over the car, okay?" Belinda nodded as the car arrived.

Adam gunned the Porsche across the I-95 bridge as they entered the District from Arlington. They had registered at the Embassy Suites near the Capitol and planned to bum around D.C. the next morning before driving back to Newark. The radio was playing and their small talk was carefully couched in case the wrong ears were listening. As they walked from the car to the hotel, Belinda said, "Whew, it's good to be off the stage and able to talk about what happened this evening. The way JoAnn handled her guests reminded me of a skilled chess player moving the chessmen around the board...with such a deft hand that no one knew they were being manipulated. Her charm is so convincing that it's hard to believe she's capable of the dark deeds attributed to her. What do you think?"

"I agree, but all of our sources point out that as head of the Right Brigade, she must be at least aware of their seamy activities. What is your take on the mysterious Mr. Ball?"

"One tough cookie. He has danger written all over him and maybe that's part of his sex appeal," replied Belinda thoughtfully. "I asked him about his background and exactly what he does for JoAnn. He danced around the subject with the confidentiality routine, but I gathered he does more than 'security' as we normally understand it. I wonder where JoAnn is going with this senator thing. Is she really trying to influence him or is she testing you, and to a lesser extent, me?"

"My guess is a little of both. I think she expects positive results from every effort and sees this as killing two birds with one stone. I'm anxious to play her little game and see where it leads. Maybe we're getting close to being let in on the mystery machine."

Before they entered the lobby, Belinda turned to Adam and asked, "What about the hotel room. Do you think they could have bugged that?"

"It's very unlikely. They would have to have followed us all the way down from New Jersey and I watched our rear very closely." She took his hand as they walked to the elevator. When they reached the suite, Adam opened the door and put his hand gently on her back as he escorted her through the door. She did not resist and said nothing as he closed and locked the door behind her. He was happy she didn't deliver her traditional 'it's only an act' speech as he surveyed the living room of the suite and his eyes fell on the sofa-bed. He knew he was doomed to occupy it for another solitary night of frustration. Since they had time to review his progress, or lack thereof at Fort Monmouth on the drive down to Washington, there was an awkward silence as they stood facing each other.

Adam broke it with, "I'm going back down and check the car. Be right back." He returned ten minutes later and smiled. "No bugs, my paranoia was groundless." He sat across from her and stretched out his legs. "Have you thought about the schedule you are going to forward to JoAnn?"

"Not really, but the first return trip shouldn't be too soon. It can't appear that I have no other clients than those in Newark. On the other hand, we want to keep the ball rolling. We won't have an opportunity to get any concrete evidence on these people until you are fully accepted into the fold. I must tell you, however, that the general is very pleased with the progress you've made so far. It's vital that we don't slip up and that you continue to burrow your way into their lair." Belinda stood and stifled a yawn. "Now, I think it's time for me to retire." She stepped up to Adam and kissed him lightly on the lips and said somewhat huskily, "Goodnight, Adam." As he had at the airport when she kissed him, he stood transfixed. His feelings for her were growing ever stronger with each contact and at last he felt that the iceberg showed signs of melting. Hope tempered his frustration for the first time as he drifted off to sleep.

While Adam slumbered in the other room, it was Belinda's turn to toss and turn. She recalled the strong sexual urges she experienced during the bodily contact in Adam's Gulf training. Those animal instincts were augmented by a growing romantic attachment. She feared she was losing control as both of these feelings were much deeper than she had ever felt before. She thought, "What if I give in to my base desires and invite him into my bed? How will I know if he shares my feelings. Is he just after my body or is it more than that with him? What about the assignment? Will an affair affect our ability to carry it out?' As she pondered over Adam, she reflected on her life, her accomplishments…and her failures, the latter primarily involving romance.

She came from an affluent family in Thomasville, Georgia. Her father was the leading family doctor in town. Her mother was an Olympic swimmer and passed her athletic ability on to her two daughters. Belinda was the younger sister and was a quiet, thoughtful child. Her sister Melanie, two years older, was much more outgoing. They had shared a loving home and were very close until high school. When Melanie reached high school, her talent for singing, dancing and drama put her in every play or musical that hit town. She was extremely popular with both boys and girls. Belinda, on the other hand, was a tomboy who played sports as well as any boy in town. Only high school rules kept her from competing on boy's varsity teams. Many boys were interested in the beautiful Belinda, but her quiet confidence was mistaken for indifference and most boys were afraid to make a move on her. She was salutatorian of her graduating class and delivered a surprisingly powerful graduation address when the valedictorian was unable to speak because of illness. She chose Georgia Tech and graduated near the top of her class in psychology with a double minor in chemistry. She joined the CIA right out of college and went through nearly a year of training before being wooed by the Army.

Her father had been an Army surgeon in the Vietnam War and one of his closest friends was then Major Arthur Rayburn. Belinda's sister, Melanie, was named after Arthur Rayburn's wife. It was Rayburn who watched Belinda grow from a tough tomboy to a strong, beautiful woman with unique abilities. It was Rayburn who encouraged her through the years to accept challenges other girls would not. It was Rayburn who persuaded her to leave the CIA to enter Army OCS. After she graduated and received the gold bars of a second lieutenant, Belinda, at Rayburn's suggestion, applied for and was accepted for Ranger training. She completed this training with the highest score of any female and exceeded over 60% of her male counterparts. She became a first lieutenant while serving in a Ranger battalion and was later sent to intelligence school at the request of now Brigadier General Rayburn. She joined his staff upon graduation and rose to the rank of major before she and Adam met. She had not had ideal relationships with men. Her beauty and grace attracted very eligible men, but her strength and confidence brought out the worst in them. It seemed that no man could resist competing with her. When they challenged her, she also could not resist that challenge, and the result was a badly-bruised male ego, and *sayonara* to the relationship. Over the years, she was hardened by this and when she met Adam, she fully expected him to fit into the mold of the others…but he hadn't.

Sleep comes when the decision that has caused the insomnia is finally made. For Belinda that decision was to show more interest in Adam without going overboard. At their next meeting, she would decide whether the time was right to play her hand…whatever that turned out to be.

May 1st, 1991,
Washington Court Hotel,
Washington, DC,
7:00 p.m....

The Washington Court is located just north of the Senate side of the capitol complex with the Capitol in the middle and the House office buildings to the south. The small but comfortable conference room on the lower level of the hotel contained a bar and a sumptuous hors d'oeuvre table. JoAnn Cleveland was definitely in her element. Dressed in a modest but elegant green gown, she offered warm greetings as she passed among some of the most powerful senators and congressional representatives in Washington. Right Brigade members Gordon Foote, Richard Thomas, and Rebecca Jacobson shared the hosting duties with JoAnn. Also present, in civilian clothes, were Major Jeffrey Randolph, Captain Adam Packard and Major Belinda Jackson, aka Lola Princeton.

It was nearly an hour into the reception before JoAnn introduced Adam and Belinda to Senator Eugene Hawthorne. The junior Republican senator from Oklahoma was average in looks, height and build, but he had a commanding presence that far surpassed his physical appearance. He had been divorced since early in his first term when life as a senator's wife was too much for his introverted wife of twenty years. At 52, he was halfway through his second term. He lacked the seniority to chair any senate committees, but had gained the respect of colleagues on both sides of the aisle. He was admired for his scientific knowledge and ability to assess situations quickly and accurately. The senator smiled broadly, as he took Belinda's hand. "It's truly a pleasure to meet such a beautiful lady. May I ask what brings you to this auspicious gathering?"

Belinda smiled back. "When JoAnn invited Adam she was kind enough to include me in her guest list. I must say I'm impressed with the important legislators such as you that are here tonight."

"Shucks, Ma'am, I'm just a country boy, but I must say, when JoAnn throws a party, there are always interesting people and outstanding grub. Since she and her bunch are big contributors, they can attract just about anybody that operates inside the beltway." He turned to Adam and asked, "Are you involved in the technical or the 'shoot-em-up' side of the Army, Adam?"

"Primarily technical, Senator. I work with communications and guidance systems at Fort Monmouth."

"I thought so. I suppose it's your job to convince me that new weapons development should get a *bigger* piece of a much *bigger* Army budget."

Adam surprised himself as he replied immediately, "That's about it, Senator. Because of our somewhat similar backgrounds, it was felt that I could talk your language. In all fairness, this is not as crass as it seems. My goal is simply to provide you with technical information on the hardware and its potential effectiveness, not to lobby for your vote on any issue."

"I appreciate your candor, Captain. In Oklahoma, we like a man who says it like it is. It's a rare quality in this place where political expediency is God. I may just take you up on your offer to educate me on the fine points of military hardware. Meanwhile, let's mosey over to the well and the chuck wagon. Only my thirst is bigger than my appetite." With that, the senator took Belinda's arm and motioned to Adam to accompany them to the bar. Both Adam and Belinda were surprised when the senator introduced them to several other members of Congress as if he had known them all his life. JoAnn, always vigilant, witnessed this without missing a beat in her conversation with a House leader. After a period of small talk with a group of 'grazers,' the senator turned to Adam and Belinda and said, "I enjoyed meeting you both. I hope we can get together again soon…and Adam, if you have a card, I'll call you the next time some lobbyist tries to pull the technological wool over my eyes."

Adam handed him his card and said sincerely, "We would enjoy meeting again and I will be delighted to provide information on military hardware to you at any time."

When the guests departed, JoAnn gathered the three members of the 'Brigade' and came over to Adam and Belinda. She began with, "That certainly seemed to go well. You two are quite a team. What is your take on Senator Hawthorne?"

Belinda began. "I was really impressed by him. He seemed very straightforward, not political at all, and I believe he liked Adam from the beginning."

Adam spoke up, "He saw through our scheme at once. The first thing he said to me was, 'I suppose it's your job to convince me to allocate more money to sophisticated weaponry.' I admitted as much, but said my only interest was to provide information, not lobby him. He seemed to be impressed with the direct answer. When he left, he asked for my card, but that's no guarantee he'll follow up."

"From my vantage point I think he liked you both. I wouldn't be surprised if he invited you out in the near future. If he doesn't, I'll make sure you're thrown together again soon." Then turning to the others, JoAnn went on to say, "You all know about the major role Gene plays on the Armed Services Committee and I think we have established an important link between him and Adam. As you know, money doesn't buy everything. Sometimes establishing relationships is more important to accomplishing our goals." Adam had to force himself not to give Belinda a knowing look at the irony of JoAnn's comment.

Adam and Belinda retired to the sixth floor suite JoAnn had arranged for them at the Washington Court. Adam scanned the suite for bugs and then turned off the lights. The brightly illuminated capital dome captured their attention. Belinda said, "I think that's the most breathtaking view I have ever seen. The panorama of the entire capitol from JoAnn's house is magnificent, but this is so close that it exemplifies everything our country stands for. At this moment, all the deception, danger and sacrifices of this operation seem worthwhile."

"I guess I feel the same. The deception I live with is my biggest problem. I'm finding it hard to dislike some of the people I know are evil and would slit my throat in a minute if they knew what I was after.

It would be easier for me to ultimately betray their trust if everyone wore the black hat Carter does. My background relied on toughness, but also on fairness. The old phrase 'it isn't whether you win or lose, but how you play the game' was drilled into me from early childhood and I need to keep reminding myself that these people are ruthless criminals that must be punished."

"When I made the comment, back in Saudi Arabia, about your mental toughness, that was exactly what I meant. I was sure you could handle all of the tasks this mission required, but I also recognized that you were a very decent man and, therefore, were saddled with a strong conscience and sense of fair play."

Belinda was silent for a time before taking Adam's hand and leading him to the sofa. As they sat down, she moved close to him and said, "I guess it's time to level with you about my feelings…and the way I've treated you from the beginning. First, I must explain that my love life has been less than outstanding. Many men have tried to get close, but I always find something wrong. Immaturity or habits often turned me off. The only men I had any kind of decent relationship with were usually older men who had a better sense of themselves. When we met in the Gulf, I found, in you, well…" She stopped, struggling to meet his eyes. "For a number of reasons that are too complicated to go into now, I have kept you at a distance. I don't know what's changed, but…" She reached over and pulled him to her, kissing him tenderly.

Adam was astounded at both her confession and actions. He responded with gentle affection even though passion was boiling in his loins. After kissing for several moments, Adam took her hands and they stood. He wrapped his arms around her and felt every inch of her glorious body as she pressed against him. They kissed with increasing passion and his tongue found her receptive mouth. Just as she anticipated him taking her to the bedroom, he broke off the kiss and in a husky voice whispered, "Belinda, I want to make love to you more than anything I've ever wanted, but you must know that I've never had the feeling for any woman that I have for you. If we pass through that bedroom door, our relationship will change forever. Are you willing to take that risk?"

"Yes, oh yes," she whispered as she led him to the bedroom. They undressed each other slowly and then embraced. Her mouth was all over him as her pent-up passion was released with a fury. On the bed, she straddled him as she kissed his mouth, neck and chest. She moved up to position her breast over his mouth and shuddered as his tongue circled her hard nipple. She moved back down and explored his mouth with her tongue as she guided him inside her hot wetness. He stroked slowly at first and as she thrust herself into him, increased the pace until they neared orgasm. Adam slowed and, without withdrawing, turned her so they faced each other. They kissed hungrily as they varied the pace and depth of thrust, always slowing short of orgasm. Belinda initiated another position change and Adam, now on top, continued to vary the motion as he kissed her breasts. He gradually increased the pace until Belinda cried out as they reached the final crescendo. When normal breathing returned, Adam kissed her lovingly and said, "Do you know how many times I have fantasized about this moment? The actual lovemaking was far more meaningful than my wildest fantasy. I fell in love with you the first day we met and it's been growing ever since, along with my frustration at your seeming lack of interest. Please tell me that this is more than a physical thing with you."

"Oh Adam, I'm so sorry for all the pain I caused you. It wasn't easy for me either, but I was so afraid to lead you on, afraid it would get out of hand. I realize I overplayed the frigid bitch role. I'm not sure what *real* love feels like even though I have been trained to appraise people's feelings. The one thing I am sure of is that I have never felt this close to anyone before. I have this wonderful sense of exhilaration and I want you close to me…in all things. Does that sound 'more than physical' to you?"

"It sounds like we will now be frustrated every hour of every day that we're apart. For my part, loving you and knowing you love me will allow me to endure any hardship I have to face." Adam kissed her and they made unhurried love with passion overshadowed by a sweet oneness of both body and spirit.

PART TWO

May 6th, 1991, Fort Monmouth, NJ, 0830 hours...

Major Jeffrey Randolph sat in his office and looked out at the beautiful spring morning. The trees were in full leaf and the brilliant green landscape was dotted with flowers that had been mere buds the week before. He felt good, in fact he felt he was about to embark on the most exhilarating and profitable episode of his life. He had met a beautiful, exciting woman with a sterling background, and income opportunities abounded between the Right Brigade and the potential of Adam Packard's inventions. Although his wealthy mother had never denied her only son, he suffered from the age-old problem of an ego that required he earn it on his own. As he mulled over these pleasant thoughts, a large gray squirrel ran across the lawn, stopped briefly to survey the scene and then dashed to and climbed effortlessly to the top of a large oak tree. He unconsciously raised both hands, simulating a rifle, and fired an imaginary bullet at the squirrel's head.

Suddenly, his childhood came back...and the pet squirrel he had fed for years before he caught and butchered it. He had thought about his 'first kill' often and the sudden impulse to end a creature's life. It had happened just after his stepfather died. The vivid memories of the past came flooding back. He recalled the insecurities of his childhood. Fatherless until his adored mother married when he was six, he went through a lot of trauma, sharing her love with her second husband, Glenn Hartford. Although there had never been any sexual relationship between them, he realized in later years that he had always had strong yearnings for his beautiful mother. He had hidden the early resentment toward Glenn Hartford and, over several years, had gradually accepted him. They developed a close relationship by the time his stepfather left for Vietnam. In fact, their closeness made it much more difficult for Jeffrey when Glenn returned...a changed man. When he thought back on those years, he realized that the radical changes in Glenn Hartford caused profound changes in himself. He had learned to trust Glenn as a role model and wanted desperately to follow his example as a successful engineer. Not only did he want to mirror his profession, he wanted to follow him in an Army career. Glenn came home from the war mortally wounded, not in body, but in mind and spirit. The once bright, enthusiastic man with so much talent as an engineer had become morose with little joy for his chosen field or life itself. The once kind, loving father-figure now displayed a mean streak that permeated his every action. Jeffrey had always been well adjusted and had never wanted to kill things until after Glenn had come back from the war. He was never sure whether Glenn had done a lot of killing himself or if the endless proximity to death had put him over the edge. His mother had accepted the personality demise of her husband far better than Jeffrey. She continued to be high-spirited and good-natured until the assassination of her beloved third husband, Senator John Cleveland. As she carried out the long-standing vendetta against the liberal elements that had killed her husband, he recognized the same ruthless quality in his mother that he found in himself. Perhaps it was always in their genes, but emerged only after a strong wake-up call.

The telephone interrupted his reverie. He picked it up and said "Randolph here."

"Good morning, dear," said the voice of JoAnn Cleveland. "I wonder if you could come up to the house this evening. I'd like to talk with you about pending social events, some including a young lady named Sela. Are you interested?"

"Indeed I am, Mother. I should be able to get away early afternoon and arrive sevenish. Will that work for you?"

"That'll be just fine, I'll have a four-course dinner waiting for you. See you then." Jeffery hung up the phone and wondered what was up. The four-course dinner meant that Gordon Foote and Sean Ball would be there for the meeting. The fact that Richard Thomas was not invited indicated an x-rated meeting to discuss a "special project."

JoAnn greeted him with a kiss and poured him one of her signature martinis from the shaker. She seated herself and said, "Please sit down,

Jeffrey. Gordon and Sean have just arrived and I'm anxious to place a proposal before you. As you all know, the Eagle is not operable and we have brought in Adam Packard to restore it. So far Adam has passed all the tests with flying colors. We are not, however, ready to entrust all of our classified information with him yet. We must devise some final tests of his loyalty in the very near future as we will need the Eagle soon. As Gordon and Jeffrey know, I have introduced Adam and Lola to Senator Hawthorne. Adam's effectiveness in gaining Gene's confidence will be important to define the extent of his future with us, but will not provide the definitive assessment of how much trust we can place in him. Jeffrey, you mentioned his talking about inventing a commercial device utilizing technology from Army equipment. Suppose we encourage him to follow through on this and file a patent through a surrogate. Wouldn't he be incriminating himself by misappropriating Army secrets for personal gain?"

"I believe he would," said Foote.

"Well then," continued JoAnn, "perhaps we could arrange a double cross by the surrogate and see how Packard handles it. Now he would not only be compromising himself by the initial act, but his disposition of the second part would give us proof that he agrees with our abiding principle that the 'end justifies the means.' I assume that Sean could provide the surrogate. He or she must be qualified to be a seeker of the patent…and must be expendable."

"The expendable part is easy," said Sean after a moment of reflection. "Finding an expendable 'scientist' may be tougher, but it can be done."

"Jeffrey, can Adam actually perfect a patentable device, and when could he have it ready for presentation to a patent attorney?" asked JoAnn.

"I have absolute confidence in his ability to deliver on any promise he makes. I know I can motivate him to finish something in two to three months. I gave him lukewarm encouragement at the time, but left the door wide open. I will have no trouble fabricating a scenario to bring up the subject and to set a early completion date."

"Are we treading on more dangerous ground here?" queried Foote. "We agreed to lay low after the 'Watergate Affair.' Will we have difficulty explaining this to the Brigade or will we expose ourselves to serious liability?"

"I understand your concern, Gordon," replied JoAnn, "but I'm sure Jeffrey and Sean can design this operation to be fail-safe. In fact, I think it would be a good idea if we had another meeting after they have completed the plan. We will go over all the details, answer any questions that may arise and approve the final plan. Are you comfortable with that?"

Foote stroked his chin. "Yes, I can live with that. How long will this take?"

Ball spoke up, "I'll start working on the surrogate right away and if you can meet with me this weekend, Jeff, we could do it within a week. You should get moving with Adam ASAP. His part will take the most time. As far as danger, this is a far simpler operation than the other and you'll be comfortable with what we come up with."

"Okay," said Foote, "I agree with JoAnn that we need the Eagle to gather evidence against the donkeys chomping at the bit to run against Bush next year. Isn't it ironic that the dummies who would give away this country to the have-nots, have adopted an animal held in such low esteem as the symbol of their party?" Foote rambled on. "That reminds me of an old New Deal joke from the thirties. 'Moses said, Pack your asses, mount your camels, we're off to the promised land. Roosevelt said, Sit on your asses, smoke your Camels, *this is* the promised land.' A lot of truth in that. Hey, I know I'm preaching to the choir here, but we all need constant reminding of the righteousness of our cause."

"Well said, Gordon," exclaimed JoAnn, as she pulled the bell cord to alert the kitchen staff. "Now I'd like to serve you a nice dinner before you return to your busy schedules. However, before we move to the dining room, I would like to propose a toast…that this evening's deliberations result in the full acceptance into the fold of a most valuable asset, Captain Adam Packard."

When the dinner was over, JoAnn turned to Foote. "Gordon, would you mind staying a few minutes? I'd like to review a few Brigade issues with you."

"I'm at your command," said Foote with a mock bow.

When the others had left, JoAnn sat on the sofa and directed Foote to a chair. "Gordon, I want to thank you for your support. Not just tonight, or this last year, but from the beginning. Do you remember that first meeting in Seattle?"

Foote replied, "Indeed I do. You know, I've always marveled at how you pulled that group of big industrialists together to form the Brigade. How did you do that?"

"I made a vow to avenge John Cleveland's death the very night he was shot. It took me several months to move from grieving to planning my revenge. I decided at the outset that simply finding and punishing the perpetrator was not enough. I needed to gather a real force and wage an ongoing war against the liberal elements of this country. Then it was simply a matter of identifying people that had similar beliefs… and substantial assets."

"You make it sound simple, but it was a gargantuan task," said an admiring Foote.

"Remember that you and the others are industrialists that have an abiding interest in the economy, and in most cases, military contracts. That made the concept an easier sell. But let's not forget, without you, Gordon, we wouldn't have had the name. Was it Richard, or Samuel, that suggested the name, Light Brigade?"

"Richard," said Foote. "I just said we didn't want to associate ourselves with a bunch of losers. The Light Brigade should have been a lesson for Custer. The dumb shits rode headlong into three times their numbers. It was a gigantic military blunder that killed every last man. With that in mind, I suggested the *Right* Brigade."

"And so right you were. But more than that, without the enthusiasm you displayed in that meeting…who knows what would have happened. You have continued to support our cause, and me, every day since." She put her hand on his and said in a tender voice, "I want you to know how dear that support…and your friendship, are to me."

Foote stood, pulled her to her feet and hugged her. "Thank you, JoAnn. I treasure your friendship and your commitment. I will support and defend you to the death. We've just scratched the surface. We'll make even bigger waves in the future…thanks to you."

As he lumbered out of the room, JoAnn smiled. For a big, hairy ape, old Gordon wasn't a bad guy to have on your side.

II

*May 9th, 1991,
Fort Monmouth, NJ,
0930 hours...*

Adam walked into Major Randolph's office, came to attention and saluted. The major returned the salute. "Good morning, Captain, please have a seat. I have given serious thought to our recent conversation on potential commercial patents. The more I think about the idea, the better it sounds. In fact, I have put some wheels in motion to find a potential surrogate to file a patent, if and when we have something to patent. Just where are we with such a project?"

"I thought you'd never ask, sir," said Adam. "It's in the works and I could have the patent application roughed out for the attorney in a few weeks, a month at the outside. I've been able to move quickly as I'm using some existing security equipment for the base. I'm including a number of modifications to the generic system to allow us to patent the entire device rather than just the laser technology. It could render most of the current systems practically obsolete and make us serious money. Have you given any thought to how this might work, the mechanics and financial arrangements?"

"First, I'm delighted with the time frame you've outlined. As far as financial arrangements, we will, of course have to pay a portion to the surrogate, but I am open to suggestions on the percentages each of the parties should receive."

Adam took a moment to reflect. "I guess the surrogate should get a generous initial payment and then a percentage of the net profits up to a certain, fixed sum."

"That seems logical. Why don't I put together some numbers and we'll go over them together. Covering all these bases will take some doing, but overcoming obstacles is the price of rich rewards."

Jeffrey couldn't keep from smiling as he thought how his plan was developing…both for the proof of Adam's loyalty and for his own financial plan.

"Adam, I like the prospects of this venture. Now I suggest you return to your workbench while I see to the details." Adam stood, saluted and left the office. Seldom, in the course of human events, have two men been so satisfied with their apparent success in manipulating the other.

Jeffrey reported his meeting with Adam to JoAnn and she expressed delight with the fast track Adam had laid out. She informed him that a reception at her home was scheduled next week to put Adam, Lola and Gene Hawthorne together once again. She suggested Sela Pierce would be a most welcome addition to the party, if he were interested.

As a daughter of a former Ambassador to Spain under President Reagan, Sela was well known in Washington political circles. Her role as a freelance fashion writer mandated that she dress well and she was consistently at the top of the best-dressed list. She was also known as a talented interior designer. Although she was quite beautiful and had been reared with all the social graces, she had always been a bit on the wild side. Men like Jeffrey, strong but somewhat dangerous, appealed to her. Unlike a number of her previous paramours, Jeffrey represented substantial money and could also show a good deal of polish when the occasion demanded.

From Jeffrey's viewpoint, she was the most unpredictable, exciting woman he had ever met. To have such a socially acceptable woman was frosting on a very succulent cake. They had met at a stuffy party for the coming-out of a debutante, the mother of whom was friendly with both of their mothers. Sparks flew immediately and they left the party early for a tour of local jazz joints. His first inkling of her kinky behavior happened on the dance floor. When the music slowed, she put her leg between his legs and roughly pulled him to her with a hand clutched to his butt. Shortly thereafter they adjourned to her luxury apartment in nearby Georgetown. The wild sex that ensued was the best of his quite broad experience. They had been together several times since that first hot night and he learned that she was not only fun to be with, but preferred sex in non-traditional settings…like the men's room at the Mayflower Hotel. Jeffery had been afraid they'd be caught in the act, but realized the degree of her resourcefulness when she found and placed a 'CLOSED FOR CLEANING' sign outside the door. Jeffrey hoped they would continue to explore variations on that theme for a long time to come.

III

May 17th, 1991, Arlington, VA, 5:45 p.m....

JoAnn felt an unfamiliar nervousness. She had two things on her mind and for some strange reason found it difficult to concentrate on either. She had used up a lot of chits to manipulate the preparations for the evening. Senator Hawthorne had changed his plan to fly home to Oklahoma City that afternoon and Anita Warwick had reluctantly agreed to break an engagement to sing at a charity function. The other major issue of the evening was the celebration of the fourth anniversary of her relationship with Tom Maxwell. The general had wanted to spend an intimate evening with her and was not too pleased to play the part of the old boyfriend at one of her social functions.

She went to the bar, selected the Bombay Sapphire and painstakingly built a martini. The cool heat of the gin had a steadying effect and she was at last able to sort out the plans for the evening. When Tom arrived, she would take him into the library, feed him a drink and her affection with a promise of delights after the departure of her guests. She would apologize separately to both Gene and Anita for changing their plans…before shooting Cupid's arrow into each of their hearts. She had prepared Anita to meet the senator, but of course, had said nothing to him about the vivacious singer. She was convinced that attacking the senator from two fronts would insure victory for her side. With Adam working on the technical side and Anita from the emotional side, how could this sophisticated cowboy possibly resist? Then there was Adam. If she were twenty years younger, she would have eaten him up. Now she saw him as a bright star in the future plans of the Right Brigade. She wanted to tell him how excited she was about his invention, but knew she must play dumb until the scheme jelled.

The doorbell shook her out of her reverie and she glanced in the mirror before going out to greet the man in her life, General Thomas Maxwell. She met him in the foyer, gave him a perfunctory kiss, took his hand and led him to the library. Once inside, she closed the door and took him in her arms. She kissed him passionately. "Dearest Tom, happy anniversary. I know you would have preferred to spend this evening alone, but I promise that I will be all yours from the time the guests leave until you decide you've had your fill of me."

"I'll never have enough of you, JoAnn. It seems impossible that it's been four years since that first wonderful night. Sometimes I feel it was yesterday and at other times, I think I've known and loved you all my life."

She brushed his cheek with the palm of her hand. "I feel like a young lover, when you first realize that you want someone more than anything else in the world. You're just as or more exciting to me than you were the first day we met. I can't wait until later on, when our private party starts, but at the moment, I can only satisfy your thirst." With that she gently disengaged herself from his embrace and filled his martini glass.

Adam had driven up from Monmouth, declining Jeffrey's offer to accompany him on JoAnn's jet. He picked up Belinda at National Airport and they checked into the Washington Court with memories of their previous stay flooding their thoughts. When they reached the room they fell into each other's arms and moved quickly to the bedroom. After temporarily satisfying their mutual lust, they dressed for the party and readied themselves for the horrendous traffic that lay between them and their destination, just over the Potomac.

Gordon Foote was the first to arrive, followed by two congressmen and a senator, all accompanied by their wives. Adam and Belinda pulled up at the same time as Senator Hawthorne and they mounted the steps together. Hawthorne greeted them with a twinkle in his eye. "Hey, you two, it's really great to see you again. I reckon fate, in the person of JoAnn Cleveland, has miraculously brought us together again."

Adam laughed. "We're delighted to see you again, Senator. I guess you could say that our fates, for the evening at least, are in the hands of our hostess."

Belinda smiled. "I appreciated your refreshingly candid approach at our last meeting and I see you have lost none of that non-political charm."

"I declare, you better be careful, lovely lady or I'll steal you away from this good-lookin' young fellah. If you didn't make such a handsome couple, I'd probably take a crack at it. On the other hand, Adam, I'd be cutting off my nose to spite my face. Should I ask for your advice, I don't guess I'd get honest answers from a jealous lover, so you're safe."

A few minutes after they were admitted to the festivities, Anita arrived. JoAnn was careful to give her an especially warm welcome, without making the others feel slighted. She arranged the introductions so that Gene Hawthorne met her last. Anita looked lovely in a dark red silk dress. Her slim figure had just enough curves that the dress clung to her seductively. She took the senator's hand, looked deep into his eyes and with her melodious contralto voice said, "I've heard a great deal about you, Senator, and I'm delighted to finally meet you."

"The pleasure is all mine, my dear. I have the advantage, however as I have not only heard *about* you, I have heard your lovely voice a number of times." He then turned toward JoAnn, but still addressing Anita, said, "I sure hope I'm not being too forward, but if our gracious hostess would permit it, I would be much obliged if you could be my companion at dinner this evening."

Before Anita could answer, JoAnn interjected, "Gene, you know I plan my seating arrangements weeks in advance and it's no small task to rearrange the table to suit any particular guest. The bad news is that the seating arrangement stands…the good news is that you and Anita just happen to have been assigned seats next to one another…isn't that a coincidence?" she concluded with a wink.

Just before seven, the stragglers, Jeffrey and Sela breathlessly entered the room. JoAnn, ever the actress, hid her displeasure with her usual skill. After welcomes and introductions, she pulled Jeffrey aside and whispered, "Where have you been? You're nearly an hour late."

"I apologize, Mother. I should have allowed more time for Sela to dress. In the future I will arrive at her abode at least an hour early." Jeffrey said this with a leer. Sela had met him at her door in a total state of undress. She had something on her mind, but it had nothing to do with clothes; in fact she had been in a dreadful hurry to relieve Jeffrey of his.

JoAnn replied cynically, "I understand, dear. I hope you had a good time."

After JoAnn seated the dinner party and wine was poured, she rose, raised her glass and proposed a toast. "I would like to thank all of you for making this such a festive occasion. I particularly want to acknowledge the members of Congress who have carved time from their horrendous schedules to be with us tonight. I also want to make a toast to my special friend, General Tom Maxwell. It was just four years ago tonight that we first met and he has brought great joy to my life for all of those four years."

The general stood and raised his glass to JoAnn. "Thank you very much for those words, and you know I share your sentiments. I would like to propose a toast to you as hostess extraordinaire. You not only bring extraordinary guests to your table, you create an atmosphere that motivates each of us to appreciate the character and values of each other." The 'hear, hear's resounded as fragile glasses were clinked with care. The party forthwith devoted its considerable energies to consumption of delectable dishes chosen meticulously by its hostess. Anita and Gene were thick as thieves through dinner and when she rendered a song from 'Oklahoma,' the Senator's eyes glazed over. He seemed totally absorbed with Anita until late in the evening when he took Adam aside and asked, "Will you be in town tomorrow, Captain?"

"Yes, Senator, Lola and I will be spending the weekend here in Washington."

"I scrubbed a trip to Oklahoma to make this shindig. As long as we're both here, it may be a good time to have a little talk. Could you get over to the Russell building in the morning…say between ten and eleven?"

"No problem," said Adam, "whatever time works best for you."

"Well, I have a reputation for cutting to the chaff, so let's meet at eleven and have lunch afterwards. I'll ask Anita if she could join Lola, you and me for a bite…who knows, we may make a day of it."

"Sounds good to me, sir. I'll be at your office at eleven sharp."

Sela Pierce knew most of the legislators casually and had, of course, met JoAnn on several occasions. She marveled at JoAnn's skill at entertaining in a society where consummate party planners were commonplace. The people that caught her eye were the general, with his handsome commanding presence, Lola, whose beauty almost tempted her to 'cross the street,' and that beautiful hunk, Adam. She could eat him alive, but Lola looked like she already had. Sela had flirted mildly with both men and noticed that both JoAnn and Lola gave her that 'don't you dare mess around with my man' look. What she really liked about Jeffrey was his lack of jealousy…in fact, it seemed to turn him on when she gave other men the eye. She was not cut out for a long monogamous relationship, but Jeffrey was by far the most interesting man that had come her way for a long time. He would ensure boredom didn't crush their relationship by introducing her to increasingly wild or dangerous pastimes. He would read her mind as adroitly as he read her body. Yes, he was a keeper, but oh how she'd like to tie that Adam up and have her way with him.

Jeffrey had observed Sela's interest in both men and, as she predicted, felt that unusual arousal that came when he thought of watching someone else make love to his woman of the moment. He knew that many men lusted after a threesome, but normally with two women. He also knew it was a bit strange to fantasize about one woman, his woman, and two men. He had no interest in a homosexual experience himself, but watching the reaction of the woman as another man did her in front of him really turned him on. He felt Sela would be game for a threesome, at the right time and with the right partners. Meanwhile, he would play out the game, watching for signals leading to the next step.

As the evening wound down, the guests trickled out and the last to leave were Jeffrey, Sela, Adam and Belinda. JoAnn called Adam and Jeffrey aside and asked, "How do you think Senator Hawthorne reacted to Anita?"

Jeffrey replied, "I think he fell for her like a ton of bricks. What was your take on it, Adam?"

"I agree. You should also know that he's asked me to meet with him at his office in the morning. In addition, he suggested that the four of us, including Anita, have lunch after our meeting. "

"Wonderful," exclaimed JoAnn. "I certainly agree that they both displayed serious interest in the other. I'm glad Gene has taken the initiative to meet with you, Adam. Perhaps we can discuss your conversation with the senator later in the day tomorrow. Please call me when you are finished with the meeting, lunch and whatever, and we'll make arrangements."

The two couples left shortly for their respective love nests, one to demonstrate their newfound devotion to one another with tender lovemaking, the other to explore new ways to satisfy their inexhaustible sexual hunger.

IV

**May 18th, 1991,
Russell Senate Office
Building, 10:45 a.m....**

Adam was shown into Senator Hawthorne's office just after eleven. The senator came around from behind his desk, shook Adam's hand warmly and invited him to make himself comfortable on the elegant leather sofa located near the large office windows. He poured coffee from a silver carafe, sat across from Adam and said, "I have a few questions about the value of some of this technology and I also want to visit a bit about some relationship issues. First, the high-priced hardware. I realize that you don't have access to information on all the military equipment that the Pentagon wants. From what you told me in our first conversation, you are conducting appraisals on equipment that includes both the effectiveness of the gear and some sort of cost/value assessment. This is exactly what I need to make sure my subcommittee, Acquisitions and Technology, sends the right recommendations to the full committee. Here's a list of a few suspect items." He handed Adam a sheet that described a dozen Army devices, both weapon guidance systems and communications equipment. He continued, "I don't know if they're on your appraisal agenda or not, but if you have time to look at them, I'd appreciate it. I don't want to be buying any goddamn $500 hammers."

Adam carefully scanned the list. "There are three items here that I have either looked at or have on my agenda for early inspection. I have no doubt that my superiors would be happy to prioritize my work to accommodate your needs. I'll take it up with them next week and contact you with their answer."

"Very good, but that brings up the second thing I want to discuss with you. That is your relationship with JoAnn Cleveland and her associates. I know it's none of my damn business, but you seem to be a straight shooter, the kind of man we see too few of around here. So, I want to level with you about these folks. I know JoAnn's a great party-giver who can charm the pants off God, and I really dig her hospitality; however, I've heard she may be involved with some bad dudes and may be willing to go to extremes to get what she wants. Do you know much about her history?"

"Not as much as I'd like. I am aware of her background generally, about her marriages and that she was devastated by the death of her husband, Senator Cleveland," replied Adam.

"That's right and it may have pushed her over the edge a bit," said the senator with a grave look. "Rumor has it that she has not only funneled mega-bucks to political candidates outside of election laws, but has been behind some plots to discredit liberal candidates. Some of these plots have involved injury and death to innocent victims. Understand that she or her associates have never been charged with any crime, but rumors persist. I'm just suggesting that you watch your back with these people. We both know they are pushing hard for more and more military strength and all the expensive hardware that goes with it. Now, with the knowledge I have, and the fact that you've been introduced by JoAnn, I should be wary of putting my trust in you. I have, however, been known to be a good judge of horseflesh and I like you and believe you will give me straight answers. Am I on target, and do we understand each other?"

"Perfectly, Senator, and I really appreciate your concern and friendship. I will do my very best to serve that friendship well…and I *will* watch my back."

"Great, I'd appreciate it if you would send me the results of your examination of those three items and, when available, a priority list for the remaining pieces of equipment. Meanwhile, I'll keep my ear to the ground for any noise on the antics of your friend JoAnn and her buddies. That should take care of our business, unless you have anything to add?"

"No, I will get the data to you early next week. The details on examining the balance of the list may take a little while to get that approved. It should take no longer than a week or so since *you* are the one requesting the information. I may ask you to verify your request to speed the process through the usual red tape."

"Just let me know and I'll grease the skids. Now, I think it's time to join the ladies. Anita is meeting us at my favorite restaurant, the Prime Rib, and we can pick up Lola on the way. Where are you staying?"

"The Washington Court, I'll give her a ring. What time should I say we'll be by?"

"Noon will be fine," said Hawthorne. "If she asks about what to wear, tell her 'business dressy.' And tell her to bring her appetite. This joint knows how to cook vittles."

As the two men left the back door of the Russell, a shiny Black Lincoln Town Car pulled up and the driver sprinted around the car in time to intercept the senator's approach. They exchanged greetings and the driver was given instructions to drive to the Washington Court. Adam followed Hawthorne's Lincoln in his Porsche and after surrendering the roadster to the valet, went in to fetch Belinda. They met in mid-lobby and after giving him a kiss, she took his arm, pressed it tightly against her and they marched toward the door, she said, "I missed you dreadfully. How did the meeting go?"

"I missed you too, love. The meeting went extremely well. In fact, he thinks I'm such a great dude, he warned me about the company I'm keeping."

"He did? I'll bet he told you that if you weren't careful, I'd rip off your clothes and take advantage of you," she said with a seductive smile.

"How did you guess?" replied Adam with a grin. "That's exactly what he said and now I'm going to be on my guard…so don't try anything." As they reached the door, he said, "I'll give you the lurid details later, while fighting you off." They drove through the noon hour traffic to K Street and the trendy restaurant. The head waiter smiled broadly as he shook Gene Hawthorne's hand and said in a middle-European accent, "Ah, Senator Hawthorne, so good to see you again. Your lovely lady has just arrived, please follow me to the veery best table in the house." Anita looked fresh and lovely in a violet dress. Her eyes sparkled like jewels when she looked at Hawthorne. She nodded to Adam and Belinda, then focused on the senator. "What's a down-home boy from Oklahoma doing in a swanky place like this?"

Hawthorne smiled. "Well, honey, I reckon I'm just a tad bit out of my element here, but ah'll try my durndest not to embarrass yo'all." Switching to a very formal tone he continued, "If Madam will allow me, I shall peruse the wine list and choose an appropriate selection to tickle Madam's delicate palate."

With a straight face, Anita replied, "Oh, please do, kind sir. And thank you for recognizing the delicacy of my palate." She turned to Adam and Belinda, pointed at Hawthorne and said, "As soon as I get rid of this stuffed shirt, we can order a coupla boilermakers and a pot of Dinty Moore's beef stew."

Belinda laughed. "I knew you acted in musical theater, Anita, but I had no idea you would be putting on a comedy act at lunch. Will the song and dance routine follow?"

"Hey, a country boy takes a bunch of city folks to a nice lunch and just like Rodney Dangerfield, gets no respect."

Anita rose and with a curtsey to Hawthorne said, "Forgive me, Cowboy Joe, my city upbringing taught me to be charitable to those less fortunate. From this moment on, I promise to always act like a perfect lady in your presence."

"Whoa, there, let's not go that far, madam. There may be a time'r two when I would choose not to act the perfect gentleman…and we would find ourselves in a conundrum." The wine steward was somewhat nonplussed as the order was given with tearful laughter. The banter continued through an excellent meal, augmented with three bottles of fine Australian Shiraz. They left in good spirits, to say the least.

After returning to the hotel, Belinda snuggled Adam in the elevator. "When we get to the room, I want you to tell me all about your meeting while I'm distracting you…being the bad influence, just like Gene suggested."

"I guess you're not too anxious to hear about the meeting, 'cause I plan to give my full attention to the 'distraction' and whatever comes up as a result."

Belinda elbowed him in the ribs playfully. "Don't forget the report you promised to give to JoAnn."

Adam replied, "If you remember, JoAnn said, 'call me when you're finished with the meeting, lunch and whatever.' I think this distraction comes under the heading of *whatever*." Adam did indeed pay attention to the joyous distraction and when they later lay back in exhausted bliss, he said, "Do you suppose all lovers feel they're unique? That no one else could possibly experience the same feelings? This is a first for me, and I can't believe it will *ever* happen again."

Belinda said in a low voice, "Me too, baby. This has never happened to me before, either and I want it to last forever. As far as being unique, I only know that I have never been so happy and I pray that nothing will ever change that."

They kissed tenderly before Adam reluctantly left the rumpled bed and dialed the number in Arlington. While waiting for the connection, he said, over his shoulder, "By the way, Gene was talking about JoAnn, not you." He dodged the pillow she threw as JoAnn picked up the phone. She asked if they had plans for dinner and Adam could hardly refuse. She suggested that she and Jeffery pick him up early for a short conference and she would send the car back for Lola a bit later. Adam showered and while he was dressing, gave Belinda the lowdown on the meeting and the senator's warning about JoAnn and company.

JoAnn and Jeffrey arrived at five in her stretch Cadillac limousine and drove downtown to the Madison Hotel on Fifteenth and M Streets. The Montpellier Room at the Madison is one of the most elegant in Washington and the only restaurant in the United States listed in the Michelin Guide. They were ushered to a round table at the back of the room and JoAnn opened the conversation with, "We'll order a drink and then you can give us a rundown on your day, Adam."

After the drinks arrived, Adam explained how Hawthorne had given him a list of devices on which he wanted an appraisal and the fact that Adam had worked on some of them. He related that he had agreed to talk with his superiors about moving the remaining items to the top of his to-do list. JoAnn was somewhat taken aback when he described the warning the senator had given concerning her and her associates. In this context he said, "If I am to gain his full confidence, I must play it straight with him regarding this equipment. With his education in technology, he will see through attempts to pull the wool over his eyes, and I will lose any effectiveness to sway him."

"I agree," said JoAnn. "Jeffrey, perhaps you should explain our strategy for dealing with the senator and his committee."

"Glad to, and you're absolutely right, Adam," said Jeffrey. "However there are two pieces to this puzzle, the technical merit on the one hand and the tactical necessity on the other. The primary reason for getting you and Hawthorne together is that through your technical assessment of equipment, you have an unusual opportunity to gain his confidence. Once that is accomplished, you will be able to exert influence on the tactical side…how important it is for our soldiers to have this particular piece of high priced equipment to fulfill their mission. From a cost-effectiveness standpoint, we will be making the argument that we can not only reduce manpower with technology, but will be able to lower the physical risks to armed forces personnel. Before you became involved, we have not been able to get this kind of info to the senator through anyone he felt he could trust. You are the key to gaining that trust and subsequently, gaining our objectives. You and I will work out the details to adjust your schedule to the senator's request. I assure you there will be no problem in accomplishing that. This may put a strain on our time frame for completing the invention, but I will assign any help you think you can use to keep both balls in the air. It may be that feeding information to the senator on a piecemeal basis will be to our advantage in that it will give you a chance to meet with him more often…more time to brownnose."

"Sounds like a plan," said Adam. "I've have been thinking about delegating some of the more mundane tasks. I'd like to review the qualifications of some of your men and assess their ability to speed up the process. Regarding that 'tactical need' issue, I'm going to need some education on that."

"Spreading out the work is an excellent idea," said Jeffrey with enthusiasm. "We'll go over both the senator's list and personnel records first thing Monday morning. On the education about tactical needs, that will come in due time."

"I'm really pleased to see you two working so well together," said JoAnn as she took Adam's hand and looked him in the eye. "As for the senator's warning, I assure you that we believe sincerely in our cause, and there are many out there that would like to discredit us. In other words, don't believe everything you hear." She moved closer and squeezed his hand. "We can offer you a world of opportunity, Adam, if you are willing to dedicate yourself to our cause!"

M *ay 20th, 1991,*
Fort Monmouth, NJ,
0720 hours...

As Adam walked to his appointment with Major Randolph, he reflected on the weekend and the hollow feeling that Belinda's departure had left inside him. They had walked hand in hand over much of Washington DC with the scent of spring filling their nostrils and love filling their hearts. Their lovemaking varied from slow and deliberate to frenzied, with each of them trying desperately to meld every part and crevice of their bodies into the other. The exceptional thing about it was the tenderness that accompanied every impassioned moment. He thought about their conversations and how they were just beginning to talk about their individual likes, dislikes and tastes. Before Belinda opened up and shared her feelings, her 'cold shoulder' attitude prevented any such intimate conversation. Now they had a lot of catching up to do and Adam was yearning for their next meeting.

He put aside his reverie as he stepped into the major's outer office. When the sergeant ushered him into his office, Adam came to attention and saluted. Randolph returned the salute and said, "Please sit down, Captain. We have some interesting work to do this morning and we'd better get right to it. I'll trade you some personnel files for the senator's list, okay?"

"Fine," replied Adam as he handed the list to the major. "Shall I look these over here and now, or take them with me?"

"Might as well study them here so we can wrap this up and dive into the work." The two men pored over the material before them, Adam reading the background of a half-dozen men and Jeffrey consulting his computer to identify the items on the senator's list. A half-hour later, Adam put down the last file and said, "Smythe looks like the one I could use. Is he available?"

"They're all available, Adam. This is the number one priority for this outfit and if you can use any more help, just say so. I can also dig into some other outfits if necessary, but I'd like to keep it in-house, if possible. Carter has some pretty good credentials, but I gather there's no love lost between you two, so I didn't include his file."

"I'm not opposed to working with the lieutenant; any animosity is on his part. If you feel he has extraordinary technical qualifications, send his file over and I'll take a look. Do you have any questions about the list, Major?"

"Decide the order in which you want to examine the devices on the list, then I'll get cracking on the approvals. That will be all, Captain." Adam rose and they exchanged salutes.

When he arrived at his laboratory a few minutes later, Smythe was there, waiting for orders. As they began working together, Adam found Smythe respectful of his rank, but hardly friendly. He was quite sure Jeb Carter had 'poisoned the well,' so to speak. Adam knew he'd have to deal with Carter soon and had mixed emotions about confronting him. He relished taking on a worthy opponent, but was concerned about compromising the mission. In his relationship with Smythe, he was careful not to deviate from either military or professional protocol. Adam gradually gained Smythe's respect for both his technical knowledge and how he treated his subordinates. He saw the change materialize steadily over the next three weeks with only minor setbacks, which he assumed came as a result of comments or propaganda by good old Lieutenant Carter. Meanwhile, the work progressed steadily. With Smythe's help, four of the items on Hawthorne's list were completed by June 7th. By working long after Smythe left each day, Adam brought the 'XR-1' security system to a point where the next step was presenting it to a patent attorney. This meant that the surrogate would have to be identified so he or she could present the invention to the attorney.

Although dead tired from three weeks of 12-14 hour days, Adam met with Major Randolph Friday afternoon to report the progress on both fronts. Jeffrey was elated with the news and promised to make the contact for the surrogate immediately. Jeffrey proposed a celebratory drink, but Adam needed to cram a week's sleep into the next two days and so asked for a rain check.

It had been three agonizingly long weeks since he had Belinda in his arms. She was in his thoughts every day and only the demands of his work load mitigated his longing for her. The telephone was his only lifeline and for security purposes, their telephone calls were relayed through her business office in Minneapolis. They had talked several times, but each phone call was a bittersweet experience. The thrill of hearing her voice was replaced by a bottomless void immediately after he put down the receiver. Now, as he lay on his bed, the most urgent tasks completed, he reflected on how completely self-sufficient he had been pre-Belinda. He had lived alone since his post-graduate days in college, and in spite of several quasi-serious relationships, had never felt alone or lonely. He had been totally frustrated throughout his 'wanna-be' relationship with Belinda, but not until their love had been declared did he feel so incomplete outside of her physical presence. He fell into a deep sleep, dreaming of next week, when he would see her again. Only then would the pain be extinguished.

VI

June 12th, 1991,
Washington Court Hotel,
Washington, DC,
4:40 p.m....

Belinda flew into National Airport on Wednesday afternoon while Adam was driving down from Fort Monmouth. She took a cab to the Washington Court and was thrilled when she was shown to the same suite, facing the Capitol dome. When she reached the suite, she found two large bouquets from Adam. As she unpacked, her hands trembled. She knew it was the anticipation of seeing and touching Adam once more. The time they'd been apart had been hell for her and he had assured her it was the same for him. The change in her had been so apparent that General Rayburn asked when she had fallen in love and, if it was any of his business, with whom? She'd blushed bright red and finally admitted it was Adam Packard. Not knowing what to expect, she was relieved when he gave his blessing to the relationship. Rayburn had laughed when he said that most men weren't that comfortable having to take orders from a woman and that they probably should promote Adam so she didn't outrank him. She remembered thinking that if Adam pulled off this mission, he would be in line for more than promotion to major.

Adam arrived at 5:45 and after entrusting the Porsche to the valet parking attendant, hurried to the suite. He knocked and almost immediately, the door swung open and she was in his arms. It was as though they had been apart for years...or only minutes. They hugged and kissed, but stopped short of the coupling they both desired. He stepped back, took her hands in his and with an admiring smile said, "You are without a doubt the most beautiful woman I have ever seen."

Belinda replied, "I want to look beautiful for you, Adam. You know, in a way, I'm glad we don't have time to make love now. This way I'll be anticipating...all evening long."

"Be careful with your tongue woman, my desire for you has a hair trigger."

Belinda put her hands on her hips and shrugged. "Too bad. This show is closed for the matinee. Check with the box office for tickets to the late evening performance."

Downstairs, they ordered a drink in the miniscule lobby bar and within minutes were joined by Gene Hawthorne and Anita Warwick. They exchanged warm greetings and after the drinks arrived, the senator said, "Anita and I have been thick as thieves since we last met and I must admit, we missed you two. Isn't that right, hon?"

Anita smiled at Gene and said, "Right on both counts. Not only do we really enjoy your company, you have a special place in our hearts for the part you played in bringing us together. How long will you be in town?"

"The rest of the week," said Belinda. "My customer in Newark is coming into Washington on other business, so I'll be able to meet with them here rather than spending time at their headquarters."

"Great," said Gene. "Adam and I have some business and I must spend a bit of time doing what the folks back home sent me here for, but we'll have time for some first-class monkey-business over the next few days." The quartet had a second drink before piling into the senator's car and crossing town to the Old Europe restaurant where they each enjoyed the spring specialty, a full pound of fresh asparagus, and a hearty variety of outstanding old world cuisine.

Adam met with Senator Hawthorne the next morning. He wished he could have met Hawthorne under different circumstances. The man was decent and would make a great friend.

Following the meeting, Adam called JoAnn from a pay phone and reviewed his conversations with Senator Hawthorne, both social and business. JoAnn was pleased with the progress in the relationship with the senator. Before hanging up, JoAnn verified the meeting that afternoon with the surrogate, Jonathon Collins, Jeffrey and himself.

Adam was introduced as Andrew Patterson, when he met Jonathan Collins at the J. W. Marriott Hotel, near the White House at 2:30 p.m. Ball and Randolph had met with him earlier and hammered out an agreement regarding the patent. Collins, tall and lanky with thinning hair and a long nose, reminded Adam of Ichabod Crane. When he introduced Adam, Jeffrey noticed an excitement in Collins. He placed his briefcase on the table, shook Adam's hand with fervor and said, "It's a real pleasure to meet you, Mr. Patterson. Your, or should I say *my,* invention is fantastic. I don't know or care why you're not filing this yourself, but I'm delighted to play a part in getting this security system on the market."

"Please call me Andy," said Adam, "and I'm pleased that you see value in the XR-1. Do you have any questions about the description or operation?"

"Yes, I have a few." He pulled a sheaf of papers from his briefcase and put them before Adam. "These are the issues I need to understand better before I present the specs to the attorney."

Adam looked over the two page list and asked, "Would you like me to respond to these in writing or just give you the answers here and now?"

"If you can rattle off the answers, I can file them away, up here, with no problem," said Collins, pointing to his head. Adam spent the next hour and a half carefully explaining each point that Collins had identified. Collins asked a few questions, but Adam was impressed by his ability to comprehend the intricacies of the project.

When the last question was answered, Adam asked Collins, "Are you comfortable with all of it?"

Collins replied with confidence, "Perfectly. I'll be ready to beat down the shyster's door in a week's time. Mr. James, have you made a decision on the attorney?"

"Yes, we'll go with the man you've used before," said Jeffrey. "He has a good reputation and it will be valuable to have the continuity. Do you think he could suspect anything, like why you have suddenly invented a far more complex device than those you have patented in the past?"

"No, though my patents were simple devices, they were somewhat unique. He was impressed with their originality. I don't think he'll give that a second thought."

"I guess we're through here then," said Jeffrey, "but before you go, we'd like to get copies of all the documents you or the attorney develop. And since this is a fairly big project, let me know if the attorney requires more money up front and I'll see that you get it promptly."

When Collins had left, Jeffrey turned to Adam and asked, "Well, what do you think. Did we pick a good man for the job?"

"You couldn't have done better. His background is good, but his performance this afternoon was outstanding. He understands this thing so well that he could walk into court tomorrow and defend the patent." Adam reached over, shook hands and said very sincerely, "Good work, Major."

"Thanks, Adam, I appreciate the compliment, even if I did ask for it. By the way, please call me Jeff, except of course, when we're on duty. When we get a little further along with the senator, I have another interesting project I'd like to get you involved with a *most interesting project.*"

When Adam returned to the hotel, Belinda greeted him with a smile. "Hey, sailor, how about taking a girl for a ride on a big boat?"

"Terrific, babe. Could that big boat possibly belong to the Queen of the Potomac, sometimes referred to as the Dragon Lady?"

"How perceptive you are for just a common sailor. I may have to promote you to seaman first class."

"Now you're talking dirty," laughed Adam. "When do we embark upon this historic voyage, fair maiden?"

"On the morrow, sir. We cast off at four bells, or whatever number of bells are rung at 1600 hours. Now are you just going to stand there or are you going to sweep me off my feet and have your way with me?"

"I sure ain't gonna just stand here," said Adam huskily as he literally swept her off her feet and carried her into the bedroom.

When they settled in the salon of the yacht the next afternoon, the men, Adam, Jeffrey, Gene Hawthorne, Gordon Foote and General Maxwell surveyed the ladies appreciatively. The light summer dresses were not only stylish, but showed off the varying shapes to good advantage. The party began with cocktails all around, wine with dinner and a special after-dinner drink, the recipe for which JoAnn refused to divulge. Adam was seated between JoAnn and Sela and found it disconcerting when Sela placed her hand on his thigh as she reached for a plate. He looked at her and received a broad smile with no hint of awkwardness. Shortly after dinner, Sela beckoned to Jeffrey and they disappeared into the bowels of the vessel. She pulled him to an empty stateroom, locked the door, and raised her skirt, revealing the absence of any undergarments. For some reason, every time she was close to Adam Packard, she felt her passions rising to a fever pitch. Since she obviously couldn't have him, she turned to Jeffrey for relief. Jeffrey, without knowledge of how deeply she was attracted to Adam, quickly took advantage of the situation. They returned to the party a half-hour later looking just slightly disheveled. JoAnn greeted their return with, "Did you have an interesting tour of the vessel, dear?"

Sela looked JoAnn in the eye, smiled and said, "We had a delightful tour. Jeffrey certainly knows his way around, the boat that is."

As the crew tied up the yacht at the pier, JoAnn said, "I hope you all enjoyed being on the water on this beautiful day. I'm sorry to say that this was my last cruise on *The Senator*. I'm donating the yacht and on-going operating expenses to replace the presidential yacht, recently scuttled for budgetary reasons. If you sail on her again, it will be at the invitation of the President of the United States."

VII

**July 10th, 1991,
Fort Monmouth, NJ,
0830 hours...**

Adam missed Belinda every day, but their meeting in Minneapolis over the Fourth of July weekend had been a huge success. He had taken her to meet his family and they had also immediately fallen in love with her. Belinda had returned the feelings and Adam's love for her continued to grow and deepen. He could not imagine *not* spending the rest of his life with her. Any thought of marriage under their present circumstances was out of the question, but he planned to ask her when the mission was completed. He had given some thought to their careers and realized that her commitment to the military was far greater than his.

The telephone interrupted his thoughts and Jeb Carter seemed quite friendly as he invited Adam to a party that Friday night. It would be held at his condo in Long Branch and he mentioned that Major Randolph would also attend. Adam accepted. A second call came, this one from Jeffrey Randolph. He asked Adam to report to his office as soon as possible. When he arrived and completed the military formalities, he noticed the grave look on the major's face as he said, "Captain, we may have a problem with our inventor. He has completed the work with the attorney and the patent application has gone in to the patent office. The problem is, he is not satisfied with the remuneration specified in the contract he signed. He claims he did not realize the potential value of this invention and wants a bigger piece. He wants to negotiate with you, and you alone. I've set up a meeting for you at the Waldorf on Monday afternoon. Does that work for you?"

"That's fine with me," replied Adam. "Am I expected to negotiate with him or play hardball?"

"Hardball. That son-of-a-bitch got more than he deserved in the first place and I don't believe he understands the people he's dealing with. I'd like to see you beat him up good, mentally, that is."

"I understand," said Adam, thinking that Jeff Randolph would be delighted if he were to dispose of the problem literally and it was entirely possible that this was a test of his loyalty *and* ruthlessness. "What time is the meeting and is it in a private room?"

"He is arriving at 1300 hours and it's in conference room F on the mezzanine floor. I'll be anxious to hear your report on the meeting."

"I'll be there. Anything else, sir?"

"No, that will be all, Captain. Oh, by the way, are you going to Carter's party tomorrow night?"

"I thought I'd drop by for a while. Are you going?"

"Wouldn't miss it. Carter's a bit rough around the edges, but he knows how to throw a party."

Adam stood at attention, snapped a salute and said, "I'll see you there, Major."

The next evening, Adam arrived in golf shirt and civilian khakis at 2030 hours, a half-hour after the appointed start. He was surprised to find Randolph, Sergeant Smythe and Carter the only ones there. Carter welcomed him with that crooked smile that Adam distrusted so completely. He was offered a drink and as Smythe delivered the martini, he spilled just a bit on Adam's chair. As Smythe leaned over to wipe up the spill, he whispered, "Watch out for the drink, Cap."

Adam took a sip of the martini and detected an odd flavor. He decided to pretend to drink, but to somehow dump what he thought to be a 'Mickey Finn.' After taking several small sips, his chance came when the doorbell rang and two 'hot' women were welcomed into the room. Adam pulled up the skirt on his chair and dumped the drink under it. He recovered as Carter turned to introduce the 'entertainment.' Adam thought quickly. Had Carter put a knockout dose in one drink or was he planning Adam's gradual decline into a black void? He opted for the first, and slurred his greeting to the newcomers. As he stood, he wavered and then as he started to say something, fell heavily to the floor.

As he feigned unconsciousness, he heard Carter say, "Don't be alarmed, ladies, he is a notoriously bad drinker. He must have had a few before he got here. Smythe, gimme a hand. We'll put him in the bedroom and let him sleep it off." They took his shoulders and feet and carried him for about twenty steps. As they tossed him onto a bed, Carter said, "Good, he went out fast. We'll go out and talk to the sluts, then come back and get him undressed so the ladies can make a little movie with our hotshot here. It'll give us a little insurance that he stays on the right track after he gets workin' on the Eagle."

A few minutes later, Carter came back and leaned over to unbuckle Adam's belt. Adam leaped up with his hand clutched firmly on Carter's throat and said in a low, but menacing voice, "Want to play games, Carter?" The lieutenant's eyes showed no fear, only hatred as he broke Adam's grip with a jarring blow to his forearm. A vicious kick caught Adam in the lower ribs and sent blinding pain through his body. Adam summoned all his strength, through the pain, and broke Carter's nose with a powerful right hand. He followed up with a left to the body and a chop to the neck. Carter fell like a limp sack and lay bleeding on the floor. Adam opened the door and found that Jeffrey had departed. He told the women, "I'm sorry, but this party is over. Smythe, do you know what we owe these ladies?"

Smythe said, "Yeah, the price was to be a grand, but they didn't do anything, so I guess we could give them a coupla C notes for their trouble."

Adam turned to the obviously frightened girls who had heard the commotion in the bedroom and said, "I think these ladies may have given up some other business opportunities to be here tonight. Would $400 be sufficient for your trouble?"

With a nervous laugh, the older of the two said, "That would be fine."

Adam peeled off four one hundred dollar bills and said with a half-smile, "Here's two hundred each. Thank you for coming." He escorted them to the door and when it was closed turned to Smythe and said, "Thanks for the warning. Now we've got a mess to clean up. Did the Major leave before the tussle in the bedroom?"

"Yeah, he took off when we were carrying you into the bedroom."

"Was the major involved in this little plan?"

"I honestly don't know, Captain, if I did I'd tell you. I just switched sides here tonight and if the lieutenant ever finds out, I'm history."

"I suspect that's true, and I really appreciate your help. Now we better take a look at Carter. I think he has a broken nose and maybe more. Let's take him to the local hospital. I'd rather not explain this to the Army medics. We'll take him in his own car and let the bastard bleed all over it. He deserves it." The two men carried the unconscious Carter to his Suburban and loaded him unceremoniously in the back seat. He was slowly regaining consciousness when they pulled him out at the emergency room. Even in his dazed and battered condition, he stared daggers at Adam as they helped him inside. All the while Adam was trying desperately not to show the excruciating pain that coursed through his side with every breath. He was certain he had broken ribs, but wanted to disassociate himself from Carter's injuries. He would have to tough it out until Monday and then see a doctor in New York. The emergency room physician told them that Carter would be admitted to the hospital and would not be released until the next afternoon at the earliest. As they returned to Carter's house, Adam said, "We'll leave the Suburban at his house. You can pick him up tomorrow, or whenever they release him. I'm going to trust you to say nothing of this to anyone. I want the report to the Major to come from Carter. I will act as though nothing happened. Are you okay with that?"

"Whatever you say, sir. As I said, I've switched sides here…and for some goddamn reason I can't explain, I think I'm now on the winning team."

"I certainly hope you're right, but you can count on my silence about your part in this. Report for work at the lab Monday morning at the regular time. I have to leave the post later in the morning, but I'll get you started on a new project before I go."

When he was alone, he could at least wince as the pain continued. He took four aspirin before lying gingerly on his bed. The bottle was empty by Monday morning, as he looked back on a quiet weekend, spent nursing his wounds. He was at the bench in the lab at 0800 when he received a call from Major Randolph. He sounded chipper as he said, "Good morning, Captain, are you ready for your meeting this afternoon?"

"Yes, sir, and I must admit I'm looking forward to it. Collins was treated more than fairly and I'm anxious to explain that fact to him."

"It's a shame that Lieutenant Carter had that accident Friday night. Did you happen to see him fall?"

"Yes, after several drinks, he missed the second step and fell face first to the sidewalk. Very unfortunate. How is he doing?"

"Both his nose and collarbone are broken. He got out of the hospital late Saturday, but will not return to duty for a week or so. He's very upset over the whole incident."

"I'm sorry to hear that, sir. Is there anything I can do?"

"No, I think you handled the situation very well, getting him to the hospital and all. I'm sure he's grateful to you."

Adam thought, 'Yeah, I bet he is, so grateful he'd like to return the favor, maybe with a knife placed strategically between my shoulder blades.' He said, "If you are available this afternoon, Major, I'd like to report the results of the meeting. Will you be in your office?"

"Yes, I'll be here, even if it's late, I'm anxious to hear your report. Good luck."

Adam stopped on the drive to New York, consulted the Manhattan yellow pages and after several calls, found a doctor to examine his painful ribs. When he described his symptoms, the doctor took x-rays and confirmed his suspicion that the two lower ribs were broken. He taped Adam's chest, prescribed painkillers and apologized for not being able to do more. Adam, who had broken ribs playing football, remembered all too well the long and painful recovery. Buoyed by the effects of a couple of powerful painkillers, Adam set out to meet with Jonathon Collins.

He arrived early and, on a hunch, swept the room for bugs. Sure enough, there was a bug in the ceiling fixture. He took a clean sheet of paper from his briefcase and printed in large letters. *THIS ROOM IS BUGGED*. ANSWER MY VERBAL QUESTIONS WITH APPROPRIATE REPLIES, BUT PAY PARTICULAR ATTENTION TO WHAT I WRITE. USE THE SHEET OF PAPER IN FRONT OF YOU FOR YOUR REPLIES OR QUESTIONS. *NOD IF YOU UNDERSTAND!* When Collins knocked on the door, Adam opened it and put the note in his face. Collins looked alarmed, but quickly recovered and with a nod said, "Hello, Mr. Patterson. I appreciate your willingness to meet with me."

"No problem, Jon, but I thought we'd agreed that my name is Andy. Anyway, please sit down. I'm impressed with the speed with which you and your attorney put the patent application together. Good work."

"Thank you, er, Andy. It went really well and I'm equally impressed with that great invention. In fact, I'm so impressed, I feel I should get a bigger piece of the pie."

Adam tone hardened as he said, "Why do you think that?"

"What we're doing is illegal and I think you people are taking advantage of me considering the risk I'm assuming here."

"You're right about the risk, but you must understand that *you* are the risk. The only way you have any liability is by confessing that the invention was not yours. May I remind you that the contract you signed and received money for was simply to sell all rights to the invention to a corporation. The only crime here is if you admit that you falsified a patent application." While he was talking Adam printed another sign and turned it to Collins. It said, THE PEOPLE YOU ARE DEALING WITH HERE ARE RUTHLESS AND WILL STOP AT NOTHING TO ACHIEVE THEIR GOALS. YOU ARE AT SERIOUS PERSONAL RISK IF YOU PURSUE THIS! Adam continued in a very stern tone, "The numbers in the contract are generous to a fault. Other principals of the corporation felt that the compensation agreed to was not only fair, but was excessive. I believe you have a sweetheart deal here and I intend to finalize any issues regarding the contract before we leave this room." Adam then said in a menacing tone, "Do you understand me*?"*

Collins swallowed hard and replied in a meek voice, "Yes, I guess I became a bit greedy after seeing the potential of the invention. Perhaps you're right, for the part I'm playing the compensation is pretty good."

"I think you'll find it more than that," Adam said in a gentler tone. "If our projections are anywhere near the mark, you will earn between a quarter and half million dollars for a couple of week's work. Now, can we shake hands on the fact that you agree to live up to the contract as it stands?"

Collins put out his hand and received such a powerful handshake that it signified not simply agreement, but an implied threat of physical retribution should he cross these people. He said, "We have an agreement. You will not hear from me on this subject again, I promise."

"I appreciate that, Jon. Call the company if you need any clarification on anything. Otherwise, the check is in the mail and you will not be sorry you've entered into this agreement. Take care." After Collins departed, Adam looked up and gave a middle-finger salute to the ceiling fixture as he gathered up his papers and left the room.

He reported to Major Randolph when he arrived back at Monmouth. Jeffrey was in a jubilant mood and suggested they celebrate with a drink at the officer's club. Adam agreed and after their drinks were delivered, he said, "Adam, I think it's time we moved on to the next level. Tomorrow morning I'm going to introduce you to my baby. Now, baby's been sick, but I think you're just the doctor who can cure her. By the way, baby's name is *Eagle*."

PART THREE

July 16th, 1991, Company A, Fort Monmouth, NJ, 0915 hours...

Sergeant Bruckberg led the two officers to the locked storeroom deep in the supply depot of Company A. He noted that this was the first 'outsider' to gaze upon the well-guarded device since the unfortunate civilian technician had breathed his last in this very room. Major Randolph seemed comfortable bringing Captain Packard in on the secret, so it should be no concern to him. After he had removed the protective cover and retrieved the thick manual from the compartment on the side of the machine, the major said, "Thank you, Sergeant. Be sure to alert me if anyone comes along looking for either of us. We do not want any surprise visitors."

"Yes, sir, I understand," said Bruckberg as he snapped a smart salute. "I'll be in my office if you need anything."

"Thank you," said Randolph. Turning to Adam as the sergeant departed, he said, "This is our baby. I think you may know something about it. But before we get into this, I understand you had a long talk with JoAnn last night."

"Yes, I did," replied Adam. "She explained the background and purpose of the Right Brigade and some of the projects you have undertaken for them." JoAnn had *graphically* described both the Right Brigade and the special operations, had stopped short of admitting to the killing of the guard in the Watergate affair, but did confess to planning and carrying out the scheme. In any event, she had accepted him into the inner circle. He had to retain their trust until the opportunity to blow them away presented itself. He went on to say, "I assure you that the goals of the Right Brigade and my goals are absolutely compatible. I want to be of service, in any way possible."

"That's great, because you can render an important service right here in this room. First, a little background. Do you remember a man named Rubin Schwartz?"

"Yes, he was a civilian contractor attached to a project I worked on over a year ago. Why do you ask?"

"He was involved with stealing the basic concept and then having the machine built by a Middle-Eastern organization. They are not known to be terrorists themselves, but are suspected of having ongoing business with them. We, the Right Brigade that is, purchased this machine through an arms dealer recommended by Schwarz. We had significant success with it before it developed a hiccup. When we commissioned Schwarz to cure the illness, he put deep bugs in it and demanded a king's ransom to put it back in operating condition. Unfortunately, the people to whom he made the demand became incensed and accidentally killed him while *persuading* him to alter his position. I know you worked on the basic technology upon which the Eagle is based and with your expertise, I feel confident you can restore it."

"I'll do my best, but before I get in there with a screwdriver and pliers, I will need to study the schematics and see how it ticks. The thing that could complicate or drag out the repair is a lack of detail or accuracy in this manual. I will make a cursory inspection now and then come back when I have an idea where to look for the bug or bugs. What kind of priority does this project have?"

"The highest," exclaimed the major. "You will still have to move forward with the remaining items on Senator Hawthorne's list, but this should take precedence over everything else. Oh, and by the way, I had a little talk with Carter. In case you're thinking he may want to thank you for last Friday night, I've recommended strongly that he need not bother. I assure you he will keep his appreciation to himself."

"Very good, sir. Now to the Eagle. I will need an hour or so for a basic examination and then I'll return to the lab and begin to formulate a diagnosis."

"Excellent, Captain. I will leave you to your work and I'll instruct Sergeant Bruckberg that you're to have unlimited access here, and are not to be disturbed."

Adam removed several panels, wincing at the pain from his ribs. As he bent over to look at her innards, he said to himself, 'Well, I finally get to meet you, devil machine. You have been the instigator of injury and death in your sordid past. If and when I fix you, I may just use you to turn the tables on your proud owners. Wouldn't that be poetic justice?'

II

*July 19th, 1991,
Arlington, VA, 2:30 p.m....*

"I have some bad news for you, JoAnn," said Sean Ball as he sat across the table in her library. "You know I have a mole at the CIA. My man tells me that your little songbird, Anita Warwick, does a little singing to the wrong people."

"What do you mean, Sean?"

"I mean she's an informer. Not a regular agent, but she does a little spying on the side, at the direction of the 'Company.' I know you've set her up with Senator Hawthorne and that he has some suspicions about you. Do you think you'll influence Hawthorne through Anita, or will Anita have *you* under surveillance for Hawthorne?"

"I'm shocked!" exclaimed JoAnn. "I would never have suspected Anita of such treacherous behavior. You may have a point as far as who's spying on who. We must consider our options." JoAnn pondered and then said, "One option is to eliminate her. Another would be feeding her misinformation that could improve my reputation with not only the CIA, but with Senator Hawthorne. Thank God I haven't taken her into my confidence and asked her to intercede with the senator. What do you think?"

"About eliminating her," said Ball, "we could arrange an 'accident' that could not be traced to you or the Brigade, but I kinda like your idea of feeding her misinformation. You could pretend to take her into your confidence, admit that you want to influence Hawthorne, but give her a hard sell on the idea that your motives are pure as the driven snow."

"Exactly," replied JoAnn. "I like that option far better than the other. I will warn the others who come in contact with her to be on their guard. In fact, I may let some 'secrets' slip out from the lips of others. The more I think about it, the more exciting the prospects become. I will enjoy this little game. Could your 'inside man' find out what she's reporting and whether any of her reports are getting to Hawthorne, either directly from her or through the Agency?"

"I don't know if he has access to her actual reports, but I'll find out and let you know." Ball sat back in his chair and said thoughtfully, "We could put a bug on her phone and her apartment and see what kind of songs she sings."

"What kind of risk would that involve?"

"Very little, my guys are damn good and we'd set up a reason for being there if they were interrupted. I may have to give them a little latitude in that case, but don't worry, chances of that happening are slim to none."

"What about bugging the senator?" asked JoAnn.

"That's more dangerous. He may have some serious security that could represent a problem. As long as the two of them are tight, I'd rather work on her end."

"That's fine. Now I'll work on some tidbits to feed our little mouse and see which rat she passes them along to."

"By the way, JoAnn, how are we doing on the Eagle? Have you given Packard the keys to the kingdom?"

"In a manner of speaking, yes. He passed my final test last week and Jeffrey has introduced him to the machine. I have no idea how long it will take if he is able to fix it, but the process is underway."

"Good, just keep a sharp eye on the captain. He's always seemed a little too slick to me, but that's your call."

"We have safeguards in place and once the Eagle is repaired, he will become expendable if he so much as blinks. He has considerable talent, however, and I hope he will prove to be a loyal member of the team." JoAnn rose and her body language ended the discussion. As Ball was leaving, she said, "Thank you for coming, Sean. Let me know when you have some of Anita's secrets to report. Meanwhile I will try to feed some information to her to see what she does with it."

She sat for a long time, thinking about the conversation with Ball. She was distressed by the news about Anita, but at the same time, elated at the prospect of playing a cat and mouse game with her. She was also concerned about Ball's remark about Adam. She had grown to like him very much...and to trust him. If Anita was any example, was her judgment of people failing? She must warn Jeffrey to keep a close eye on Adam. Perhaps he should also be put under surveillance, he and Lola both. One couldn't be too careful.

III

August 6th, 1991, Company A, Fort Monmouth, NJ, 1530 hours...

Adam was in the second stage of a four-step project to return the Eagle to operating condition. He had first studied the schematics to determine what technologies had been employed in building this ingenious machine. He now was verifying that the schematics, and the circuits shown therein, were one and the same with the circuits under the hide of the Eagle. The third step would involve tracing the activity through the machine and lastly, checking each circuit board to ascertain if it not only worked, but was fulfilling its particular role in the machine's operation. He wiped the sweat from his brow. Halogen lights added heat to the already stifling storeroom. Unfortunately the air conditioning in the supply depot was confined to Sergeant Bruckberg's office.

He found it difficult to concentrate between the heat, his sore ribs and anticipating Belinda's arrival on Friday. The month since they'd been together had seemed like a year and the work, although intriguing, was no substitute for her loving arms. They had once again been invited to JoAnn's for a formal party on Saturday. Belinda would arrive in Newark Friday morning, meet with her 'customer' and then drive with him to Washington that afternoon. He forced his thoughts back to his work, resolving to complete phase three by Friday and dive into the final stage the following week. Although the last part would be the most difficult and time-consuming, he had set the end of the month as his goal to complete the repair. An hour and a half later, he put down his tools and quit for the day. After a shower at his BOQ and a meal at the officer's mess, he returned to his quarters to call Belinda. When he placed the call to her company in Minneapolis, his extraordinarily sensitive ear caught something in the sound of the phone. When the receptionist said that 'Lola' had gone for the day, but she would attempt to patch the call through to her home, Adam said, "Please don't bother. I can call her tomorrow. Do you expect her to be in the office in the morning?"

"Yes," replied the pleasant female voice, "I believe she'll be in all day. Would you like her voice mail?"

"No, just tell her Adam called and I'll try to catch her in the morning." Adam hung up and while holding down the button on the cradle, unscrewed the mouthpiece. He was startled by the size of the bug. It seemed little more than a large speck of dirt and smaller than any transmitter Adam had ever seen. He unscrewed the earpiece and found another. 'I'll be damned,' he thought, 'they invite me to join the club and immediately show their trust by bugging my phone, and probably my room and car. What they don't realize is that I wrote the book on these devices and I will use them to help sink their ship.' As he finished putting the phone back together, he gave it a mock salute and said to himself, 'Thanks for helping me bring you down, Dragon Lady.'

The next day, after a 0630 start on the Eagle, working in the cool of the morning, Adam returned to his quarters at 0900 hours and placed a call to Belinda. After the normal delay with the switching from Minneapolis, he heard her lovely voice and nearly forgot that they were not alone on the phone. He opened with the code that put her on alert that something was amiss. "Good morning, Lola. How's the weather in Minneapolis?"

"Hello, Adam, The weather is clear, hot and humid here, what's it like there?"

"Just hot. I've been sweating all morning. Regardless of the workload and the heat, I can't stop thinking of you. I look forward to this weekend more than you know. When do you arrive in Newark on Friday and when can I see you?"

"I get in at 10:15 and we have a luncheon meeting at the Brady office," said Belinda in a soft, loving voice. "I should be through about two o'clock."

"I'll be waiting outside the office when you come through the door. I'm counting the minutes 'til I see you!" replied Adam a bit huskily.

"Me too. I'll get away as soon as I can. And I must say you've never been out of my thoughts. I guess that's what happens when you truly love someone," she whispered and he heard a click as she hung up the phone.

Adam floated on air as he returned to the 'oven.' He looked up in search of clouds that might provide cooling rain, but realized that a temporary cooldown would be accompanied by still higher humidity, if that was possible. As he entered the office of the supply depot, he met Jeb Carter for the first time since that fateful Friday night. Carter had been back on active duty for over two weeks, but their paths had not crossed. Carter's nose looked almost normal and he had shrugged off the arm sling he had worn for three weeks. Carter, the consummate soldier, came to stiff attention and saluted smartly. As Adam returned the salute, he saw the anger smoldering in the lieutenant's dark eyes. He said, "Lieutenant Carter, I'd like to have a word with you." Adam led Carter to Bruckberg's office and asked the sergeant to give them a few minutes. As Bruckberg left, Adam said, "Please sit down. I want to talk to you about our altercation last month. I'm sure you're aware that I could bring charges against you for your behavior. I do not intend to do that, however, I do want to know just what's behind your attitude."

Carter, sitting stiffly in his chair, said through clenched teeth, "I don't know what you mean by attitude, Captain."

Adam leaned forward and said in a low, menacing tone, "You know exactly what I mean, Carter, and if you try anything like that again, you will be history. Do you understand me?"

"Yessir. Will that be all?" Carter said with no fear or sign of regret in his manner or voice.

Adam stood and said, "That will be all, Lieutenant." The warm, fuzzy mood that had enveloped him from Belinda's call evaporated. Rather than return to the storeroom in his present state of mind, he looked for Smythe and found him at work on a piece of equipment on Senator Hawthorne's priority list.

Smythe looked up, smiled and said in a cheerful voice, "Morning, Cap."

Adam replied, "Good morning, hard at work?"

"Yessir, I like this duty…and working with you."

Adam looked squarely at Smythe. "I appreciate that. By the way, you mentioned changing sides. Are you really serious about that?"

Smythe thought about the question. "Sure am. I'm sick and tired of the kinda shit that's been goin' on around here."

"Just what kind of shit are we talking about?" asked Adam.

Smythe looked around and said in a low voice, "I'd rather not talk about it here. Can we find someplace…private-like?"

Adam replied in a normal voice, "Sergeant, I need some parts for the Eagle. Do you need anything for your work on the senator's priorities?" When Smythe gave an affirmative reply, he continued, "Make a list, then you can check out a truck this afternoon."

"Yessir, I'll go down to the motor pool right after noon chow."

As they drove out of the Fort, Adam turned on the miniature tape recorder hidden in his pocket, and asked, "Okay, now what's been going on around here that been bothering you, Smythe?"

"We had this real deal goin'. We were doing some spying with a hotshot machine called the Eagle. We stored it in the supply room and because it was secret stuff, we all got a nice bundle of extra cash every month. Sweet deal, huh?"

"Sounds great. Did something happen to change it?" asked Adam.

"Yeah, it all started when a little black guy named Champ McRae got transferred into the outfit. He got into a broohaha with Sergeant Jimmy Swanson and later wound up stickin' a shiv in ole Jimmy…did him in."

"He killed him? What happened to McRae?"

"Nothin', Lieutenant Rogers of the MPs, a guy from CID, I think his name is Leach, and guy from the DA's office asked us all a lot of questions, but they couldn't pin it on McRae."

"How do you know McRae did it?"

"He did it all right. I was there. McRae followed us when we were moving the Eagle one night. Lieutenant Carter ran him off the road and Jimmy went down the embankment to finish him off. McRae brought a knife to a gun fight, and the little sonofabitch won. We torched the car with Jimmy inside, but they found the cuts in his body anyway."

"Why didn't you put the finger on McRae for killing Swanson?"

"He worked for the supply sergeant, Bruckberg. He knew about the Eagle and we couldn't let him run off at the mouth about that shit. The lieutenant let him in on the deal afterwards. To keep his mouth shut."

"What happened after that?" asked Adam.

"The night he killed Swanson, McRae had borrowed his bunkmate's car. Carter didn't trust the little fairy, so they grabbed him, strangled him and dumped him and his car in a lake up where he came from. Guy's name was Harris."

"Who's *they*?"

"Carter and Albertson. Pollard and I were there when they did him, but we didn't go up to the lake."

"How did they find his body?"

"I dunno, some kid was fishin' and snagged his cap. He called the cops, those cops called the cops down here and Lieutenant Rogers and the D.A. guy went up and pulled 'em out of the lake. They questioned us again, but Carter gave us all alibis, so nothin' happened."

"Is that it?" asked Adam.

"No, a while later, after McRae was in the loop, Pollard slipped up and told him about Harris. McRae flipped his lid, pulled a knife and Albertson had to shoot the little bastard."

"Did McRae die?"

"Yeah, after a coupla days. Carter wanted to finish him off before he could squeal, but he musta died without telling, 'cause they never pinned it on anybody."

"Three murders and no one was arrested? That's quite a record, don't you think?"

"That's not all. When the Eagle started acting up, they brought this Heinie, named Schwartz, in to fix her. He screwed her up good and then wanted a bunch of dough to fix it. Carter got mad and roughed him up…a little too good, the guy died. We buried him out in the country. Next thing, you come on the scene. Now that I think of it, Cap, you oughta watch your ass once you fix that machine. These bastards don't like leavin' any witnesses layin' around after they've got what they want."

"I see your point," replied Adam, and in a confidential tone, continued, "and I appreciate your telling me the whole story. Now let's keep this between the two of us. We'll be very careful and just see what happens, okay?"

"Okay by me, as I said, I'm on your side all the way."

As they neared the shopping area, Adam said, "Why don't you drop me at the mall? I need to get some tools at RadioShack. You can hit the depot and pick me up in an hour." At RadioShack, Adam made a copy of the tape he had just recorded, bought a meter and a few small tools. At the mailing center, located a few doors away, he mailed the original tape to General Rayburn and the copy to himself at the Washington Court Hotel. He threw the recorder in a trash can and went to meet Smythe. His mind was relieved by getting the tapes in the mail, but deeply troubled when his worst fears about his enemies were verified. He slept little that night and only the task at hand took his mind from the danger that drew closer each day. He managed to make good progress, with no further conflicts for the balance of the week. When Friday morning finally dawned, he estimated that he'd complete phase three in about four hours. He grabbed a bagel and coffee and was at work at 0630 hours. Forcing Belinda from his thoughts, he concentrated on the task at hand and by 1015 hours was reinstalling the panels that protected the delicate innards of the Eagle. He returned to his quarters with a spring in his step, showered and dressed in a golf shirt, lightweight khakis and tan loafers. He was in the Porsche by 1140 hours, speeding toward Newark and the love of his life.

IV

August 9th, Newark, NJ, 1300 hours...

When Adam reached the outskirts of Newark, he made a number of turns with his eye on the rearview mirror. When satisfied he was not being followed, he pulled into the parking lot of a small office building, then scanned the entire car with an electronic probe that would detect and locate the position of any listening device/transmitter. He was rather surprised to find the car clean. As he pulled out of the lot, however, he resolved to re-scan the car every time he let it out of his sight.

He arrived at the Baker Building at 1340 hours and let the powerful engine idle to keep the cabin cool. He knew the joy of their reunion would be interrupted by a serious conversation about the events that had transpired during their time apart. Putting that aside, he eyed the door she would walk through like a hungry dog waiting for his dish to be filled. It seemed like an eternity before she swished through the door, into the car and his arms. The lingering kiss was like a bridge over the river of loneliness in which they had been drowning for weeks. With weak knees and a somewhat forced grin, Adam finally rallied himself to the task of driving the car. His first intelligible words were, "I love you Belinda, and I may tell you that a million times before the weekend is over, but we do need to discuss the little project we've gotten ourselves into."

"I love you too," Belinda said with tenderness and an unusual concern in her voice, "but you seem upset. Are you all right, honey?"

Adam's demeanor was deadly serious as he continued, "I warned you the other day because the phone in my quarters had been bugged. Even though I seemed to have been accepted into the club, they obviously have doubts about my loyalty. The day after I found the bug,

I had a pleasant chat with my friend Carter. I warned him about any future shenanigans and he was about as civil as a rattlesnake ready to strike. For the sake of the mission, I hope I can avoid working too closely with Carter when we take the Eagle into the field. The inevitable explosion between us could compromise the mission."

"Yes, and if he blindsided you, I would lose more than the mission. Please be careful, I don't know what I'd do if I lost you," said Belinda with a frown as she gently touched his injured side.

Adam put his hand over hers and said, "My good mood, created by our phone call, was destroyed by the confrontation with Carter. I didn't feel like returning to the Eagle, so I went over and checked on Smythe. Fortunately, he has proven to be a friend, not a foe. What started with his warning at Carter's little 'party,' continued big time that afternoon. He told me about all the bad deeds this outfit has done. Unfortunately the actions he described made me more concerned than ever before. Between the bug, Carter and Smythe's tale, I was a bit shook up."

"Oh, Adam, you went through such a terrible ordeal in just one day. I can't see how you were able to concentrate on your work."

"If it weren't for the intensity of the project and anticipating seeing you again, it would have been pretty tough. As it turned out, I was able to get into it and the Eagle should be operational in less than a month. Once that's accomplished, assuming they don't find me expendable, I have to find excuses to be a part of any operation in which it's deployed."

Belinda bit her lip as she said, "Sometimes I wish we could just walk away from this, but if you're still convinced you can do it, I do have some good news. We're going to bring in some reinforcements."

"I really don't have any choice. We can't let these people get away with what they've done. Now, what's this about reinforcements?"

"General Rayburn and I agree that you need closer support than either he or I can provide. We'd like to bring Mack Rogers into our confidence. We have done additional checking on him since he brought this issue to our attention and we both feel he is not only trustworthy, but a most capable man in every sense. I have arranged a meeting with him in Washington tomorrow. We will bring him up to date on all of your activities and what we have learned about the Right Brigade. He will be working undercover and his superiors will not be informed of any of his activities related to this mission. When it comes to the final showdown, the general wants him involved for your protection and to assure that we have solid testimony against these people. Oh, and another thing, Anita Warwick is more than just a songbird friend of JoAnn's. She has been working with the CIA for several years and is currently gathering background material on the people surrounding JoAnn. The high command has not decided whether to confide in Senator Hawthorne at this time, but he may be brought into the 'anti-Right Brigade' campaign before the final curtain."

Adam squeezed her hand and said, "Thank you, love. My confidence is growing by the minute. I look forward to meeting Rogers. His appraisal of the situation and willingness to stick his neck out were gutsy to say the least. What time is our meeting?"

"Eleven o'clock at the Smithsonian. He'll have his wife Amy with him. We will both do a circuitous route on the way to eliminate any opportunities for them to tail us. I have arranged a private room at the Institute where we won't be disturbed."

"What about the wife?" asked Adam.

"She's been cleared to attend and hear the story. She was a police officer for nearly ten years and carried the gold shield of a detective in Syracuse, NY before she married Mack and moved to New Jersey."

The twinkle returned to Adam's eye as he said, "You have washed away all my dark clouds. Now, if we're through talking business, how about telling me how much you missed me?"

She put her arm across his shoulder, gently stroked his neck and said in a low, sexy voice, "Every day in every way. I thought of you with my mind, missing your voice and just your presence, and I thought of you with my body, missing your touch, your lips and the feel of you inside me. Other than that, I didn't miss you much." As she said the last words, she pulled his head toward her and kissed him on the cheek.

"Words cannot explain how I have missed you. When I consider the pitfalls of this project, I also think that without it, I would never have met you. Whatever happens from here on out, it will have been worth it to have learned to love you the way I have."

"What do you mean – 'whatever happens'?" said Belinda in a pouty voice, "We're going to get through this and live happily ever after!"

V

August 10th, 1991, Washington Court Hotel, Washington, DC 7:45 a.m....

Belinda completed her makeup, turned to Adam and smiled. "I suppose a stud like you could use a little fodder. Are you ready to chow down?"

"In a minute, but first, please listen to this." Adam turned on a tape recorder and they heard the voices of Smythe and himself.

Belinda listened intently and, when the tape ended, said, "You must have been devastated when he told about these twisted people. Thank God we're bringing the Rogerses into this thing to back you up. I'm *really* anxious to meet with them this morning."

After breakfast, Adam and Belinda took a cab to the Mayflower Hotel. Entering on Connecticut Avenue, they rode an elevator to the mezzanine floor and walked to the back of the hotel, then took the rear elevator and exited on the side street just short of 17th Street NW. They slipped into the back seat of a dark gray Ford Taurus and were whisked away to the Smithsonian with a number of twists and turns on the way.

A knock on the door of the small conference room signaled the arrival of Mack and Amy Rogers. Mack made a strong first impression with his good-natured smile and powerful physique, Amy for her dark Irish beauty and confident, open bearing. They both seemed highly competent, 'what you see is what you get' type people. They shook hands all around and Belinda and Mack, old soldiers together in Ranger training, hugged. Adam began the conversation with, "Mack, I want to compliment you on your tenacity and courage in pursuing this case. Not many men would hang in there the way you have."

Mack blushed slightly as he replied, "Shucks, t'wernt nothin'. Actually, Amy came up with the idea to seek outside help. I immediately thought of Belinda, and here we are."

"I agree with Adam," said Belinda. "You really put yourself at risk to send that information to me. Now I'm going to ask you if you're willing to assume additional risk by helping Adam take down these people. First, however, we'd like to fill you in on everything that's happened. We will tell you where we've been and where we hope to go, including your potential role. Then, and only then, will we ask you to consider playing a part in this."

"I can't wait to hear the story," said Mack, "but be warned, they don't call me 'bulldog' for nothing. I can't think of anything you could say to stop me from riding shotgun on this stage."

Belinda smiled as she began with her introducing Mack's story to General Rayburn, the search for and recruitment of Adam, his qualifications, the training period in Saudi Arabia and his assignment to the 44th at Fort Monmouth. Adam then took up the story and told about being introduced to JoAnn and how Belinda, as Lola, joined the group. He told them about the relations with Carter, Randolph and the others and how he had finally become accepted into their confidence and began work on the Eagle.

Mack and Amy were transfixed as the story unfolded. The final chapter was delivered by both Adam and Belinda as they discussed the surveillance on Adam, Smythe's confession, the plan for the take-down and Mack's role as backup, participant in the showdown and witness for the prosecution. When the one-hour-plus presentation concluded, Belinda asked Mack, "What do you think? Are you willing to help us get these guys?"

"Wild horses couldn't drag me away from this fight. I've been so damned frustrated by the power and audacity of these people that I'll do anything to see 'em get what they deserve. One question, do we need any additional manpower to assist Adam?"

Adam replied, "It's hard to say, but it would be smart to have someone waiting in the wings, just in case. Do you have somebody in mind?"

"The two men I worked the case with know everything that happened up to your coming aboard. D.A. Investigator Jim Young and Warrant Officer Al Leach of the CID are my guys and they both want this take-down as much as I do."

"That sounds good," said Belinda. "But I suggest we give them minimum information and put them on a stand-by basis. I'm sure they're not security risks, but the fewer people that know, the less chance of any leaks. If Adam's cover is blown, he's a dead man." As she said the last words, the color drained from her face.

"I understand," said Mack. "I will tell them there is activity on the case and I may be calling on them for help. We also need to discuss communications. I'm sure you don't want Adam and me to become drinking buddies at the officer's club. I need to be able to safely get in touch with you too, Belinda. Any suggestions?"

"We've already put together some procedures and codes. To begin with, Adam's phone is bugged and we dare not remove the bug," said Belinda. "If it's an emergency, call as a wrong number and ask for 'Harry.' Adam will then know to call you from a secure phone. It's more likely that Adam will need to reach you. Is it safe to call your office or your home?"

"Yes, to arrange a meet which should also be in code. I wouldn't want to discuss any classified info over either phone. We can establish some codes for meeting places or phone destinations."

Amy spoke up, "I have a neighbor who is on the Long Branch Police Force. She is as incorruptible as they come and would be happy to provide a meeting place or a safe phone for you two to talk. If you like, I'll clear it with her and get you the number and address. How should we contact you?"

Belinda said, "I like that idea," as she handed a business card to Amy. "Call me at my 'company' in Minneapolis. We have an arrangement that any calls for 'Lola Princeton' are forwarded to my office at Fort Benning. If you need to send written material, send it to 'Lola' at the company's address in Minneapolis. Anything else?"

"I think we're on the same page," said Mack. "I'm going to do more than propose a toast when this is over, a drunken brawl would be more like it. Call me anytime, Adam. In the meantime, good luck and good hunting."

Amy and Mack left the building first. After a fifteen-minute delay, Adam and Belinda followed and slipped into the gray Ford around the corner. After being dropped off at the rear entrance of the Mayflower, they retraced their steps through the mezzanine and reappeared from the front elevators. The circuit completed, they returned by cab to the Washington Court. Adam had scanned the suite for bugs the evening before, but went though the process again when they returned. Finding none, they were able to discuss the meeting and agree on additional codes and safeguards with which to communicate with the Rogerses.

VI

August 10th, 1991, Arlington, VA, 7:00 p.m....

They arrived at JoAnn's mansion to find Jeffrey and Sela as the first guests on the scene. In the exchange of greetings, Belinda noticed the very long and close hug Sela bestowed on Adam.

Jeffrey was expansive in his praise of Adam's work. He directed his remarks to Belinda as he said, "You have your lovely claws in a man among men. He has accomplished near miracles with electronic gadgetry. I believe he will go on to great success in the Army or, God forbid, as a civilian."

"Why thank you for those nice words," replied Belinda, with a glance at Sela. "I have every intention of keeping my sharp claws firmly embedded in him."

"Whoa, you two," said Adam with a smirk, "I appreciate the praise, but it's getting a bit deep in here and I feel like a rabbit clutched in the talons of a hawk."

JoAnn laughed. "Yes, I think it's dreadful of them to characterize you in such a manner. Shame on both of you. Now, I'd like to discuss something with Adam and Jeffrey. Would you two beauties mind excusing us for a moment." JoAnn led Adam and Jeffrey to the library and closed the door. She said, "Tell me about the progress on the Eagle."

Adam said, "It's going well. I am ready to begin the last stage of the repair and I am incorporating some upgrades that will increase the accuracy and the reliability of the machine. At some point you may want to consider a total redesign to make it as portable as a professional television camera. When the Eagle was designed, little effort was made to minimize its size. That, combined with subsequent advances in circuit miniaturization, would allow a significant reduction in size and weight. It would be a major task, but if your needs justified the effort, it may be worth considering."

"I guess you now understand why I was singing Adam's praises earlier, JoAnn," said Jeffrey. "I have asked him for an estimate of the time and expense to create a *baby* Eagle, but only after he completes the task at hand. Tell her your time frame to get the Eagle running, Adam."

"I believe it will be ready by the end of the month," replied Adam.

"Wonderful," said JoAnn. "The wanna-be candidates for the Democratic nomination for president are coming out of the woodwork and we must begin our surveillance of their dirty deeds as soon as possible. Will you need to be involved personally in the operation of the Eagle, Adam?"

"I will have to conduct exhaustive testing initially and, yes it would be valuable to oversee the operation under actual field conditions." JoAnn had just offered him the entrée into the field-use he needed. "The more I work with it, the better able I will be to develop a second generation machine. I will give you a more accurate estimate later, but a rough guess for its development would be three to six months and somewhere in the neighborhood of a quarter million dollars."

"That sounds very doable. When you finish your current task, we should investigate building the new Eagle at once," said JoAnn. "We have a number of fish to fry and we surely can use more than one pan. Now we must rejoin your ladies and see if any of the others have arrived."

Upon their return, the festivities were progressing nicely and when the dinner bell rang, twenty-four carefully chosen guests answered the call. At the end of the evening, JoAnn asked Jeffrey to stay a minute and when they were alone, she said, "I sincerely hope Ball's suspicions of Adam are unfounded. I can see a larger and more vital role for him in my plans for the future. I assume that since you came here with glowing praise, you have nothing negative to report from your surveillance?"

"No, we have nothing, but will continue to watch him until everyone's suspicions are satisfied. I agree that he has a great deal of potential, not only in the clandestine operations, but with his inventiveness. Who knows? This outfit could become self-supporting."

Adam and Belinda continued their 'Let's assume somebody's listening' routine during the ride back to the hotel and until Adam had scanned their suite. What had previously been clean was now dirty. A listening device had been planted in the bedroom and another in the living room of the suite. He rechecked the bathroom carefully to find a place where their words would not reach outside ears. Once inside with the door closed he told Belinda, "Honey, we're going to have to keep a notepad handy to communicate the things we don't want the wrong ears to hear. Hopefully the radio will drown out any bedroom sounds, just in case any lovemaking should occur during the night."

"Or, we could have some fun and give the listeners a thrill with some screaming orgasms à la 'When Harry met Sally.' They would be more likely to believe we don't know about them if we're honest," said Belinda with a wicked smile.

"That movie, my dear, dealt with *fake* orgasms. In the interest of realism, I intend to provide adequate stimulus to create the genuine article."

VII

August 29th, 1991, 44th Signal, Fort Monmouth, NJ, 1540 hours...

Adam picked up the phone in Sergeant Bruckburg's office and called Major Randolph. When the major answered, he said, "Major, this is Packard. I have the news you've been waiting for. The piece of equipment we have been working on is now operational. It will require field-testing before being put into active service. Could you recommend the appropriate people and location for the tests?"

"That's great, Adam," said Jeffrey. "Meet me at the officer's club in an hour and we can discuss the tests over a celebratory drink."

"That will be fine, sir. See you there."

Jeffrey was seated at his favorite table in the back of the club when Adam arrived. He gestured at the drinks, already delivered, rose and shook Adam's hand vigorously as he said, "Good work, Adam. You not only accomplished the impossible, you did it on schedule. JoAnn will be extremely pleased. I suspect she may shower you with more than praise for your outstanding achievement. As to the testing, there are several people who have operated the Eagle. Carter, Albertson, Smythe and Pollmer on my side, and a couple of Ball's people."

"Who is the most capable and experienced in its use?" asked Adam.

"Ball's people have conducted most of the field work. Probably the most savvy technician in the whole bunch is one of Ball's men, Jason Bark. We may need him to verify that the machine captures the same or better images and audio as before the sabotage."

"Good," said Adam. "Since I assume this phase carries the same priority as the repair, I will be available anytime to pursue the tests."

"I'll make the contact tomorrow and we'll get this show on the road," said Jeffrey with a smile as he raised his drink. "Here's to your work on the Eagle and more importantly, to a long and very profitable relationship."

Adam clinked his glass. "I'll drink to that. I can't tell you how anxious I am to participate in this great effort. I thank you for your support and encouragement. May we bring down the bad guys and keep the good guys on top." Adam said this with the fervor only available when expressing one's true beliefs, which he *was*. The Right Brigade and Jeffrey were the bad guys.

The following Wednesday morning, an Army 6x6 arrived at the supply depot with Smythe at the wheel. Bruckburg helped Smythe load the Eagle into the truck. Smythe drove out of the base and rendezvoused with Adam and Jason Bark in a secluded wood east of the Fort. They transferred the machine to an unmarked van and Smythe returned to Monmouth. Bark drove the van north and stopped on the outskirts of Newark to affix 'Copiers Plus' magnetic signs to each side of the van. During the ride, Adam questioned Bark about technical issues, being careful not to touch on the specifics of his past escapades with the Eagle. Bark began to open up as he became aware of both Adam's knowledge and his acknowledgment of Bark's 'nerdy' but substantial expertise. Their entire conversation was taped on a miniature recorder under Adam's shirt.

They set up the machine in the Hilton Newark Gateway hotel and aimed its beams at the office building across the street. They would not only record the images and sounds from the target, but would dub in details of the 'shoot' as they scanned different portions. The dubbing would define the distance to the building, the structure itself and the depth of each image within the building.

After half a day together, Bark was talking to Adam like an old friend, with technical computer language as their bond. Adam adjusted the controls and when they had established an image of an office, Bark remarked, "I don't know what you did with this machine, Captain, but the linear depth adjustment is much better than it was before. The picture is clearer and so is the audio. I have to take my hat off to you. This is a better machine than the one I operated before."

"Thank you, Jason, but I simply substituted some more recent technology and changed some of the circuit paths to improve the general operation of the machine. I believe you could have done it yourself.

Tell me how it compares specifically. What were your results in past operations?"

Bark considered the question and replied, "When we did the surveillance of the Democrats for the 'Watergate clone,' the depth control was a problem. The image moved deeper and shallower in the room so that we lost some of the action. When we recorded the 'perps' in the safe house, we wanted to use the Eagle again so the tapes we gave the newspaper would have the same characteristics. Since we were taking it at closer range and through just one frame wall, the results were quite different. I think that would not be the case with the *new* Eagle."

"Interesting," said Adam. "I didn't consciously work on that problem, but the circuitry I substituted in the depth resolution section may have cured it. Sometimes chance mated with dumb luck are the parents of invention."

"You said it," Bark said as he adjusted the depth control and scanned an office deeper in the building. "See how perfect the image comes through? I'm revved about the improvements. I hope we can work together to get the goods on some of these scumbags. The liberal dorks we've scanned preach about helping their fellow man in public, but in private, they lie like rugs and will do anything to stay in office *and* line their pockets."

"Ain't that the truth," agreed Adam, "I imagine you got an earful when you tuned in to their meetings at the Hyatt?"

Adam referred to the scandal known as 'Watergate II.' A group of liberal, 'behind the scenes' politicians planned and executed a break-in at the Democratic Party Headquarters. The Right Brigade spied on their meetings with the Eagle, followed the hired burglars, entered the building after they'd left and killed a security guard. The Right Brigade captured the hired thugs and the 'mouthpiece' for the operation, recorded their confessions and turned the evidence over to the press and authorities. Many political pundits credited the backfire of the plan with helping George Bush win the 1988 presidential election.

"You can say that again. I told Jolson that we were almost Snow White compared to these liberal bastards. We kinda lost our squeaky-clean image when we wasted the little lady guard, but at least we weren't parading around as Goody Two-shoes like they were."

"Well, you have to do what you have to do," said Adam. "That really made a story of it. I would have planned it that way from the get-go, but I suppose it was accidental on your part?"

"No, we had orders to off her," said Bark. "Ball led us to believe that he got the order from the very top, whoever that might be."

"I'm glad to hear that. It shows that the leadership of this group concentrates on the ultimate outcome and is willing to do what it takes to accomplish that most effectively. We've done enough testing in this environment, so let's try a longer shot, in case we can't get this close to the target. Try that building in the next block," requested Adam.

"Okay, I'll take one last, deeper scan here and then go long range." Bark adjusted the controls and after getting a good image, aimed at the distant building. The result was surprisingly good. The machine performed better than they expected and Adam was anxious to hear the reaction of the Right Brigade when the news came back to them through Ball.

The Eagle was put back in storage at the supply depot after duplicating the transfer with Smythe. When Adam returned to his quarters, he listened to the tape with earphones. The conversations with Bark were clear and complete and represented the second piece of solid evidence in his quest to dismantle the Right Brigade. Adam drove off-post, made a copy of the tape and mailed the original to the general and the copy to Mack Rogers at their contact person's home.

The next morning Adam reported to Major Randolph's office at 0800. He gave a run-down on the performance of the Eagle and certified it ready for a real assignment. After completing his report, he walked back to his lab. As he walked through the early fall sunshine, he thought, 'If I'm ever going to pirate the Eagle away to actually use it against JoAnn and company, I need to get it off this base, to a place where I can access it without Army security. Perhaps Mr. Ball can become an unwitting ally to accomplish that goal.'

September 9th, 1991, Arlington, Virginia, 2:45 p.m....

They assembled in JoAnn Cleveland's library for a strategy meeting regarding the 1992 election campaigns. JoAnn served coffee rather than cocktails, casting a serious note to the proceedings. It was the first time Adam had been invited to a meeting of the executive committee of the Right Brigade. This meeting would carry a PG rating as Richard Thomas was in attendance. Of the regular Brigade members, only Gordon Foote sat in on the x-rated meetings where details of serious undercover work were discussed. Sean Ball and Jeffrey Randolph attended as the people who would carry out operations the group would discuss and approve for action.

JoAnn began. "Thank you all for coming. The time has come for discussion of the upcoming elections and what part, outside of contributions, we may play to assure success for conservative candidates. I am happy to report that the Eagle has been restored to operating condition, thanks to Adam, and we are ready to assign targets for its use."

"I assume we are talking about projects with less disastrous consequences than the Watergate II affair?" asked Thomas.

"Absolutely, Richard," replied JoAnn. "We are simply gathering evidence, the disposition of which will be decided by this committee. In addition to looking for inappropriate behavior, we will be trying to determine the strategies of various political committees, particularly in tight races."

"I believe it is essential that we achieve our goal of presenting a conservative Republican Congress to George Bush," said Foote. "As far as the President is concerned, the Gulf War has given George phenomenal ratings, but the election is over a year away and we must remain vigilant and do everything possible to insure that he's re-elected."

"Hear, hear," said JoAnn. "I have people working the Democratic front runners. We either already have or will have moles in each of their campaign headquarters. Based on their intelligence, we will dispatch the Eagle to whatever events seem most likely to yield damaging information about their candidates. There are a dozen or more House and Senate races that we also need to monitor carefully. Adam is beginning to develop one or more second-generation Eagles that will be much more portable and allow us to keep a watchful eye on an even greater number of liberal candidates."

Gordon Foote stood. His six-foot seven-inch height and commanding look was punctuated by a mop of unruly black hair and bushy eyebrows. His deep voice boomed, "That's interesting. How long before you complete these devices, Adam?"

"I've done some preliminary research and depending upon the availability of generic circuitry, with luck, they could be operational in three to five months. The more we have to custom fabricate, the longer it will take."

"That makes sense. Are you going to be able to devote most of your time to this project?" asked Foote, "Perhaps I should ask your boss that question. What about it, Jeff?"

Jeffrey responded, "Yes and no, this will be one of his primary tasks. However as an officer in the Army, he will also have to spend time on a number of 'Army' projects appropriate to his current duties. Unless we can squeeze sixteen-hour days out of him, we'll have to be content with half-days on this venture. He also will be involved in some of the Eagle assignments to maximize his understanding of both the machine and its applications. The good news is that he is not a clock-watcher."

"Adam's record for delivering the goods on time has been excellent to date and I believe that will continue," said JoAnn. "We will use the Eagle initially to watch the shenanigans of Mr. Willard Fenton, Governor of Kentucky. My sources tell me he can't keep it in his pants and we'd like to catch him in the act. His schedule calls for him to be in Frankfort all next week and my source will provide details of his schedule and her take on the most likely times for illicit activities. Is it too late to implement an action for next week?"

"I don't see any problem if Adam is willing to work on the weekend and Sean can line up the shooters," said Jeffrey.

"I will be happy to do whatever is necessary," said Adam. "I have a suggestion, however. Since we may be using the Eagle on a fairly regular basis, wouldn't it be wise to find off-base storage to lessen the possibility of detection during transport off and on Army property?"

"That's a good point," said Ball. "We had a secure location before and only moved it to the Fort when we were expecting little activity for awhile. Now that you plan to use it a lot, it makes sense to find it a new home. If you like, I can have a cozy place ready when it returns from Kentucky."

"I agree," said Jeffrey. "Now let's consider the trip. If your man Bark can be available this Friday, we'll transfer the Eagle to a van and he can drive it to Kentucky. Adam can fly out Sunday morning and meet him for the shoot. Does that work for everybody?"

"No problem on my side," said Ball. "I would, for security, like to send Jolson with Bark. It's a long drive and the cargo is precious."

"I like that," said JoAnn. "And, I agree with moving the Eagle to off-base storage until further notice. I believe we have covered all of my agenda. Richard or Gordon, do you have anything you'd like to discuss before we adjourn?"

"Only that I'm counting on all of you to use extreme caution in all of these activities," said Thomas. "I was very upset with the Watergate thing and we must not jeopardize the sanctity of the Right Brigade with foolhardy escapades."

"I second that motion, Richard," said Foote, pointing his large, stern face at Jeffrey and Ball. "I'm sure the message has been well received by all of the parties to this meeting. That right, boys?"

The 'boys' shook their heads and JoAnn bid them goodbye with, "I couldn't agree more. Now, Godspeed and good luck."

On the drive back to Fort Monmouth, Jeffrey said, "It's too bad JoAnn can't find somebody with balls instead of that pussy Thomas to fill out the executive committee. He's afraid of his shadow, but she insists he provides confidence to some of the other faint hearts on the

Brigade. As far as this assignment goes, don't be afraid to be aggressive. If we have to push a few people around to get the goods on these guys, it's perfectly okay, comprende?"

"Si, señor," replied Adam. "I understand Jolson is the muscle in the Bark-Jolson team. Does he have anything but muscle between his ears?"

"He's not as savvy on the technical side as Bark, but he's no fool and he's been around the block a few more times. He's a particularly good man to have around if there's trouble. I prefer to use Ball's people more than my own men because, as civilians, it's easier to shake them loose when we need them."

Adam reflected, "Hmm. I was impressed with Bark. He's a computer junkie, but he seems to have some common sense, a rarity in that category. I was just thinking, I could use him to help me develop the new Eagle, but it would mean establishing a lab off-post. Probably involve renting a place to house a lab, and me. That way, we could both come and go with no problem. It's too bad he isn't a woman, he could pose as the wife."

"Come on Packard, first you want fancy digs in town, now you want me to supply you with pussy too? No way. I have to think about letting Bark get his nose under this particular tent. But how do you propose to work on this baby in the Army lab and at home at the same time?"

"That's the best part. I can divide the work and do certain phases in the lab and others at home. This way Bark will only be exposed to a portion of the technology. Does that give you any comfort about Bark's becoming involved?"

"I guess so," said Jeffrey, "but I want to sleep on it. If I decide to let you do it, I'll have to talk with Ball to see if he's willing to give us Bark full-time. We'll see..."

September 15th, 1991,
Frankfort, KY,
5:30 p.m....

Adam arrived in Louisville at 1:25 p.m. on Continental Airlines. He rented a Pontiac Bonneville from Avis and was in Frankfort before three o'clock. He joined forces with Bark and Jolson in the back lot of the local GM dealer. He parked his car in a row of Pontiacs, entered the van and they drove to the governor's mansion downtown. Bark introduced him to Jolson with, "I want you to meet the guy that wrote the book on electronics. Wait till you see what he's done with the Eagle."

"How you doin', Captain," said Jolson, putting out a beefy hand. "Bark here has been singin' your praises all the way from New Jersey. I can't wait to see the results."

"Good to meet you, and I'm as anxious as you are to see how this works in a real operation. Did you have any trouble getting the one-way glass installed in the van?"

"Only with the timing," responded Bark. "We had to drive up to New York to get the glass from the manufacturer. Once we brought it to the windshield shop, it only took a couple of hours to install. It looks good, but we won't know how the Eagle will like it until we make the shoot tonight. Do you plan to hit the Governor's mansion first thing?"

"We may as well experiment with the actual target," said Adam. "We should stop and get enough food and drinks to last us through the evening, then we'll drive right over to old Willie Fenton's place and see what he's up to." After a stop at Burger King, they pulled up a block from the mansion with the 'window' side of the van facing the long side of the building. Two additional automobile batteries had been installed in series with the van battery to provide up to three hours of operation without running the engine.

They fired up the Eagle, then Adam made some adjustments and showed Jolson how to calculate and adjust the range. When the picture came in, Jolson remarked, "You're right, that goddamn picture is a lot clearer than before and we never tried it at this distance. I have to hand it to you, Captain."

"Thank you," replied Adam. "It looks like the glass is not a deterrent to the picture quality. Now let's scan the entire building, see if we can find anybody home. Here are pictures of Fenton, his wife and son. We also want to determine which rooms are which, so you can anticipate where to look for him at the times shown in this schedule." Adam passed the pictures and schedule to the two men.

"There he is," said Bark triumphantly. "In the bathroom of what looks like the master suite. This could be pretty good duty if we record some good looking babes during their bath or shower."

"Cool it, Bark," said Jolson. "We're not here to satisfy your warped sexual fantasies. Isn't that right, Captain?"

"I have no problem with you watching an orgy as long as it doesn't interfere with getting the evidence we need. Remember, we're looking for any kind of deviant behavior that we can use against this guy. To prevent the van from becoming too conspicuous, rent a hotel room whenever the shoot allows. I'll leave it to your judgment as far as when you have gathered sufficient evidence to terminate the surveillance, but you must not stay active for more than a few days. I don't have to tell you the consequences of being busted by the law."

They surveyed the mansion and the Governor's family for several hours before driving back to the car dealership. Adam left Frankfort at 11:10 p.m. and pulled into the Marriott Courtyard at the Louisville Airport at midnight. At nine a.m. on Monday morning, he lifted the receiver of a pay phone in the Newark airport and dialed the Minneapolis office of the Baker Company. After the customary delay, the voice, sweetest of all voices to his ears, said, "Good morning, Lola Princeton here. May I help you?"

"I certainly hope so," said Adam. "I'm calling from a pay phone in the Newark Airport so we're okay to talk. How are you, baby?"

"Hearing the sound of your voice, I am ecstatic. Before you called, I was a bereft, lonely woman ready to go out and give myself to the nearest thing in pants. How about you?"

"I only miss you about twenty-two hours a day. The other two comprise the sleep that doesn't include you in my dreams. If I don't get an invitation from JoAnn for the two of us in the next week, I think we should arrange a few days in Minneapolis. Missing you has my tank almost on empty."

"Mine is dry," replied Belinda. "Let's try to make it this weekend. We could spend some time with your folks, that is, after I have my way with you alone."

"Sounds wonderful, providing I don't have to play peeping Tom. I'm returning from Frankfort, Kentucky, where we are currently sneaking a peek at Willard Fenton and company."

"How is the Eagle working?"

"Great. Jeffrey even hinted that JoAnn may show how much she appreciates my efforts beyond saying 'thank you.' As well as getting approval to supervise at least some of the shoots, my suggestion to move the Eagle off-base was approved."

"Do you have anything in mind for the final take-down?"

"No, but I would like to use the Eagle to do it. I don't know if I'll get a chance to review all the footage from the shoots, much less be able to copy it. I think the best chance is to borrow the Eagle and record one or more meetings of the Brigade. At this point I have no idea where they'll store it or what kind of security will be put in place. I may have to wait until the new ones are built. I'm toying with the idea of building one more than they think I'm building. What do you think?"

"I think that sounds a lot safer than trying to pirate that big tank out of their secure storage. I'm concerned about blowing the mission, but even more so, about your safety. There's no urgency that justifies taking foolish risks. I'm sure General Rayburn would agree."

"Check with him and we'll make a decision this weekend. I also have to check with Jeffrey about renting a place off-post, establishing a second lab and enlisting Jason Bark to help build the new Eagles. The kid is bright and it would cut the time to develop the units nearly in half."

"He may be bright," cautioned Belinda, "but remember, he was in on the brutal murder of that security guard. How could you trust him?"

"He may be ruthless, but he's also an electronics guru and I have become his God. If only I could encourage the worship from you that this lad willingly bestows upon me, I would truly be in heaven."

"Wrong," she exclaimed. "People like that only want what you can give them. Make one slip and he'll cut your throat with a smile on his face. However, you're the guy in the trenches and the final decision is yours. I'll brief the general on all this and we'll discuss it over a drink on Friday night. Do you think all your brilliant work and your overtime this weekend might entitle you to a three-day pass?"

"I wouldn't be surprised. When I hang up, I'll hop in my car and whoosh directly to Major Randolph's office. After making my report, I will plead my case for rest and recuperation. With any luck at all, I should call you by noon with the answer. Until then, parting is such sweet sorrow."

"Parting is horrible, but the thought of seeing you in five days makes my spirits soar. Drive carefully. I'll be sitting by the phone waiting for your call."

Adam drove carefully, but swiftly, and was sitting in the major's office at 1030 hours. After giving the details of the operation in Frankfort, he asked, "Have you given any further thought to Bark's getting involved with the new Eagle at a house in town?"

"As a matter of fact, I have. I discussed it with the appropriate people and you have a go. You may recall that I suggested JoAnn might reward you for repairing the Eagle. She has decided to show her thanks by setting you up in something more than a trailer house...in Long Branch. If you have time this afternoon, I would be pleased to introduce you to your bounty."

"Thank you, sir, I'd be delighted," Adam exclaimed with genuine excitement. "I am at your disposal." As he said this, Adam thought that he would indeed be at Jeffrey's *disposal* if the major found out what his real mission at Fort Monmouth was about.

As they drove to the seaside town of Long Branch, Jeffrey told how JoAnn had taken the bit in her teeth when he told her of Adam's plan for an off-post residence/ laboratory. She had sent Sela Pierce down to

Monmouth to search out an appropriate place, one that would satisfy Adam's needs and also serve as a secondary meeting place for Brigade business. Sela, no tightwad when it came to spending other people's money, declared that she had found the perfect place and absolutely no other would do. Jeffrey relayed that he had no idea if JoAnn had swallowed hard when she wrote the check, but he knew there were a lot of zeros behind the number. In spite of Jeffery's comments, Adam was shocked at the elegance of the sprawling seaside home that lay in front of Jeffrey's hood ornament.

He gasped as he said, "Wow. You must be pulling my leg. This place looks like a million dollars…literally."

"I told you there were a lot of zeros," said a smirking Jeffrey. "For all I know she may kick you and Bark out occasionally and fuck the general's brains out while she's enjoying the view of the sea."

"If that's the case, I'm going to have to be a tidy housekeeper," said Adam.

"Oh, that's been taken care of too. There's a live-in cook/housekeeper that JoAnn hired temporarily from the previous owners. They're living in Florida and the maid doesn't like the heat, so she's staying for a couple of weeks at least."

"Great," said Adam, but he thought it might be too coincidental and the 'maid' might want to keep track of more than the dust on the furniture. "When do we take possession of this grand abode?"

"Right now. The people had previously moved to Florida and JoAnn bought it furnished. All you have to do is bring your pajamas and toothbrush. After you have a gander at the place, we'll look for an appropriate spot to build your lab. We want to get it operational as soon as possible so you can get to building those little suckers."

"I'm overwhelmed," Adam said with feeling as they entered the large foyer of what appeared to be a one-story house from the road. After walking through the large beautifully furnished rooms on the main floor, they descended a large curved staircase and found another level with large windows facing the sea.

The end of the tour found them on the third or ground level. Jeffrey said, "This looks like the perfect place for the lab. We'll have to build just one wall and the others are well protected from enemy eyes."

"Exactly," replied Adam. "We should complete the design and start as soon as possible. I will also prepare a list of tools and equipment. By the time the lab is completely built and stocked, I should be ready to start ordering parts for the machines. I plan to order three of everything to build two machines. This will give us a spare for every part in the device."

"What do you see as the biggest stumbling block from a timing standpoint?" asked Jeffrey.

"Locating all of the parts. I have to replace all of the original Eagle components with miniaturized versions. This will involve a lot of searching with a lot of manufacturers. Once found, ordering will be simple. The tough part will be either fabricating or farming out for custom-making the parts we cannot buy in the marketplace. The delay is doubled because we cannot begin this phase until we have exhausted our search of the electronics market. Another factor is the housing. I can't begin to design the housing until *all* the parts are assembled. At this point, I have no idea of the size or shape that will accommodate the necessary components."

"That all makes sense," said Jeffrey. "I want you to call on me for whatever help you need to move this project forward at maximum speed. The trip to Frankfort with two men and a van is an example of inefficiency and danger from a security standpoint. Remember, cost is no object."

Adam asked for and obtained a three-day pass for the weekend. As he looked back on his magnificent new house, he concluded that, in spite of the dangers he faced, he had been successful in achieving every goal he'd set so far. All in all, this was undoubtedly his finest hour at Fort Monmouth. The thought made him nervous. How much longer could things continue to go so well?

September 30th, 1991, Long Branch, NJ, 9:30 a.m....

Adam surveyed the scene as the concrete contractor dug footings after jack-hammering openings in the concrete floor. An electrician was installing a 200-Amp service box and the plumber was chopping for floor drains after running water lines into the soon-to-be laboratory. Although he was finalizing the plan for the layout and furnishings, his thoughts kept coming back to the three days at home...three days with Belinda.

His father, mother and sister had all given them a hard time about their *too* obvious, mutual love. The family finally relented when they sensed he was ready to move to a hotel for more privacy. In the infrequent intervals when they had not been talking or making love, they discussed the progress of the mission. General Rayburn had approved the concept of waiting for the new Eagles rather than attempting to spirit the bulky original away for counter-espionage against the Brigade. He also agreed with the idea of building an extra machine. He suggested that the fourth set of parts be ordered by the Belinda's "Company" in Minneapolis rather than risk discovery by ordering them through the Brigade.

Adam forced himself to return to the task at hand and put the finishing touches on the plan for the workbenches and drawer units. After making sure the contractor had no additional questions for him, he climbed wearily into the Porsche and drove to the Fort. He sighed as he thought about the work ahead. He must satisfy the requirements of his assigned workload, lay out the design for the new Eagle, begin the search for components and complete the construction and installation of equipment in the new lab. His concern was for his mental stamina. Could he operate for 12-14 hours a day at the level of efficiency necessary to create these complex devices? Perhaps he should mandate that Belinda receive his update in person on a regular schedule, like every other week. Yes, that would give him the incentive to work like crazy, to always have that pot of gold at the end of a close-at-hand rainbow. He had described his new home to her, but the thought of showing her through it was not only pleasant, but downright erotic. The sunshine that had been prevalent all day suddenly burst into his consciousness as he resolved to call her and present his plan. He would devise a long list of reasons why frequent personal contacts were absolutely necessary to the success of their mission. With the tasks that lay before him this day, he might have to postpone the phone call to allow time to develop a list of *most* persuasive arguments. That was the answer; he would work on the list tonight and call her tomorrow. With that decision made, he focused on his schedule for the day with renewed vigor.

After an early morning call to establish her availability, Adam called Belinda from a pay phone on the way to the Fort. He was quite business-like in his quest for regular and frequent meetings.

The carefully conceived plan was skillfully delivered, at the end of which Belinda replied, "My, I don't think I've ever heard you present such an orderly and well-concocted strategy, and in such detail. One argument that is most compelling for me is that you'd like to be able to press your head to my breast and have me tell you 'it's all right.' On the other hand, I probably should leave that one out when I present this to the general."

"With your talk with the general in mind, I purposely left out page after page of erotic reasons for this schedule to be adopted," said Adam. "To maintain our cover, I could meet you in Newark every other time, otherwise at my house. Should we get further invitations from our lady JoAnn, of course, they would count as report meetings."

"Aren't you at all afraid that we'll tire of each other with all this togetherness?" said Belinda in a teasing voice.

"There is zero chance of that," said Adam so seriously that it surprised Belinda. "My feelings for you have grown steadily since we first met and that ain't gonna change."

"Adam, I was only teasing. I feel the same way and depending on the general's decision, would like nothing better than seeing you every other week. I will discuss it with him today. If I call you tonight and suggest coming up next week, you'll know he agreed. Feel better now?"

"Much," said Adam. "I'll be waiting for your call." The phone rang at seven that evening and Adam was delighted that the general had agreed with his request. The message was delivered as Belinda announced she would arrive in Newark at noon on the fourth for an afternoon meeting with her 'client.' Following the meeting she would drive down to Long Branch and have a look at everything he had, including the house.

Adam's frame of mind after the phone call was extremely positive as he sat back in the recliner and reflected upon the project ahead. What had seemed like a gargantuan job at first sight was really quite manageable when he calculated the tasks he could delegate to Smythe on post, and Bark at his home lab. The workflow crystallized in his mind, assigning searches for a portion of the components to Bark and the balance to Smythe. He had laid out the lowest floor, containing the lab to allow access from the ground level with no access to the rest of the house. He envisioned Bark arriving early in the morning, getting instructions and working alone as Adam worked with Smythe in the Army lab. Adam would return in the afternoon to review Bark's progress before dismissing him for the day. Regarding his ongoing review of various Army communication devices and sophisticated weapons, he would ask the major to provide one or two others to assist in that effort. Suddenly the project he had approached with a degree of dread became not only doable, but a challenge he looked forward to. The confidence garnered while laying out his development strategy was tempered when he reminded himself of the inherent danger in his every move. He could never relax until the deed was done. He would have to assemble the secret, *third* Eagle at night and leave no evidence of its existence. He would also secure the working blueprints for the machine as a little insurance, so they'd think twice about his disposal. That is, unless they discovered his true mission.

The week flew by with Bark exceeding Adam's highest hopes as he performed his assigned tasks with speed and accuracy. Smythe did well at the base, beginning his part of the component search while helping Adam in training two new recruits for the ongoing equipment appraisal. As he worked in the Army lab on Friday morning, Adam received a surprise call from JoAnn. She opened the conversation with, "Good morning, Adam. I hope things are going well with all of your projects. I have not yet seen your off-post quarters. Are they satisfactory?"

"That is the understatement of the century," replied Adam. "How can I ever thank you enough for putting me up in such a splendid place?"

"If you continue to perform at current levels, I'll do more than 'put you up' in that house, but for now, any chance you could show me around the place? We could even combine business with pleasure by having a little meeting."

"Your wish is my command, m'lady," said Adam. "When would you like to come up?"

"I don't mean to rush you, but how about tomorrow?"

"Wonderful, Lola is coming out later today, and I know she'd love to see you."

JoAnn practically gushed as she said, "Oh, that would be fantastic, dear. We could invite a few guests and have a party. I have a caterer that will put the entire party in her van and deliver it to your house. I can fly a group up from Washington in the morning and Lola can entertain them while we talk business. It will be ideal."

"I'll look forward to your arrival. Would you like me to arrange transportation from the airport?"

"I will take care of everything," said JoAnn. "You concentrate on your fine work and leave everything else to me. I'll see you elevenish tomorrow." As Adam hung up the phone, he thought about the meeting. He had found no bugs in either his phone or the house. It seemed strange that they would bug his BOQ and not his new home. He thought about bugging the rooms himself to record the meeting and then wondered if they would sweep for bugs and destroy his credibility, among other things. He decided to play it straight for the time being.

The sun was slanting through the west windows as Belinda pulled into the driveway. Adam recognized awe in her expression as she viewed the subdued elegance of the property. As she stepped from the car, he took her in his arms and their bodies and mouths met in joyous reunion. They walked hand in hand as they carried her luggage to the house. Adam had given the maid the evening off and insisted that, as king, he would pour a glass of fine champagne to accompany them on the grand tour of his castle. That accomplished, they began the tour. When they finished, they settled in the family room and Adam brought her up to date on his progress and JoAnn's call that morning. Belinda listened thoughtfully. "Everything sounds good. I'm anxious to see who she invites and what the meeting is about. Did she give you any clue to either?"

"Absolutely none," replied Adam. "She caught me by surprise with her last minute arrangements. She is sending her caterer up with all the food and drinks and is flying people up in her jet. I have no idea who will be here, but I do know that you are expected to entertain the guests who are not part of the meeting."

"No problem, but that's tomorrow," she continued in a low, sexy voice. "What are your plans for tonight?"

"My train of thought goes off the track when you talk in that tone. I had planned a nice candlelit dinner in a nearby restaurant, but now I can't get the idea of us naked in bed out of my mind."

"Well, maybe we could do both," Belinda said in an even more throaty whisper. "Did you hear a swishing sound? I think my panties just fell to the floor."

He rose immediately, took her hand and pulled her toward the master bedroom. His only words were, *"*Let's see if we can hear some more *swishing.*"

XII

October 5th, 1991,
Long Branch, NJ,
11:30 a.m....

Belinda poured champagne and orange juice into glasses for Sela Pierce and Alyce Foote. The day was unseasonably warm and they basked in bright sunshine on the deck overlooking the ocean. As she took the glass from Belinda, Alyce said, "My, what a wonderful view. This is very lovely house."

"It is indeed and I understand Adam has you to thank for it," Belinda said addressing Sela. "How did you find this gem on such short notice?"

"More luck than skill," replied Sela. "The house went on the market the day I arrived and I took one look and knew it was the one. It's not often that a house of this character comes along, and to find it so tastefully decorated and furnished makes it a truly rare find."

Meanwhile, in the large den, JoAnn opened the meeting by expressing concern over the time necessary to achieve results during the Eagle voyage to Kentucky. She said, "I don't know how long we can maintain surveillance on any of these people without risking discovery. You were there, Adam. What do you think?"

"I think there's a real danger when operating from the van. When we can establish a fixed base such as a building overlooking the target, the risk goes to near zero. Then the only possible exposure is transporting the machine in and out. When the new, smaller machines are available, that issue will practically disappear."

"It seems to me that we're being too impatient," boomed Foote, standing somewhat awkwardly and pacing. "The primaries are months away and all we need is one little slip and we can skin this guy alive."

"That's true, Gordon," said JoAnn, "but Fenton's just one of several people we need to discredit. To be certain that both houses are not only under Republican control, but that we install some strong conservatives in that group, will require more effort than we've ever put forth in the past. With that in mind, do we have adequate personnel to operate three Eagles?"

"We have two experienced teams in place," said Jeffrey. "One staffed by my men and the other with Ball's. If necessary Adam and I can fill in, but we will expand the group when the Eagles are ready. We can split the teams using one experienced man with one newcomer. I know Adam is working at warp speed to complete the new machines and we'll be ready when he is."

"Good, now I'd like to talk about another matter. It has come to our attention that one of my close friends, that you all know, has a cozy relationship with Sean's old employer. Our little songbird Anita has apparently been singing more than love songs for some time. We have bugged her apartment and phones and now are ready to feed her some well thought-out misinformation. In order to convey this information most effectively, we feel it should come from more than one source. Although I will bear the heaviest responsibility, I have prepared a few comments for each of you to drop at our next gathering. Don't be surprised if they include some uncomplimentary references to yours truly, although the ultimate message is always positive. I am most anxious to see how she handles the intelligence we give her."

"What have you gotten from the bugs so far?" asked Foote.

"We now have a new, better bugging device and they're now in place. The results so far have been just gossip, but we only have a week's worth of eavesdropping," said Ball. "She has a big thing going with Senator Hawthorne and he's the target of most of the news JoAnn plans to feed her. We'll give her some dope and see what she does with it."

Adam took note of the comment about the new devices. He had been scanning his home from the beginning and had found nothing. Could it be that his scanner failed to pick up the new bugs? Or perhaps they had waited until this meeting to install them. In any event, he would warn Belinda and confine their conversations to topics they could afford to share with the enemy. He broke into the conversation with, "Do you have a date in mind for the gathering with Anita?"

"Yes," replied JoAnn, "I'm planning a little Halloween party on the 26th of this month. It will be strictly costume and I plan to ask the guests to dress as their wildest fantasy. It should be quite interesting. This group will arrive early and we will meet to discuss progress on several fronts. Now I would like to move on to the primary purpose of bringing you here today. Last week, thanks to Adam's wonderful restoration of the Eagle, we literally uncovered our friend Willie Fenton. While a reception was being held on the front lawn of the governor's mansion, we caught him balling one of his campaign workers in a guest bedroom. We now need to discuss the disposition of that information. If we play our hand now, he could withdraw from the race and throw his support to another candidate. If we wait, he may throw some valuable mud at his rivals, mud that will not wash off sufficiently for him to effectively endorse any recipient of such mud. The third, and most dangerous option, is to actually support his nomination and drop the bomb on him during the election campaign. Please give me your reactions."

Foote folded his huge frame into a barely adequate chair. His rugged features softened with his reply. "I like option two. It's the best overall, but with it we also leave option three open in case we change our mind."

The others nodded agreement and JoAnn said, "That's settled then. For the last order of business, I am pleased to announce that Adam's patent has been filed and Gordon has completed a prototype, done preliminary testing, and will finalize the design for a production model before the end of the year. This means the system will be on the market in late spring. I compliment all of you that had a part in this, but particularly Adam. I realize we are putting a lot of stress on you, but if you can fit in one more project, consulting with Gordon's people on the production model, you'll be out of the woods in a short time."

"As long as there's light at the end of the tunnel. I can handle it," said Adam with a smile, "particularly when the light is as bright as this one."

"Wonderful. That's the attitude we expected from you," said JoAnn. "The Brigade will be pleasantly surprised when the money starts flowing in. Although they have contributed huge sums without complaint, they will appreciate some funding from within. Unless anyone has an issue to discuss, this meeting is adjourned. Let us join the ladies and enjoy our host's splendid picnic site."

The beauty of the day, the elegant surroundings enhanced by champagne and superb food, created a festive mood that delayed the departure of the guests. Adam carefully hid his impatience to scan the house for bugs while playing his role as host with good humor and aplomb. After they'd gone, he scanned the entire house carefully. He was disappointed to find several bugs, but was relieved that his scanner was able to detect this *new* generation. Had it failed and they had been installed earlier, he and Belinda would be totally and perhaps fatally compromised. When he completed the task, he and Belinda had a conversation in the yard. He explained the location of the bugs and suggested they each keep pad and pencil handy to write notes when in the 'hot' areas of the house. Discovering the bugs dampened their spirit somewhat for the balance of the weekend, but heightened their caution.

Belinda drove out of his driveway at three p.m. on Sunday. He watched her car until it disappeared in the distance. He stood there for some time, motionless. A sense of dread gradually came over him. The weight of his onerous work schedule intertwined with the pressure of the deadly game he was playing nearly overwhelmed him. He recognized the depression born each time Belinda departed, but this time the feeling of aloneness was more pronounced. It was as if the entire world was in sync and he was standing as odd man out. As he walked into the house, he straightened up and made a decision to look beyond all of this, to a day when he wouldn't have to look over his shoulder constantly and be alert every moment of the day and night. All he had to do was tough it out for a few weeks or months…and by God, he would do just that.

**December 11th, 1991,
44th Signal, Fort Monmouth,
NJ, 0820 hours...**

A weary Adam Packard answered his phone, "Packard here."

"So, is today the big day?" asked Major Jeffrey Randolph. "You've been saying 'any day now' for a week."

"It could be, sir," replied Adam. "I have a few calibrations to complete and 'Teeny Eagle I' should be ready to test. Do you want to be here for the big event?"

"Nothing could keep me away. By the way, I have some interesting news about our surveillance on the songbird. Do you happen to know a person named Belinda?'

Adam caught his breath and thought quickly, "It's Lola's middle name. I call her that once in a while to get her goat. Where did you hear it?"

"In a recorded conversation with the person we have under surveillance, she mentioned Adam and Belinda. I thought you had another babe on the string, but I guess not, right?"

"Right, Lola's the only one I've got going," said Adam with a sigh of relief. "With my workload, I barely have time for her, but that should improve very soon. With the work on the patent out of the way, and if our baby enters the world without complications, I'm putting in for a long holiday leave."

"You've certainly earned it. Call me when you're ready for the unveiling."

"Yes sir, I really think it will happen this afternoon." Adam hung up the phone and went back to work worried about Anita's slip. With all the precautions they had taken, to be threatened by such a stupid mistake. She should not have divulged that name to the senator at all, much less used it in a phone conversation. If only it were a common name like Mary or Jane, but it was not and she could be identified through either the CIA or the Army. Damn, their cover could be blown, and just when they were so close. He knew he had to put it out of his mind and concentrate on the final steps to make the little Eagle a reality. When he finished, he'd slip away and call Belinda with the bad news.

At 1430 hours, Adam called Major Randolph and announced that the machine was ready for preliminary testing. Jeffrey said he'd be over at once and the test began at 1500 hours. The first shot had good sound, but a faulty picture. Adam made several interior adjustments and the picture improved. With additional adjustments to the exterior controls, the picture became crystal clear. The Eagle was aimed at several targets at varying range and the results were perfect. Adam then took the machine from his shoulder and dropped it about 8 inches to the top of the work bench. He picked it up, turned it on and there was no loss of performance. He turned to an amazed Jeffrey and said, "That was a test of durability. I tried to isolate as many components as possible to reduce the damage from dropping or other mishaps. I also made an attempt to waterproof the entire unit. I'm certain a little rain won't affect it, but with only two units, I'm not ready to drop it in a pool. Perhaps when this year's mission is complete, we can give it the acid test."

"Adam, I am most impressed. What does it weigh?" Adam handed the Eagle to Jeffrey and he put it on his shoulder. "Man, this is fairly light. I could record for a long time without putting it down."

"It weighs a little more than the old M-1 rifle, just over ten pounds, but in most cases you'll scan from a tripod. The socket is right here," Adam said as he pointed to the center of the machine. "To keep the new Eagle light, we have incorporated a short-lived battery in the housing. For normal use, a separate battery pack or 110 volt AC current will be used. We also use a remote recorder to store the video and audio signals. Before long, data storage devices will be miniaturized to the point that all recording can be incorporated in the Eagle housing."

"I think this calls for a celebration. How long will it take you to finish up here?"

"About an hour, but I need time to shave and shower. I've taken little time for grooming these last weeks. I can be ready at about 1800 hours if that's all right with you." He thought about the call to Belinda and realized that he might not be able to *safely* make the call until the next day.

"Perfect," said the major. "I'll pick you up at your BOQ at 1830." Jeffrey arrived on the dot in his silver BMW 540i and they drove to the Manhattan Steak House, an upscale supper club seven miles from the Fort. As he negotiated the road at speeds that tested the superb roadability of the sleek machine, he talked casually, asking Adam, "Where do we stand with the second Eagle?"

"All the parts are ready to assemble. It should be ready in a week or ten days. I would like to train the people on the first one and get it into action, then put the other together. What do you think?"

"Sounds good," replied Jeffrey. "We can start the training as early as tomorrow. I also want to demonstrate it to JoAnn, Foote and Thomas. Perhaps we can get together this weekend and show off a bit."

"That's fine with me," said Adam. "Lola's meeting with her client in Newark on Friday and we'll be happy to meet with the group anytime."

"If the players are available, I'll set it up tomorrow," said Jeffrey as he pulled into the restaurant's parking lot. "Now let's concentrate on a bottle of champagne and a pound of rare steak."

Following the celebratory dinner, Adam asked to be dropped off at the BOQ. He told Jeffrey that he would stay on the base that night and be ready to start training on the Eagle in the morning. The major agreed to issue orders for the Company A personnel first thing in the morning and to contact Ball's men regarding their availability. Although physically and mentally exhausted, Adam slept fitfully. That someone might discover his true purpose had suddenly become a very real possibility. He arose nearly as tired as when he went to bed, but forced himself to go through his morning ritual including a four-mile run.

His run deviated from normal on this morning as Adam stopped and stuffed quarters in a pay phone for a direct call to Belinda. He could hear the dismay in her voice when she heard about Anita's slip. She agreed to discuss this development at length with General Rayburn that morning and call him with a coded message later in the day. She closed with a whispered, "Until tomorrow, hang in there, my love."

Carter, Albertson, Smythe and Pollmer arrived at 0830 hours for training on the 'baby' Eagle. Before noon, they were thoroughly familiar with both the operation and care and maintenance of the device. Bark and Jolson arrived at 1330 hours and completed the same course by 1700 hours. Major Randolph sat in on the afternoon session and was also 'checked out' on the new Eagle.

When Ball's men had departed, the major turned to Adam and said, "I have arranged the meeting we discussed last evening. JoAnn's plane will pick us up at Newark International at 1000 hours on Saturday morning. We will fly to Chicago and be guests of Gordon Foote. We'll all fly back early Sunday afternoon. Does that work for you and Lola?"

"That's perfect," replied Adam "We'll stay overnight in Newark and drive to the airport in the morning. Perhaps JoAnn will even drop Lola off in Minneapolis on the way back?"

"You never can tell. Even if she can't, we'll be back in time for a commercial flight. Perhaps I should haul the Eagle and related equipment. You hardly have room for the two of you and a toothbrush in that little Porsche."

"Good," said Adam. "Otherwise I'd have to haul it up to the room. There's no way I'd leave it in the car overnight. Where will we meet you at the airport?"

"Pull your car into the valet parking. We'll leave instructions with their desk. Now I must make haste, the lovely seductress Sela awaits my presence and her patience has finite limits."

Adam checked the Porsche twice for bugs before picking up Belinda in Newark. When she entered the car and was given the 'all clear,' she said, "Adam, I am so sorry Anita made that slip. I discussed the situation with the general at length and he feels we should alert our backups and establish closer liaison. He is afraid that the Brigade will act swiftly if they associate my name with my true identity. What are the chances of turning the tables on them and setting up some surveillance on JoAnn and possibly Jeffrey?"

"I'm afraid that's almost impossible. Her home is so large, it would require a myriad of devices. After the new security system is in production, I could suggest that she install it in her house. The bugs could be built in. The problem is timing, because we're talking several months. If they pursue the name, we could be compromised in weeks or even days. We need to accelerate our timetable and take them down before they take us down."

"General Rayburn had the same idea," said Belinda. "He suggests we arrange a meeting with Mack Rogers and his people ASAP. What do you think?"

"It may be a bit premature to call out the cavalry. I'd like to lay low until I get some sort of signal from them that our relationship has changed."

The weekend was show and tell. After Friday's long-awaited togetherness, Adam and Belinda reluctantly left their love nest and boarded JoAnn's sleek silver jet. JoAnn served Bloody Marys to her guests Jeffrey, Sela, Adam, Belinda and Sean Ball. Belinda could not ignore the looks she received from Ball. If ever there was animal magnetism, it was exemplified in this man's eyes. She finally resorted to reading a novel to avoid his intense stare. She was so absorbed in avoiding the silent attention of Ball, she failed to observe a similar eye-stalking of Adam by Sela. Adam, although flattered by the attention, had an uncomfortable feeling that Jeffrey might take offense. This was no time to add any rifts to their relationship.

They met the Thomases at O'Hare and were whisked away in two limos to Globe Electronics northwest of the airport. Gordon and Alyce Foote greeted them in the executive office suite and invited them to be seated in his lavish board-room. Foote gave an impressive multi-media presentation on the company followed by the grand tour of his large and sparkling-clean production facilities. He made a particular point of showing the area designated for the production of Adam's security system. He winked at Adam and cuffed him on the back with a huge paw. "We have room to expand this area as you come up with more inventions, hey, boy?"

Adam smiled and nodded, but was not anxious to have a close relationship with the likes of Gordon Foote. He suspected Foote's 'good nature' was a thin veneer covering a heartless bully.

After lunch, Alyce Foote guided another tour for the ladies, while the Eagle demonstration brought ooh's and ah's from the men and

JoAnn. The rest of the afternoon was devoted to a tour of Chicago and after checking into the Palmer House Hotel, they dined at the famous Pump Room on the North side. Adam and Belinda, anxious to be alone, finally reached their room at ten o'clock. The incredible tension they both felt interfered with their lovemaking. Their lack of passion, however, was replaced by a greater sense of togetherness than they'd ever felt.

At breakfast the next morning, JoAnn stood, raised her glass and said, "I propose a toast to Adam Packard for your outstanding work in restoring the original and designing the new Eagles. I salute you!" After the 'hear, hears' died down, she continued, "As a small token of our appreciation, we hope this gift will help you continue to meet all your commitments on time." With that she handed Adam a gold, diamond-studded Rolex watch.

Adam stood and said, "Thank you very much. Although the last few months have been harried to say the least, the results and more importantly, the benefits to the cause, have made them well worthwhile. I would like to toast you, and the important work to which you are all committed. Thank you for allowing me to play a small part in it."

The route home was by way of Minneapolis to drop off Belinda. Adam watched wistfully as Belinda walked, with her extraordinary grace, across the tarmac to the terminal. He was unaware that another pair of eyes were glued to the same walk. The difference was, Ball's eyes watched not with love, but with pure lust.

January 6th, 1992,
Company A, Fort Monmouth,
NJ, 0915 hours...

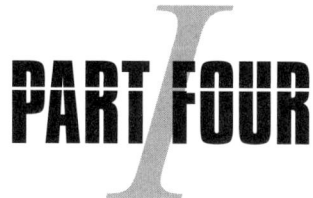
PART FOUR

Adam sat in his office/lab with a hangdog look about him. He had just returned from a meeting with Major Randolph. His keen judgment of character and ability to read attitudes left him dismayed. Jeffrey had seemed pleasant enough on the surface, but the open friendship he had displayed for many months was forced. The 'Belinda' slip by Anita Warwick now obsessed Adam. He felt certain they *knew* and would take action against him sooner rather than later. He saw his chances of accomplishing the mission going up in smoke and his life given in a fruitless cause. The time had come to bring in Mack Rogers, as the general had suggested. Adam had entrusted the third Eagle to Rogers in mid-December and had trained Rogers, Al Leach and Jim Young to use it. He went through the motions of checking the projects he had left for his subordinates and watched his rearview mirror carefully as he drove to his home in Long Branch.

He stopped at a gas station, bought gas and called Rogers from the pay phone. He gave him the code and called him back at the safe house a few minutes later. When Rogers answered, Adam said, "I have bad news. In my meeting with Randolph today, I sensed a change in his attitude toward me. We had a major problem arise in December when a person that knows our story let Belinda's name slip on her bugged phone. When Randolph confronted me with it, I covered it the best I could, but, after this morning, I have a strong suspicion our cover's been blown."

"Damn," said Rogers. "Just when we're really getting close. What do you want me to do, Adam?"

"Watch my back and have the Eagle ready to record any meeting I have with the Brigade. I will try to anticipate their moves and will keep you informed. If I call your beeper, come running. One beep for my office at the Fort, two for my house and three for JoAnn's house. Bring help and some firepower to storm the gates if necessary."

"Gotcha. I'll inform the troops and we'll practice on the Eagle. I want to get in close and give you some real backup."

"We'll let them make a move and hope we can counter it...and come up with the evidence. If they confront me, I'll try to get them to incriminate themselves. It's up to you to get it on tape."

"I'm gonna do more than wait for your beep," said Mack. "I'll have Leach plant a device on your car and in your shoe so we can track you wherever you go. Call me at this time tomorrow and we'll discuss the details."

"I don't think that's necessary. Why don't you just wait for my beep?"

"Look, Adam, if you want me to back you up, you're going to have to do it my way. If those bastards get you, it's gonna be over my dead body!"

"Have it your way, and thanks. Frankly, I can use a little reassurance right now. I'll call you tomorrow."

Adam then called Belinda and told her of his suspicions. She said, "I think we should pull you out. You are in great danger, Adam. I couldn't stand it if anything happened to you."

"I know that, love, but we can't just throw away our investment in this mission. We have to try to finish it. We always knew there was danger and I have alerted Rogers. He's calling out his troops and intends to follow my every step. They're good and will get the evidence we need...and protect me."

"I agree that Mack is good, but so are the people on the other side...and they've got him outnumbered ten to one. Keep your head down until I can discuss this with the general. I'd ask you to go out and call me later tonight, but you need to stay buttoned up in the house after dark. Call me on your way in tomorrow and we'll discuss what the general had to say. And Adam, please be careful. I love you."

When Adam arrived home, he went to the closet, withdrew his 9mm Glock, checked the magazine and chambered a round. With the gun in his belt he carefully checked all doors and windows and double-checked the alarm. He had installed a prototype of the alarm he had designed for the Brigade and had purposely coded it so the bypasses set up for the production model would be inoperative. Unless they hit the house with a missile, he felt safe. He had no appetite, but knew he must eat to maintain the strength to face the forthcoming showdown. Two chicken breasts and a pot of vegetables later, he sat down and tried to put himself in the place of his adversaries. What would their first reaction be? Would they act rashly, or would they carefully consider their options?

If Randolph and his minions acted on their own, a knee-jerk, violent action would result. If Randolph went to JoAnn with it, she would insist on a thorough discussion before any action. Ball would shoot first and ask questions later, but he would likely wait for JoAnn's call. Adam concluded he must be prepared for anything, so he placed the Glock, with a cartridge in the chamber, under his pillow.

As he lay wide awake in the early hours of the morning, Adam recalled the twelve days of Christmas he had spent at home with his family and Belinda. Oh God, Belinda. Lovely, wonderful Belinda. She had loved him, loved his family and tearfully accepted the diamond he had presented to her on Christmas Eve. He vowed not let her come back under these circumstances. When they talked in the morning, he must make that clear and warn her that he wasn't the only one that had to watch his back. After a too-short, fitful sleep he arose and forced himself to go through his exercise and nutrition ritual.

When the sun spread its brilliant beams over the shimmering ocean, Adam took heart and the demons of the night were banished…at least for the moment. He shaved, showered and dressed. The Glock felt good in his coat pocket and when he climbed into the Porsche, he found that the gun fit neatly between his seat and the console. Ready for a quick draw, but unseen should he be forced to leave the car suddenly. As he drove toward the Fort, he was convinced that his paranoia had reached a serious level. He saw danger in every car, truck or motorcycle traveling in either direction.

When he reached his first destination, a Perkins Restaurant, he forced himself to walk in casually, eyes front. He called Belinda and was buoyed by the sound of her voice. He struggled to sound confident as he said, "Good morning and how was your night?"

"Of course it was sleepless and terrible. I suppose you'll tell me you slept like a baby?"

"Yeah, I cried all night long," Adam quipped with a forced laugh. "Did your conversation with the general upset you?"

"No, I felt good about his reaction. He is leaving it up to you. If you decide to fold up the tent and come home, he will support that decision. On the other hand, he will supply additional backup should you opt to carry on. He will transfer a small elite, special-forces unit to Monmouth for training. These people are a match for the likes of Ball and company and will cover your butt. He'll assign part of the unit to work off base in civilian clothes to augment Rogers group. What do you think?"

"I'm impressed," said Adam. "What about timing? We wouldn't want to lock the barn door after the horse is gone."

"As soon as you decide, he'll put the plan in action. He will back-date orders to send the unit over. They're on 24-hour combat ready call, so they'd arrive in two days. Now do you want to hear my feelings on the subject?"

"I'm impressed with the general's commitment and it gives me a great deal of assurance, but of course, I want your opinion."

"The Army officer in me says, 'go for it.' The woman in me says, 'get out quickly and save yourself for me.' And the psychologist in me says, 'if Adam walks away, will it have a lasting effect on his psyche?' I have to admit that the general's plan impressed me too. In the final analysis, I will support you completely, whatever you decide."

"I'm a little confused here. You've just told me, as a soldier, I should forge ahead. As your lover, I should head for the hills, and, as a man, I'll feel like shit if I give up. Two out of three say, go for it...and that's what I have to do. I know you love me and I want to always deserve that love. Between the role the general has agreed to play and your support, my path is clear. Tell the general to put his plan in motion. In the meantime, I promise to walk on eggshells. Now I must get going."

"Goodbye, my darling," Belinda whispered. "You'll be in my thoughts and prayers every minute of the day and night."

Just after Adam reached his office, the phone rang. He picked it up and said, "Packard here."

"Good morning, Adam," said a somewhat reserved JoAnn Cleveland. "I trust you had a pleasant holiday?"

Adam was dismayed by the lack of warmth in her greeting. After a brief delay, he replied, "Thank you, JoAnn, I did indeed have a fine holiday. I hope Santa Claus was good to you, too."

"Yes, we had several parties and I'm told everyone had a splendid time. In fact, I'm planning another for this weekend and I do hope that you and Lola can come down on Saturday. We can combine a little business with pleasure. Are you two available, say fiveish?"

Adam thought fast. If he made up an excuse, they'd suspect he knew something. If he accepted, they could always plead an emergency at the last minute. He answered, "Thank you. I don't see any reason why we can't make it. I'm sure Lola will be delighted. I can call her this morning to verify her availability."

"Good, please call me when you find out. It wouldn't be a special party without the *two* of you."

"I'll call you later this morning, and thank you for the invitation."

Knowing that his phone was bugged, Adam called Belinda, through Minneapolis and began with, "Lola, how are you this morning? I hope you're in the mood to say 'yes,' because I have a party invitation for this weekend. JoAnn has invited us and I hope you can make it."

"I'd love to come, Adam," said Belinda, catching Adam's 'yes' in the invitation. "When and where?"

"Saturday at five p.m. at JoAnn's house. If you could fly into National early in the day we can spend some time looking at the sights."

"Great, I'll call you as soon as I get a flight reservation and you can pick me up at the airport. I can't wait to see you."

II

*January 7th, 1992,
Arlington, VA, 4:30 p.m....*

JoAnn paced back and forth, obviously frustrated. She whirled on Sean Ball and said, "Are you absolutely certain that Lola is really Major Belinda Jackson? And if she is, that Adam's a spy in our midst?"

"I sent the pictures to you two days ago, there can be no doubt. When I looked through her service record with a fine-tooth comb, I found that she trained with another soldier who has also been in our hair, Captain Mack Rogers. Interesting coincidence, don't you think?"

"Yes," replied JoAnn, "but isn't it possible that she's been playing Adam and he's not a part of any plan to injure the Brigade?"

"Think back, JoAnn. When Anita slipped and called 'Lola' by her real name, Adam told Jeff that 'Belinda' was her middle name. If he were innocent, why would he make up an excuse? I've always told you he was too slick. Now we need to take him down before he takes you and the Brigade down. I need a little private time with him and I guarantee we'll find out whose side he's on." As Ball said this, he thought how much he'd like to interrogate Belinda, but put that aside. He'd bide his time until the opportunity arose to move on the gorgeous 'Lola.'

JoAnn said, "You could be right, and we cannot afford to make a mistake here. As you know, they're invited down here this weekend. Meet with Jeffrey and come up with a plan, but under no circumstances are you to take any action without my approval. I am committed to meetings tomorrow, but I want to resolve this thing no later than Thursday morning. Is that a problem for you?"

"No, I'll call Jeff right now and we'll put together some options, but we have to work fast. If he suspects we're on to him, he may either run or worse, go public with what he's got. Even without hard evidence, the wrong kind of publicity could sink your ship."

JoAnn had a pensive look as she said, "All right, Sean, call me as soon as you have a plan. I'll be available anytime after four p.m. tomorrow." She rose and saw him to the door of her library. As he headed for the front door, she said, "This could be the most important assignment you've undertaken for me, so don't let me down."

As he turned the corner entering the foyer, he called back, "Don't worry, JoAnn, you can count on me."

When Ball reached his Audi, he called Jeffrey Randolph's office at Fort Monmouth. Learning from his assistant that he had left for the day, he dialed his pager and put in his car phone number and a code that spelled URGENT. Within three minutes, Randolph was on the line. Ball said, "We need to have a heart to heart about our little problem. The chief wants answers in twenty-four hours. Can you get to a secure phone and call my special number right away?"

"Will do," said Randolph.

Twenty minutes later, Ball's phone rang and he activated the scrambler that would eliminate any trace or record of the call. He said, "I'm sure you've guessed that I've just come from a meeting with JoAnn."

"Yes," replied Jeffrey. "From the urgency, I assume she's on the warpath."

"Well, not as much as I am. She's still giving your prize pupil the benefit of the doubt. I'm so goddamn-sure he's a ringer, I want to take him down now. Your old lady, on the other hand, wants us to concoct several scenarios so she can play eeny, meeny, miney, moe. We may have to sugarcoat what we really plan to do."

"Easy, you don't want to cross JoAnn on this. You're dealing with her fair-haired boy and if you're wrong or even go at it differently than you say, she'll eat you alive."

"Don't be an ass. I'm not suggesting we go way outside the plan, just make it a bit easier for JoAnn to accept. I've already told her I want to do some serious interrogation, and you know what that means."

"You bet I do," said Jeffrey. "Have you come up with any plans or are we starting with a blank page?"

"I don't care how we get him, I just want to get him to a safe house and have twenty-four hours to work him over. I can't see any value in pussy-footing around…asking him to 'fess-up.' He'll just deny everything. I suppose you know that JoAnn invited the two of them down for the weekend?"

"Yeah. I wonder if he has any idea that we're on to him. I tried to act as friendly as ever when he got back, but he did seem a bit stand-offish. Are you thinking of taking him at JoAnn's?"

"That might be a problem. If people know where he's going and he disappears, it could implicate JoAnn. It would be better to take him either before or after the weekend. I assume he's still living in that fucking mansion JoAnn bought for him."

"Yes, as far as I know, he goes home every night. We'd almost have to catch him at the house, coming or going. I wouldn't want to abduct him from the Fort."

"I agree. The question," said Ball, "is *when*? I'd like to do it before the weekend. We'll have to convince JoAnn that this can't wait until next week. When we get him, you'll have to come up with a story how he seemed upset, not himself when he returned from leave. Some hints as to why he might have gone AWOL."

"I can do that. Who do you want to carry out the snatch, some of your guys or mine? Carter would dearly like a crack at old Adam."

Ball responded, "I'd like to sleep on that. I can see some advantages and drawbacks either way. Your guys would be available on short notice, mine may not be."

"I know you're convinced he's dirty, but what if he isn't? You're going to have to lay out a scenario for JoAnn that deals with that possibility."

"I'm sure he's a mole, but I suppose we have to cover that base if only to mollify JoAnn. We'll tell her we'll treat him gently…if we're wrong, we'll give him one hell of an apology."

"Okay, suppose he does confess, what do you plan to do with him after you work him over?" asked Jeffrey.

"That's a dumb-ass question. I sure ain't gonna crown him Queen of the May. We're gonna kill the son-of-a-bitch. After that, we'll dump him in a fucking swamp. Do you have any problem with that?"

"Of course not. We just need to spell it out for JoAnn. Why don't we each draft a strategy and compare notes in the morning. We can decide who makes the grab when we put together the final plan. We should meet with JoAnn tomorrow afternoon if we're going to get it done before the weekend."

"Sounds good to me," said Ball. "Call me at this number in the morning and we'll compare notes. Get crackin,' compadre."

When Ball and Jeffrey explained the plan to JoAnn that they'd finalized earlier, she absolutely refused to allow Adam to be 'taken' before the weekend. She insisted that they go through with the party and watch both Adam and Lola's every move and inflection to determine if they suspected anything. They would send Adam back to duty and make their move during the next week. She outlined a plan to send Adam on an Eagle mission that week and 'take him' in a distant location. Ball and Jeffrey reluctantly agreed that his disappearance from a strange locale might cast less suspicion on any of his Army colleagues or JoAnn Cleveland. They decided to do the shoot in a sleepy little Mississippi River town, called New Orleans.

III

*January 9th, 1992,
Fort Monmouth, NJ,
Officer's Club, 1710 hours...*

Adam put on his best nonchalant face and bearing as he walked into the club. As instructed, he went to the bar and ordered a Glenlivit on the rocks. He traded quips with the bartender until he heard a gusty voice say, "I'll be goddamned, is that old Adam Packard holding up that bar?"

Adam turned and grabbed the hand of a major in Ranger's uniform. He slapped him on the shoulder and said, "Rusty Cochrane, you old devil. What brings the likes of you to this civilized environment?"

"Strictly temporary duty, m'lad. My boys and I are here to see what you geniuses have conjured up for us. I guess you have some new ways to deliver messages, both the informative and lethal kinds."

"We do indeed," said Adam. "Although I'm not sure they're designed for barroom brawlers like you guys. These are very sophisticated devices. I seem to remember you preferring a knife in the dark, to even using a rifle."

"You offend me, sir!" said Cochrane, trying to look hurt. "I am a modern warrior. I conduct war from air-conditioned bunkers by pressing buttons with my delicate fingers."

"That'll be the day," laughed Adam. "Why don't you stow the bull and tell my friend here what poison you'd like today, I'm buying and the sky's the limit."

"If you put it that way, how about a double 'Jack' on the rocks, my good man."

"Comin' right up, Major," said the bartender with a crooked grin. "It's a pleasure to serve a real soldier. Cap'n Packard here is 4 square, but we got a lot a toy soldiers around this place."

"You don't say. Well I know about Packard, but I'll keep my eye open for these 'toy soldiers' of yours and give 'em a wide berth." Cochrane picked up his drink, turned to Adam and asked, "Should we find ourselves a table, mate?"

When they were settled at a remote table, Adam leaned over and said, "Nice acting job Major, I feel like I really do know you. Are we to share information here or do you want to arrange a more private meeting?"

"Speaking of actors, you're not so bad yourself. As far as our logistics here, it's your home turf and you know the bandits. I'd like to have you meet my entire team, but I don't know what kind of surveillance you may be under and what risks that may entail."

Adam considered and then said, "I believe I can shake a tail and meet somewhere off-post. Are all of your men billeted at the fort?"

"No, I have assigned six of my people to act as 'outside' guard. They will be dressed in civilian clothes and will watch your back from the time you leave the Fort at the end of the day until you are safely back inside the next morning. That of course assumes you're safe inside, and the rest of my troop will insure that."

"That's *most* encouraging! I'm sure you've been briefed on my local support team. I have a man from the Provost Marshal's Office, one from CID and an investigator from the County Prosecutor's office. They need to meet your people and establish a working relationship. They will operate the Eagle to try to get the goods on the Brigade and I know they'll welcome your support."

Cochrane smiled and said, "Good, I have rented rooms at the Holiday Inn in Tinton Falls for the outside guys. They have a decent-sized meeting room. Could you and your team meet us there tonight for a briefing?"

"It's short notice, but I'll try," said Adam. "There's a fairly private pay phone in the back. Why don't I give them a call right now. What time do you have in mind?"

"Anytime after 1900 hours will work for us."

Adam left the table and made a call to Mack Rogers. He explained the situation and Mack said he would contact Leach and Young and asked Adam to call back in another ten minutes. When he called back,

Mack said they would meet at 1930 hours, but he would arrive early and make sure Adam wasn't followed.

At the Holiday Inn, after introductions were made, Cochrane outlined the plan to protect Adam. They'd keep him under constant surveillance and should he be taken, they'd follow rather than intercede. The Eagle team would be alerted and follow the strike force to gain evidence against the Brigade. Beginning that evening, three chase cars would work in and out of his tail to keep him in sight with little chance of discovery. Adam left the meeting with renewed confidence knowing his new 'outside' protectors were right behind him.

IV

*January 10th, 1992,
Arlington, VA, 8:30 p.m....*

"Well, my dear lady," said Sean Ball as he stood facing JoAnn in her library. "The shit has really hit the fan! A strike team has been suddenly assigned to the Fort with no good reason. We may have to change our plan and take your boy this weekend."

"Why?"

"Because Jeff and I are convinced that this team could have only one mission at Monmouth and that is to protect one Adam Packard's ass. If we're right, he will see through our plot to send him to New Orleans and refuse, or he could take a few bodyguards along. This development will also make it difficult, if not impossible, to snatch him at the Fort. We have no choice but to grab him here."

"I thought you and Jeffrey had decided it was too risky to have him 'disappear' from a weekend party at my home."

"We suggest you go ahead with the party as planned. After *your* party, I'll throw a little party of my own for Adam and Belinda. I will be through interrogating them on Sunday. If they're clean, I'll send them off with my apologies. If not, we'll arrange an 'accident' involving his sleek, but vulnerable little Porsche. I'll take them after they leave your house, so you can claim ignorance of the whole affair, if they're innocent, that is."

JoAnn rose and paced for what seemed like minutes to Ball. When she finally faced him, he was surprised to see tears welling up in her eyes. He stepped forward and took her in his arms. JoAnn didn't resist, in fact, she put her arms around his neck and began to sob uncontrollably. Ball murmured words of consolation to hide his shock in seeing this strong woman literally fall apart in his arms. He held her until the movement of her chest against his subsided.

When she pulled away, she said in a shaky voice, "I don't know how much more of this I can bear. I feel my confidence and strength slipping away a little more each day." She shook her head sadly and continued, "Ever since my husband John was killed, I have been given great strength from the vendetta I made to avenge his death. I have done everything with a clear conscience, because the end always justified the means. But lately I have had nightmares that leave me terrified. I have tried alcohol and barbituates, but nothing seems to help."

Ball took her by the arms and said, "JoAnn, you have been a valiant fighter for a cause you totally believe in. It's natural that you should have some concerns when some things don't go your way, but this 'darkness before the dawn' will pass. The emotional attachment you have for Adam Packard is making this much harder for you. Once we resolve this issue, you'll feel better. Now let the doctor mix you a therapeutic tonic in the form of a martini and calm all of your fears."

Major Jeffrey Randolph was otherwise engaged when his beeper sounded. His immediate reaction was, "Who the fuck is after me at eleven o'clock on Friday night?"

"Why don't you get up and find out, big boy?" whispered Sela in her sexy voice.

Jeffrey reluctantly left the warm bed and checked the number on the beeper. He said, "I'll make the call in the other room. It may be awhile and I wouldn't want my baby to miss her beauty sleep." He pulled on his pants, went to the kitchen and after opening a Michelob, dialed the familiar number.

"Yes," said Ball. "Is this the party I just beeped?"

"Yeah, and the timing was less than ideal. What's so goddamn important that you have to wake me on a weekend?"

"I doubt you were asleep and I have a damn good reason. I spent the evening with JoAnn and I'm concerned about her. Have you talked to her lately?"

"Of course, we discussed the weekend yesterday. What are you getting at?"

"I mean, talked about her attitude or how the events of the last two weeks might be getting to her?" queried Ball. "When we went over the latest developments, she broke down and cried. I was goddamned shocked. Have you *ever* seen her do that?"

"Not since I was a boy," said Jeffrey with concern in his voice. "She's always been the strongest person I know. I can't believe this is getting to her after all she's done over the years, and all the crap that went with it. What set her off?"

"The news of the arrival of Adam's 'bodyguard team' and my insistence on grabbing him this weekend seemed to knock her for a loop. After she shut off the waterworks, I mixed her a couple of drinks and fed her an hour of my most comforting B.S. By the time I left she had pulled herself together pretty well, but we need to keep a sharp eye on her. If she had to face a tough situation in the shape she was in tonight, she might crack."

Jeffrey's concern was replaced by anger. "Dammit, the last thing we need is female problems right now. We may have to level with Foote and have him pull her out of the loop until things quiet down. We should meet before the party tomorrow and talk about it, say three p.m. at the Hyatt bar?"

Ball agreed and as he hung up, his thoughts turned to getting rid of enemies. Would security dictate that he add the leader of the Right Brigade to his hit list?

V

January 11th, 1992, Long Branch, NJ, 5:30 a.m....

Adam awoke to what would become a gorgeous morning. The sun, hiding its rays below the horizon, would add its warmth to mild southerly winds and simulate a day in spring. When he had shaken off a troubled night's sleep, Adam realized that this day could be one of severe consequences. For whom, he could not be certain. Adam watched the sun peek over the nearly still ocean as he sat drinking a protein drink at his kitchen counter. He had dressed for the evening following a hard workout, shave and shower. Although he was not scheduled to appear at JoAnn's until five p.m., he decided to leave the house and head for National Airport as if to pick up Belinda. They had debated whether he would call JoAnn in the morning to inform her of Lola's sudden attack of the flu or to announce it upon his arrival. The latter was decided upon, but he wanted to be incommunicado until that time. Belinda and his protectors had wanted him to 'carry' or at least wear an ankle weapon. Adam had insisted that he go in unarmed.

At 6:45 a.m., he stepped into the Porsche and drove out of his garage and headed south. He parked in the short-term lot at National Airport and arrived at the Northwest Airlines World Club counter at 10:25. When he was told that flight #312 was thirty minutes late due to snow in Minneapolis, he asked if there were any messages for him. The attendant checked her computer and said she had a message and would print it out for him. Adam read, "Dear Adam, I have come down with a nasty virus, no sleep last night. I just cannot make the trip. Please give my apologies to JoAnn. Love, Lola." Expressing surprise, Adam thanked the attendant and climbed the stairs to the balcony and the phones. After consulting his address book he dialed a Washington number. The phone rang five times before a sultry feminine voice said, "Hello."

Adam said, "Sela, this is Adam. How are you?"

She replied, "Well, I'm a lot better now than I was ten seconds ago. What prompts a hunk like you to call me on a dull Saturday?"

"I thought I'd check to see if that furniture we ordered had come in. I'm a bit anxious to complete the decorating project we started a couple of months ago."

"Where are you calling from, dear man?" Sela queried with that come-on in her voice.

"I'm at National Airport. I came here to pick up Lola, but she called in sick and won't make the party."

"I have an idea. Why don't you just scoot over to the Prime Rib on K Street. I'll tell you all about the delivery over lunch. Are you on?"

"Sure," said Adam. "Can I pick you up?"

"That would be delightful. I'm at 1820 N Street, a little old brownstone. It's only a few blocks from the Rib. I'll be ready in an hour and I'll make a reservation. Just ring the bell."

"Done," Adam responded. "I'll see you in an hour."

Sela hung up and after checking her telephone directory, made another call. "Nathan? This is Sela Pierce. I need a favor. I need a picture at the Prime Rib this noon." After a pause she continued, "I know you only do restaurants in the evening, but this is important to me. Does a hundred bucks on top of your usual fee interest you?" A pause and then, "Wonderful, we'll be there about noon. Don't make a fuss, just come up to the table and shoot. Oh, and be sure to put the place and date on the print."

Adam pulled up in front of the brownstone at 11:45 and was relieved to see Sela open her door and head for his car. Knowing her passions and bent for intrigue, he feared she'd insist he inspect her home, particularly the bedroom. He moved around the car and opened the door for her, she gave him a warm smile with none of her usual sensuality attached and said, "Thank you, love."

Adam surrendered the car to the valet parker and they were greeted cordially by the maître d´. When he took Sela's coat, he couldn't help notice the elegant dress and the superb form that it encased. He was surprised at the total class she displayed in every word and movement. When they were seated, Adam chose a fine Riesling wine and suggested the salmon with bread pudding and hot bourbon sauce for dessert. Sela agreed and complimented him on his choice. She thought, 'I enjoy Jeffrey, but this man's really a keeper. I will have to continue to play the lady if I'm to have any chance with him, but I will have to eliminate Lola.' As Sela was proposing a toast, a photographer came up and said, "Look this way and smile." He snapped three photos and said he'd return with the prints. He went on to another table and repeated the performance. After what Adam regarded as a most pleasant lunch, including Sela's promise to have his home complete in fifteen days, the photographer returned with a framed print. Adam said no, but Sela insisted and they each left with a very flattering picture of them touching glasses in a toast.

They pulled up before her home at 2:45 and she invited him in for coffee. Adam would ordinarily refuse, but since she had abandoned her wanton behavior and he had nearly two hours to kill, he accepted. He expected elegance in the décor of her splendid home, but what he saw was far more. She had combined furniture styles from several periods to contemporary with wall coverings and hangings that said 'I'm an original.' What was so special was the comfortable air of welcome that he felt everywhere, a feeling that was usually missing from such luxurious furnishings. Sela asked him to make himself comfortable and returned a few minutes later with coffee. As she poured, she said, "I'd like to clear something up. When I'm with Jeffrey, we do a little play-acting, but I'm really not the slut I pretend to be."

Adam said, "I must admit I thought I was in the company of a different person today. If you don't mind my saying so, I much prefer this Sela."

She laughed and they talked away the afternoon.

Although the party was scheduled for seven o'clock, the inner sanctum of the Right Brigade was asked to arrive two hours early for a meeting. As Adam parked the Porsche, he looked around for signs of his backup. He was gratified that they were professional enough to be well hidden, but at the same time, concerned that they were in position to fulfill their part of the takedown. He walked up the steps, pressed the doorbell and took in a deep breath as he steeled himself for whatever lay on the other side of that imposing door.

The butler smiled as he ushered Adam into the foyer and took his topcoat. He said, "Good evening, Captain Packard. Mrs. Cleveland requests that you join her in the library."

"Good evening, and thank you."

When Adam stepped into the library, Ball, Jeffrey and Gordon Foote were already seated. JoAnn rushed forward, eyes wide, face pale and shouted, "Where's Lola?"

Adam said, "Unfortunately, she came down with a terrible virus and is confined to bed. She didn't even make it on the plane. She asked me to convey her sincere apologies."

JoAnn's eyes widened even farther and she shrieked, "It's true, you are a traitor. They said if Lola didn't show up, it would prove that you're working against me! How could you do this to me after all I've done for you?" Her face was scarlet with rage as she began pounding her fists on Adam's chest.

He grabbed her wrists and fairly shouted, "JoAnn, please, what are you talking about? Who says I'm a traitor?"

"I do!" shouted Jeffrey as he leaped from his chair and wrestled Adam from JoAnn.

They stood facing one another as Jeffrey said with venom, "We know all about Lola. She's Major Belinda Jackson and you're hooked up with that bastard, Mack Rogers. He gave my boys a hard time over the demise of those two little shits, Harris and McRae. We know you are trying to take down the Brigade and that's not gonna happen."

"Hold it, Major," said Adam in a commanding voice. "If you say Lola is somebody else, I don't know about it. I can't believe you've poisoned JoAnn against me. Your boys have admitted killing both Harris and McRae, and have I done anything about it? Bark told me you ordered the hit on that security guard in the Watergate affair, but did I do anything about that? If I were a spy, I could have turned you guys in long ago."

"So you claim they admitted these things to you?" asked Jeffrey. "Well, I'm glad we wasted those crumbbums, but you have no proof and none of them will ever testify against us."

"Hold it, Jeff," said Ball. "Before you say too much, where are the new Eagles, and are they secured? I'd hate like hell to have this conversation recorded."

"They are all under lock and key and are guarded by both my people and electronics. Don't worry about them, let's get to the bottom of this!"

"All right," said Ball. "I guess it's time for you and I to take a little ride, Packard. I have a memory-expert that would like to verify that you are telling the truth and if you are, we'll all give you our most abject apologies. If not, well that's another matter."

As Ball reached for him, Adam grabbed Ball's arm and pulled it behind him in a half-Nelson. This put Ball between Adam and the others. As he applied upward pressure on Ball's arm, he said, "This is by no means a confession of guilt, just the opposite, but I'm not about to have some Agency goons work me over. Is that clear, Sean?" As he asked this, he increased the pressure and Ball gave a grunt for a reply. With further pressure, Ball gasped, "Okay, no interrogation. Now let me go."

As Adam maintained the pressure, he saw a Beretta automatic in Jeffrey's hand. He said, "Drop the gun, Major or I'll break your partner's arm and he's going to blame *you* for that."

"Not a chance, Packard. If I have to shoot him to get to you, so be it." Just as he said this, the butler slipped silently behind Adam and brought a sap down on his head with crushing force. Adam folded and fell limp to the floor.

Ball clutched his sore arm and said, "All right, let's get him into the trunk of my car. I'm going to turn him over to old Dr. Death. We used him at the Agency and he never failed to get a confession, except when the perp couldn't survive the questioning."

JoAnn, who had collapsed into a chair after her confrontation with Adam, now struggled to her feet and said in an uneven, raspy voice, "Wait, Sean. We still don't know that he's guilty. If these people admitted everything to him, why didn't he do anything about it?"

"Dear, naïve JoAnn, we have no proof that anybody admitted anything to him. Don't you see, he's just blowing smoke?" said Ball.

Jeffrey stepped forward, stood over Adam and pointed the Beretta at his head. "Why don't we just finish this right now?"

Ball grasped Jeffrey's gun hand and said, "Don't be a fool. We can't have any traces of a struggle with him in this house. I'll take care of him, but I want to know who all he's working for first."

Just as Ball said this, Rogers and Young, followed by three members of Cochrane's team, burst into the room. Rogers shouted, "Freeze!" Jeffrey fired three bullets from his .25 caliber weapon into the chest of Mack Rogers. Rogers fired just one round from his Colt .45. Jeffrey was thrown back and lay motionless on the floor. JoAnn shrieked in horror and Foote stood with his mouth hanging open. Ball took two steps and a leap, crashing through the window to the bushes nearly twenty feet below. Seconds later, outside, several shots rang out and then there was silence.

Time seemed to stand still for a moment with the acrid smell of gunpowder permeating the room. Finally Young asked in a worried tone, "Are you okay, Mack?"

"Yeah, the vest stopped that peashooter with no trouble. It's a damn good thing he didn't do a head shot." Before he went over to Adam, he said, "Get on the radio and find out about Ball. We can't let him get away!" After feeling the pulse in Adam's and then Jeffrey's necks, he gritted his teeth and ordered, "They're alive, call an ambulance, then cuff these two goddamn socialites and the butler. Jail's too fucking good for them, but without a gun in their hands, I can't finish the job."

Foote regained his voice and shouted in his deep booming voice, "You bastards. I'll get you for this. Every last one of you!"

Mack felt an involuntary shiver when Foote made his venomous threat. He spoke harshly through gritted teeth, "There'll be plenty of time to think about that where you're going!" He turned to Young and hissed. "Make the cuffs extra tight on that big sonofabitch."

VI

January 12th, 1992, Walter Reed Medical Center, Washington, DC, 1145 hours...

Adam came fully awake after several hours of sliding in and out of consciousness. He had no idea where he was or how he got there, but more importantly, he didn't know *who* he was. The pain in his head was constant and when he tried to move, he found he was strapped down with a number of tubes invading his body. In a panic, he discovered the call button and, with difficulty, managed to press it. A middle-aged, wide-bodied nurse with a pleasant smile appeared almost immediately and inquired, "How are we doing?"

Adam said weakly, "Can you tell me where I am…and who I am?"

"Oh, dear," said the nurse, "have you lost your memory?"

"I have a terrific headache, and nothing else," said Adam weakly.

"You are in the Walter Reed Army Hospital. You were admitted last night with severe head trauma. Your name is Captain Adam Packard and the doctor will have to take it from there. I'll get you something for the headache and notify the doctor of your condition. I'll be right back." She returned in three minutes and changed the IV bag hanging above his head saying, "There now, we've put a little kick in your saline solution so your head should feel better in a few minutes. I have put in a call for the doctor and someone will be in to see you soon. Is there anything else you need?"

"Could you release me from these straps? And my throat is drier than a desert." She released the straps and helped him drink two glasses of water. As she was leaving, a man in a blue coat with a stethoscope around his neck stepped into the room and asked, "How are you feeling, Captain?"

"Not good," said Adam. "My head is empty, except for the pain."

"Well, you did receive a blow strong enough to crack your noggin, otherwise known as a fractured skull. You are lucky to be alive. Let's have a look." The doctor looked into Adam's eyes with a pinpoint light source and remarked, "Good, your eyes are beginning to react to light which signifies an easing of the concussion. We have performed multiple brain scans and believe that you did not suffer any permanent damage. Now, what's this about your memory?"

"I am a blank. I have no idea who I am or how I got here," said Adam. "You and the nurse called me *Captain.* Captain of what?"

"Your name is Adam Packard. You are a captain in the U.S. Army, stationed at Fort Monmouth, NJ. Does any of that sound familiar?"

"No, I'm a total blank. Am I married? Children? What else can you tell me about myself?"

"According to the records I have, no to both questions, but before going into any further detail, I'd like to have our Doctor Anderson examine you and work on that memory problem. Just relax and rest. I'll get him in here as soon as possible."

Adam drifted off again and when he awoke, another doctor-type person had entered the room and was sitting quietly by his bed. He said, "Good afternoon, Captain Packard. My name is Sam Anderson, and I'm here to talk about your identity."

"I'm sorry, Doctor, but that seems to be missing."

"I'm here to help you locate it. We may not bring it all back immediately, but I'm confident it's out there and with a little patience, you'll find your past. The brain has marvelous recuperative powers and I believe you will recover completely. The unknown factor, however, is time. We will gradually introduce you to all the elements of your life and you will begin to recognize them, slowly at first and then with increasing rapidity."

"I'm okay with that," said Adam. "When do we start?"

"You have three visitors waiting outside. I will allow them to spend a short time with you after I've briefed them on your condition. We'll talk further after they've met with you. I'll send them in shortly."

Adam fought to keep his eyes open and was rewarded by the entrance of a beautiful black-haired woman and a stocky, red-haired man. The man said, "Adam, it's me, Mack Rogers, and this is my wife Amy. Do you remember us at all?"

"I'm sorry to say that you're strangers to me, just like everybody else. How do we know each other?"

Mack told the story of their relationship and a brief recap of the mission in which they were engaged. He filled in the details of the battle after Adam had been knocked unconscious. When he finished, Adam said, "Well, at least I don't seem to be a couch potato. Thank you for breaking in at the opportune time. I guess the people you described didn't hold me in high regard."

"On the contrary," said Rogers. "They had nothing but praise for you until they found out you were there to destroy them. A slip by a professional singer named Anita Warwick led them to the real identity of Lola. By the way, she should be here later this afternoon. She's flying in from Georgia."

"You say Lola, or Belinda, is my fiancée. Is she pretty?" asked Adam with a hint of a smile.

"No, she's knockout gorgeous," piped in Amy, "not to mention smart and most competent. Once you see her, you'll fall in love all over again."

The nurse appeared at the door and said, "I'm sorry, but the doctor has put a limit on the visiting time and I'm afraid you've reached it." After Mack and Amy said their goodbyes and left, the nurse said, "Are you up to another visitor? There's a very beautiful lady out there."

"I'm tired, but the suspense is killing me. Please show the lady in."

She was indeed beautiful, tall and shapely in a dove gray knit that cried out good taste and high bucks. Adam said, "Don't tell me. Belinda?"

"No, Adam, I'm Sela. I'm what you might call *the other woman.* You and I have been working together on the décor of your house and we developed a strong mutual attraction. I hope you will recall the times we spent together. The last time was just yesterday, our lunch date at the Prime Rib and the wonderful time at my house afterward. Please tell me you remember?"

As she said this, she gently caressed his cheek and leaned over to kiss him lightly on the lips. Her perfume was light, but it enveloped him and he found himself putting his one free arm around her neck and holding her close. She purred, "Oh Adam, I love you so much." She stepped back and said, "Whatever happens, I want you to know that your happiness means everything to me. I will come to see you every day and when you're better, I want a chance to reawaken your love for me. I can't bear to lose what we've shared. Is that fair?"

Adam, almost overcome by emotion, said in a whisper, "Yes, that's more than fair. I will look forward to seeing you, anytime." Sela left and before Adam fell into a deep sleep, exhausted from the two visits, he thought about Sela. If he was engaged to Belinda and was having an affair with Sela…what kind of man was he?

He had no idea how long he slept, but as he gazed out the window, he noted the daylight had been replaced by moonlight. He turned and in the dim light, saw an angel sitting motionless by his bedside. He was startled when she smiled and took his hand. "Oh, Adam, darling. I was so worried about you. I would have given anything to be there…maybe I could have prevented them from.. injuring you. How do you feel, my love?"

"Belinda?" he managed to ask.

"Yes. Do you know me at all?"

"I'm afraid not. I want desperately to recognize people, but I'm a blank."

"I will spend every waking moment with you. Tell you everything that's happened. I know you'll remember…in time. Now I must leave and let you rest. I'll be back first thing tomorrow. Just remember, I love you more than anything on earth." She kissed him tenderly and left the room. Her wonderful scent and presence remained and Adam's mind whirled in conflict as he thought of these two outstanding women who professed their love for him. He must regain his memory soon and sort out this impossible dilemma.

The next person to enter his room was a tall statuesque woman with auburn hair and what Adam remembered as the face of the angel. Her beauty took his breath away. When he found his voice, he confessed, "Good morning, Belinda. When I woke up last night and saw you sitting there, I thought you were an angel."

She came to him, sat on the edge of the bed, kissed him and said softly, "Thank you, dear." Belinda looked at him tenderly. "We will work together to bring your memory and the memory of our love back." She then spent over an hour telling him their story, but when Adam's eyelids started to droop, she said she realized he needed rest and would return that afternoon.

When Adam awoke, Sela Pierce was sitting next to his bed. She came over and caressed him in that special way. His thoughts returned to the question of whether he had betrayed Belinda with this woman. Adam broke the silence with, "Sela, did you and I…I mean, did we have…relations?"

Sela blushed slightly as she replied, "I thought it was so special that you would never forget. Let me be perfectly honest. We met through your boss, Major Jeffrey Randolph. He and I had been an 'item' for nearly a year. I had eyes for you from our first meeting, but each time we were thrown together at a party or meeting, my feelings for you changed…grew. I admit I've been a little wild and I initially viewed you as a real hunk. But as time went by, I began to compare your qualities with Jeffrey's and realize that you were so much more…a person I could spend my life with. Our precious time together happened after I realized that I had fallen deeply in love for the first time. I came down to your house by the sea several times…and we made passionate love together."

The demure manner and apparent sincerity with which Sela told her story dismayed Adam. Although the throbbing in his head had subsided somewhat, he was certain this apparent triangle could only lead to even more severe headaches in his future.

January 13th, 1992, Provost Marshal's Office, Fort Monmouth, NJ, 1130 hours...

Mack Rogers hung up the phone, turned to Al Leach and exclaimed, "Damn, they haven't found any trace of Ball and now Carter seems to be AWOL."

"How long has he been missing?"

"Only a few hours, but he's such a gung ho soldier. He'd never just 'not show up'."

"We better get a court order to search his apartment in town," said Leach, "Have you looked at his room in the BOQ?"

"I've got a request in the works for the warrant. My guys are headed for his BOQ room as we speak. I suspect with quarters off-post, he'd not keep much here. I had Young send a squad to drive around his condo to see if his Suburban was around, no luck."

"What about our other buddies, Albertson, Bruckberg, Smythe and Pollmer?" asked Leach.

"We've had their CO suspend them all from duty. Bruckberg and Smythe are confined to quarters and I've got Albertson and Pollmer in the pokey. Pollmer isn't the brightest star in the sky and I have a feeling he may spill his guts if we offer him a deal. Of course, we'll have to work that out with the Adjutant General or the D.A., depending on who gets jurisdiction."

"Of course," replied Leach with a heavy hint of sarcasm, "but we should question him right away, tell him it could go easy on him if he tells us the truth, without making any specific promises. You and I can play 'good cop – bad cop,' whata you say?"

"I'm good with that, as long as you don't try to play 'good cop.' When Major Lampert gets in, I'll ask permission to interrogate them.

By the way, Jim Young gave the evidence we gathered on the Brigade to the District Attorney's office in Arlington. I told him to ask about the status of JoAnn Cleveland and company, when he talks to them."

"Yeah, I'm anxious to get a heads-up on those bozos. I'll be in my office, so call me when you get dope on either thing," said Leach as he rose and headed for the door.

Seconds after Leach departed, the phone rang and Jim Young said in an excited tone, "Mack, I have good news. The D.A. in Virginia is planning to arraign JoAnn and Jeffrey for first degree murder, Foote for conspiracy to commit murder and the butler for attempted murder. The District's D.A. is charging Bark and Jolson on the security guard murder. How are you doing with the boys from Company A?"

"Nothing so far, but as soon as my boss shows up, I'm going to request that Leach and I have a go at them, offer them a deal to give evidence against the others."

"Good luck. It would really help if we could get one of them to talk. We can probably put them away for a time, but I doubt if we can get a murder conviction with what we currently have. By the way, any word on Adam?"

"Unfortunately, no," said Rogers. "I called this morning and he has not recognized anything or anybody. The good news is that, other than his memory, he's in good shape. His family is flying in today and they may be able to kindle a spark in his mind. Speaking of people with injuries, did the D.A. give you an update on JoAnn and Jeffrey?"

"Yeah, it's bad. It looks like Jeffrey will never walk again. The bullet all but severed his spinal cord, he's lucky to be alive, well, maybe not, considering what lies ahead of him. JoAnn is being held in the psychiatric ward. She seems totally out of it. They think she may talk if they can get her back to some kind of rational state. They're getting a court order as we speak, to seize all the records of the Brigade. Hopefully they'll find some incriminating evidence there. What about her boyfriend, General Taylor?"

"Nothing has happened on that front. He may be safe until the whole affair gets into court. The trial or court marshal of the boys under his command might drop a little crap on him, but it's too early to tell. Let's talk again late this afternoon."

"Sounds good. I'll be talking to Arlington and Washington later, so I'll call you about five," said Young as he hung up.

Major Lampert approved the interrogation of the suspects and said he would monitor the questioning through the bug installed in the room. They agreed upon signals when the major had a problem with or wanted to expand the questioning on certain points. With a tape recorder running, Leach and Rogers began with Albertson and went through a line of questioning that began with the death of Sergeant Swanson, covered the deaths of Corporal Harris and Private McRae and the whole Eagle story. Albertson denied any part in any of the deaths and played down his knowledge of the Eagle. Next, they put Pollmer in the hot seat. Leach said, "I'm going to level with you, Corporal, we just talked with Sergeant Albertson and we discussed your involvement in the deaths of Corporal Harris and Private McRae."

"That son-of-a-bitch," exclaimed Pollmer. "Carter did Harris and Albertson pulled the trigger on McRae. I had nothin' to do with either one!"

"Well, Corporal, the fact that you were part of the group that carried out these slayings makes you an accessory," said Rogers. "You could get the same punishment as the actual perpetrators. Now if you cooperate and tell us the whole story, we could work out a deal to go very light with you. Why don't you tell us what happened, from the beginning?"

"I dunno," replied Pollmer, "I hate to rat on my buddies. I don't think I can do that."

"Yeah, swell buddies you got, they're ready to serve you up on a platter," said Leach with venom. "And leave you holding the fucking bag!"

Pollmer thought this over for just a few seconds and then blurted, "Okay, dammit, it all started when we got the Eagle. We agreed to do some 'special work' and we got paid double our Army pay – on top. Everything was good until that little prick McRae showed up. He had a beef with Jimmy and after he got sent to the supply depot, he wanted in on the deal. He followed us one night and Carter forced him off the road and down an embankment. When Jimmy went down to finish him off, he stuck Jimmy. Carter was afraid Harris would buckle under, so he offed him and we put him in the lake. Then this Jew came in to fix the Eagle and tried to hold us up. Carter killed him, by accident, I think. We buried him way out in the woods. McRae worked his way into the group and was okay until I told him about Harris. The dumb shit went nuts and Albertson put a bullet in him to shut him up. That's about it."

"What about Major Randolph?" asked Rogers. "Was he part of all this?"

"I 'spose so...sure, he's the one who brought in the Eagle and he backed up Lieutenant Carter all the way. I'm sure he knew about everything that happened, probably ordered it."

Leach and Rogers went over a number of details with Pollmer and then gave him coffee while the tape was being transcribed for him to sign. They informed him that in order to get his 'deal,' he would have to testify at a court marshal or civilian court. He expressed concern over this, but finally agreed as he signed the statement. When Young called later that afternoon, he was overjoyed with the news of Pollmer's confession. He told Rogers that the FBI, with the unlikely cooperation of the CIA, had placed Sean Ball and Jeb Carter on their 'most-wanted' list.

**January 13th, 1992,
Walter Reed Medical Center,
Washington, DC,
1445 hours...**

A short time after Sela left, Belinda returned. The tenderness she displayed earlier was replaced with a hard, distressed look. Without touching Adam, she said, "I just met Sela Pierce in the hall, and she made some remarks…have you been seeing her? I mean, do you remember anything about her?"

Adam sensed jealousy in her words, but her tone seemed more one of despair. He said. "Belinda, I honestly don't know her and with the love you say we have for each other, I can't believe I ever had anything to do with her…*but I just don't know.*"

Belinda turned away to hide the tears that she could not stop. When she had composed herself, she said in a soft voice, "I believe you, Adam, but I just can't imagine losing you." She broke down as she buried her face in his chest.

He caressed her gently and said, "Belinda, I feel such strong emotions, I would give anything if I could get my head on straight. Will you be patient with me? I don't know how long it will take, but I will be true to you until that day. That's all I can give you right now."

"That's all I could ask for," she replied, "and I will be patient. In the meantime, let me tell you a bit more about *your* and *our* past." She recounted his being recruited for the special mission and more details about their training together. This time she pointed out the emotional side of that training how he had indicated interest in her romantically or sexually and how she had totally rejected him. She admitted that she was drawn to him from the beginning, but built a barrier due to her previous, unsatisfactory experiences with men. She had brought the story up to Adam's transfer to Fort Monmouth, when his eyes once again began closing involuntarily. She kissed him tenderly and left with the promise to return that evening. As Belinda walked down the corridor toward the elevators, she was intercepted by Sela Pierce. "Lola...er, Belinda, could we have a cup of coffee in the cafeteria? I have something important I'd like to discuss with you."

Belinda looked at Sela with mistrust in her eyes, but agreed to hear her out. They sat down with strong coffee in styrofoam cups and Sela began with, "I know you were upset by what I said earlier about Adam and me. I also know that you consider my behavior with Jeffrey to be crass, to say the least. Jeffrey is an entirely different man than Adam. He thrives on sex and every word or action that has any relation to sensuality. I played a game with him and in doing so, came off as something of a slut. There is more to me than you have witnessed. As I watched Jeffrey and Adam together, the differences between them became more and more apparent."

"When I told you about Adam and I, it was not Sela the temptress that spent time with Adam, but Sela, the woman seriously in love. While you were meeting with him on weekends, I was filling out his love life during the week. Ever since I found the house by the sea for him, I've been going down there and accepting his appreciation...and he really appreciates that house. He told me that he would have admitted our affair to you, but since you two were working together...perhaps our love is apparent in this picture taken just last Saturday during our lunch at the Prime Rib."

Belinda looked at the picture and winced. They were apparently proposing a toast and although she was not surprised at the loving look in Sela's eyes, she was devastated by the look in Adam's. Perhaps it was true, Adam *had* dallied with her. Knowing him as she did, she was sure he would never betray her for just sexual gratification. He would have to have feelings for this woman. She felt like a knife had been driven into her heart. She was unable to take her eyes from the picture and finally heard Sela say, "Are you all right?"

Belinda took a deep breath and said in a shaky voice, "No! I'm not all right. You have shattered the only relationship that ever mattered to me!" She rose, tore the ring from her finger and threw it at Sela saying, "Here, take his ring...if he has no more loyalty than this, you can have him!" Belinda stormed out of the cafeteria and headed for the front door of the hospital. As she opened the door, Adam's parents and sister climbed the steps.

George Packard said, "Belinda, how good to see you. How's Adam?"

Belinda, blinded by tears, ran down the steps and called back, "Ask Sela!"

IX

October 8th, 1992, Mack Rogers Home, Eatontown, NJ, 7:30PM...

Mack Rogers raised his champagne glass high and exclaimed, "May our foes forever ponder the question, 'Did the end justify the means?' as they look at the world through prison bars."

"Hear, hear," said Al Leach as he touched his glass to Mack's then Adam's, Jim Young's and finally, Amy Rogers'. "I must admit there were times when I thought this day would never come...that we would put 'em all away!"

"Me too," said Adam who had gradually recovered his memory over a period of three months. "If JoAnn were coherent, I believe she would agree that she'd do it all over again...to advance her cause. I doubt that Jeffrey and Gordon Foote would be willing to suffer their punishment if they had a chance to re-live their past. Thomas and the rest are a question mark. In spite of some pretty heavy fines for illegal contributions, they got off easy considering no one is serving any time."

The reason for the celebration was the end of the last trial of the Right Brigade. The jury had come back with a verdict in the trial of Jeffrey Randolph that afternoon. Some thought Jeffrey's condition, confined to a wheelchair for life, would influence the jury in his favor. That did not happen as the jury returned a verdict of 'guilty of murder in the first degree' for the death of Jamie Harris. His sentence was 'life with no possibility of parole.'

Earlier, JoAnn Cleveland had been judged incompetent to stand trial and was confined to the high-security section of the Virginia State Mental Hospital. Should she recover and be judged sane, she would stand trial for several crimes, including accomplice to murder in the first degree. Gordon Foote was given a sentence of ten years for complicity with several crimes. JoAnn's butler was given six months for assault with a deadly weapon. Jason Bark and Henry Jolson received life sentences for the murder of the security guard.

"You all were very effective with your testimony," said Mack. "Adam was brilliant as usual and Belinda made the defense attorney look like he'd gotten his law degree that morning. I hate to admit it, but even Leach came through with flying colors."

"Hey, hold on there," said Leach expansively. "Without my superior detective work and inspired testimony, these guys would all be on the outside, still doing their dirty work—and that's just the Brigade. Need I remind you that I was very instrumental in Harry Albertson receiving a life sentence at hard labor for the murder of Champion McRae. With minor assistance from Captain Rogers, I obtained the confession of Billy Pollmer who was given a mere twenty-year sentence at hard labor due to his cooperation. I decided to let John Smythe off with five years due to his cooperation with both Adam and the prosecution. I also saw to it that Frank Bruckburg received only a dishonorable discharge from the Army due to his being cooperative plus the fact that he wasn't directly involved in any of the Eagle-related crimes."

"That's the biggest crock I've ever heard," said Rogers. "I suppose you're taking credit for the end of the Cold War as well as General Maxwell's giving up his post at Fort Monmouth and resigning from active duty? Those private discussions with General Rayburn had nothing to do with it?"

"No, we have to hand it to Rayburn for that," admitted Leach, "but when we start handing out credit, without one guy, none of this would have happened. Adam took all the risks and deserves all the gravy…by the way Adam, what are they giving you for all this?"

"Hey, they're giving me the best gift of all, letting me return to civilian life. They plan to pin gold oak leaves on me when my time-in-grade is up, but otherwise I can do my own thing. Fortunately, I did learn a thing or two that will help me on the outside."

"You make the Army sound like prison, Adam," quipped Mack. "Remember some of us found a home in the Army and never had it so good."

"For the unenlightened that may be true, but for those of us that want a *life*, you gotta look for it outside of this man's Army."

"Without throwing any more old Army clichés around," said Rogers, "I am proud to serve my country and will continue to do so. My lovely wife would have it no other way. Ain't that true, honey?"

"If you say so," said Amy. "Seriously, Adam, did you talk to Belinda?"

Adam's smile faded. He nodded.

"What did she say?" asked Amy.

"She just congratulated us on the success of the mission, said she's happy for all of us, and then said…goodbye."

Amy Rogers came over to Adam, put her arm around his shoulder and said softly, "Is there any chance she'll change her mind…that you two can get back together?"

Choked with emotion, Adam whispered. "No…no chance at all.*"*

Amy put her arms around Adam and said tenderly, "I'm so sorry."

1999

PART ONE

May 27th, Edina, MN, 10:30 p.m....

Adam decided the definition of serenity was lying in bed with a soft blossom-scented breeze wafting through the window and the chirping of crickets as the only sound. He was finally back in his own house and it felt good. As Adam drifted in and out of a light sleep, the perfume of the night reminded him of *her* perfume, but the scent no longer brought as much pain. At long last perhaps his demons had faded away. The 9mm Glock automatic pistol was resting in a dresser drawer rather than under his pillow as it had for so long.

Adam was jolted awake as an explosion ripped the quiet of the night. He jumped up, dressed quickly, put the Glock in his belt, and let himself out the back door. Two doors down, fire and smoke poured from the remains of the Sandell home. He heard sirens in the distance as he searched the gathering crowd for a face that didn't belong, but realized he didn't know the neighborhood well enough to do so. No one could have survived had they been inside when the explosion occurred.

As the emergency vehicles and fire trucks turned into the other end of the block, Adam backed away, returning to his house. It was virtually impossible that George and Mary Sandell would be targets for such a vicious attack, but he, Adam Packard, the resident of the Sandell home for the last three weeks, was another story.

He had purchased his house through Mary and they had become friends. While they toured Europe, Adam lived in the Sandell home. He had put his redecorating project completely in his decorator's hands and had not set foot in his own house for over two weeks. On this day, the project completed, he had returned from his electronics company's office at 6 p.m., driven into the Sandell's garage and closed the door. He cleaned up the portion of the house he had occupied, packed his belongings in his Beamer and drove two doors away to his own house at 8:30 p.m. He unpacked the car and went to bed. The next thing he heard was the explosion.

Adam knew there were people out there who had both the motive and the capability to end his life. Now, in a matter of hours, the assassin would realize he had failed…and that Adam was now aware of the threat to his life. Suddenly, they came back…the old demons were once again upon him.

Adam ran up the stairs to his bedroom, quickly packed a bag with clothes and necessities, another with a notebook computer and a third with an M-16, grenades, an ankle pistol and ammunition for all the weapons. He shouldered the bags and headed for the garage. After loading his black BMW X5, he opened the garage door and slipped outside to survey the scene.

Pandemonium reigned down the street. The glare was so intense, he knew he was invisible in the darkness of his driveway. He jumped into the Beamer, backed out and hit the street slowly with no lights. In the next block, he turned on the lights and made several turns with an eye on the rear view mirror. When he turned onto I-494, he put the pedal to the metal and the BMW's powerful V-8 responded with authority. He stayed on the freeway through Minneapolis, St. Paul and eastward over the St. Croix River into Wisconsin.

At the top of the hill in Hudson, he turned off the freeway and pulled in at the Hudson House Inn. The parking lot wrapped around the building, which allowed him to park the BMW out of sight of the freeway and frontage road. He withdrew a blond wig streaked with gray and a matching mustache from his bag and affixed both. Adopting a somewhat stooped posture and a shuffle step, he entered the lobby and registered as Steven Stellner, an assumed name for which he had complete identification. Once inside his room, he removed an electronic transmitter from the bag and affixed it to the top of the door. He placed the companion receiver next to the bed and turned it on. He picked up the Glock, chambered a round and put in under his pillow. Secure for the moment, he removed his clothes, wig and mustache and stretched out on the bed. Between the adrenaline and the need to develop a plan of action, sleep was not an option. After a short time, he got up, fired up the laptop computer, and dialed up his desktop computer at home. After downloading all the pertinent files to the laptop, he erased any information from the desktop that could help his adversary. Several more hours of searching his mind for answers would precede sleep, which arrived just before dawn.

Adam awoke with a start at 11:45 and hastily shaved, showered, and dressed as Steven Stellner. He read the newspaper account of the explosion and fire in Edina as he munched on a bagel. 'No cause had been determined, but an investigation was underway.'

The Hudson newspaper advertised a storage area just three blocks from the motel. Adam walked over and rented a 12' x 24' unit. Back at the motel, he checked the phone book and found a Ford-Mercury dealer a few blocks east. He walked to the dealership and looked at, drove and completed the paperwork on a used Mercury Marquis. After driving his new wheels back to the motel, he cranked up the laptop and checked the elaborate alarm system at his house. The signals indicated no entry to his house…yet.

Adam Packard was no stranger to alarms, or for that matter, electronic devices of any kind. He had a reputation as a guru's guru in the field. Since leaving the Army, he had developed a number of sophisticated alarms and surveillance devices. With more than a dozen patents in his name, he had sold manufacturing rights to several large companies including 3M and Honeywell. He also consulted with and designed devices for a number of law enforcement agencies and the military. Substantial royalties, in addition to income from his thriving electronics company, allowed him to splurge on his hobby of collecting and restoring classic airplanes. As an accomplished pilot, he flew his favorite 1930 stub-winged racer in several pylon races each year.

The television was tuned to CNN and Adam paid little attention until a news flash boomed across the screen. He stared at the screen with disbelief. The anchor had just announced the death of several high ranking U.S. military officials in a plane crash over the Mediterranean Sea. He reported, "The C-130, four-engine, turbo-prop military transport had taken off from Milan, Italy and was still in sight of the airport when it suddenly exploded and disintegrated in a huge ball of flame. The cause is unknown, and no bodies have been recovered at this point. The passengers included top intelligence officers from the Army, Navy and Air Force. Names are being withheld pending notification of next of kin." Adam had a sinking feeling that one of the officers on that plane could very well be General Arthur Rayburn.

He consulted his phone directory and dialed an Arlington, Virginia number. When the phone was answered by a strange male voice, Adam said, "May I speak with Melanie?"

The voice replied, "I'm sorry, but Mrs. Rayburn is unavailable at this time. May I ask who's calling?"

"An old friend. I wanted to express my sympathy for her loss."

"I'm sure she would appreciate your condolences. May I tell her who's calling?"

Adam hit the 'End' button on the phone and sat staring blankly into space. He realized he must have been correct in assuming that his mentor and friend had perished in the plane crash. Was there a connection between that *accident* and the attempt on his life?

His normally steady hands trembled as he again referred to his directory. He dialed an Atlanta number and after five rings heard that rich, familiar voice, "You have reached Belinda. I'm sorry I'm not available to take your call at this time, but please leave a message at the tone."

His gut wrenched at the sound of her voice. How could she have this effect on him after all these years? Just hearing her voice had occupied all his attention. Had he missed a coded message in her greeting? He called back and this time listened carefully to her words. The 'I'm sorry' in her message was their code for *danger*. Suddenly a plan crystallized in his mind.

Adam turned off the TV and began packing. After dark, still disguised as Steven Stellner, Adam checked out of the motel, loaded the Mercury and drove around to the parked BMW. He drove the BMW to the storage area, and walked back to the motel. It was 10 p.m. when he drove the Mercury down the frontage road to the freeway entrance and headed East on I-94.

The first streaks of light appeared on the eastern horizon as he pulled into the parking lot at O'Hare Airport in Chicago. He parked, took his bag out of the trunk and affixed an electronic transmitter to the trunk lid. He registered at the O'Hare Hilton under the Stellner alias before crashing and sleeping soundly until 11:30 a.m. He showered and once again dressed as Stellner. He ordered a hearty lunch from room service. After finishing his meal, he consulted the directory and walked to a cellular store within the sprawling airport.

He bought an expensive satellite cell phone under a name taken from the phone book with a suburban Chicago address. He returned to his room and made a reservation on Delta Airlines for the next flight to Atlanta.

II

May 29th, Atlanta, GA, 9:00 p.m....

Adam sat in the rented black Ford Taurus down the block from an impressive town house complex. He had arrived in Atlanta two hours earlier, and after several unanswered calls, drove to Belinda's house. He drove through the neighborhood twice before taking up his current position, waiting for the cover of darkness.

At 10:45 p.m., he left the car and walked to number 716. He had changed into dark clothing and applied makeup which transformed him into a mere shadow as he approached her condo. The front door was set back from the double garage and allowed him to take the time necessary to pick the lock with gloved hands. As he opened the door, he activated an electronic sensor of his own design that transmitted a range of frequencies to the alarm system. The sensor detected the code and automatically responded with a signal that shut off the alarm without a single beep.

After re-locking the door, he put on night vision goggles and made a quick circuit of the town house. He found nothing out of order. He located and pressed the message button on the answering machine. There were several messages and from the date and time log, she had not listened to them for at least four days. He felt he was intruding on her privacy as he listened to her messages. The feeling heightened as he walked into her bedroom. Was her perfume still in the air, or did he imagine it? His mind was filled with images of Belinda as he stood motionless in the center of her most private place. After several minutes, Adam forced himself back into action.

He found her computer in the den and turned it on. He found only non-descript files and no address book. He found a section that required a security code for access. He typed in the code they shared from the assignment in 1991 and it opened. Here he found an address book with numbers for General Rayburn, several other officers and to his surprise, his own current number. He searched the files and found recent letters to Rayburn. The latest letter was dated May 21st, 1999. 'Dear General Rayburn, I'm glad to hear that you are enjoying your European vacation. I hope you won't have to do any serious work while over there. There always seems to be loose ends to tie up. I'm sorry Melanie couldn't make the trip with you, but I know how she is about flying. Take care of yourself. As ever, Belinda.' Did the words 'Take care of yourself' have special meaning? Was Belinda aware of danger to the general...or herself?

He removed fingerprint equipment from his bag and dusted all the places a resident would normally leave prints. Everything had been wiped clean. Had Belinda been abducted? Everything pointed to that conclusion. Was she being questioned, or had they finished the interrogation...and possibly her?

Adam locked the condo and returned to the Ford at 11:50 p.m. After looking up the number, he called Mack Rogers on his cell phone. After several rings, a sleep-drenched voice said, "Hello."

Adam said, "Mack? This is Red Dog. Do you understand?"

"Understand? What the hell oh, yeah. I gotcha."

"I need to see you, pronto. Meet me at your *favorite* place at 0600 hours. Okay?"

"It's Sunday, for Chrissakes."

"Just *be there!*" growled Adam.

"Okay," said a resigned Mack Rogers. "I'll see ya'."

Adam drove to the outskirts of Columbus, Georgia and rented a room in a mom-and-pop motel. At 4:45 a.m., he rose, shaved and forced himself awake in a cold shower.

III

*May 30th, 1999,
Fort Benning, GA,
0550 hours...*

Adam drove to the south gate of the Fort in a well-tailored navy blue suit, gleaming white shirt and gold tie. At the gate, he presented his Army ID card to a sleepy-looking guard. After checking his identification and snapping to attention, the corporal asked, "Can I help you locate anyone, Colonel? It's a bit early."

"I'm here to see Colonel Mack Rogers. Can you tell me where to find him?"

The corporal replied, "Colonel Rogers is the Provost Marshal of this command, sir. His office is here." He pointed to a building on a map of the fort. "But I hardly think he'd be in his office on Sunday morning."

"We have an appointment. Thank you, Corporal. I can find my way."

The corporal came to attention again and saluted. Adam returned the salute, drove to the appointed building and parked in a visitor space near the door.

Mack Rogers met Adam at the door like a linebacker aiming for an opposing quarterback. He lifted Adam off his feet with a bear-hug and shouted, "Adam, it's great to see you. Even if it is Sunday morning."

When he recovered his breath, Adam said, "I'm sorry about the bum's rush, but I had to get to you right away. I have bad news." As Adam talked, he swept the office with a detection device that would divulge the presence of any bugs. "...and I'm happy to report that your office is clean."

"It must be pretty serious for you to barge in here at this time and suspect that my joint's bugged. Are you paranoid, or what?"

"When you hear what I have to say, you'll appreciate just how paranoid I am. I just accidentally survived an attempt to whack me. Then I got the news about General Rayburn. His death came as a huge shock. Within hours of that, I discovered that Belinda Jackson seems to have disappeared. Paranoid is a mild word, stark terror is more like it. Have you heard anything about a resurgence of the Right Brigade?"

"Son-of-a-bitch, I thought we'd put that all behind us!" exclaimed Rogers. "This really sucks. Rayburn is gone? Jesus, Amy and I were devastated by the death of Jim Young in a car accident last week. I didn't put any special significance on it at the time, but now it looks like it's part of a conspiracy to take all of us out."

"I'm afraid that's it, Mack. I'm really sorry to hear about Jim, I know the three of you were really tight. How *are* Amy and the kids?"

"She and the kids are great, I'd brag about them, but right now, we've got to get to the bottom of this doomsday deal."

"Exactly," said Adam. "We have to concentrate on covering our butts. You and Amy are in serious danger. If you could find a safe place for the kids, I'd like you to join me to try and sort this thing out. What is your situation, can you and Amy get away until we get to the bottom of this?"

"We don't have much choice, do we? We can stay here and be sitting ducks or join your little team and at least be moving targets. I should be able to arrange two or three weeks by tomorrow and I'll get Amy and the kids out of the house as soon as we finish here. Any bright ideas about where to start?"

"First, we need to contact Pat Conroy and Al Leach before the bad guys do. Can you give me any info on how to get in touch with them?"

"The information I have is a couple of years old, but we can give them a try," Mack Rogers said as he pulled up an address book on his computer. "Here are the phone numbers I have."

The number for Conroy had been disconnected with no further information. Leach answered his phone after five rings. He listened to Adam's description of the recent events and after letting out a deep sigh said, "I knew about the General, but the rest of this comes as a real fucking shock. What do you have in mind, Adam?"

"Do you have a family, Al?"

"No, just me…and the parade of gorgeous women that flock to my house."

Adam smiled. "Pack your bag and get out, right now. Find a safe place, out of your area. When you're secure, call 800-254-4548. It's a message center. Leave a message for Red Dog with your phone number. Meanwhile, I'll set up a command center. A place to get together and decide how to attack the problem. One other thing, do you have a recent number for Pat Conroy?"

"Negative on Conroy. I haven't talked to him in years. Thanks for the heads-up," said Leach. "I'm outta here. If you don't hear from me by tomorrow, come-a-lookin'." The connection was broken.

Adam thought for a moment and then said to Rogers, "After I find a safe house, I'll try to locate Conroy and bring him in. Call me at the 800 number and I'll give you an address. Then our first objective must be Belinda. God, I hope we can get to her in time!"

IV

**May 30th, 1999,
Hartsfield-Atlanta Int'l
Airport, 1310 hours...**

Adam ate a heavy breakfast at the officer's mess with the portly Mack Rogers before returning to Rogers' office to change identities.

Adam then drove to the airport and returned the Ford, which had been rented in the name of Adam Packard, to Hertz. He picked up a copy of the *Atlanta Journal* on his way to the National Car Rental booth where he rented a Cadillac DeVille under the name Steven Stellner.

Before leaving the terminal, he scanned the real estate section of the paper and the yellow pages. After choosing several real estate firms that advertised both sales and rentals, he called until he found one open on Sunday. He drove directly to the office and was ushered into the office of one of the partners, Karen Green. She pointed to a chair and said, "Please sit down, Mr. Stellner. What can I do for you?"

"I appreciate your helping me on Sunday. I have a big order. I'm looking for a home to lease, preferably in the country, but not too far out. I need something large, preferably isolated and I need to take possession immediately. Price is not an issue."

"Well, you do have quite a list of requirements, but the difficult we do right away, while the impossible may take a bit longer."

"Sounds like my kind of operation. How do we proceed?"

"For starters, how long you will need this home?"

"I'm willing to sign a lease for three to six months," said Adam "Whatever works."

"The next question is the rent. You mentioned price not being an issue…we are probably talking in the $15-30,000 neighborhood, is that all right?"

"Yes, for the right property, I'm willing to spend that or more. The main thing is availability. I need to move in very soon."

After satisfying herself that she understood Adam's request, Karen Green stood and once again extended her hand. "I will put all else aside and work for you exclusively…until we have you in your home. Where can I reach you?"

"I have not taken care of that little detail. What is the best hotel? Downtown preferably."

"I'd recommend the Grand Hyatt. It's right in the heart of downtown and the manager is a friend of mine. I'd be glad to call ahead and assure you of a reservation."

"Why, thank you. Please ask for a suite," replied Adam. Ms. Green made the call, nodded with a smile to Adam and gave him directions to the hotel.

The suite at the Hyatt was somewhat more comfortable than the Dew Drop Inn in Columbus. As soon as the bellman left, Adam called Belinda's number on his cell phone. He was frustrated by the sound of her answering machine. The message became more ominous each time he heard it. He fired up his computer and did a search on Pat Conroy. Another fruitless effort. He unpacked, opened the mini-bar and made himself a scotch and soda. He paced back and forth twirling the ice cubes in the glass. 'Have I missed anything? Is there any more I can do today?' He feared the lack of rest and stress of the last two days were catching up to him. He ordered a fish dinner from room service and after eating, stretched out on the bed.

Belinda reached out to him, but he couldn't touch her. Her eyes pleaded as her hand stretched to his chest. He took her hand…to pull her to him, but her hand disengaged from her wrist. She fell away from him, falling in a slow spiral, looking at him, her eyes beseeching him to save her, and then she was gone. He looked with horror at her hand, still in his. He yelled as he sat up, sweat pouring from his face. He looked at the bedside clock. Four in the morning. He'd slept for over ten hours. He was refreshed, physically. As soon as he could shake the terror of the dream, he would be ready to get back to work…to unravel the mystery that had already cost two comrades their lives.

*May 31st, 1999,
Grand Hyatt Hotel,
Atlanta, GA, 9 a.m....*

Adam did a heavy workout in the Hyatt gym before picking his way through the hotel's extensive buffet breakfast. When he returned to his suite, a message was waiting from Senator Hawthorne. When he reached him, the senator was shocked to hear about Jim Young's death, the attempt on Adam's life and Belinda's apparent disappearance. Adam asked about Anita. He and Anita Warwick had been married in 1993, the year after he lost his chairmanship of the Senate Armed Services Committee due to the change in control of the Senate. He remained as Ranking Member on the committee and had since moved up to a similar position on the Senate Select Committee on Intelligence. After saying that Anita was just great, he asked Adam what he could do to help. Adam asked, "How well are you connected with the CIA?"

"Very well indeed. The Director hails from my home state. We've crossed paths often over the years and I consider him a close friend."

"That's really good news, Gene. As you're well aware, there were elements within the Company that weren't necessarily on our side in the past. I need to establish contact with someone we can trust in order to finish the job we started in 1991. Could you possibly arrange a meeting with the Director, away from Langley?"

"Adam, you know I respect you and trust your judgment implicitly. I'll be happy to set up a meet. What's your time frame?"

"Just as soon as possible. I'm in the process of gathering my troops, but this is the highest priority."

"I'll give the Director a call this morning," said Hawthorne. "I'll let you know at once."

"Great, there is one point I must insist upon. Nobody can know about this but you, the Director and me. We have no idea who we can trust in the Agency, so he must agree to share this with no one."

"I will make that point clear when I talk with him," replied Hawthorne. "We'll communicate on a secure line only. Anything else?"

"No, but I want you to know how much I appreciate your willingness to help. We are facing a formidable foe with very little to go on. Your assistance is vital. By the way, you and Anita may want to watch yourselves until this is over. The people behind this may have you in their sights, too."

"Thanks for that, Adam. I want to see those bastards behind bars, or preferably dead, as much as you do. I will do anything in my power to make that happen."

Adam hung up the phone with the most positive attitude he'd had since the house bombing. He suspected Sean Ball had a hand in all of this, but he also felt the CIA was involved somewhere…if not everywhere along the way.

His spirits ratcheted up another notch when Karen Green called. "Are you in your office? Don't you know this is Memorial Day?"

Karen laughed. "No wonder the traffic was so light on a Monday. And yes, I am working. I have good news for you. It so happens that one of my partners has a friend who is taking a sabbatical to Africa for three months. He is a nationally known cardiologist who is partially retired. He had no intention of renting his house, but when my partner mentioned a number, he had a change of heart. How does $20,000 for three months sound?"

"If the house fits my requirements, it sounds perfect."

"Like a glove," she said with a smile in her voice. "It's over 5,000 square feet on three acres with five bedrooms, four and one-half baths…and a four-car garage. It's in a gated community with an alarm system. We can look at it this afternoon if you're available."

"I have no higher priority," Adam said.

They drove North on I-400 to Buckhead. About a mile from the divided highway, she turned into a well-landscaped entrance and pulled up to the guardhouse. After gaining clearance, they drove four blocks and turned into a brick driveway that wound gracefully uphill for several hundred feet. The home was perched on the crown of the hill with a commanding view in all directions. Perfect, thought Adam. He asked, "Is the owner still here or has he left for Africa?"

"He's here. Since he is not in the habit of renting his home, he wanted to meet the renter before signing the papers. Do you mind?"

"Not at all. Do you think I'll pass muster?" said Adam with just a hint of a smile.

"Absolutely. You have such an honest face that I doubt you could tell a lie."

"Thank you," Adam said, chuckling to himself as he stroked his fake mustache. "This place is beautiful. I certainly hope the good doctor looks at me through your rose-colored glasses."

She laughed and rang the bell. After a moment, it opened and a short, plump, but robust, white-haired man greeted them and asked them in. He made a quick appraisal of his guests and said, "Welcome, please make yourselves at home. If you like, I will give you the grand tour, or you may wish to conduct it on your own?"

Karen answered quickly, "Oh, we'd like you to show us. This house is too outstanding to have anything less than the grand tour."

The doctor laughed as he fell into a fast waddle and said with a wave of his hand, "Follow me." The house was indeed grand. The doctor was quite interested in technology as evidenced by his pride in explaining his electronics and security system. When the tour was complete, he invited Adam and Karen into the kitchen eating area, whose circle of casement windows afforded a panoramic view of the gardens and the countryside beyond.

The doctor asked, "Will you take coffee or tea?" After both had opted for coffee, he meticulously ground beans and started a coffee-maker right out of Star Wars.

Adam inquired, "Where did you find such an unusual coffee maker?"

"Ah," said the doctor, pleased with the question. "It is my own creation. There are a number of my inventions working throughout the house. My late wife thought my hobby was pure folly, but every now and then, to her utter amazement, one would actually work. This is one of my successes."

"It's wonderful," exclaimed Adam. "As somewhat of a technocrat, I'm fascinated by the inventive mind."

"What is your line, Mr. Stellner?" asked the doctor.

"I'm an engineer by training and I do consulting in the field of thermodynamics. I have a contract with a firm here in Atlanta to oversee developing a somewhat complex new process."

"Your work must have high value judging by the level of housing you have chosen for your stay," the doctor quipped.

"Let's just say that the company I am working with stands to make huge profits if it can successfully develop this process, and they believe I can be of some help in that effort. I am fascinated by your hobby. What other devices have you incorporated here?"

The doctor, sensing a kindred spirit, smiled broadly and said in the voice of a conspirator, "There are several gadgets, but my pride and joy is a secret passage in the library that leads to an equally secret room in the basement; in fact, it's under the garage. It is a bomb shelter and has a tunnel that opens into that small shed, down the hill there." He pointed to a small building, with an exterior matching the house, about a hundred feet away. "The cold war was still very much alive when I built this house so I went a little overboard. My wife never knew of its existence. I also have a lookout in the attic. From the outside, it looks like a cupola, but one can view the entire countryside from there. Someday, I'll mount television cameras in it and watch the neighborhood on TV." As the coffee was poured, Adam resolved that his lookout would be activated sooner rather than later. The doctor rose and said, "Bring your coffee, we'll adjourn to the library and I'll divulge its secrets." After he had proudly shown his innovative secret panel and the clandestine elements beyond, they returned to the library where he stated, "Now that you are privy to all my clandestine places, perhaps it's time to get down to business."

Karen smiled and said, "Does this mean you are agreeable to leasing your home to Mr. Stellner?"

"Absolutely, I would hardly bare my deepest secrets to someone I couldn't trust in my home. Where do I sign?"

After the documents were signed and a check delivered, Adam asked, "When may I take possession?"

"I leave in the morning," said the doctor, "so you can move in anytime after noon tomorrow."

As they drove away, Adam said, "I don't know how I can thank you for the splendid service you have rendered here."

"It has been my pleasure. If you need any help in finding anything in our fair city, I am at your service."

Adam looked at this charming woman and realized that under other circumstances, he might consider that offer, but finding Belinda was his priority…his only priority.

After she dropped him off at the Hyatt, Adam immediately called his message center, giving them his ID and code. He called the number Al Leach had left and the phone was answered immediately with one word, "Yes?"

"Al, I have a place. Give me the description of your vehicle."

Leach replied, "Black, 1999 Ford Explorer, New Jersey license JLL683."

"How far are you from Atlanta?"

"About six or seven hours. Is that where you're holed up?"

"Yes, and I want you to arrive after dark. Do you have a cell phone?"

"Sure, you know me…up to date on the latest tech crap, a regular James Bond."

"Yeah, I bet," said Adam with mild sarcasm. He then gave Leach detailed directions and asked him to arrive after 10 p.m. the next evening. He gave him his cell phone number and asked him to call when he turned off I-400. He was to use the name 'French' at the gate.

His next call was to Mack Rogers at his office at Fort Benning. He asked Mack to get to a pay phone and call him. When Mack returned the call an hour later, Adam said, "I have found a base of operations in Atlanta. Have you taken care of the kids?"

Mack replied, "Yes, they're off to a safe place…one that no one would suspect. Amy is packed and ready to leave at a moment's notice. I'm cleared to leave on the same basis."

"Okay, drive to La Grange and find a garage to park your car… long term. Then rent a dark Suburban and drive into Atlanta. Maybe you should have Amy rent the SUV. Keep that carrot-top of yours out of sight. When you reach Atlanta, pick up some supplies, food, liquor, at least a week's supply. Then drive out here after dark. Give the name 'MacFarland' at the gate. Here are the directions..."

Satisfied that his troops would arrive at the 'safe house' the next day, Adam decided to get a head start on *other* preparations. He called the concierge and asked about a men's shop that did rush orders. He left the room and took a cab to the address. In less than an hour, he selected a wardrobe consisting of three suits, two sport coats, slacks, sweaters, shoes and several shirts and ties. All would be delivered the next day. He returned to the Hyatt, had a solitary dinner courtesy of room service and retired early.

Adam arose at 5 a.m., worked out in the hotel gym and shaved, showered and dressed before seven o'clock. He located Packard Electronics' purchasing guru working out at a Minneapolis gym. After cutting his workout short, he raced to the office to search his files for security equipment and other suppliers in the Atlanta area. A series of phone calls followed to alert selected suppliers that a certain Steven Stellner was authorized to purchase, without limit, equipment to be charged to Packard Electronics. Adam was given a list of names and addresses of providers with the specific range of technology each carried. He called for his car and drove away from the hotel at 9 a.m.. His new clothing had been delivered before he returned to the hotel. He packed and checked out of the hotel at 1 p.m. and drove a circuitous route to the house on the hill. Before unpacking, he called his company in Minneapolis and ordered them to rig two panning cameras that would integrate a daylight and a nighttime infrared system and automatically switch between them according to available light. Holding his subordinates' feet to the fire, he insisted they be shipped air express in no more than three days.

By 10:30 that evening, two additional vehicles were parked in the garage and a reunion of sorts was underway. Mack Rogers had insisted they unpack only the frozen food, perishables *and* the liquor supply. When drinks were distributed, Adam raised his glass in a toast. "My friends, it's wonderful to be with you again. We have a difficult task before us, but we have faced tough challenges before, and we will do it again."

"I've really missed you birds," said Leach as he clinked glasses. "I can't wait to clobber these bastards. What's the skinny, Adam?"

"First, I must meet with CIA Director Rains. We need his cooperation to start our search for Belinda. In the meantime, we'll set up a foolproof defense, right here. Then we go looking for those bastards. Hopefully, when we find them, we find Belinda."

"Now you're talkin', Adam," said Mack. "Let's rustle up some grub, turn in and hit it hard first thing in the morning."

"Yeah," said Leach. "As long as it's after 8 a.m. I need my beauty sleep, ya' know."

Mack looked at Leach with a crooked smile and said, "You sure as hell do!"

Adam installed motion sensors the next morning. By Friday, the house had become an armed camp. The special cameras installed in the cupola on the roof were attached to real-time video screens and provided a 360° view of the perimeter, twenty-four hours a day along with floodlights activated by motion sensors. Screens had been removed from selected windows, the windows raised and plexiglass panels inserted. The panels were removable instantly to provide a gun port to cover every inch of the yard. Now, the question remained, should they seek out the foe or should they lure their prey into attacking them…in their fortress.

VI

June 4th, 1999,
Mayflower Hotel,
Washington, DC, 1 p.m....

Adam opened the door of the suite to CIA Director, Dennis Rains. He held out his hand and said, "Thank you for coming, Mr. Director. I am Adam Packard. Please come in."

The Director shook his hand. "Good to meet you, Packard. Senator Hawthorne speaks very highly of you." Looking past Adam, he said, "Hello there, Gene. How are you?"

"Terrific, Denny. Have a chair. Would you like coffee or anything?"

"Coffee, black would be fine, thank you." The director sat at the table in the foyer of the suite and said, "What's this all about?"

Gene Hawthorne related the story of the Right Brigade and the recent deaths of General Rayburn and Jim Young, the attempt on Adam's life and the suspected disappearance of Belinda Jackson. He then told of the role his wife Anita played and how her CIA connection was betrayed from within.

Adam then said, "The reason I have asked for secrecy is that I suspect that a person or persons within the CIA are in league with your ex-agent, Sean Ball. I feel certain he is behind these tragic events. We need your help to seek out Ball, wherever he is, and identifying a potential mole at the CIA may be an integral part of that effort. We must also neutralize the threat to the remaining team members from the 1992 takedown. We are prepared to release information on our whereabouts to lure the perpetrators into showing their hand. To determine the identity of the mole, this information can be fed piecemeal to key elements within the Company…I'm sure you know the best way to do that."

The director scratched his chin as he mulled over the information he'd received. Finally he said, "I cannot deny that Ball may have had a pal at the Agency back in '92, but I hardly think you've made a case that he has a conspirator working for him today. Is there anything in particular that speaks of the CIA being involved?"

"The crash of General Rayburn's plane is the most probable tie. It was definitely sabotaged and the details of his trip were highly classified. Other than 'need-to-know' military personnel, the CIA was the only agency with knowledge of his itinerary."

"What about the people with whom he was to meet?" asked the director. "There were a number of opportunities for a leak outside the Agency. I understand your concern and I will respect your request to keep this top secret, but I must ask you to bring me more definitive evidence of a mole before I undertake a witch-hunt within the Company. I'm sorry."

Adam was sorely disappointed, but carefully hid his feelings. "Can you give us any help in locating Ball?"

"I have no idea what has become of our rogue agent, but I will make inquiries. I will let you know if I learn anything."

"Thank you," said Adam. "I appreciate your help on that, and your willingness to remain silent. We will just have to try smoking him...or her out. I trust we can keep the lines of communication open and should we uncover definitive evidence, you will cooperate in identifying the mole."

"I have no problem with that. In fact, I will keep my eyes and ears open for any sign of malfeasance within my organization." The director rose. "It's been a pleasure and your story is most interesting. I shall be in touch. Shall I contact Gene if I have information to share?"

"That would be fine, sir," said Adam. "And thank you for your time and cooperation."

When the director had gone, Hawthorne turned to Adam. "I'm sorry that didn't work out as you'd hoped, but you can trust him...both his silence and his agreement to watch for signs. Do you have a plan to smoke out the mole?"

"Not exactly, I was hoping the Agency could help me bait a trap. The only other way is to *become* the bait by showing myself conspicuously in public. That, of course, provides an easy target for our assassin."

"You can't do that, Adam. Is there anything I can do to gather more evidence for Dennis?"

"Not that I can think of at the moment. I'll have a powwow with my people and see if we can point you in some direction. Just having you on our side is a huge benefit and we all appreciate it!"

The Senator rose and shook Adam's hand. "Good luck and don't become a sitting duck. You are the vital cog in the wheel that's going to take these people down…don't forget that."

Adam once again donned his identity of Steven Stellner and left for Ronald Reagan Airport and the flight to Atlanta. Before boarding the airplane, he made a call to Mack and asked him to pick him up at the airport at 6 p.m.

As the wheels touched down in Atlanta, Adam thought of Belinda and the deep love he'd felt for her. Where was she now…and was she still alive? His mood was somber when he arrived at the house and told about the meeting with CIA Director Rains. He paused. "We've hit a stone wall before. I guess it's time for us to get back to the drawing board. How is your plan coming, Mack?"

"I have a tactical plan that would make Robert E. Lee proud. Now that the security is in place, we can detect entry at the outer perimeters and track movements anywhere on the property. We'll then have a choice of taking them out with converging fields of fire or letting them reach and/or occupy the house while we escape though the library and position ourselves behind them."

"What about arms, ammunition, vests and so forth?"

"All in place, Boss," said Amy. "In addition to your list, I added a bazooka to take out any vehicles we might find offensive. They are deployed as you asked with appropriate ammunition. Unless they bring in tanks, we can hold off a substantial force."

"Great, now if we could just identify the enemy, other than Ball, we'd be set," said Adam. "Let's all consider ways we can bait the trap, without help from the CIA."

June 7th, 1999, Ranchero Grande, Paz de Rio, Colombia, 10:15 a.m....

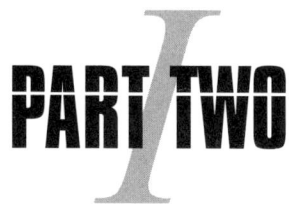

The smoke from his cigarette curled toward the ceiling as he looked off into the distance. His thoughts strayed from the problem at hand...he didn't really need to finish the job for JoAnn. What did he owe her? He recalled the time he'd offered to make love to her...her obvious interest, but ultimate rejection. Bitch! She deserved her years in the loony bin. Now that she had her mind back, she thought he should jump through hoops for her. Well, hadn't he taken care of most of her enemies? If it weren't for that damn Belinda. If only he had simply killed her in the beginning. Taking her hostage seemed like a good idea at the time. Now she was eating him up. When he had the right drugs in her, he could have her body, but when her head cleared, she expressed such hatred for him that he wanted to kill her, but he just couldn't bring himself to do it. In dying, she would defeat him...he had to find a way to get at least *some* respect from her.

His thoughts were interrupted by Jeb Carter's stern voice. "When are we gonna make our move, Sean?"

"I assume you refer to a move against Packard and his cohorts?"

"Yessir," said Jeb Carter. "You know I really want a crack at that stuffed-shirt bastard. We don't want 'em to get too prepared. I figure the sooner we hit 'em, the better."

"Well I'm giving the matter some serious thought. I have already called in some chits at the agency. The guy who has taken care of some people for us still owes me big time. He *was* pretty high on the hog before, but he just got a big promotion. Why dirty my hands when I can make a phone call and get it done?"

"You mean we won't be going back to the States…get involved ourselves?" asked Carter in a disappointed voice.

"Maybe, maybe not. Don't tell me you're getting homesick? Remember, if a cop stops us for going through a red light, we could both go up on the murder charges hanging over us. Besides, you've never lived in such luxury. The decision whether and when we risk it to go back depends on how much my friend at the CIA values his new job. He's been very cooperative to date, but for this mission…I might have to apply a little pressure personally. That could involve a return to Washington, and possibly playing a little cat and mouse game with our friends."

"What do you plan to do with Jackson if we make a trip back, leave her here?"

"I haven't thought that one through, Jeb. I rather doubt she'd be a willing traveling companion. I could leave her with a local babysitter…or I might ice her."

"I'd have done that long ago. She's a real pain in the ass," said Carter, "I s'pose that's what you keep her around for…her ass."

"That's none of your goddamn business," said Ball, suddenly heavy with menace. "Keep your yap shut about the lady."

Carter put his hands out in a sign of resignation, "Jesus, Sean, take it easy, I was just makin' conversation."

"That mouth of yours will be the death of you someday. How about doing something useful for a change? You know we have a big problem with transporting the next shipment to Miami. If we don't get it there by next Tuesday, we have a good chance of losing that distributor. Go check with Miguel and see what luck he's had in finding pilots."

"It's not easy to get a straight answer out of that little spick," said Carter, back to his usual sullen tone. "How about I rattle his cage a bit, let him know who's boss?"

"Maybe *you* need to remember who's boss around here. When somebody needs discipline, I'll let you know. Miguel is an important cog in this wheel and you keep your lousy mitts off him, understand?"

"Yeah, I'll not only keep my mitts off him, I'll handle the asshole with kid gloves," Carter muttered as he left the room.

Ball sat for a moment, then rose, walked languidly down to the end of a corridor and knocked softly on the door. Hearing no response, he took a key from his pocket, unlocked the door and swung it wide open. Looking carefully on both sides of the door and seeing nothing, he moved into the room and said loudly, "Belinda?" There was no sound, so he walked through the living room and cautiously opened the door to the bedroom. The bed was made with the spread neatly in place. The furniture was all in place, so he went to the closet and again, threw open the doors, ready to repel the attack she had launched against him before. There was no attack…there was no attacker. She was gone.

How could this be? The drugs she was given last night should have kept her out of the loop until noon today. He hurled back the bedspread – the sheets and pillowcases were gone. He ran to the living room and checked the locks on the windows…there it was, one of the locks had been removed from the window and the sheet-rope was attached to the window handle. The windows were connected to the alarm system. How did she deactivate the alarm? He ran back to the main room and yelled into the intercom, "Jackson is missing. Everyone drop whatever you're doing and find her. Carter and Miguel will organize the search…Move!"

II

June 7th, 1999, Town Square, Paz de Rio, Colombia, 10:45 a.m....

Belinda was careful to stain her face, arms, legs and even feet to match the natives' skin color. She had, with the help of Maria, dyed her hair jet black and dressed in native garb. With her CIA training in the art of disguise, she had copied the walk and mannerisms of the Colombian village women. She had one disadvantage; she was 5'8" and nearly a head taller than the local women. She stooped to minimize the difference. In the two weeks she had been Ball's captive, and when the drugs weren't in charge of her very being, she had worked on her Spanish. Maria coached her daily on the local accent and she now felt confident that she could get by as long as she limited her conversation.

What would she have done without Maria? She recalled the many kindnesses, but most important were the reduced drug doses that Maria had risked her very life to administer. The only downside had been forcing herself to submit to Ball while feigning a drugged stupor. That had been key to crystallizing her plan…her one goal in life… escape, and eventually, ridding the earth of Sean Ball.

Her immediate goal was getting out of Paz de Rio. Ball had connections everywhere. The power of his drug money was absolute and she wouldn't last twenty-four hours in the city. Local authorities were nothing but pawns to the drug lords. Maria had given her the name of a cousin who might be willing to smuggle her to the city of Tunja, capital of the province of Boyaca. There, she would seek transport to Bogotá and the American Embassy. Juan was a trucker and was gone for the day, so she must find a safe haven until she could contact him that evening. Maria had sketched out the downtown and its relation to Juan's business.

Maria had executed all the details of her escape the night before. After giving Belinda a false dose of drugs, she had provided tools to remove the lock from the window and disabled the alarm for that section of the house. Maria had then boarded the bus that transported the day workers from the Ranchero to the city below. At 3 a.m., Belinda removed the window lock, descended hand over hand on the sheet-rope and crept to the garage. There she found the hair and skin dye, clothing and the blanket left by Maria in the back of the bus. She transformed herself and hid beneath the blanket. When the bus drove into the city the next morning to pick up the workers, she silently opened the back door at the first stop and slipped out into the early morning darkness. Now she was on her own in a strange country, determined to escape the clutches of Ball and reestablish her life.

Avoiding the main thoroughfares, she walked down the narrow streets of the old city. She found a small shop with a crystal ball painted on the sign hanging over the door. Inside, several people drank coffee under the watchful eye of an elderly, overstuffed woman. Belinda ordered coffee and asked if she was the fortune-teller. Her face lit up in broad smile displaying remarkably white, even teeth as she affirmed that she was the one and only true forecaster of the future in all of Colombia. Although she had little money, Belinda saw an opportunity to delay her return to the street and agreed to submit to Madame Cordoba's star-guided scrutiny. They passed through a curtain dividing the coffee shop from a dark room with navy blue velvet draped haphazardly over the ceiling and walls.

She motioned Belinda to a chair opposite her, and gazed back and forth between Belinda's eyes and her crystal ball. At length, she said, "I see a great sadness. You have been in bad company and have been very unhappy. You will be rid of this for a time, and then you will be betrayed, and the bad times will return. In the end you will rise up and be victorious. At this moment you are in great danger."

Belinda was shocked at the perception of this would-be prophet and said, "Do you have any suggestions for my immediate future?"

"Only to provide you with safe haven for a short time…until the cover of darkness." She rose and beckoned Belinda to follow her through another curtain to the very rear of the shop. She pointed to an old, but clean-looking rattan sofa and said, "Rest here, dear. If you fall asleep, I shall wake you when the sun leaves the sky."

"Thank you, you are very kind."

"Thank the stars, they are watching over you...it is *they* that brought you here to me." She left the room and Belinda, to her surprise, fell into a deep, drug-free sleep. She awoke hours later to a pungent, but delectable aroma. She opened her eyes and found a steaming bowl of chili and heavy dark bread on a table by her side. Every last morsel fell victim to her ravenous hunger. She pushed the dark window curtain aside carefully and saw the long shadows of late afternoon. Minutes later, Madam Cordoba returned and smiled at the empty bowl. "Good, you have eaten. Now you must wait for the light to depart. When the stars appear, it will be safe for you to continue your journey."

Belinda thanked her profusely, then asked directions to an address near Juan's garage. An hour later, she slipped out, while the streets were still crowded, but the darkness would hide her true identity. When she arrived at the garage, she was dismayed to find it locked. The neighborhood was very poor and rough, but she made her way around to the back of the building and sat down on a pile of old tires. The only sound was an occasional scratching that she assumed were rats seeking their evening meal. After an hour of expecting that the animals would soon feast on her, she heard a noisy engine and loud rattles as a large vehicle lumbered down the alley. She scrambled behind a fence and watched as the truck stopped outside the garage and a small man left the cab and opened the ramshackle doors. She said tentatively, "Juan?"

He was startled, but replied, "Si, who is asking?"

"Maria sent me. She said you could give me a ride out of town."

"Come inside. I will park the truck and then we will talk." She entered the garage and after he had pulled the truck in and closed the doors, he turned to her and said, "I know who you are running from… they are very powerful people. There is great risk in helping you."

Belinda heart pounded. "I realize that, but I am prepared to reward you handsomely for your help. I don't have money now, but if you will get me to a safe place, I will pay you $10,000 American money."

"That will not benefit me if I am dead," said Juan. "And how do I know you will pay me?"

"I can guarantee payment if you take me to the American Embassy in Bogotá. A wire transfer should take less than a day. Isn't $10,000 for a day's work worth a little risk?"

"You do not understand, senorita. If I do this, I must leave this place for good. I must take Maria and her family with me. They would hunt us down and kill us for helping you. They have eyes and ears everywhere."

"I know, believe me, I owe everything to Maria. I would never do anything to harm her." Belinda was desperate, but said simply, "How much do you need to relocate *both* families?"

Juan did some calculating on his fingers. "It would require nearly three times your offer to get us far enough away from these people."

"Well, I owe a great deal to Maria, and if it will insure her safety. Would $25,000 be enough?" Juan thought for a moment and then nodded. Belinda said, "Since you are leaving for good and to get the money right away, can you take me to Bogotá?"

Juan frowned in thought, then brightened. "We will find a way. Now, I will go to Maria's house and ask her to pack. We will all leave very early in the morning. What makes me very sad is…we can never return to Paz de Rio."

"Juan, I promise you I will come back and defeat these people. It may take time, but someday, you will be able to return to your home."

Belinda slept in the truck and although it was reasonably clean, the smell of sweat permeated the cab. She awakened before dawn to the sound of the creaking hinges of the garage door. Maria and her two children carried their meager possessions to the back of the truck. Juan, his wife Rosita and daughter also loaded parcels and boxes in the truck. After wishing her a good morning, Juan said, "Pack everything at the front of the truck-bed. I will pick up a load to be delivered in Tunja. You will all ride between our things and the cargo. We must not do anything that will arouse suspicion."

Belinda considered Juan's plan. "Isn't Tunja on the road to Bogotá?"

Juan replied, "Si, it is the direct route. Why do you ask?"

"If Maria fails to show up for work this morning, how long will it take for them to connect her with you, check your customers and realize where you are heading? Could you pick up a load to deliver in a different direction?"

"You speak sense," said Juan, scratching his meager chin whiskers. "Instead of the load to Tunja, I will pick up food at the market and tell the other truckers I am heading north instead of south. That will be good. We must hurry, we can leave the market at 6:00 and travel the 200 kilometers to Bogotá by 9:00. Maria will not be missed until after 8:00…after that, they will not be able to catch us."

The mountain air of the early morning was cool, but the huddled mass in the truck-bed soon generated heat that, combined with the old truck's bumping over potholes, created their own version of Hell. When Juan stopped the truck on the outskirts of Bogotá three hours later, a sore, sweaty group thankfully climbed out of their cramped quarters. Belinda said, "I think you should drop me off a block or so from the Embassy. It may not be wise for them to identify your truck. But, before that, let us find a place for all of you to stay. I will call you there when I have the money."

"I don't know," replied Juan cautiously. "You could just forget about us…when you are safe."

Maria spoke sharply, "Juan, I told you she can be trusted. Don't you think I know her after all the time we've spent together? We will do as she says."

They located an old motel that offered a place to park the truck out of sight. Juan went in and registered for two rooms. He came back with a phone number which he presented to Belinda. He then walked a block to a service station to get directions to the Embassy. After locating it, Juan dropped Belinda a block away. She walked briskly to the gate. The Marine guard asked her business. She replied that she was an American citizen who had been kidnapped and taken against her will to Colombia. It was just after 10 a.m. when she walked through the gates of the American Embassy.

III

June 8th, 1999, Ranchero Grande, Paz de Rio, Colombia, 4:45 p.m....

Ball sat in the large, comfortable dining room of the sprawling mansion that had been his home for the past five years. Like a fortress, it commanded the highest point for several miles in every direction. One road wound its way up from the valley below and other than that road, the terrain was rocky and forbidding to even the most ambitious 4-wheel drive vehicle. The house was luxuriously furnished and floor to ceiling windows provided panoramic views of the surrounding mountains. The man who had built the house had amassed a fortune in the drug business and was among the top twenty drug lords in Colombia...that was before he met head on with a bullet from Ball's .357 Magnum. The law of the jungle prevailed in this country and if one had the audacity and muscle to overthrow a drug kingpin, he inherited all of his victim's assets...until another interloper came along.

To prevent meeting a similar fate, Ball had assessed his predecessor's weaknesses and shored up his defenses accordingly. With the many contacts he had made over the years as a CIA operative, he gathered expertise from around the world to protect both himself and his illicit and outrageously profitable business. His staff members were talented in electronics, demolition, computers and, of course, handling a myriad of weapons. He hired several pilots who were known for their flying skills and ability to avert the law. Unfortunately, the life expectancy of an airborne drug-runner is unusually short. A high percentage experienced prison bars or a cemetery headstone after a short but highly profitable career. Ball had expended his pilot contacts and was now relying upon the persuasive talents of the chief lieutenant he had inherited from his predecessor, Miguel Santana.

As he waited for his drink to be served, the phone rang. "Yes?"

The voice on the other end was familiar. "She's at the Embassy in Bogotá. Her reservation, tomorrow, is under the name of Janet Dayton. Delta Airlines, Flight 299, departing at 4:05 p.m. for Atlanta. She will be driven to the airport by one or more CIA operatives." There was a click and the line went dead.

Ball leaned back in his chair, a smile curling his thin lips. He thought, 'Well, my lovely, you don't know it yet, but you're coming back to Papa. Then you'll learn what it means to walk out on Sean Ball.' As his drink was put before him, he reached for the phone and punched three numbers. "Jeb? How about joining me for a cocktail. I have an interesting project for you." When Carter arrived a few minutes later, Ball invited him to sit down and ordered him a drink. When it was delivered and the server dismissed, Ball gave Carter a series of orders to be carried out the next day. Carter left with a purposeful stride and a hint of a smile on his otherwise sullen countenance. Once again, Ball leaned back in his chair and reflected on his good fortune. He was rich beyond his wildest dreams. He wielded vast power over just about anything or anybody he chose to control. But it hadn't always been this way.

His English father, Douglas Ball, had enlisted in the Marines in 1942 and had a merciless tour of duty in the South Pacific. He came home, wounded severely. After a heavily morphine-assisted recovery, he was discharged and soon struck out across the country in a shiny 1941 Ford convertible.

He woke up one morning in El Paso, Texas. As he opened his eyes, his blurred vision beheld what he thought was an angel. Broke and broken from drink and drugs, he allowed Juanita, his angel, to nurse him back to health. He proposed marriage three months later. She had not confided in him, about the baby boy growing inside her. That December, Sean Douglas Ball entered the world in a snug little home on the outskirts of El Paso. Sean inherited the golden skin and dark hair and eyes of his Hispanic mother. By the age of fifteen he excelled at sports and was a good student. Over the years, Sean received his share of physical abuse from his father when he was drinking. When sober, Douglas had given Sean boxing lessons, but as Sean grew in stature, the once-friendly lessons became more of a prizefight. Sean was awakened by loud voices one night, and found his father slapping his mother. For the first time he struck his father in anger and in his rage, beating him unmercifully. His father never hit his mother again. He also never forgave his son.

The daughter of a wealthy stockbroker, Shirley Adams caught up with Sean after an October football game and made it clear that she wanted to get to know him better. They began a nearly clandestine relationship due the difference in their stations and by November, Shirley was pregnant. Sean tried frantically to raise money for an abortion. Failing to gather the money by lawful means, he broke into the home of one of El Paso's wealthiest families. He successfully evaded capture during the robbery, but was arrested when he tried to fence stolen jewelry. Upon hearing of his arrest, Shirley confessed to her father, who was a friend of the family Sean had robbed. He convinced them to drop the charges with the proviso that Sean immediately leave town via an enlistment in the Army. It was the fall of 1964 and the Vietnam kettle was heating up. He would arrive when it came to a boil.

He scored high in the Army's tests and with his considerable physical skills was assigned to Ranger training after basic training. His performance in Ranger training was, once again, outstanding and he was chosen for inter-service training with Navy Seals. His unit was cited for bravery on several occasions and Sean won bronze and silver stars for valor in battle. He later was chosen to leave the Army and join the CIA. His record was exemplary until he became involved in the Iran-Contra scheme. With his excellent command of Spanish, he was chosen as a go-between in passing American dollars to the Contra leaders. The problem was a disparity between the funds he received and the funds that were transferred to the Contra. An informer of this disparity, a mere $350,000, was murdered and although positive proof of Ball's part in his death was not forthcoming, his superiors decided to terminate his career with the CIA rather than prosecute a man who knew too much about this highly illegal operation. Aware that the 'Company' had meted out ultimate termination on occasion, he insured his future by informing his superiors that, should he disappear or meet with an accident, lurid details of the Contra affair would find their way to the media.

With a hefty bankroll of Contra money, Ball gathered a floating crew of primarily former soldiers with which he had served. These men possessed a variety of talents, all violent. Once he had established a group of clever, hard-nosed associates, he put the word out that they were available to undertake virtually any kind of mission with skill, speed and utmost secrecy. His enterprise began working with the Right Brigade in 1988.

Many women had succumbed to his charms over the years, but until Belinda only one had awakened the emotion of love. Shirley Adams, torn from his embrace by social circumstances, represented the only crack in his otherwise rock-hard psyche. That is…until Belinda. What began as simple lust gradually developed into a gnawing need for her approval. His treatment of Belinda varied from harsh cruelty to a tenderness he believed himself incapable of. His lovemaking with her, always accompanied by drugs, followed the same pattern. When she was free of drugs, her hatred for him was ever apparent. Again and again, he became enraged and vowed to end her life, but he could not bring himself to do it. He thought about his options when she was returned to him. She must be punished…but how? How could he teach her a lesson and yet show her a different side of him?

The decision came to him in the middle of the night. She would suffer the guilt of having brought several people to their deaths unnecessarily. He would not personally be the bearer of bad tidings, but would make the information available to her…a piece at a time. He would also make alcohol and drugs readily available for her to appease her sorrow. If she were strong enough to resist, he would see to it that she became dependent…first on the drugs and ultimately on Sean Ball.

On Thursday morning, Ball woke to good news. His Belinda had been brought home, and was once again where she belonged, locked in her quarters. A cart in the living room of her suite was set up with sandwiches, wine, ice, scotch and several lines of cocaine. Ball delighted in playing the spider with the beautiful fly caught in his web. Although sorely tempted, he resisted visiting her for the entire day. He allowed a butler who had been friendly with Belinda to 'sneak' a copy of the Bogotá newspaper to her that evening. The headline read: "THREE AMERICANS PLUNGE TO FIERY DEATH." The story followed with the description of two U. S. State Department officials and an American woman who died when their embassy car went off the road and crashed on a mountainside near the Bogotá International Airport.

When Ball knocked softly on her door the next morning, there was no answer. As before, he cautiously unlocked the door and entered. She was not in the living room. The bedroom door was closed. Again he knocked softly and asked in a conciliatory tone, "Belinda, may I come in?" Hearing no reply, he opened the door. She was in bed, facing away from him. He asked, "Are you all right?"

"You murderous bastard," she shouted as she turned to him, "How could I be all right? Can you possibly imagine that I could ever regard you as anything but the lowest form of life? You can hold me here, you can drug me, rape me, but you'll never, ever change my feelings for you…I hate you with a passion you'll never understand!"

Ball had not intended to throw the deaths in her face, but his rage at her words overcame his calm and he shouted, "You bitch, don't you know who's responsible for those deaths? It's you and *you alone*. And when I find the people who helped you, there'll be more blood on your hands…that's right, *your hands!*"

Belinda threw back the covers and leaped at Ball with the ferocity of a wild animal. Had it not been for the bodyguards that stormed into the room, she may have had her revenge. When she was handcuffed and Ball recovered, he slapped her hard across the face. "If you ever try that again, I will kill you. But it will not be a nice quick death…you will suffer untold agonies while pleading for the end." He turned to a female assistant and said, "Keep her sedated until I tell you otherwise."

IV

June 10th, 1999, CIA Headquarters, Langley, VA, 11:25 a.m....

Clyde Johansen did not relish phone calls from Colombia. Sean Ball, his blackmailer, had asked for and received hefty favors for the knowledge he had of Johansen's past. Recently appointed CIA Deputy Director, he had accepted the current request with the caveat that this would be the *final* payback. His new position afforded him more power, but he could not exercise that power without increased scrutiny from above and below. He had called in a lot of chits to take care of Jim Young, General Rayburn and the kidnapping of Jackson. The hired assassin succeeded with Young and Jackson, but failed to silence Adam Packard. Johansen rewarded this failure by paying him off in hot lead, thereby covering his tracks.

Now, there was just one person he could depend upon to do this last job, and keep quiet about it. He picked up the phone and dialed a Washington, DC number. When the answering machine came on he said, "Urgent meeting, place: Apple, time: Charlie, date: Whiskey, response: David," and hung up. One hour later his phone rang. He picked it up and said, "Johansen."

A female voice said, "Your supplements came in. Shall I send them to your home or office?"

Johansen replied, "Very good, please send them to my home. Do you have the address?"

"Yes, I'll get them in the mail today."

"Thank you for the prompt service," said Johansen as he hung up. He sat back in his chair and smiled. He always looked forward to meeting with an assassin who brought such passion to the trade.

His reverie was interrupted by a buzz on his intercom. "The director would like a meeting in his office at 11 a.m. Are you available, sir?"

"Yes," replied Johansen. "I'll be there. Thank you."

When he arrived at the director's office, the other two deputy directors were already seated at a conference table with Director Rains. Johansen declined the offer of coffee and was disturbed by the serious expression and tone of the director as he said, "Gentlemen, we have a serious problem. I believe the incident in Bogotá yesterday was the result of a leak within the Company. I'm sure you are all aware that Colonel Jackson's airline reservation was made under an assumed name and a priority-one security classification. I want each of you to supply me with the names and security clearance data on each and every person who had access to this information. I have no doubt who is behind the killings, but right now, I intend to ferret out his contact within this organization. Please have this information on my desk by tomorrow morning. Any questions?"

No questions were forthcoming and as the deputy directors filed out of the room, only one felt the weight of the director's words slice into his inner being. His mind raced and by the time he'd reached his office, he had come up with a daring plan to extradite himself from the situation. At lunchtime, he drove to the city and put in a call to Colombia from a pay phone, using a calling card. He instructed Ball to transfer $50,000 to a numbered account in a Swiss bank in the name of Colin McReady. The account was to be backdated to June 8th and it was to be disclosed that the funds had come from Colombia. He returned to the office and carefully forged McReady's handwriting on a note. The note contained the name of a Swiss bank and one number, Ball's Colombian telephone number.

Johansen was wearing a nondescript jacket and an Orioles baseball cap as he slipped into the seedy bar in Georgetown at 8:30 that evening. He walked to the back of the room and slid into a booth across from a dark-haired woman. Her features were classic, but hard. Without makeup and with baggy clothes, she attracted little attention. Johansen smiled as he said softly, "Rita, how nice to see you again."

Without returning his smile, she said in a businesslike tone, "Let's skip the bullshit and get down to business."

After the waiter had taken his order for a beer, Johansen said, "I have two assignments for you. One is urgent, the other can take a while. I need an agent to suffer a fatal accident on the way to work tomorrow morning. The fee is fifty. The second involves three fairly tough clowns. You will have to research this one, but you'll get a hundred for each providing all go down."

"What's with this *urgent* shit! You know I don't work that way. A quick hit, sure, but when you want an 'accident,' it takes some planning. Unless, of course, you have it all laid out."

"When will you learn, my dear, that I always have a plan. He takes the Metro and is picked up at the West Falls Church station by a shuttle to Langley." Johansen reached into his coat pocket and after looking around, produced a small package which he passed to Rita under the table. "You hold, in your hand, a powerful drug that will stop his heart in less than a minute and will be untraceable in his bloodstream in five. You simply bump him as you board the train and stick him in the neck…the carotid artery."

"Yeah, the other passengers and particularly the mark are not going to notice me sticking a needle in his neck and having to hit an artery? Give me a break. With a long enough needle, I could jam it up his ass, but his *neck*?"

"Patience, my love," said Johansen, as if talking to a child. "When you examine the syringe, you will see that it is 16" long and will fit perfectly in a folded newspaper. Only the mark will notice it and I know you will disappear like a puff of smoke immediately thereafter. As far as hitting the artery, it's right here," he said pointing to his neck. "If it only had to go in his ass, I wouldn't need your unique skills."

"How old is this guy? Is he likely to drop dead like this?"

"He's only 51, but he has family history of heart disease. He takes medication for high blood pressure and that is why I have chosen him for this singular honor."

"You know, you're a real prick, Clyde, but I like the color of your money. It'll cost you seventy-five with half up front…have you got some pictures of this bird?"

"There's several in the packet, with front and side views. He'll be wearing a suit with a white shirt and tie. He will transfer from the Blue to the Orange line at Rosslyn. You stay on the Orange platform and wait for him. He should arrive at about 7:45. As far as the money goes, I'll go sixty tops, but I'll give you a bonus of fifty on the other job – providing you get all three."

"Deal. What's the arrangement on the money and the skinny on the other job?"

"I'll wire-transfer the sixty to your Swiss account by 1 p.m tomorrow. I'll have a packet on the other job delivered to your mail drop by Saturday morning. We'll meet here again on Monday night to work out the details…after you've had a chance to familiarize yourself with the marks."

"Done. Now I'm taking a trip to the ladies' room. I'll expect you to be gone when I return. And, Diamond Jim, don't forget to pay the bill before you leave." She rose, folded newspaper in hand, and slid out of the booth with the lithe movements of a jungle cat. She looked back and favored him with a slight wave and the broad smile he had waited for all evening.

Johansen arrived at his office at 6:30 a.m. on Friday morning and made it a point to say hello to several acquaintances on his way in. The executive floor was deserted at this hour and he slipped into McReady's office. He put on rubber gloves and placed the slip containing the bank and Ball's phone number in a book in McReady's bookcase. He removed the gloves, wiped the doorknob and returned to his office. He fidgeted from 7:30 until 8:15 when the phone on his desk finally rang. He grabbed the phone impatiently, and forced himself to answer in a calm, normal voice. "Johansen here," he said.

"Mr. Johansen, this is Sergeant Porter of the Capitol Police. I'm sorry to inform you that your associate, Mr. Colin McReady, suffered a fatal attack this morning on the Metro. His wife asked me to call you."

"Oh, no," said Johansen with disbelief and grief in his voice. "I can't believe it. Are you sure it was Colin?"

"No question about it. His ID was in his wallet and he matches the description and picture. His wife asked if you could come to the morgue and identify his body. She is too broken up to do it."

"I'll be glad to do that for her. I will talk with her later, and thank you for informing me." Johansen wrote a short memo to the director indicating that his personal assistant, Sheila Andrews and Colin McReady were the only persons in his section that had access to the Bogotá information.

The trip to the DC morgue offered a perfect cover for the delivery to Rita's mail drop and for the phone call that would make her $60,000 richer for the morning's work. After identifying McReady, he returned to the office where a message from the director awaited. The director asked for another meeting of deputy directors at 1 p.m. He dialed Director Rains' office and informed his assistant that he would attend the meeting as requested.

Rains began with, "I think you all know that we lost one of our valued agents this morning. Colin McReady had a fine record and will be sorely missed, particularly by your section, Clyde." He looked at Johansen and continued, "I trust you will do the proper thing toward his widow."

"Yes, sir," replied Johansen. "At her request, I identified the body earlier and I will pay a personal call on the family this evening. His death was a terrible shock to everyone."

"Good, now I'd like to thank you for the information you all provided on Bogotá. Have any of you personally or, to your knowledge, have any of your subordinates with access to the information ever served with a former agent named Sean Ball?"

One of the deputy directors said he had run across Ball back in Nam, but had never worked directly with him. The other had heard of his discharge from the Company, but had never met him. Both said they knew of no contact between Ball and their subordinates. Johansen said he had served briefly with Ball in Laos while Ball was still in the Army. He couldn't say about McReady. He knew they had both been in Vietnam about the same time, but without checking personnel files, could not put them together.

The director concluded with, "We need to make certain about any possible relationships. Please scrutinize the personnel records of every person involved and if they've had any contact, check their financial situations, bank accounts and anything else that might tie them to Ball. You all know the drill, so go to it!"

Late that day, the slip of paper was discovered in McReady's office. The CIA, one of the chosen few who can gain access to information on inviolable Swiss bank accounts, discovered the $50,000 deposit in McReady's name and that, in the eyes of the director, closed the book on the mole.

PART THREE

**June 10th, 1999,
Buckhead, GA, 9 a.m....**

"Oh no," said Adam into the phone. "Are they sure?" He listened, face ashen, his gut cramped in fear. "No, it couldn't be...have they recovered the bodies?" After another pause, he said in a resigned voice. "I see." He took the phone away from his ear and took a deep breath. "I can't believe it...I want to have a DNA check before I accept this. Will you follow through on that? And, Gene, do you think this gives the director enough cause to look around for moles?" He listened again. "Thank you, Gene. I'll really appreciate it if you'll get right on it...this has got to be his smoking gun."

Mack looked at Adam's face and said, "Bad news?"

"The worst. Belinda escaped from Ball and made it to the Embassy in Bogotá two days ago. She was on her way to the airport with two State Department men yesterday. Their car went off a mountain road and, according to the report, all were killed. I just can't accept that she's dead. I won't accept it!" He was over her. She wanted nothing to do with him. Yet the thought she might be dead took his breath away. Some part of him had held out hope Belinda would be his again one day. But if she was dead, that hope would die with her.

Less than an hour later the phone rang and Senator Hawthorne informed Adam that CIA Director Rains had agreed to request a DNA sample from the body in Bogotá and that he would pursue, with vigor, Adam's suspicion about a mole within the agency. The defense work came to a screeching halt for the rest of the day while four of Delinda Jackson's best friends remembered her and mourned. Early the next morning, Adam called a meeting and announced, "I propose that we go forward today as if nothing happened. I refuse to accept Belinda's death until the DNA is matched. I ask you to do the same and even if we later learn that she is gone, it will not change our mission…it will fill us with an even deeper resolve to avenge her death." A few leftover tears were shed before they resumed the tasks, but resume they did…with increased energy and a renewed sense of purpose.

He had talked with Belinda a few times over the last seven years, but they had met face to face only once. She steadfastly refused to hear his denial of wrongdoing with Sela Pierce and with Sela's refusal to admit her lies, he had finally given up trying to prove his innocence.

The phone rang and Gene Hawthorne said, "I have good news, Adam. Denny has found the mole and he's dead."

"Great, tell me the details."

"Denny met with his deputies on Thursday and asked who knew about Belinda's travel plans. On Friday morning, a top aide of one of the deputies dropped dead on the Metro. Later that day they found evidence in his office including a Swiss bank account number. They found that $50,000 had been transferred to the account on Wednesday, the day after the accident in Colombia. Denny has closed the case on the mole."

Adam took a few moments to digest the information. "Gene, doesn't that sound a little too pat for you? The guy just happens to die the day after the search for the mole is instituted…then he conveniently leaves incriminating evidence in his office? Maybe you should ask Denny if they did an autopsy on the alleged mole. Am I being too paranoid here?"

It was Senator Hawthorne's turn to reflect. At length, he replied, "I've never questioned your thought processes, and I won't now. I want to discuss this with the director in person. I'll call him now and see if we can huddle this weekend. Any other thoughts?"

"You might remind him about Belinda's DNA and if he buys into our theory at all, let's talk about setting a trap for the *real* mole. We're about ready to 'invite company' and we could kill two birds with one stone."

"Right on. I only wish I could get these guys in my gun-sight, but I know you'll do the job. I'll call you as soon as I've talked with Denny. We may need another meeting. Any problem making another trip up here?"

"None, assuming the director is ready to play ball," said Adam. "I'm anxious to get this done and Gene…thanks again."

II

June 14th, 1999,
Washington, DC,
7:45 p.m....

"You lousy son-of-a-bitch!" exclaimed Rita Garrett, pointing her long slender finger at Clyde Johansen. "Setting me up to take out some real players who have gone underground and are just waiting for little old me to show up with my cap pistol."

Johansen held up his hands in a sign of surrender as he said, "Hold on, Rita, I was given names and some background, but I know nothing about their current location or status. How do you know they've 'gone underground'?"

"Come on, Clyde, you're supposed to be in the intelligence business. All one needs to do is make a few phone calls to find out what's going on here. When everyone is on vacation or not answering, it creates a pattern. You should have hit them all at the same time, but no, you take out enough to warn the others and give them time to prepare for the next wave. These people are capable...they took down an Army unit and some big hitters. Well, if little Rita's gonna play in this league, the price is going up...way up. I have to hire me some soldiers and make sure I don't make the same mistake you did. I have to get 'em all in one shot. By the way, there's four, not three. My spies tell me that Rogers' wife is an ex-cop and she's probably with him."

Johansen put his hands up in surrender. "What's your proposal? How much do you need to do the job right?"

She sucked on her cigarette, drew the smoke deep in her lungs and slowly exhaled. "A million bucks...take it or leave it."

"Shit, Rita, I could maybe double the fee, but a million?"

"That's not all. Besides the money, I'm looking to you to find out where these birds are holed up. That's the deal, and it's not negotiable."

"How sure are you that you can get the job done?" asked Johansen.

"Dead sure, just get me the money. One quarter down for expenses with the balance after the deed is done."

"How long will it take?"

"That depends on you. From the time I get the money, I need a week to gather troops and gear. After that I will deliver the goods within a week. That is, after you give me the address."

"Okay, I'll have to make a call. If it's a go, I'll transfer a quarter to your numbered account and let you know it's been done. Anything else?"

"Just this, Clyde," said Rita with an icy cold smile. "Don't ever play me for a patsy again. I might have to do a little pro bono work…just to satisfy my ego, get it?"

Johansen fought the rage he felt rising like bile in his throat and said through clenched teeth, "I don't appreciate threats, Rita, but I hear you." He left the bar with one resolve. He would pay Rita off with the currency of *her* realm…hot lead.

He called Ball later that evening and explained Rita's demands. Ball said, "Is she the only goddamn fish in the sea?"

"No, but she's the best. She's normally a lone wolf, but when the occasion arises, she knows how to pick the right people *and* lead them into battle."

"All right, but let's not have any slip-ups."

"Don't worry, you pay good money, you get good results. One other thing, Sean, do you have any intelligence on their current whereabouts?"

"Jesus Christ. I should think a ranking official of the CIA wouldn't have to ask such a stupid question. Just get it done, Clyde." There was a loud click as Ball hung up. Johansen felt foolish. He'd been treated like a schoolboy by two people in an hour's time. He thought, 'They will pay dearly for their little victories. When the smoke clears, I will be the last man standing.'

*June 15th, 1999,
Buckhead, GA, 9:35 a.m....*

The 'Ball-busters,' as Leach had adroitly named their group, were busy at their respective tasks when the call came in from Washington. Amy handed the phone to Adam.

"Adam, this is Dennis Rains and this is an absolutely secure line. I thought it would be more efficient if we communicated directly rather than through Gene. First, I apologize for doubting you about a mole within the Agency. Gene and I had a long meeting early this morning and he's convinced me to consider your theory that we may still have a traitor in our midst. He told me you had a plan to seek out this person as a part of baiting your trap. Would you care to share that plan with me?"

"Thank you for your cooperation, Mr. Director, and yes, I'd be happy to give you my thoughts. The first part is the trap. We have prepared ourselves to invite an attack by persons unknown and need to inform such persons of our location. How this information is disclosed is the key to identifying your mole. I would suggest that you give info to likely suspects and then keep them under surveillance to see if they pass the information on. You also may identify the hit man in the process. The XK-13 Eagle may be helpful in that surveillance. The mole could be taken down any time after that, but we should discuss the pros and cons on that timing. That's it in a nutshell."

"Sounds straightforward to me," said the director. "What is your time frame? Are you ready to initiate this action?"

"In a day or so. Once we disclose our location, we need to button up and not leave the premises. We can't afford to let them pick us off one at a time."

"Contact me when you're ready. I will not ask for the location until that time, to be perfectly safe. I'll have my end of the plan in place and execute upon your call. One other thing. We have taken DNA samples from the female body in Colombia and they are on their way to our lab for comparison with Colonel Jackson's DNA. I've put 'highest priority' on it, so we should have an answer in a few days."

"Thank you…for all your help. If our plan succeeds, we will put some very dangerous people out of circulation…for good."

Adam relayed the news to the others and asked their opinion on a date to invite an invasion. "If we spread the news on Thursday, we could have company as early as Saturday or the first part of next week. My guess is, they'll take at least two or three days from the time they get the intelligence."

"Yeah, they'll have to get to Atlanta and set up a base of operations," said Leach.

"They'll know we know they're coming and they'll have to do some serious recon before walking up to the front door. That timing sounds okey-doke to me."

"Everyone agree?" asked Adam, and after getting nods of agreement from Mack and Amy, he said, "I'll call Rains tomorrow and give him some time to set up a meeting with his suspects. That means we do all of our outside work before Friday noon."

Mack rubbed his hands together in anticipation. "They can't show up too soon to suit me."

"Yeah," agreed Leach. "It's gonna be like shootin' fish in a barrel."

June 18th, 1999,
Langley, VA, 10:00 a.m....

"Good morning, gentlemen," said Director Rains with a broad smile. "I have good news tempered by bad news this morning. I have just received a DNA lab report that proves conclusively that Colonel Belinda Jackson did not perish on that Colombian mountainside. Apparently a surrogate was inserted in her place. The bad news is that she is likely back in the hands of our renegade ex-agent, Sean Ball. Under other circumstances, this Agency would take responsibility for her apparent captivity and mount a rescue. In this case however, for reasons I am not at liberty to divulge, we will take no action." A buzzer sounded and Rains pressed his intercom button. A female voice said, "Mr. Rains, I have Senator Hawthorne on the line, you asked to be interrupted for his call."

Rains said, "Thank you. Excuse me. Gene, I have great news for you. The remains at Bogotá are definitely not Belinda Jackson's." There was a pause and then the director said, "I'd be glad to send the specifics to Packard, just give me his address." Rains picked up a pencil and wrote an address in large letters on his memo pad. "I'll see that this gets out today. Sorry for the interruption, gentlemen. Now where are we with the Bosnian situation?"

V

*June 19th, 1999,
Hyatt Regency Hotel,
Arlington, VA, 9:40 a.m....*

Rita Garrett picked up her cell phone. "Yes?"

"Okay, I'm on a secure phone, what's the emergency?"

"You stupid bastard! I suppose you don't even know we were followed to our meeting last night. You're some kind of asshole spy." Rita spit out the words.

"You're full of it, Rita. I watched your back all the way out of the store and there was no sign of a tail."

"Clyde, I can't believe you're that naive. There were three of them, sweetheart." Her voice dripped with sarcasm. "It took me a couple of blocks to spot the tail and a half-hour to lose them. I have no idea whether or not they heard anything we said, but I can't afford to risk it and am going to change the plan completely. I'll call you if I need anything...otherwise, watch the newscasts." She hung up before Johansen could reply and quickly dialed another number. "Juan?"

"Yes, what are my instructions?" said a gruff Hispanic male voice.

"The plan is changed. Pack and meet me in two hours, at the Greenville Airport."

"We'll be there. Is this a charter, can we bring the...stuff?"

"Affirmative to both, now get going!" Rita dialed another number. "Is Red Robin there?"

"May I inquire who is asking?" said a very polite, high-pitched male voice.

"The Hare...like in four legs with long ears."

"How are you, darling? It's been too long, but I suppose you called for something more urgent than my silly chit-chat."

"Yes, Cedric, I have a most urgent request. I need you to look into a gated community in Buckhead and tell me how to get around the gate and get to an address. I need it today."

"My, my," exclaimed Cedric. "You know of course, this will require doubling my usual, ridiculously high fee. However, if you provide the details, I shall render a blueprint of the entire layout in five to six hours."

"You're a sweetheart, and I will pay your price with a minimum of sobbing." She then gave the name of the complex and the address of the house. "I'll call you late this afternoon to exchange goodies. Get me complete information for an attack on that house. I plan to hit them tonight."

VI

June 19th, 1999,
CIA Headquarters,
Langley, VA, 9:20 a.m....

Director Dennis Rains put the call through on his secure line. When the call was answered, he asked, "Adam Packard there? Rains calling."

"Yes, Mr. Rains," answered Amy Rogers. "One moment, sir."

Adam picked up the phone a few seconds later and said, "Good morning."

"I believe you will indeed find it a good morning. We not only uncovered the mole last night, but identified the hit person and the plan. The traitor is a man recently promoted to deputy director. A man with an outstanding record, but that's of no consequence now. The hired gun is a woman named Rita. We have nothing on her yet, but are working on her identity as we speak. I had intended to keep her under surveillance, but one of my best teams lost her. This may be an indication of her ability. Her plan was to fly in immediately with one or more confederates while others drove down in a van carrying the ordinance. Assuming this plan is still valid, they probably won't be knocking on your door for two or three days."

"Congratulations," said Adam, "this information is just what we need to set up our defense. May I ask your plan for the mole?"

"I plan to keep him in the dark and under surveillance until your operation is concluded."

"Good," answered Adam. "Is there any way to intercept any communication he may have with Ball?"

"Good question. I'm reminded of the words of an old saw, 'fool me once, shame on you, fool me twice, shame on me.' I could try to follow him with an Eagle, but I assume his cohort informed him of our tail…and he probably has a pretty good idea that we're on to him."

"Are you doing any follow-up on Rita?"

"I've had to bring in our good buddies at the FBI. They take a dim view of our operating on their precious turf. They are circulating her picture to the airlines to identify the flight she takes to Atlanta. They'll pick her up at the other end."

"When you say 'pick her up,' do you mean arrest her?" asked Adam.

"No, they've promised to follow her and keep me apprised of her activities on a real-time basis. I will relay the information to you as I receive it," said Rains. "For security purposes, I have not revealed your name or location."

"The plan sounds good…unless she shipped out before the information was received by the airlines. She could be in Atlanta now. In any event, we are going to button up and go on full alert immediately," said Adam. "Thank you again for your outstanding support. I have one other request. As soon as we deal with this problem, we must begin the search for Belinda Jackson. Can you gather some intelligence on Ball and his complex in Colombia?"

"I'm committed to help in any way I can. Now that it's certain that Mr. Ball has a hand in all this, I will put all of our Colombian assets to work on it. I'll keep you informed…and good hunting." As he hung up the phone, Rains thought, 'You don't know it, Packard, but you'll be doing me a big favor by killing Sean Ball, if he doesn't kill you first. As a betting man, I'd say the odds are about fifty-fifty.'

VII

June 19th, 1999,
Buckhead, GA, 9:40 a.m....

The mood of everyone had evolved from morose to jubilant with the news about Belinda. Although tempered by her apparent re-capture, the group held a modest celebration the night before.

After talking with Director Rains, Adam called his team together and announced, "Show time! Mr. Rains has ferreted out the mole and intercepted his conversation with our foe. The leader is a woman named Rita. We know little about her other than the fact that she shook an experienced three-person CIA surveillance team. The plan they discussed had a couple coming down from DC by air with the others driving with the artillery."

"How sure can we be that they'll follow that plan?" asked Mack.

"I don't think we can count on it," said Adam. "We need to make our final preparations right now. After we've checked out all the systems and weapons, we will do a run-through to insure that both the hardware and software are in sync."

"By software, you talkin' about us?" asked Leach.

"You got it, Al," replied Adam. "All the hours we've put in at the fitness center, on the firing range and designing this fort are about to be tested. Amy, would you check the weather for tonight and the next few days? The darker the night, the more likely they'll attack. You all know your areas of responsibility, so let's get started. We wouldn't want our guests to be disappointed with the reception we've prepared."

Mack went to the cupola on the roof and carefully oiled and wiped the circular rods upon which were mounted the surveillance (daylight) and infra-red (night) cameras. The system, including searchlights, was triggered by sensors located throughout the property. Amy, the operator, monitored the entire scene on a screen located in the concrete bunker below the house. Any movement on the property was detected by the sensors. The operator had radio contact with the three gunners whose weapons covered the entire perimeter. The operator also controlled dummy weapons on both floors that simulated the muzzle flash and report of the M-16s.

A quarter moon rose, shielded intermittently by clouds. Not a perfect night for stealthy activities, but passable. Although audible alarms were activated 24/7, full alert to computer screens and visual observation had begun at nightfall. It was 2:45 a.m. when vehicle noise was detected in the distance. No headlights appeared and the engine sounds died some distance from the house.

Adam triggered the talk button on his radio and said, "Get ready! This may be it. If the vehicle that stopped a block or so away were a neighbor, we would have seen lights. I expect company any minute! Remember, try to avoid a killing shot on the *smallest* target. I want 'Rita' alive if at all possible."

It was nearly 3:30 when the first target was detected by the sensors. Adam ordered a 'hold fire' to allow the leader to further commit her force. Two other blips appeared within moments, about 100 feet apart. The three advanced slowly. They had covered half the distance to the house with no other bandits in sight when Adam gave the order to fire. The searchlights suddenly transformed the yard into day as the staccato roar of three automatic weapons shattered the stillness of the night. Silence returned in seconds as all three intruders lay motionless on the lawn. Adam gave the order to kill the searchlights.

The continued silence cast an eerie mood while the adversaries waited and watched. After several minutes, one form moved and slowly crawled back toward the road. Adam ordered, "Let him go. We need them out of here so we can clean up the yard before any local authorities check out the noise." Apparently sensing a 'cease-fire' from the house, a van with no lights pulled up when their wounded comrade reached the far side of the road.

Leach's voice crackled sharply over the radio, "Shall I take out the van?"

"No!" Adam snapped. "They may have a second vehicle and we could be ambushed while we're getting rid of the van."

After a brief stop, the van roared away. Mack drove a four-wheeler out of the garage and Adam covered him as he approached a still figure on the lawn. After checking for a pulse and finding none, Mack loaded the dead man onto the vehicle. He repeated the process for the other and returned to the garage.

The garage door had barely closed when Leach announced on the radio, "Cops are coming! Amy, get into your nightdress and don't forget to put on a sleepy look when you answer the door."

Amy hurried to her room and donned a nightgown and robe. She left the room, scrubbing makeup from her face as the doorbell rang. After an appropriate pause, she turned on the outside light and observed two uniformed policemen through the peephole. She opened the door just far enough to poke her head out and said in a sleepy voice, "What's the trouble, officer?"

"Sorry to bother you in the middle of the night, Ma'am, but neighbors heard loud reports from around here…like gunfire. Did you hear anything?"

"Yes, at first I thought it was thunder, but then it stopped. It only lasted a little bit and was quiet again," said Amy.

"Could you tell what direction the noise came from?" asked the taller cop.

"No, but it was quite loud, and I heard a car right afterward."

"What direction was the car going?" asked the other officer.

Amy said, "I have no idea, my bedroom is in the back of the house,"

"Is there anyone else at home?"

"My husband, but he could sleep through a nuclear attack. He never moved during the noise or when you rang the doorbell."

"Well, I guess that does it. Sorry to disturb you," said the taller cop. As he turned to leave, he added, "The station may send somebody out to follow up tomorrow…er later today. Will you be home?"

"As far as I know, I'll be home all day," replied Amy. "Perhaps they could call before they come…just to be sure."

"I'll ask them to do that. Thank you." He gave a small salute as he turned and walked across to the police cruiser in the driveway.

Amy gave a sigh of relief as she closed the door. Mack and Adam joined her in the foyer. She asked, "Did you hear that conversation?"

"We sure did," replied Mack. "We were just around the corner, ready to blast those cops if they turned out to be fakes."

"You were superb, Amy," said Adam. "Now we have to get outside at first light and repair any damage to the lawn or driveway. Let's get a little sleep before that. I'll wake you in a couple hours and we'll have a critique after we clean up outside."

"Sounds good to me," said Leach who had joined them. "We gotta have a powwow to figure out their next move."

The cleanup began at dawn, and at 8 a.m., they sat at the kitchen table eating an egg omelet Adam had concocted. Amy and Al kept their eyes on the four TV screens that displayed a 360° view of the property. As Mack wiped his mouth from the last forkful of eggs and salsa, he said, "Okay, Adam, what's your take on the situation?"

"My mind keeps going back to Belinda. If I could fly down to Colombia this morning, I'd do it. But, of course, we must not only finish this job, we have to develop a well thought-out plan for her rescue. Back to the business at hand. I've been trying to put myself inside Rita's mind. If I were her, I'd try a whole new approach. Instead of trying to storm the gates, I'd either fire-bomb the place or try to worm my way in pretending to be someone else. What do you think, Al?"

"Well, if she's still in the game, she sure knows what doesn't work. I guess I'd go with destroying the house, figuring we'd stay in it. By the way, Adam, what are you planning to do with the stiffs in the garage?"

"I've called Rains. He's sending a meat wagon to pick them up. He wants to try to identify anybody involved in this operation. He's taking more responsibility than I expected because of the involvement of his subordinate."

"I hope he gets here before the cops come back," said Amy. "I wouldn't like to have to explain two dead bodies resting in my garage."

"Don't worry, honey," said Mack, "they're in body bags that'll pass for golf club carriers. Speaking of cops, we'd better check out any that show up at our door. They could be bad guys."

"You're right, Mack, I've even asked Rains to call me with the description and license number of the vehicle he sends for the bodies, just to be safe. Now, Amy what would you do in Rita's shoes?"

"I agree with your assessment, Adam. The question we need answered is, what's the most likely way for them to do it? They could hit us from the street, the back way or even with a chopper." Amy paused a moment and then added, "Since they know we're prepared and cautious, I think there's less chance they'd try to infiltrate our base."

Mack spoke up, "Although I don't want to appear a 'yes' man to my lovely wife's ideas, they make the most sense. If I had to do it, I'd go with a chopper. They could fire armor-piercing incendiaries into the roof and even with the sprinkler system, the house would be gone in minutes."

"Okay," said Adam, "let's plan a defense based on your assumptions. No matter how they attack the house, we will be safe in the bomb shelter. We can continue to monitor the property from there and use the guns if they repeat a frontal assault. If they decide to mop up after hitting the house, we must be prepared to fight them outside. We'll keep the night glasses along with a full complement of equipment at the ready. I will add a night scanner to detect any movement at the outside perimeters of the property. Mack, we need a couple of heat-seeking missiles and a radar aiming system. If you have a problem, I'll ask Rains for them. I'm also going to ask Rains if he'll put a government chopper down nearby. One that could be ready to take off at a moment's notice and trail or shoot down the bandits. It's asking a lot, but he's been so committed, it's scary. I suspect he'd like us to do some dirty work for him…like taking out Ball."

June 20th, 1999, Safe House, Atlanta, GA, 4:15 a.m....

"Cedric, we ran into a fucking machine-gun nest. Two dead, one wounded. I need a doctor fast. My guy's losing too much blood to last more than another hour."

"Now, now, sweetheart, has Cedric ever failed you? I'll have someone there in thirty minutes. I'll call you back right away to see if you're doing everything possible." Seconds later, Rita's cell phone rang. "Where was he hit?" asked Cedric.

"In the upper chest and leg. I have a tourniquet on the leg and we're applying pressure on his lower neck. Any other suggestions?"

"Just keep him warm to ward off shock," said Cedric. "My man should be there in twenty minutes. Remember, he doesn't carry an MRI machine in his little black bag. Your man's chances are far less than if he were in a hospital environment…but, of course, you cannot afford that."

"Yeah, I know. I'll tell you, Cedric, this job was just a job until now…it is now a vendetta. I'm gonna kill these bastards if it's the last thing I do!"

"There, there, my dear. With that attitude it very likely will be the last thing you do. One must plan carefully and execute flawlessly. There is little room for excess emotion in our business. I know you will adopt a cooler head when the firefight retreats from your immediate consciousness."

"You do have a way with words, but you're right. After I take care of my man, I'll get some rest and then I'll put on my coolest head and present a new plan for your comment. Thank you, I'll call you in a few hours."

The 'doctor' looked like a homeless junkie, which under the circumstances, was entirely possible. Even his black bag looked like a refugee from a dumpster. His deep, melodious voice, however belied his shaggy appearance. He looked at Rita appraisingly and asked, "I need to scrub, where's the sink?" She led him to the bathroom and then to the wounded man. He moved swiftly and deftly and in five minutes, announced, "I have done everything that can be done...his fate will be decided within the next two or three hours." With that, he packed his bag and headed for the front door.

Rita exclaimed, "Where are you going?"

"I'm out of here. I told you I've done everything I can. Unless, of course, you want me to hold your hand...or some other succulent body part?"

"Don't get smart with me," said Rita in her most venomous tone. "If I felt like playing Doctor, it wouldn't be with a filthy loser like you."

"Don't judge a book by its cover, lady. I have good reasons for my appearance and if you're concerned about the medical attention your friend received, he got the best possible under the circumstances. Next time be a little smarter about making cannon fodder out of your people."

Rita looked at him carefully and for the first time, noticed strong features under the shaggy look. She spoke in a conciliatory tone, "You're right. I apologize. Please stay and do everything possible to save my man. I'll pay handsomely for the favor."

"Money is not the issue. I need to be out of here...and his life or death is out of my hands. If he survives the morning, call our mutual friend and we'll see about follow-up treatment." As he turned and walked out the door, his parting comment was, "Better luck next time."

Rita turned to her wounded comrade whose shallow breathing seemed to come at decreasing intervals. She sat by his side, watching until her eyes closed involuntarily and her head began to nod. She had no idea how long she'd dozed when she awoke with a start to the telltale gurgling of death. She sighed deeply as she drew the blanket over the warrior's face. Unable to rest, she began to mull over her options for another attack.

He picked up the phone at 8 a.m. sharp. Rita's voice was calm and assured as she said, "I need to meet and discuss my plan."

"There's a small coffee shop at Peachtree and 17th. Back booth at 10 a.m. Need I remind you to watch your back?" Rita walked four blocks watching carefully for any sign of a tail. She took a bus past the location and walked back, stopping several times to browse in shops along the way. It was apparent why Cedric had chosen this place as it was dark and contained large booths that afforded privacy for its patrons. As she slid into the booth, she said, "Nice place. Is it secure?"

"Such a silly girl," Cedric replied. "Would I invite you to a place that wasn't? I own this place and the employees are my people. So, how can I help you?"

"First, thanks for the doc. My man died, but I've decided that was inevitable. I need to bomb the house in Buckhead. Destroy it in a way that will insure that all the occupants will be eliminated. I obviously can't get close enough to set charges, so I need to attack from a distance. What do you suggest?"

"Hmm," mused Cedric as he thoughtfully stroked his thin van Dyke beard. "The most innovative weapon will be a drone."

"A what?" asked Rita.

"A small unmanned airplane that is radio controlled and, in this case, would be loaded with explosives and flown into the side of the house. It's the same technology as small model planes, simply on a larger scale."

"Is one immediately available?"

"That depends on what you define as immediate," said Cedric. "To my knowledge, none exist in the Atlanta area, but I could have one shipped here in two or three days."

"Who would handle the flying, the radio control? And how long would it take to turn it into a missile?"

"I can find a 'pilot' and the appropriate explosives can be readied while the aircraft is being shipped. Don't you think a little delay would be to your advantage? To let your adversaries sweat a bit?"

"I agree with that. So what's the damage to put this together, including the pilot?"

"I'd normally ask one hundred, but for you, dear lady, the package could be delivered for a mere pittance…say eighty thousand."

"Come on, Cedric, I'm not looking for a 747. You can do better than that."

"Absolutely. Give me two or three weeks and I can cut the price in half. You demand speed, you pay top dollar. Tell you what...I'll guarantee the eighty as the ceiling and if I can put the package together for sixty or seventy, that is what you will pay. You know I'll be fair with you."

"Okay, get to it, I really don't have a choice," said Rita in a resigned tone. "Keep me informed on the timing. I need a little notice to ready my part of the operation."

"Progress reports shall be forthcoming promptly. You will not regret this decision."

June 23nd, 1999, Buckhead, GA, 10:25 a.m....

"Hey, Chief," exclaimed Al Leach in his droll manner, "when am I going to sleep in a proper bed again? This camping out in a damp basement is the shits."

"Al, you're welcome to sleep in your bed upstairs," said Adam. "I know it's been quiet for the last two nights, but one never knows when the firestorm may begin. I sort of like the idea of being around for a while…even if I have to sacrifice a few creature comforts, but it's up to you."

"Yeah, yeah. I get the point, but aren't you getting tired of waiting for something to happen?" complained Leach.

"Of course I'm anxious to have it over with," Adam replied. "I can't wait to get on with the next mission, Belinda. No matter what happens here, I'm going to call Rains tomorrow and see if he has any dope on Ball."

"*Dope* on Ball. That's a good one," said Leach with his cracked smile. "Back to our sweet little killer, Rita. What are ya' thinking?"

"I'm mostly suffering from an abundance of curiosity. How we will be attacked? If by air, will the new radar pick up an incoming bandit in time? Will the radar aiming system and the heat-seeking missile get off in time to bring down a flying object? Will they mount a ground attack with or without an attack on the house itself?"

"Whoa there, fella," admonished Mack. "Second guessing at this point will only drive you crazy…or crazier. We've prepared for every contingency we can think of, now we just have to wait…and do our thing when the time comes."

"You're right, of course," Adam responded with a faraway look in his eye. "Doubting the effectiveness of our plan has few rewards, but

I can't help thinking there should be other ways to stop them. I have to get inside her head…try to think as she would. What about remote-controlled four-wheelers? Mount a shield in front and either detonate on impact or with the remote. They've had two days to rig something. I just feel they're going to do something 'out of the box.' Make any sense?"

"Like I said, Adam, we need to relax and wait. We've pretty much taken the destruction of the house for granted. All we have to do is mount a counter-attack after they make their move."

Mack got up from his stool at the breakfast bar and added, "I'm off to relieve Amy on the monitors. Why don't you two get some rest? It could be a long night."

Adam lay with his hands folded under his head for a long time. The preparations he had so carefully planned seemed inadequate somehow. After mulling them over for what seemed like the hundredth time, he finally fell into a deep sleep. In his dream, he suddenly woke to the sound of gunfire all around him. He saw a woman he assumed was Rita heading toward him, a flame-spitting Uzi in her hands. He heard his name called from a distance and saw Karen Green running toward him, then another voice and Belinda Jackson was coming from yet another direction. Inexplicably, his thoughts turned to explaining his non-existent relationship with Karen to Belinda. Everything stood still for a moment. When the action resumed, Belinda fell to one knee, aimed an Army Colt .45 automatic with both hands and dropped Rita a few feet from where Adam stood. She then turned and aimed the pistol at Karen. Adam shouted, "No, no, Belinda don't shoot!"

He was shaken rudely and from a vague distance heard Al Leach say, "Adam, wake up, you're having a nightmare."

Wet with sweat, Adam came fully awake and realized he was dreaming. It was all so real. As the details flowed back into his consciousness, he pondered the importance of the dream. Was his smoldering love for Belinda waiting to be kindled into the fire it once had been? If he were able to rescue her and if she forgot the past and offered her love to him, how would he react? And, most importantly, why were these thoughts invading his mind when it should be totally occupied by the physical invasion he expected at any time? He looked up, saw Al Leach looking at him quizzically and said, "Okay, Al, I know I was dreaming. The good part was that Rita was taken out. The bad part was that it was Belinda Jackson that did it. I don't think I can count on Belinda to eliminate Rita."

"You got that right. Dreaming about Belinda, eh? Maybe that's good. Maybe she gets a little extrasensory perception and forgives you for the past. Who knows? Speaking of perception, my gut is sending a message. How about a little grub? I could wake Amy, you could cook something or I could open a can or two…what's it gonna be?"

"Let Amy sleep, I'll throw something together. Maybe you should relieve Mack. I'll bring dinner down to you when it's ready."

Darkness fell, the moon rose and waned…that was the extent of nocturnal activity for yet another day. Thursday brought increasing tension after the phone call from Dennis Rains announcing the FBI helicopter cover would be cancelled the following day. If the strike did not happen that night, any chance to follow or destroy an attacking aircraft would be lost. The day was overcast with humidity thick enough to bottle. As evening approached, the weather cleared and a light breeze whisked away the soggy air. The light from a quarter moon outlined the house without defining shadowy forms that would appear in Buckhead that night.

A small engine sound broke the stillness at 1:15 a.m. Friday morning. The radar set off an alarm, but no one was sleeping. The screen showed a blip and indicated the speed and distance of the approaching aircraft. When the distance narrowed to 350 yards, Adam gave the order to fire. The missile belched flame as it streaked toward its target. Almost immediately, a tremendous explosion rocked the house. Radar had shown the distance at 240 yards at the time of detonation. Another alarm indicated action by the sprinkler system in the house. Mack raced up the stairs and other than broken windows, could see little damage. The thump-thump-thump sound of the FBI helicopter whirling its way into the air immediately followed the explosion. Adam slipped on his headset and fingered the switch to contact the copter. He said into the mike, "BB1 to BB2, incoming bandit was destroyed short of target. Either suicide or remote-controlled. Speed 65MPH. My radar shows only your blip. Do you see anything on the ground? Over."

The radio crackled and a voice replied, "Negative, no, wait, there's a cherry-picker down there. It looks like it's being retracted. Due north from your house, about 500 yards. It's pulling out now—heading east on the street behind you. Over."

"Roger, we will pursue. I'll get back to you from my vehicle, keep them in sight. Over."

"Roger, we await your call. Out."

Adam and Mack screeched out of the driveway in the Suburban. Mack floored the big V-8 and the super-sport suspension allowed the heavy vehicle to corner like a Corvette…well, almost. Adam contacted the helicopter and within five minutes, they had the cherry-picker truck in view. Adam asked for FBI cars to pick up the chase so the copter could drop back and the truck could be followed without their knowledge. The FBI agreed and the two cars that had been standing by were on the street within three minutes. The helicopter patched the cars through to Adam and the three vehicles began alternating in the chase. The non-following cars kept well back until their turn came to tail the suspects directly. The trail led south to a run-down commercial area less than a mile from Hartsfield International Airport.

The bandit truck pulled through the garage door of a two-story building. Adam, Mack and two FBI agents surrounded the building while two agents stayed with the cars to pursue anyone driving out of the building. The FBI SWAT team arrived forty minutes after the stakeout began. Adam met with the team leader and urged him to take the woman alive if at all possible. With agents covering all four sides of the building, the heavily armed and armored SWAT team broke down the door at 2:40 a.m. Automatic weapon fire broke out immediately and continued sporadically for the next two minutes. Adam and Mack, along with the two FBI agents, entered the building behind the SWAT team. When the lights were restored, two bodies were lying on the concrete floor. The sound of gunfire continued from the second floor.

Adam had reached the steps, ready to climb when he heard several shots from the rear of the building. He turned and hurled himself out the rear door, rolling with his Glock at the ready. Dim light from the windows illuminated a figure running toward the end of the building. He jumped to his feet and raced after the fleeing form. With his sprinter's speed he gained quickly and was less than twenty feet behind when the suspect stopped and whirled. Adam saw the gun come up and instantly dove to his left. The bullet screamed by as Adam took quick aim and fired. The second shot kicked up dirt a few inches to his right, but there was no third shot. The suspect lay motionless, but Adam stayed in his prone position. After half a minute, he rose slowly, keeping the crumpled figure in his sights. As he cautiously approached, it was apparent that the form was that of a woman, undoubtedly Rita. He feared that after pleading with the SWAT team to spare her, he may have killed her himself. He heard footsteps coming up behind him as he bent over and checked her pulse. "Thank God," he said. "She's alive."

Ambulances took Rita and two others to the hospital under FBI guard. One was the 'pilot' of the drone that had been aimed at the house, the other was her next-in-command. The meat wagon followed and the lifeless bodies of three perps and one FBI agent were quietly and efficiently sent off to the morgue.

X

June 25th, 1999, Atlanta General Hospital, 9:35 a.m....

Later that morning, Adam conferred with FBI Agent-in-Charge Les Goodrich, with his battle-weary troops, Amy, Mack and Leach looking on. Adam had commended his decision to keep a lid on the events that transpired earlier that day. He then asked to be included when they interrogated the remnants of Garrett's team. Goodrich said, "I know you have other fish to fry and these people may have information to help that effort, but the Bureau has jurisdiction here and I can't allow you to participate."

"Agent Goodrich, I understand your position," said Adam, "but there are certain facts that I cannot reveal, even to you, that make it absolutely vital that we participate. I have to make a call... and please don't think I'm going over your head, but this transcends normal protocol." With that, Adam turned walked to a private portion of the waiting area and dialed a number on his cell phone.

Fifteen minutes later, Goodrich received a call on his cell phone. "Yes, sir, I understand. I'll give them complete cooperation. Thank you, sir." He turned to Adam and said in a less than pleasant tone, "You went over my head all right. That was the Deputy Director himself. You're in the game."

Goodrich, Adam and Amy went in to interrogate Rita Garrett, accompanied by an FBI court reporter. Although lightly sedated to relieve the pain from her chest wound and sprained knee, her eyes opened wide when the contingent entered. Goodrich began with, "We'd like to ask you a few questions, Miss Garrett."

"Am I under arrest?" was her simple question.

"No charges have been filed as yet," replied Goodrich. "However, it is likely that you will be charged with murder in the shooting death of FBI Agent David Samuels."

"In that case, I have nothing to say other than I want to call my attorney."

"That is your right," said Goodrich. "However, if you answer a few questions regarding your activities before the shooting, you may help yourself overall."

"Go fuck yourself!" was her straight-to-the-point reply.

Goodrich, red-faced, left the room abruptly and ordered his assistant to facilitate Garrett's *one* phone call. Adam gave him a few moments to cool down and then asked, "What about the other two?"

"One is in critical condition and a coma, the other is my next project. Come this way." Goodrich moved down the hall and stopped before another guarded door. He turned to the group and said, "This guy looks more like an engineer or driver. I doubt that he's one of the soldiers."

Adam motioned toward Leach and said to Goodrich, "I think Leach should be in on this one. He's very good at playing the bad cop."

Leach rolled his eyes as he followed Goodrich and Adam into the room. The man, George Sands, had suffered a bullet wound in the thigh. After serious interrogation that included thinly veiled threats by Leach, Sands admitted to being the 'pilot' of the drone. He convinced the questioners that he had been told that the plane was to simply buzz the house as a prank. Just before the flight, upon threat of death, he was directed to fly the plane into the house. He gave up the name and address of the person who had contacted him for the job and Goodrich immediately sent agents to arrest the go-between.

When the exhausted foursome returned to their damaged, but livable house, a unanimous decision was made to get some rest before critiquing the battle.

XI

*June 25th, 1999,
Buckhead, GA, 1:40 p.m....*

They assembled one by one and Adam opened the discussion with, "I believe the immediate danger is over. I plan to call Rains concerning his mole as soon as we finish this discussion. I think he should be taken out of the picture immediately, before he learns of Garrett's failure and puts out another contract on us. Next, we must put everything else aside and concentrate on a plan to attack Ball and rescue Belinda. The longer we delay, the more chance that Belinda will be harmed or even killed. Last, we need to arrange for repairs to the house and grounds. Give me your thoughts."

"Okay, let's start at the beginning," said Leach as if he were teaching a first-grade class. "After Rains, I want to follow up with Goodrich and see if he's taken down the guy that contacted the pilot. He may lead us to someone else…someone who may have an interest in finishing what Garrett started. After that, I *may* agree that the immediate danger is over."

"I see your point, Al, and I don't disagree," said Adam. "I'll call Rains first, then Goodrich. Any thoughts on the second issue, the plan for Ball?"

"While you're talking to Rains, you should ask him to give us everything he's got on Ball," interjected Mack. "He promised to dedicate substantial assets to this effort and I'm sure the embassy staff in Bogotá would be more than willing to gather information for us, after losing two of their people."

"Good idea, Mack," said Adam. "What about you, Amy?"

"I agree with what's been said, particularly about making haste with Ball's takedown. Perhaps you should stress the urgency of the situation when you talk to Rains."

"I'll do that," said Adam.

His call to Rains was very productive. Rains said he had received a call from Goodrich about the takedown early that morning and he had sent operatives to the mole's house within the hour. Johansen was being held incommunicado until further notice. He also explained that he had significant data on Ball and would have a packet delivered to Adam later that day. The packet would include information gathered as recently as the day before.

Adam called Goodrich and learned that they had arrested the pilot's contact and found a trail that led to a well-connected arms dealer named Cedric Williamson. They didn't have enough evidence to arrest Williamson, but were putting him under surveillance. Williamson had never been known as a contractor, but simply a supplier. Adam was encouraged by Goodrich's comment that he had contacted Williamson, told him he knew about his connection to Rita Garrett and warned him that if any further attempts were made on certain parties, the FBI would come knocking at his door.

After giving a heads-up to Mack, Amy and Leach, Adam shaved, showered and put on clean sports clothes. Leach remarked, "Don't you look like the cock of the walk?"

"Could be," said Adam with a smile lighting his handsome face. "You could use a little work, yourself. Spruce up that old frame of yours and maybe, just maybe, some misguided older woman may look your way."

"Listen, buster, if I looked any better, I'd have to fight off dames all day long. I am what is oft described as tough on the outside and tender on the inside. Sort of a Humphrey Bogart type."

"Pardon me, Bogie," said Adam, "but I've failed to notice any screaming hoard of female admirers trying to grab your bony butt."

"Leave my well-muscled posterior out of it," said the self-proclaimed womanizer.

At that point, Mack showed up with his usual he-man's appetite and Adam's energies were once again devoted to culinary pursuits.

After satisfying ravenous appetites, the foursome began disassembling the weapons systems. They put in four hours before exhaustion, born of weeks of heavy stress, took its toll. By 8 p.m. the only sound was an occasional snore from Leach's room. The special messenger arrived with the parcel from Rains at 9 p.m. A sleepy and exhausted Adam accepted the packet, but put it aside until morning.

Saturday morning dawned without a cloud in the sky. The stress-free night's sleep combined with the sunshine buoyed everyone's spirits. Adam opened the packet from Rains as they gathered at the kitchen table. Detailed plans of Ball's compound and its buildings were included, but satellite pictures revealed difficult, if not impossible terrain surrounding it on all sides. Intelligence indicated that sophisticated surveillance equipment was in place. The report noted that the system had been upgraded after Belinda's earlier escape. The report went on to detail business dealings with both locals and the drug traffic into the U.S. and Canada. This seemed superfluous until one sentence jumped out at him, "Informants in Miami reported that Ball's chief of operations, Miguel Santana, is seeking pilots to fly between Colombia and Southeastern United States…"

"That's it," exclaimed Adam. "That's our way in. I'll go down to Miami and sign on as a drug-runner. Once I get inside, I can appraise the situation and formulate a plan to take them down."

Mack put his huge hand on Adam's arm. "Hold on, Ace. Do you have any idea how dangerous it is to fly that route? Besides that, even if you got the job, who's to say you'll be invited up to the mansion for dinner? Let's say all that happens. Won't Ball blow you away the first time he lays eyes on you?"

"Now you're sounding like our pessimistic friend here," Adam said, nodding his head toward Leach. "I'm aware there's some pitfalls here. A couple of Ranger squads dropped in by chopper would be ideal, but that's not an option. From a practical standpoint, do any of you have a better suggestion?"

Leach finally broke the silence. "I agree that infiltration makes more sense than a frontal attack. The question is, how? I think we oughta consider Adam's plan, but we should brainstorm some alternatives. Anybody have an idea?"

Amy stood, twisted her well-formed torso, tossed her head back and said in a sexy voice. "Perhaps Señor Ball could be influenced by a woman's charms, no?"

"No!" said Mack loudly. "At least not with *my* woman's charms as the bait. There may be, however, other options regarding infiltration. We could put a sombrero and a serape on Leach and send him up on a donkey."

"What's this, bash Leach week?" inquired the self-styled successor to Bogart. "What about luring the bad guys out of the fort and whacking them on neutral ground?"

"Good thought, but how do we get them out?" asked Adam. "And even if we take them down outside, we still have to get to Belinda. They would obviously leave troops behind to guard the goodies. I still think going in as a pilot is the best solution. I'm not suggesting a solo operation here. You guys can fly to Colombia early and establish a base to back me up when we're ready to make our move."

"I'm concerned about you being recognized, Adam," said Amy.

"I learned a lot about changing appearance from Belinda. I will dye my hair black, grow a mustache and darken my skin. With colored contacts and a small nose alteration, none of you will know me."

"I'm not convinced," offered Leach, "but I'd go along as far as laying out the details, with the proviso that we keep other options open. Anybody have a problem with that?"

Mack agreed with a nod and said, "What's the first step, Adam?"

"I need to find out what airplane they're flying and make sure I'm checked out in it. I'll have to build an identity including passport and pilot's license. Then, and only then, can I walk into Ball's Miami office and apply for a job."

Adam put through a call to Rains and requested details on the pilot's job, including the type of aircraft to be flown. The group spent most of the day disassembling the surveillance and weapons systems.

Late that afternoon, after a shopping trip, Adam dyed his 'Stellner' hairpiece and mustache black, applied makeup putty to his nose, darkened his skin and inserted dark brown contact lenses. The effect amazed the group...building their confidence in Adam's plan.

Amy took several photos of the *new* Adam in different clothing and backgrounds. When darkness fell, Leach took the photos together with an artfully concocted bundle of fictitious information to the lair of a highly competent forger in southwestern Atlanta.

It was 10:45 the next morning when Adam received the call from Director Rains. "I suggest you travel to Miami and call this number: 697-4822. Ask for Andy and tell him RD is calling. He will brief you with everything we know about the target and the path to him. I have replaced the CIA contingent at the embassy in Bogotá with some of my best. Feel free to use them as a resource. The mission you are about to embark upon will be a serious challenge, but I have every confidence that you are the man to pull it off. Good luck and good hunting!"

Monday morning dawned with a lazy sun that, in spite of its heavy haze, brought oppressive heat and humidity to Atlanta. Amy contacted a bevy of contractors to repair the house while the three men finalized the plan. Adam made airline and hotel reservations for the next day.

June 29th, 1999,
Americana Hotel, Miami
Beach, FL, 11:35 a.m....

PART FOUR

The sun shimmered off a nearly calm sea. The oppressive heat and humidity outside were masked by the quiet whir of the air conditioning. Adam Packard, aka Bryce Bentley, gazed out the floor to ceiling windows, his mind far away. His hair was dyed coal black, as was the false mustache covering the growing mustache beneath. Sunless tanning had been augmented by makeup and his nose and eyes were altered. He was abruptly returned to reality by the ringing of the telephone. He answered, "Bentley here."

"Good morning, Mr. Bentley. May I ask if you are sometimes called something else?"

"My nickname is Red Dog and some people shorten that to initials," replied Adam.

"Good, our mutual friend asked me to assist you in any way possible. My name is Andrew Scheffer. I would be happy to meet with you, at your convenience, of course."

"Thank you, I appreciate the assistance of our mutual friend. I would like to meet as soon as possible. Do you have a location in mind?"

"Let's see," said Scheffer. "Could you browse at the men's toiletry counter at Saks about 2 p.m. this afternoon?"

"Do you mean the Bal Harbour Saks?" inquired Adam.

"Yes, right across the street. I'll be wearing a tan suit and straw hat. We'll exchange the ID passwords when we meet."

"I'll see you at two," Adam said, then hung up.

Adam arrived just before two and made conversation with the attractive sales clerk, asking her what cologne she preferred. She replied in a sultry voice, "Dolce & Gabbana is my favorite. I have a hard time resisting a man that wears it."

"Is that your only requirement?" asked Adam, flirting to keep his mind off Belinda.

"By no means, but something tells me you would have a good chance to pass the entrance exam."

"If I were interested, where would I take this exam?" Adam teased and as he said it, he saw a flash of tan out of the corner of his eye. He turned to see a tall, slender man in his early fifties in a tan suit and straw hat. The man did a double take and said, "Charlie, is that you? I haven't seen you since we worked on that project in South Carolina."

Adam grabbed his hand enthusiastically and said, "Mark, you old devil, but it was North Carolina, remember?"

"Let's go get a cup of coffee and you can give me a geography lesson…that is, if you're through with the pretty lady here?"

"Well, I was about to buy some Dolce & Gabbana." Turning to the woman, he said, "Please wrap up one of your largest bottles."

"Can you believe it, I'm fresh out. If you could come back tomorrow, I'll have some for you. Would that be possible?"

Adam smiled and said, "Of course. I'll come back just before lunch." He turned to Scheffer. "Lead on Mark, I'll flip you for the coffee." Scheffer led him out of the store and into the parking lot. He seemed to have misplaced his car, but finally stopped at a white Buick LeSabre. He looked back as he unlocked the car and asked Adam to get in the front seat. As he drove out of the lot, he stopped under a portico on the building and a woman quickly entered the back seat. She had been in the shadows and when Adam turned and saw her, she said, "How about taking that exam now, honey?"

Scheffer laughed. "Meet Abby Munsen, she's one of ours. Abby watched our back to make sure we didn't have company. We'll go to my office for our meeting. I have materials there that will be of particular interest to you." They drove into downtown Miami and pulled into the underground garage of a medium-sized office building. As they walked to the elevator, Adam noticed an unusual number of security cameras covering the entire garage area. In the elevator, Munsen inserted a card and pushed the button for the fourteenth floor, the highest number on the panel. The elevator opened into a small, smartly furnished lobby with yet another security camera gazing at them through its glass eye. Munsen stepped up to the only door and put her eye close to what looked like a small peephole as she inserted the card in a slot below. Scheffer repeated the procedure and then asked Adam to look into the small aperture. The door buzzed and Scheffer opened the door to another small room with another camera. After a moment's delay, another buzzer sounded and the three entered a spacious office.

Scheffer led the way into an interior conference room and poured coffee. "We can dispense with the aliases now, Adam. Considering your work with the Eagle, you'll be glad to know that this room is shielded by a magnetic field from floor to ceiling that disrupts the wave lengths of any Eagle-like beam. If you're wondering about this office, the Agency doesn't have elaborate field offices such as this in every big city. Miami is sort of the center of the universe for almost everything illegal. Everything from jewels and drugs to human contraband finds its way to or through the city. Our security is higher because we are up against drug lords with unlimited resources and money can buy sophisticated security-busting equipment. But, enough about us, I know you're interested in getting at our friend Ball. By the way, he and I worked together in Cambodia, so I know what you're up against. What's at the top of your agenda?"

"Getting a job flying for Ball's enterprise. I understand his lieutenant has advertised for pilots."

Abby spoke up in a business-like manner. "He didn't exactly put an ad in the help-wanted column, but our sources tell us he's quite anxious to find additional pilots."

"How does a willing candidate apply for a job?" Adam looked at Munsen and said with a smile, "I hope it's not as difficult as taking that exam."

"No, in this case we leak a name through our source and he sets up an interview," said Munsen, ignoring Adam's last comment. "Miguel Santana is his name and as of yesterday, he was in town. We'll call our source and we could set up a meet as soon as possible. Are all of your papers in order?"

"The sooner the better and, yes, I have a passport, driver's license, pilot's license and flying logs, all in the name of Bryce Bentley. I would like to know the make and model airplane they're flying and if you have any additional information on Ball, beyond the dope I received from Dennis."

Scheffer nodded and handed Adam a sheaf of papers including maps, pictures and information on the business dealings of Sean Ball. He said, "I'll have our source ask about the plane."

Adam reviewed the information at some length. "Can I take these with me?"

"Yes," replied Scheffer. "Do you have any questions on this information or anything else?"

"No, it seems fairly straight forward," said Adam. "I just need to get back to my hotel." Looking back to Munsen, "By the way, shall I show up at the perfume counter tomorrow?"

Munsen smiled and adopted her teasing voice, "Not unless you really want to buy some Dolce & Gabbana."

Scheffer looked at Munsen and laughed. "Hey Abby, admit it. You really enjoyed playing that little game." To Adam he said, "We're going to send you back with a different driver and car. We will call you later tonight or tomorrow morning on the meet with Santana. If I don't see you again in person, it's been a pleasure and good luck."

After being introduced to a young black man named George Franks, Adam shook hands with both agents. "Please come this way," said Franks, motioning him to follow. "We'll take you back to the Americana." They went back through the labyrinth of lobbies and security and left the garage in a Lincoln Town Car. Adam noted without comment that they headed in the opposite direction from Miami Beach. After a dozen blocks, Black pulled the big Lincoln into the covered entrance of the Marriott Hotel. As Adam turned to him with a quizzical look, Franks said, "You are switching to a cab here. Yellow cab number 197 should be in the lineup. The driver is one of ours. Have a good day, Mr. Bentley."

Adam got out and spotted the cab in question, second in line. He walked to the bell stand area and was asked if he wanted a taxi. He replied, "I'm trying to decide whether to ride or walk." Just then, a couple came out of the hotel and claimed the number one cab. Adam walked quickly to the bellman and said, "I guess I will take that taxi you offered." He put a five-dollar bill in the man's hand as he was ushered into the back seat of Yellow Cab #197. A pretty Latina face attached to a large body turned and asked, "Where can I take you, señor?"

"The Americana Hotel, Miami Beach, please."

"Si, I know it well. Please sit back and relax. The traffic at this time of day is not *bueno*, but I shall deliver you safely to your destination."

Adam looked at the identification on the visor which indicated his driver's name was Juanita Juarez. He smiled and said, "Thank you, Juanita." Anticipating a long, slow ride, Adam removed some of the material from the folder Scheffer had provided and studied it carefully. He memorized key locations in both Bogotá and Ball's city of Paz del Rio. Although the trip took nearly an hour, Adam was so engrossed with his reading that it seemed like no time before the cab stopped under the portico of the Americana. He asked for the fare and received a wonderful smile as she said loudly, "Twenty-five dollars, señor." He handed her two twenties and waved off the change. She said, "*Gracias*, please take my card. Call anytime you need a cab. *Adios*."

Adam retired to his room and continued his study for another hour. At 5:30, he rose, stretched and opened the honor bar. He withdrew two mini-bottles of Chivas Regal and poured them over ice. He sat contemplating the sea while he sipped the scotch. His thoughts turned from the task in Colombia to Belinda and the mixed emotions he felt about confronting her. The ache resulting from Belinda's stab to his heart had never totally healed. He looked at the glass in his hand and found it empty. He refilled with Johnny Walker Red and called room service. After ordering a halibut dinner, he stretched out on the bed and closed his eyes. The knock on the door awakened him and though disoriented and a bit woozy from four shots of scotch, he answered the door and tipped the employee who delivered his meal. The fish dinner was unusually good and it cleared his head.

The telephone rang. Adam picked it up anxiously. "Mr. Bentley, can you give me another name?" asked the sweet voice of Abby Munsen.

"Some folks call me Red Dog or by the initials R.D.," replied Adam.

"Thank you. We have a meeting arranged for tomorrow night at nine o'clock. You are to board that certain vehicle you returned in this evening at the door from which I joined you this afternoon…at 8:15 sharp. You will be briefed at that time."

"Were you able to get any dope on the airplane?" asked Adam.

"Yes," she replied, "it's a Mooney, model M20J." Do you know it?"

"It's a fast, single-engine plane with good efficiency, meaning it has a good combination of speed and range. For a prop plane, it's a slick machine. You can do me another favor in the morning. Call around to uncontrolled airports and find one of these I can rent. I'll feel better at the meeting with a couple hours in a Mooney under my belt."

"I can do that. Anything else?"

"No, but I really appreciate your help." An early bedtime led to his rising at 5:30 a.m. and taking a five-mile run on the beach. He followed this with a half-hour of weights and was shaved, showered and eating breakfast in his suite by 7:30. He pored over the documents Scheffer had provided until the phone rang at 8:45. Munsen gave him the name and directions to a private airfield in Pembroke Pines that had the airplane he sought. They would rent it for $150 an hour with a minimum of two hours and she had made a tentative reservation for him at 10:30 that morning. Adam thanked her and said he would rent a car and drive to the airport. She offered to drive him and accompany him on the ride. He demurred, saying that he would be putting the plane through its paces and it would be a rough ride with the possibility of tearing off a wing or two. Her response was a mixture of disappointment and relief.

He arrived at the North Perry Airport at just after ten. The small airport in Pembroke Pines was composed of a number of mismatched hangars and a single runway. He spotted a hand painted sign whose oddly shaped letters spelled FLIGHT BUSINESS OFFICE and quickly found the man who rented airplanes. 'Junior' Harrington was a tall, rangy man with a shock of gray hair and a twinkle in his eye. He examined both Adam and his papers before asking, "Did you ever fly in the service, son?"

"No, I spent several years in the Army, but did most of my flying after I got out. Were you a military aviator?"

"Sure was. I flew F86s and later, F16s in that little engagement over in southeast Asia. I been flyin' these little butterflies so long, I'd like to put one of those F-16 cannons under my ass one more time before they punch my ticket."

Adam laughed. "I know the Mooney is no jet, but I wouldn't call it a butterfly either."

"Yeah, you're right. It's a pretty hot little plane. This one has all the latest Lopresti speed mods installed. I s'pose you'd like to can the crap and mosey out to that little beauty out there?" He pushed a form across the desk.

"I am itching to get my hands on that yoke," Adam replied as he filled out and signed the rental agreement and plunked down three one-hundred dollar bills.

"Okay, now where do you plan to fly the Mooney?"

"I plan to head out over the Everglades to Naples and down the West Coast following the old Tamiami Trail back here. I may tarry a bit over the Everglades, see if I can spot any gators."

"Sounds good. I don't like people flying over the water until I get to know 'em pretty well. Flying a plane like this too far over the water can raise suspicions…if you get my drift. I'll go through the pre-flight with you and then we'll take it up. The owner of this airplane insists that I go along on a shake-down flight before sending his baby into the wild blue yonder with a stranger. That okay with you?"

"Fine," said Adam. "Let's go." Adam hadn't flown for a few months and was just realizing how much he missed it. He had his private pilot's license before the Army, but it was after his discharge that he logged most of his hours in the air. They went through the pre-flight, warmed up the smooth 200HP Lyc engine and Adam taxied out to the end of the strip. He lowered the flaps and pushed the throttle home. The Mooney leapt forward and was at takeoff speed in seconds. Adam lifted her off the tarmac and raised the flaps and gear. He eased back on the throttle as he did a slow climbing turn. He turned to Harrington and said, "If you have a little time, why don't you fly with me for a half hour? We'll head out over the Everglades and do a few aerobatics…are you game?"

"I am, but the owner isn't," said Harrington. "This airplane is not approved for aerobatics, but if you're planning to just punch a few *mild* holes in the sky, I'll be happy to ride along. Let her rip." They were soon over the vast river of grass known as the Everglades. Adam climbed to ten thousand feet and put the Mooney into a steep dive. The airspeed reached 250 and he pulled back hard on the yoke and pulled out into a climbing turn. When he again reached ten thousand, he performed a series of tight turns and a barrel roll. When Adam returned the plane to level flight, he turned to Harrington and said, "This airplane handles like a dream."

Harrington replied, "Indeed it does. That little performance would make a pretty good commercial…Mooney might want to show something like that to prospective buyers. By the way, you have convinced me of your flying ability. How about taking me back to the ranch?" There was little wind so Adam was able to make a landing known as a "squeaker." He approached at only 65 knots and used only half the runway to bring the plane to a stop.

When Harrington opened the door, he turned to Adam. "You are one of those rare birds that have that special touch. I've flown with hundreds of pilots, but only a handful have the rare gift I see in you. You should spend more time in the sky, Mr. Bentley, it is very friendly to you."

Adam thanked Harrington for his kind words and took off again. He headed west again and flew over to Naples and the many boats plying the inland waterway. He then headed south over Marco Island and then turned east, back over the Everglades. He performed a few aerobatics…a substantially more severe test of the airplane than those he'd done with Harrington. Satisfied that he knew exactly what the airplane could do, he headed back to the field in Pembroke Pines. When he turned the airplane back to Harrington, he asked, "That was great. If you don't have other plans, I'd like to buy you lunch."

Harrington replied, "You know, I'd like that. I'll have my man put the Mooney away and I'll be with you in a minute." At Harrington's suggestion, they ate at a small bar a few blocks from the airport. The place was dark and a bit smoky, but had old barroom charm. They ordered a beer and what Harrington described as 'the best hamburger in Florida.' Adam asked, "How long were you in the Air Force?"

"Twenty-six years. I would have stayed longer, but it became clear that I was at the top of my game. I would retire as a bird colonel, but the only star I'd ever see would be in the sky. What about you? How long were you in the Army?"

"Only four years of active duty. I went in before the Gulf War as a shave-tail, from ROTC. They bumped me to major when I left active service, and later gave me a pair of silver oak leaves in the reserves. I spent most of my time in the Signal Corps, working in electronics."

"Where the hell did you learn to fly like that?" asked Harrington, with a degree of awe in his voice.

"I guess I had a bit of a personal problem when I left the Army and for some reason, bouncing around in the sky seemed to ease the pain. I started normal flying, then graduated to aerobatics and finally got into pylon racing. I'd love to show you my stubby little Ryan racer."

"That explains it. Other than flying with the Thunderbirds or Blue Angels, pylon racing is probably the most demanding of any flying skill. Where do you keep your Ryan?"

Adam realized he was giving more information than was prudent, so he lied. "I keep it in Dayton, Ohio, which as you know is the home of pylon racing. I don't have any business cards with me, but I'll send you one and if you're ever up that way…"

After lunch, Adam dropped Harrington off at the airport on his way back to the hotel. When he walked into his suite, he went over to the window. Looking out over the ocean, he was reminded of the oceans between Belinda and himself. There was the actual body of water that separated them. And there was the ocean or psychological barrier, that had kept them apart these many years. A barrier built on lies he could not refute, but one that was all too real to her. He sighed and resumed his studies. He put down the last page three hours later, confident that he had committed all of the pertinent material to memory. Adam stretched, walked into the bath and touched up his makeup. He dressed in a short-sleeved shirt, tropical slacks and loafers. Upon the concierge's advice, he dined on swordfish with a crab garnish at a beachfront tiki bar next to the hotel.

As he walked the beach following dinner, he watched the sun setting over the buildings. It sparkled on the gleaming white boats tugging at their anchor chains in the breeze. His thoughts ranged from anticipating the evening ahead to JoAnn Cleveland and the Right Brigade. He experienced the return of an uncomfortable feeling that could be described as something between desire to do battle and naked fear. He realized that no matter how well prepared they might be, a certain element of luck could be the difference between success and failure. And failure was almost certain to be fatal...to him, to those who relied on him, *and to Belinda.*

II

**June 30th, 1999,
Mansion del Colombia,
Miami, Florida, 9:00 p.m....**

Adam's illuminated watch showed 7:45 as he strolled across the highway to Saks Fifth Avenue. He browsed through the men's department until 8:10, when he walked casually out the west door and stepped into Yellow Cab #197.

"*Buenos noches*, Señor Bentley," said Juanita as she pulled out of the shopping center on to A1A. "I trust you've had a good day?"

"Excellent, thank you. Do you know where we're going by any chance?"

"*Si*, and I have a small gift for you," she said as she passed a .25 caliber automatic pistol and an ankle holster back to him. "It seems puny compared to my .40 caliber Colt, but for a fine marksman such as yourself, it is quite adequate."

"Thank you for your confidence in my shooting skills. Will anyone from the agency be attending my interview?"

"You are welcome. The pen I am providing for your shirt pocket will bring me quickly to the scene. Also, our source, Pedro, will be either present or nearby." Juanita drove another twenty minutes in silence before stopping at a closed gate between two impressive stone pillars. She said in a soft voice, "Roll down your window and do everything they ask."

Adam rolled down the window just in time to hear a metallic voice from the pillar, "Please state your name and business."

"My name is Bryce Bentley and I have an appointment with Mr. Santana."

"One moment please" was the reply. Seconds later, the voice said, "You may proceed. Stop under the canopy at the front door."

Adam closed the window as Juanita began to move through the opening gates. He said, "You may be nearby, but if you leave the gates, will you be able to get back in?"

"Ask them if the cab can wait for you. They are unlikely to suspect a fat, Spanish woman of being any danger to them." She continued with a sly smile, "Of course, they will be mistaken to assume that."

She pulled under a large brightly lit canopy and two large Latino men in well-fitting suits stepped to either side of the cab. The one on the passenger side said in perfect English, "Good evening, Mr. Bentley. Mr. Santana will see you shortly."

"Thank you," said Adam. "Can the cab wait for me?"

The man bent down, looked at Juanita and said, "Yes, she can wait," as he pointed her across the driveway to several marked parking spaces. He turned to Adam and said, "Please follow me, Mr. Bentley." He led Adam through an elegant hand-carved door of gargantuan dimensions.

They passed through a large foyer and his guide knocked on a door halfway down the hall. "Enter." They entered a large room furnished as an office. A Latino man sitting behind the desk rose as Adam approached. Adam thought he must be standing in a hole. He was small in stature, but had impressive good looks and a rich baritone voice which said, "Ah, Mr. Bentley, is it?"

"Yes, and you are Mr. Santana?"

"Indeed I am and it's a pleasure to meet you, sir," he said with a crisp British accent as he extended a small hand which was engulfed by Adam's. He wore a pencil thin mustache and a chalk stripe navy suit. His gold Rolex watch was obviously a woman's model and his gold cuff-links were appropriately downsized. He said, "Please sit down. May I see your credentials?" Adam passed a small folder that contained all of his Bryce Bentley information. Santana examined the documents carefully and then looked up to the guide. He came over to the desk and accepted the documents. Santana said to him, "Please make copies." He returned his attention to Adam. "Everything seems in order. Tell me, Mr. Bentley, have you ever broken the law?"

Adam was surprised at how comfortable he felt with this very sophisticated little man. He would have to be careful not to let his guard down. "Are you referring to taking an action that was against the law, or being caught and punished for a crime of some sort?" asked Adam.

"I am not referring to cutting the label off a pillow. Have you ever committed what could be described as a felony?"

"Yes, I have transported items whose entry into the destination were prohibited."

"Were you detained, arrested or convicted of a crime in connection with such transport?"

"No to all three. I have never been arrested, other than for speeding in an automobile," Adam replied.

Santana nodded his head approvingly and asked, "May I ask the nature of the item or items you transported illegally?"

"Money and gems," Adam replied. "Large amounts of currency and uncut precious stones…on several occasions."

"Was this enterprise lucrative to you?"

"Yes, very, but I chose to walk away when others in the enterprise became careless and became a threat to me and my future. I am only interested in working with competent professionals. In fact, Mr. Santana, I am investigating *you*, much as you are investigating me. I have a clean record for one reason…I choose my associates very carefully."

Santana's eyes lit up. "Very interesting. I must say your attitude is refreshing. Can you give me any references, on your illicit activities?"

"I'm afraid not. If I work with you and decide to leave for any reason, no one will ever hear about you…from my lips. I would be happy to elaborate on some of my adventures, but no names or faces."

"Hmm, an interesting viewpoint. I will have to ponder that attitude. For the moment, I am favorably impressed. Are you available to make a test flight, as soon as tomorrow?"

"Certainly, just name the time and place," said Adam.

Santana stood and extended his hand and nodding toward the guide said, "Please give Ricardo your address and phone number. You will be contacted in the morning. It has been a pleasure meeting you, Mr. Bentley. Assuming everything checks out, I suspect we may do significant business together."

"Thank you. The pleasure has been mine." Adam said as he carefully shook the small hand, smiled warmly and added, "Good night." He turned and followed Ricardo, who held the door for him and guided him to a hall table. Ricardo returned the Bentley documents and asked for his address and phone number. Adam gave him the information and was escorted through the front door to his taxi, now waiting under the canopy.

Ricardo held the door and as Adam entered the cab, he said with a pleasant smile, "Good night, Mr. Bentley. I hope we see you again soon."

Adam smiled back and said, "Good evening. That is my hope as well."

When the door closed, Juanita headed for the front gate. "Did it go well? I assume you didn't have to use the little persuader?"

"No, it went extremely well. Everyone acted like real gentlemen. I must have passed the first test as I have been invited to take an aviation exam tomorrow."

"*Muy bueno*. What are the details?"

"They'll call me in the morning, that's all I know."

"You were, what you say, a big hit? Or they plan to dump you in the big drink *mañana*. You have to wait and see."

"You're right," said Adam with a note of sarcasm. "And thanks for the encouraging remark."

"*No problema*, I think you may be a match for them. Now I drive directly to your hotel. Should anyone follow us, I shall allow it. When you get to the hotel, I suggest you go directly to your room."

"Why would you suggest that. Can I expect visitors in the night?"

"Who knows?" said Juanita with a sly smile. "It just seemed like a good idea. Security, you know."

Adam made no reply, paid Juanita, and took the elevator to his floor. When he let himself into the suite, he found Abby Munsen sitting comfortably on his sofa, watching the rerun of a classic college football game. She looked up and asked, "How did it go, did you pass muster?"

"If an invitation to a test flight tomorrow is any indication, I passed."

"Tell me all about it, every detail." Adam recited his interview chapter and verse, including his surprise at the civility and manners displayed by all the players.

Munsen listened without comment. When Adam finished, he asked her, "What about your man, was he there?"

"Yes, Pedro was the other guard, with Ricardo, and you must understand, the money these people possess is beyond belief. They may be thugs at heart, but they can afford to hire very cultured people to work for them. Do not mistake their good manners for good intentions. They are ruthless and will cut your throat with pleasure. What are the plans for your test flight?"

"They asked for my address and phone number and simply said they'd call in the morning. That's it."

"I took the liberty of bugging your phone," said Munsen. "We'll be nearby in the morning."

"You realize if they spot a tail, it could jeopardize this whole operation," said Adam in a concerned voice.

"Don't worry, we'll find a foolproof way to cover your ass. We are totally committed to this project and will lay off if we can't be sure to be undetectable."

III

July 1st, 1999,
Americana Hotel, Miami Beach, FL, 8:15 a.m....

Adam picked up the phone. "Good morning, Mr. Bentley, Miguel Santana speaking. I trust you had a pleasant night."

"I did indeed, Mr. Santana, Thank you."

"I appreciate your willingness to indulge me by making a short flight this morning, but I will be unavailable beginning tomorrow. Would it be convenient for my car to pick you up at ten o'clock?"

"That would be fine. I will be in the lobby at that time."

"Excellent. Be sure to bring your helmet and goggles," Santana said with good humor before hanging up.

At precisely 10 a.m., a shiny Silver BMW 750IL arrived for Adam. The chauffeur held the door for Adam, then took his position in the driver's seat, started the big V-12 engine and pulled out onto A1A heading north. Adam asked, "Are we going directly to the airport?"

"Yessir, we will be there in about twenty minutes." They arrived at Fort Lauderdale Executive Airport at 10:17 and pulled up to a sparkling new hangar.

Adam was directed into the hangar where he found Miguel Santana in elegant casual attire. Santana had one foot up on a chair and was smoking a cigarette as he waved a greeting to Adam. "The day is perfect for aeronautical exploration, wouldn't you agree?"

"Absolutely, blue skies provide an open door that invites all aviation lovers to climb into them and leave the cares of the earth far below."

Santana smiled. "Poetic. Perhaps we should depart from our descriptive language and get to the matter at hand. Please step this way." He led Adam to a new-looking Mooney as he requested that the hangar door be opened. "Have you flown a Mooney, Mr. Bentley?"

"Yes, I have," replied Adam. "And please call me Bryce."

"Very good…Bryce. Let's climb aboard and have at it." They did the pre-flight check with Santana in the right-hand seat. Adam started the engine and taxied out of the hangar and, with permission from the tower, to the end of the east-west runway. When he received clearance and opened the throttle, the sound and power of the engine were obviously not standard Mooney. As they climbed out, Adam said, "Hey, this is not your average, run-of-the-mill Mooney."

"No, this may be a bit hotter than the Mooneys you've flown. It is called a Riley Rocket, with a 250HP 6-cylinder in-line engine. It is capable of over 300MPH and, with other modifications, has a 1,600-mile range with two passengers. We also carry some unique instrumentation to assist low altitude flight."

Adam followed the flight plan and did a gradual climb as he headed over Coral Springs and out over the Everglades. After attaining 15,000, he performed a few mild aerobatics to get a better feel of the airplane. He remarked, "The extra weight has surprisingly little effect upon the maneuverability of this airplane. I'm impressed."

"We have tried various airplanes including a Marchetti Meteor, but we always come back to the Mooney. Why don't we do a little hedge-hopping, take her down to about 50 feet and check out our 'stay-out-of-the-drink' technology." Adam dove down and pulled out at 100 feet then eased it back down to 50. The altimeter-controlled surface sensor started a slow beep at 90 feet and increased as the earth moved closer. At fifty feet, it was moderate, and as he slowly edged lower, the beeps increased until it became a steady sound at 25 feet. Dropping below 25 feet, the sound changed and increased in volume and pulse rate as the plane inched ever lower. When Adam laid it on the deck, leveling off at about 15 feet and dodging a few scraggly trees, Santana said, "I believe that's low enough, you've convinced me of two things…your skill and your nerve."

"I was prepared to shear off a few rushes with the prop, but perhaps another day," said Adam as he climbed to three thousand feet and turned northeast toward Fort Lauderdale. Adam landed with the same skill that had so impressed Junior Harrington and as they disembarked, Santana said, "You passed the flight test with flying colors, Bryce. Providing my spies find nothing untoward in your background,

I look forward to a most interesting and mutually profitable relationship. I will be leaving Miami tomorrow for a few days and will contact you immediately upon my return." He turned smartly on his heel and walked away before Adam could reply. During the return trip to the Amaricana, Adam thought about his plan and decided it was time to bring in reinforcements.

It was 3:15 in the afternoon of July 3rd, when Yellow Cab #197 deposited a stooped old man at a medical office building in downtown Miami. Leaning heavily on his cane, the man shuffled into the building and took the elevator to the seventh floor. A handsome woman greeted him as he stepped off the elevator. They reentered the elevator and the woman inserted a card as she pressed the button for the fourteenth floor. Moments later they entered a conference room and Adam shed the wig and hat as he shook hands with Mack Rogers and Al Leach.

Adam said, "Fancy meeting you here. I understand you two are headed for a little vacation down South America way. I thought I'd stop by to wish you *bon voyage*!"

July 3rd, 1999,
Ranchero Grande, Paz de
Rio, Colombia, 7:05 p.m....

Miguel Santana walked into the large room with his usual formal bearing. He nodded at Jeb Carter as he stepped over to the bar and made himself a drink.

Sean Ball sat at a beautiful hand-carved desk, engrossed by the papers before him. Several minutes later, without looking up, he said, "Well, what do you have to report, Miguel?"

"My intelligence informed me that our client in Philadelphia has been approached by one of our competitors. The contact is new to the trade and has been taught just how we conduct our business."

"Whatcha mean is," interjected Carter, "you snuffed him."

"My, my," said Santana in his cultured voice, the one he knew really aggravated Carter. "I prefer to make a report that does not assess culpability to anyone in or out of this organization."

"Very good, Miguel, continue with the report, as you wish to present it," said Ball with an irritated glance at Carter.

"Thank you. I talked with our client in Chicago and a telephone call from you may be in order. He is questioning the new pricing and could use a more forceful explanation of the need for the increase. I also have two new candidates for our air transport operation. One is marginal, but the other seems to be particularly resourceful. They are currently being investigated and I will either hire or send them home when I return to the U.S. That completes my report."

Carter, irked by this confident little man, couldn't resist. "By sending 'em home...you mean, to their maker, right?"

"Let me put it this way," replied Santana, addressing Carter like a schoolteacher. "I cannot examine the background and talents of such candidates without disclosing more than I like about our business. So, we either allow them to join the team or *discourage* them from joining…let us say, the wrong team. Is that clear enough for you?"

Carter's reply was cut off by a look from Ball. "Very good, Miguel. Let's head for the dining room. I expect our *sometimes* guest may join us for dinner this evening," Ball said as he rose and walked out of the room. They sat at three sides of a long table set for four with sparkling silver and fine china.

Ball turned to the formally dressed waiter and said in Spanish, "Please ask the Señorita if she cares to join us for dinner." Twenty minutes later, Belinda, dressed in a fairly low-cut gown, which displayed her deep, seductive cleavage, walked into the room. Ball rose and held her chair. She was somewhat pale and the makeup didn't quite cover the bruise on her cheekbone.

Santana had also risen and bowed as he said, "Good evening, *Señorita*. It is such a pleasure to have you dine with us. May I say you look particularly lovely tonight?"

Belinda raised her eyes and said with a thin smile. "Thank you, Miguel, you look very dapper yourself." She glanced at Carter and saw the disgust he felt for the exchange…and for she and Santana. Ball retained a neutral expression that gave away nothing.

After she had been recaptured by Ball, Belinda realized that she must adopt a new attitude to survive. She told him that she would grant sexual favors providing he would stop forcing her to take drugs. He was delighted with the proposal at first, but as she had hoped, he soon wearied of her passionless acquiescence to his demands. Her lack of response had put him into a rage several times and she would fail to appear at dinner for a time, when the results of that rage were too apparent. She disliked the sexy wardrobe provided by Ball, but accepted it as part of her sentence. Other than his frequent temper tantrums, Ball treated her with increased respect and granted her requests for reading material and amenities. She used the well-appointed gym every day and was rapidly regaining her tone and strength. In return, she emerged from her shell and tried to make conversation during social activities. She retained a degree of hope for rescue, but as the days slipped by, her expectations diminished. Miguel Santana was a bright spot in her life.

Although she suspected he was also a hardened killer, his charming manner and obvious affection for her buoyed her disheartened spirit. She had considered proposing an escape with his help, but discarded the idea as he consistently showed his steadfast devotion to Ball.

With an expansiveness seldom exhibited at dinner, Ball picked up Santana's cue, saying, "You're right, Miguel, Belinda is absolutely radiant this evening. To what may we attribute your glow, my dear?"

"I have no idea," replied Belinda, pleased. "I am duly flattered by all this attention. The next thing I know, Carter will pay me a compliment."

Carter expressed himself with, "Hmmh."

Ball looked at him and said, "Perhaps I have misjudged you, Jeb. I thought you could appreciate dining in the company of a beautiful woman, but if this is distasteful to you, other dinner arrangements can be made, like the kitchen." Ball said this lightly, but those at the table recognized the implied threat.

Carter, though clearly furious, bit his lip, bowed, and said, "My apologies, Ms. Jackson. You look very fine tonight."

The conversation was unusually pleasant following Carter's reprimand and Ball personally poured excellent wine during dinner followed by an ancient, marvelous port. He rose to pull out Belinda's chair and asked if she would like a stroll in the garden. Whether it was the wine or the desire to be outside, she was not sure, but she accepted his offer. As they walked through the lavish, scented gardens, the moon shone brightly and Belinda felt a sense of peace and contentment come over her. When Ball took her arm, she didn't resist. Later, when she opened the door to her bedroom to him, he had a sheepish, tentative manner. She allowed him to take her in his arms and kiss her tenderly. Her breasts pressed against his chest with only the sheer gown and his silk shirt between their bodies. He led her to the bed, lay beside her and stroked her body gently. He removed her gown and as he circled her nipples with his tongue, she felt them harden for the first time since Adam had touched them. Ball kissed her body from her breasts to her stomach. She opened her legs, pulled him up and guided his rock-hard shaft into her warm wetness. Her response to his slow, rhythmic thrusts grew slowly and tears streamed down her face as she began to thrust her hips into him. The intensity of their motion increased until a crescendo of passion was released. They lay panting and Ball said softly, "You have no idea how I have longed for that response from you." He brushed a tear from her face and asked, "I may not like the answer, but why are you crying?"

Belinda felt a final tear on her cheek as she said bitterly, "Because I've surrendered… to my enemy…lost my self-respect."

Ball sighed. "I want it to happen again. My desire for you could change to something more. I could be a different man, if you'd let me."

"I don't want to talk about this, please leave." He said nothing as collected his clothes and left the room.

Belinda lay awake with distressing thoughts whirling through her mind. She thought, 'How could I give in to Sean Ball…with such wild abandon? What happened to that strong woman he dragged here months ago? What about tomorrow? Will I resolve not to let it happen again? The minute he puts his hand between my legs, will I let myself go again…like a bitch in heat?' The tears returned as she thought of Adam. Good, wonderful Adam. Even if she could forget and forgive his fling with Sela, had she damaged herself irreparably tonight? She suddenly realized that the self-confidence she had from early childhood, that had never deserted her…even after losing Adam and after Ball's savagery, was shaken, maybe lost…Belinda sobbed for what seemed like hours before falling into an exhausted, troubled sleep.

WHEN RIGHT IS WRONG

**July 5th, 1999,
Americana Hotel, Miami
Beach, FL, 11:15 a.m....**

Adam smiled as he hung up the phone. *He was in...* a member of Sean Ball's drug empire. Miguel Santana proposed a luncheon to finalize terms and conditions of his employment. As he dressed for the meeting with Santana, he thought about the upcoming face-to-face with Ball. Would his disguise be adequate? Or would he be recognized? He could alter his posture and walk, but what about his voice? He picked up his cell phone and plugged it into the scrambler the Company had provided. He hit two-four-six and the phone rang after the usual delay. Abby Munsen answered, "Good morning, Bryce, how are you?"

"Wonderful, Abby, I just received a call from our friend and we are a go."

"Outstanding," said Munsen with a lilt to her voice. "What's next?"

"I am lunching with the principal today to discuss my role and the compensation. He will give further instructions at the meeting. He didn't seem to consider the possibility that we would *not* come to terms."

"That's not surprising. If you turned him down at this point, we'd be looking for you underwater... wearing a pair of concrete shoes."

"Nothing like an uplifting motivational speech to start my day," said Adam with appropriate sarcasm. "What do you hear from my pals?"

"Sorry about the wise-ass remark. They're living the life of Riley in Bogotá. Last I heard they were recruiting some soldiers to bolster your little Army down there. I guess you're aware the director sent a couple of our hot-shots down to give them a hand. You should be in good shape."

"I can contact them through the Embassy, right?"

"Right, ask for Middleton Oakes, nickname Middy. He'll know how to patch you through to your boys. Anything else I can do for you?"

"Perhaps. I'm a bit concerned about my disguise...if it's adequate to fool people who really know me. Do you have anything that will change the timbre of my voice?"

"I'd hate to change that lovely voice of yours, but there's an herb made of tree bark from Chile that will deepen the voice. I'll get you some. Where are you having lunch?"

"I have no idea. After my initial interview, they have always picked me up at the hotel. My ride will be here at noon."

"Well, they're not likely to expect you'll abandon your belongings, so you will at least return to the hotel after lunch. I will have the herbs delivered to your suite while you're gone. They'll be at the bottom of a bottle of Advil in your bathroom."

"Thank you, Abby. If I'm unable to talk to you again before I become completely entangled in their web, I want you to know how much I appreciate your help."

"It's been a pleasure." Her voice became low and personal as she said, "Take care of yourself."

The big silver BMW was waiting at noon and Adam wondered if the CIA had added a tracking device to it. He was delivered to an old, but elegant restaurant in Key Biscayne. Santana's man Ricardo was waiting inside the door and escorted Adam to a booth near the back door. Although the restaurant was busy, Adam noted that the tables and adjoining booths were empty. Santana rose and greeted him warmly. Adam refused his offer of wine, saying he never mixed pleasure with business. Santana's smile told him he was pleased with that response. They ordered lunch and Santana immediately began the business discussion with, "You are something of a mystery man. I was unable to trace your background very far. Can you explain that?"

"Although I have no record with the law, I chose to adopt a new identity when I began my...shall we say undercover work. It is my plan to reclaim my real name when I retire from such business pursuits."

"May I ask if you plan such retirement in the near future?" asked Santana with genuine interest.

"That depends largely upon the results of this discussion and our subsequent relationship," replied Adam.

"That would lead me to believe that your expectations of compensation from us are substantial. Am I correct?"

"You are correct. I believe I can bring substantial benefit to your organization and would expect to be rewarded accordingly."

Santana smiled and said, "I do like your style, Bryce. May I ask your real name?"

"No, it is absolutely crucial to my long-range plan that no tie can be made between Bryce Bentley and my true identity. If that is a deal-breaker, so be it."

"It is not that easy for me to abort a potential relationship at this point. There are those in my trade that end such negotiations with, shall we say…finality?" He looked Adam in the eye, stroked his goatee for a moment and then said, "Of course, we are far more civilized than that. I believe I will take the gamble that you are as you say and invite you to join our organization. We pay $15,000 per trip, and bonuses for extraordinary service. If you fly three to four runs a month and provide the extras I believe you are capable of, you could earn upwards of three-quarters of a million dollars in a year."

The conversation was interrupted by the arrival of their food and Adam gave no hint of his reaction to Santana's offer. After a few bites of his grouper, he asked, "Can the compensation be deposited to an overseas account of my choosing, no tax liabilities?"

"Of course," said Santana with a smile. "We also provide extremely comfortable living quarters at both ends." Small talk accompanied the meal and when they put down knife and fork for the last time, Adam agreed to the proposal. They shook hands and Santana asked him to report at nine the next morning.

At the Americana, Adam opened the door to his suite and to his surprise, found his sofa graced by Agent Abby Munsen. She rose and took his hand, saying, "I thought we should talk over some last minute details…oh, and I've taken the liberty to bring you a going-away present…a suitcase. This is a very special suitcase. Instead of the traditional false bottom, the tubes for the retractable handle are hollow and accessible from under the lining. In these tubes you can store hair dye and other makeup items that would give you away if discovered. They also will hold some insurance. Tiny transmitters that will allow you to identify yourself to U.S. agencies that otherwise would shoot you down. Just in case you aren't stealthy enough."

"Sounds terrific, but what if they x-ray the suitcase?"

"No problem. The alloy in the tubes will block the x-rays. We have loaded two of them in one of the tubes. The only time you face exposure is when you remove one from the case. We assume you will always have the case with you, so you can remove the transmitter after you're in the air and replace it before you land."

"Looks like you've thought of everything. Thanks again."

"You can repay me by getting the job done…and coming back safe and sound." She gave him a hug and a kiss on the cheek.

Adam arrived at the mansion at 8:45 a.m. accompanied by two bags and a fair degree of apprehension. He was told to report to Mr. Santana's office at 9:30.

He was introduced to three pilots, all males, two white and one Hispanic. Miguel Santana asked them to sit and he said, "Gentlemen, we are adopting a new procedure. In the past, we have flown our airplanes to and from the United States over water to Florida. Between runners of drugs and illegal aliens, U. S. government watchdogs have blanketed the approaches to Florida and we are as likely to be apprehended on the return flight as on the delivery of our cargo. Henceforth we will fly interior routes from Mexico to destinations in western and midwest states. We will employ duplicate aircraft in the U.S. to confuse and confound those authorities that object to our business practices. Our product will be flown in bulk into the base airfield and then reloaded into your aircraft for the border crossing. You may be aware that we have suffered losses in the past and we believe the new routing and procedures will reduce that possibility substantially. The new ground-detecting radar will allow very low flight patterns with minimal danger. The radar signal is very short range and therefore virtually undetectable. We will fly the Gulfstream to the new base tomorrow morning. There you will practice low level flying over the actual terrain you will experience on your flights. Because of the proximity to the border, you will often deliver your cargo to destinations deeper into the U. S. Any questions?"

The oldest pilot asked, "Does this mean we will be based in Mexico rather than Florida or Colombia?"

"Yes, this base of operations will be closed down. Those of you that have established residence in Colombia may commute in our supply aircraft. The rest of you will live near the new base in Mexico. I assure you that the quarters available will be more than adequate in every way."

Adam kept a straight face in spite of the devastating news. His entire plan depended upon infiltrating Ball's headquarters in Colombia. He must now play along and wait for an opportunity to either jump ship or somehow talk his way into the drug kingdom that had become Belinda's prison.

When Adam climbed the ladder of the shiny new Gulfstream jet the next morning, Santana called out to him, "Bryce, why don't you fly right seat?"

Adam managed his first smile since the disastrous notice of the Mexican base as he replied, "Thank you. I haven't flown this configuration, so I'm anxious to see what this baby's all about."

"You've flown jets before?" asked Santana as Adam settled in his seat.

"Yes, some of my pylon racing buddies owned Lears and such. We batted them around the sky a bit. I suspect the insurance providers wouldn't be too happy with some of the stunts we performed with their high-priced birds."

"Interesting. Perhaps you'd like to test your skills on this airplane. We wouldn't want to cause airsickness among our passengers or take the airframe to the breaking point, but I do enjoy an occasional thrill. Let's go through the pre-flight and you can take the wheel from the get-go."

Adam acclimated himself to the controls and when he received clearance for takeoff, pushed the throttles forward. He felt the raw power as the Gulfstream accelerated to flying speed less than halfway down the runway. He pulled back on the yoke and the airplane shot up at more than twice the rate of climb of the most powerful propeller-driven aircraft. For the moment Adam left the worries of Ball behind and after raising the flaps and gear, turned to Santana. "Even though you've flown jets, stepping into one from props is always a fresh experience. This machine is truly a rocket."

"Yes, it can reach nearly 50,000 feet and fly at over 600MPH. Take her up to 40,000 feet and hold on 172° until we get well out over the Gulf. Then we'll go down to about 15,000 feet and see what she'll do." Adam did as instructed and as he descended, Santana informed the pilot passengers to snug up their seat belts. At 20,000 feet, Adam pushed the yoke forward and put them into a steep dive. He pulled out at 14,000, still well short of the number of Gs necessary to cause the occupants to black out. He eased back on the throttles and climbed until his airspeed slowed to 200 knots. He turned the wheel hard right, gave a slight right rudder and the Gulf turned over into an aileron roll. He toyed with the idea of climbing to stall and letting the airplane fall into a tailspin, but quickly discarded the notion and returned to level flight.

The first sound uttered came from the cabin. "Holy Christ, this is no goddamn fighter. Are you guys trying to take the wings off?"

Santana spoke on the intercom, "Just a little sport. We wanted to practice evasive maneuvers in case we met any fighters. If we mount a couple of 20MM cannon or a missile or two, we might be ready to take on the U.S. Air Force."

Another voice said, "You gotta to be kidding. I'd like to watch that battle…from the ground, that is."

Santana turned off the intercom and said to Adam. "That was an impressive display of flying. Now let's go back up to cruising altitude and head for Mexico…I'm anxious to give this crew a tour of their new home."

Adam thought, '*Their* new home? I'm sure you intend that to include Bryce Bentley. You may be stationing me in Mexico, but I'm going to find a way to fly this bird to Columbia. Hold on, Belinda, I'm on my way.'

VI

**July 7th, 1999,
Hotel La Grande, Bogotá,
Colombia, 9:45 a.m....**

Mack Rogers paced the floor of the elegant suite in silence. Al Leach watched patiently for a time, finally he said, "Ya know, they're gonna charge us if you wear out that fancy goddamn rug."

"Don't be a smart-ass," replied Mack. "When did Oakes say he'd have some dope for us?"

"He said this morning, and he's got two and a quarter hours before we can call him a liar," Leach added in his sardonic tone. "I don't know why you're so fuckin' edgy. He said there *might* be a problem with the other drug lord. That doesn't mean the guy is sending a tank column up Ball's damn hill this morning."

"No, but it could mean that Ball might take it on the lam and take Belinda with him. If they did attack, she could be killed or captured by Dominguez. Either way, we're screwed as far as finding and rescuing her."

"Yeah, but 'til we hear from Adam, we got no choice but to rough it in this crummy joint... and force down caviar and champagne," Leach responded.

"Under normal circumstances, I'd agree, but depending upon Oakes' report, we may have to think up a new plan...speed up the process. I wish he'd call," said Mack as he continued to pace. Twenty minutes later a knock on the door signaled the arrival of 'Middy' Oakes. Mack checked the peephole before admitting the CIA's Columbian chief. "Oakes, we've been waiting patiently for word from you. Get in here and give us the story."

Leach said, "*I've* been waiting patiently, Rogers here has been as nervous as a bridegroom at a shotgun wedding. Take a load off and tell us all about these bastards."

Oakes, six foot three and two-forty, looked like a thirty year old athlete as a result of a good diet and religious exercise regimen. He smiled conspiratorially as he slid into a chair across from Leach. "I have good news and I have bad news. Which do you want to hear first?"

"Bad news, of course," said Mack, sitting next to Leach with a worried look on his broad freckled face.

"Enrico Dominguez plans to raid Ball's complex to kill Ball and his higher-ups and take over his business. Our informer attended a meeting that put together the preliminary plan."

"Wait a minute," exclaimed Mack. "What good news could counter that?"

"Timing, my friend," said Oakes. "They plan to attack somewhere between the 23rd and the 26th of July. That gives us over two weeks to take care of our business…and if we can do it quietly enough, we could leave some calling cards for Mr. Dominguez, killing, so to speak, two birds with one stone."

Mack scratched his head and said, "We still have no idea when Adam will be here and ready to make a move, but I suppose we can put together and fine-tune our part of the operation while we wait."

One could almost hear the gears meshing in 'old fox' Leach's head as he proposed, "Maybe we should consider a different plan. If we could get our hands on Belinda, we could save ourselves the trouble… let those assholes kill each other off."

"I suppose you have a magic scheme to accomplish such a feat?" asked Mack with sarcasm.

"Pretty much," replied Leach. "All we need is for Mr. Oakes to get us all the dope about the complex. We go up with a few well-armed guys, break in and spring her."

"My, my," said Oakes with disdain, "I'm amazed that you were able to formulate such an inspired and comprehensive strategy…right off the top of your head. Perhaps you could provide details on how I am to gain this dope?"

"Hey, you're the spook. This is what you guys do…right?" asked Leach.

"Indeed it is. However it takes time to insert a mole and still more time for that mole to gather the necessary information. More time than we have. We are relying on your man, Adam, in this case."

"What about Maria, the one who helped Belinda escape before? She would have information on the complex," suggested Mack.

"We have no idea where she is or even if she's alive," said Oakes. "If we could find her, Ball could find her and the rules are quite strict on betrayal down here…you must be killed to set an example. It works rather well if you have the scruples of a drug lord."

"That pretty much closes the door on your idea, Al," said Mack. "We don't want to wind up the way our attackers did in Atlanta. We must wait for Adam and let him open the door for us…there's no other way."

VII

July 8th, 1999,
Lampazos, Mexico,
6:45 a.m....

The day dawned bright and sunny with light winds...a perfect day for flying. Adam returned from an hour-long run through the lush lawns and gardens of the estate that was Ball's new headquarters. Each of the pilots had been assigned a small suite with a sitting room, bedroom and lavish bath. Last night's dinner had been extraordinary and the female help looked as though they had come directly from the Miss Universe pageant. Adam shaved, showered and dressed and was drinking coffee in the dining room long before the others showed up for a breakfast meeting. Santana, a fashion plate whether dressed formally or casually, as this morning, was next to enter. They sat in a long room with a huge, elegant light fixture emanating from a oval ceiling that soared twenty feet above the marble floor. He greeted Adam warmly and ordered a special egg omelet for each of them. The other pilots and an office manager and security chief completed the breakfast party. A lively conversation accompanied a sumptuous meal and when they finished eating, Santana dismissed the non-pilots, then stood.

"Gentlemen, I trust you enjoyed a restful evening and are ready to practice some low level flying. We have two Moonies ready to go and another will be ready shortly. The route you will fly will be the same as your payload route except that you will turn around forty miles short of the Texas border. You will take off and attain an altitude of five thousand feet heading southwest or 180° from your destination. After 50 miles, you will turn around and take it down to the deck. The flight plan has been carefully calculated to avoid population centers and topographical obstructions; therefore it is imperative that you follow it unerringly. Make your original flight at a minimum of 100 feet. We will work our way down from there after you're completely familiar with the route and the equipment. Any questions?"

"When do you propose to begin actual operations?" asked Adam.

"In a day or two. I will check each one of you out after you've had some practice. When I decide you're ready, we'll begin the first night that affords the proper conditions." They were driven to the airstrip in a Lincoln Navigator and each pilot, flying solo, made three trips before noon. They had a siesta after lunch to avoid the extreme heat and resumed flying at four in the afternoon. Santana climbed into the cabin with Adam after his sixth flight. When they returned, the recorder attached to the ground-sensing radar showed an average altitude of nineteen feet after the turn-around. Santana turned to Adam and said, "I'm asking the others to stay above twenty-five feet, but since you are the 'ace' of the group, I will only caution you not to dig any furrows with your prop. You and I will fly the whole route after dinner and you'll carry a payload tonight, okay?"

"Absolutely," replied Adam. "Will we be flying treetop for a long way in the States?"

"That, my friend, is my bright idea. An identical aircraft, including numbers, will take off from a towered field in Texas; you will intercept that aircraft and take over their flight plan at normal altitudes. They will land at an unmarked field near the rendezvous while you fly to a distant city. On your return, they will intercept you for the return flight to their Texas airfield. You will then hedge-hop back over the border before early morning light."

"It's brilliant," exclaimed Adam. "I assume you will fly the decoy from different airports and to various destinations."

"You have it," replied Santana with an admiring grin for the insight of his prize pupil. "This flight will originate in San Antonio with Aspen, Colorado as the destination. It's wise to fly in to places that have a lot of private aircraft traffic. You will arrive and depart in daylight, but darkness will cover the switch at both ends. Your cargo will contain mountain equipment that will be carefully packed with extremely concentrated product. Since no customs are involved, the cargo will easily pass normal inspection. We even add hard-to-detect scents that throw off drug-sniffing canines."

Adam flew the practice run to the field where the decoy would land and returned without incident. He turned in at 7 p.m. and was dressed ready to fly at 3:30 a.m. He took off at 4 a.m., one hour before daybreak and rendezvoused with the decoy at 4:45. He climbed to 12,000 feet, turned on his lights and set his course for Aspen. The transfer of product was completed by 7 a.m. and he was driven to an excellent hotel for breakfast and a day's rest. At 8:30 p.m., he took off and rendezvoused with the decoy at 10:45. He touched down at the estate's airstrip at 11:30 p.m., $15,000 richer. When he showed up for breakfast at 7 a.m., Santana greeted him with, "Well Bryce, I'm surprised to see you up so early. How did it go?"

"Like clockwork," replied Adam. "The decoy arrived at the exact time and place and there was no problem in Aspen. We rendezvoused perfectly on the return trip and I had no incidents coming back over the border."

"I have one other pilot ready to go tonight, but the others need work. Would you like to take another run tomorrow night?"

"No problem, but at some point, I'd like to fly that jet down to Colombia…just to see the lay of the land. Would that be possible?" asked Adam.

Santana considered the request as he stirred sugar into his coffee. "I don't see any reason why not. If we can successfully make three more runs in the next three nights, I'll need to replenish product. You could accompany Matthew and me as we journey south on Wednesday."

"I'd like that," said Adam.

Matthew Purves, a veteran drug-smuggling pilot, completed that night's run without a hitch and Adam flew to Kansas City the following night. At 10 a.m. on Tuesday morning he hitched a ride into Lampazos with Annabelle DuPrey, the business manager, and the chef. Ms. DuPrey, although most proper, had glanced at Adam in that certain way that he interpreted as interest. He had smiled cordially without either turning away her interest or leading her on. His excuse had been to pick up a few toiletries and he was dropped off at a pharmacy near their food supplier. Adam walked to the back of the store and handed a prescription for a stronger version of Advil to the pharmacist. The middle-aged, white-coated man nodded and filled the prescription. Adam's Spanish was far from perfect, but passable, and after paying for the medicine, he inquired of the pharmacist if he was on the internet. Getting a positive response, he asked about emailing his mother who was in ill health. The man agreed readily and Adam sat at the somewhat antiquated computer and put in the email address *Cbentley111@aol.com* before typing 'Dear Mom, I hope you're feeling better. I am vacationing in northern Mexico. Weather's hot, but area is beautiful. I plan to travel south tomorrow and will head home to see you as soon as possible. Love, Bryce.'

Adam picked up shaving cream and toothpaste before strolling down the street toward the wholesale grocer. Twenty-four hours later he was at the wheel of the Gulfstream rising off the tarmac, destination: Paz del Rio, Colombia.

VIII

July 13th, 1999,
Hotel La Grande, Bogotá,
Colombia, 11:15 a.m....

Al Leach energized the scrambler, picked up the phone and said, "Hello, if you're a beautiful woman, the coast is clear."

"You really are a dirty old man," said a provocative female voice. "Have you taken precautions?"

"Not so old, but the other words apply, and yes, this is a safe-sex call. Would this be the lovely Abigail?"

"Of course, and I have good news. Our long-lost friend has surfaced. He sent an email to his *mother*. He's currently in Mexico, but is heading for Colombia tomorrow. I'm having Middy arrange to get a satellite cell phone to him as soon as he makes contact. It will look identical to the phone he's been carrying around, the one that's worthless in either Mexico or Colombia."

"Great, this is Mack, on the speaker. We have rehearsed our roles and are ready for the curtain to go up. We'll go into Paz del Rio before the action day, so we can make sure our plan is foolproof. Your guy down here has been terrific. He's working on a new angle that sounds great...if he can work it out. I hope Adam can do his part quickly, since we only have ten days before the other operation is scheduled to go down."

"I know and we will inform Adam as soon as we make contact," said Munsen. "We'll expedite matters as much as possible from this end. Meanwhile, keep your powder dry. I'll call as soon as I hear any more...Bye."

"OK, Al," said Mack. "Let's go over the physical layout once more."

"Shit, I can draw the whole thing to scale...in my sleep," complained Leach.

"Don't bitch," said Mack as he tossed a blown-up version of a satellite reconnaissance picture onto the table. "We have to assume that the checkpoints at the bottom and midway up the mountain are in contact with the headquarters. We must get through the first one by stealth. My guess is the second one may require the people to get out of the van and possibly be searched. If that's the case, we have to blow them away and rush the place from there. If Adam can disable the alarms, we're home free, otherwise we could have a tough fire-fight."

"You know, if I were in their shoes, I'd lay some mines in the road. Mines I could activate if the security point is breached," suggested Leach. "We should tell Adam to check that out if he can. Speaking of Adam, how sure are you that he can fool Ball with that disguise?"

"Pretty sure. He'd damn better," replied Mack. "If he gets taken, they're really going to beef up security. We may have to wait for Dominguez to go in and hope for the best, but let's look on the bright side. We're going in with eight men including you and me. Body armor, silenced automatic weapons and handguns. Smoke and tear gas grenades. Have we forgotten anything?"

"No, we're well prepared…for what we expect. Who knows what we'll run into that we don't expect. I think we should brainstorm the whole plan one more time…try to think like Ball."

"He could set up weapons like we did in Atlanta. The key is for Adam to cut the communications. If he fails, we could be dead meat," said Mack in a less than cheerful tone.

"What about a diversion?" Leach supplied. "Send a chopper in close just before the van heads up the hill."

"That could put them on higher alert …No, I think we're better off maintaining a normal routine. On the other hand, if the chopper could stay out of earshot and come in if we trigger an alarm and are in trouble…they could provide some covering fire on the opposite side of the compound. Let's run the idea by Oakes."

The meeting with Middleton Oakes and Travis Campbell, his CIA partner, was held over dinner in their suite. After dinner, Mack said, "I don't suppose you guys have a spare Huey and a crew lying around?"

"Oh sure," said Oakes. "We keep a couple in the garage at the Embassy. Have you changed your plan of attack?"

"We were thinking more of a backup," offered Leach. "To be called in only if we have a problem getting in on the road. It wouldn't have to be an attack helicopter. Just somebody to give us a little diversionary fire...if we need it."

Campbell shifted in his chair and said, "Getting an ordinary helicopter is a lot easier than a Huey, but as you know, we can't be directly involved. You'd have to make arrangements on your own. We would, of course, be happy to steer you in the right direction...for both the machine and some drivers."

Oakes looked at Campbell with some disdain before adding, "We have some sources, but I'm not sure how reliable they are. As we discussed before, the drug lords have unlimited resources and the power of life or death over their enemies. You can get sold out pretty easily."

"I'm not too concerned about that," said Mack. "We're paying top dollar and we also promise a fatal payoff for traitors. Why don't you look into it, without making any commitment, and get back to us...like tomorrow."

IX

July 14th, 1999, Ranchero Grande, Paz de Rio, Colombia, 2:45 p.m....

Jeb Carter's somewhat harsh voice brought Ball out of his reverie. He had been absorbed by a problem that consumed much of his attention for almost two weeks. He was disgusted with himself for allowing a woman to so completely dominate his thoughts. If only she hadn't given in to him with such passion. And then shut it off. He tried to replicate all his moves from that special night, but her response never returned. The anger that had been so apparent in her since her capture had turned to a resigned sadness. Her spirit, which had always attracted him, was slowly ebbing away. "Damn her," he muttered as he turned toward Carter. "What is it?"

"Santana's coming in. Want me to bring him up when he gets here?"

"Certainly," said Ball curtly. "Have some refreshments brought in. I'm anxious to hear the details of the new operation."

Santana could barely reach across the huge desk to shake Ball's proffered hand as he said with a wide smile, "Good afternoon, *Señor* Ball. I trust the world is smiling upon you?"

"Indeed, Miguel, but more importantly, is it smiling on your new operation?" Ball said with as much of a smile as he ever managed.

"It is truly a jewel, my *capitan*. We have made five deliveries without a hitch...and to final destinations. We no longer slip into the fringe of the country and then find ways to transport to distant markets. We now fly either direct or to a destination with easy access to the end-user."

"I'm impressed," said Ball earnestly. "Your new method of delivery will be most welcome as we add a few new customers...converts from our friend Dominguez."

Santana's smile disappeared, replaced with a frown. "Do you think it wise to escalate the conflict with him at this time? He is not one to turn the other cheek if he feels injured in any way."

"Miguel, do not underestimate me. At this moment, he is formulating a plan to attack us and take over *our* business, just as I did to my predecessor several years ago. What he doesn't know is that I have someone in his camp and we will attack him just before his planned attack on us is scheduled. When our empires are combined, the importance of your function will grow enormously."

"Please accept my apologizes for doubting your infinite wisdom," said Santana, bowing gracefully. "I look forward to transporting ever larger quantities and the addition of two new airplane drivers will accommodate such increases. My star pupil flew the Gulfstream down here. I am anxious to have you meet him."

"Perhaps we should invite him to dinner," mused Ball. "Does he have proper attire?"

"I believe so," replied Santana. "I suggested he bring a suit…just in case."

"It's settled then. We will serve cocktails at seven-thirty with dinner at eight. I shall inform the lady that you look forward to her presence this evening. Good afternoon Miguel."

Adam had been assigned to a comfortable room and bath on the ground floor of the hacienda. He immediately hung and steamed his suit and shirt that would be worn if…and only if he were invited to dinner. An hour later, Santana called and told him to be ready for cocktails at seven-thirty. Two hours before the appointed time, he nervously prepared for the ultimate test…fooling Ball. Although he had re-dyed his hair and mustache black two days before, he repeated the process. After a shower, he carefully applied makeup to his entire body, darkening his skin several shades. He took two of the voice deepening pills that also added a husky timbre to his otherwise clear voice. He added small 'Godfather' puffs to his cheeks and applied facial putty to his nose. False eyebrows and deep brown contacts completed his facial makeover. Satisfied with his look, he put on a medium gray silk shirt with a black, small patterned tie. An Italian-cut Armani suit in shimmering black stood above patent leather loafers. The look was complete, now the movements. He practiced walking with exaggerated fluidity…almost a swagger. He thought back to his training with Belinda and her insistence that one must change his mannerisms or be unmasked.

At 7:25, he left his room and ascended the wide staircase that carved its way majestically through a grand entrance hall and deposited its climbers onto a marble floor that supported elegant teak walls and soaring ceilings. A young man dressed in a tuxedo stood at the top of the stairs. He exuded a rare combination of breeding, grooming and toughness. A classy bodyguard in Adam's opinion. The man smiled and asked in slightly accented English, "May I help you, sir?"

"I am Bryce Bentley. I'm invited to take cocktails with Mr. Ball."

"Yes sir, please follow me." Adam noticed just a hint of a bulge in the back of the man's well-tailored tux as he was led into a comfortably sized reception room. Santana was just inside the door and grasped his hand eagerly as he led him across the room. Ball was standing with a martini glass in his hand, clothed in a finely tailored suit with a lavender shirt and a tie that so closely matched the colors of the suit and shirt that it had to have been made for them. He extended his hand as Santana said, "May I present Mr. Bryce Bentley," and turning to Adam, said, "This is Mr. Sean Ball."

Heart pounding, Adam shook his hand. "It is a genuine pleasure to meet you, Mr. Ball."

Ball showed no sign of recognizing Adam. "Thank you, Mr. Bentley, Mr. Santana speaks very highly of you. Welcome. I hope we may have a long and mutually profitable association."

"Thank you, sir," said Adam. Santana led him to a small bar in the corner of the room and motioned to the attractive young barmaid to serve Adam. Adam was careful to avoid his favorite single malt scotch, and ordered Royal Crown on the rocks. Santana, resplendent in a monochromatic off-white suit, shirt and tie, opted for a glass of chardonnay. As they drifted back toward their host, Jeb Carter entered. He had gained a measure of class, at least in his dress, since Adam last saw him. Santana introduced them and once again, no sign of discovery was apparent. Adam breathed a sigh of relief, two down, one to go. He had no doubt Belinda would identify him immediately if and when she came upon the scene. His fear was that his cover could be blown if she failed to hide her surprise at seeing him in Ball's lair. Carter hit the bar before joining the rest at Ball's corner of the room. The conversation was general and Adam picked up no intelligence that could be used in their upcoming action, but his anticipation and anxiety grew as the dinner hour approached with no sign of Belinda.

A white-coated waiter opened carved double doors at precisely eight o'clock and Ball ushered his guests into the opulent dining room. He directed Adam to the side of the table facing Carter and Santana, on Ball's right. A vacant chair remained at the opposite end of the table from Ball. The wine steward arrived at once and poured a choice of an outstanding red or white wine. Ball proposed a toast to Santana's new distribution system and to the newest member of that system, Bryce Bentley. Even Carter smiled as he joined in the toast. As they returned their glasses to the table, a door opened and Adam caught his breath as Belinda swept into the room in a gleaming green dress, cut low, revealing deep cleavage. When she came and took his hand when introduced by Ball, he was literally rendered speechless. Belinda, however never missed a beat as she smiled and welcomed him. Her eyes revealed that she saw through his disguise and he prayed no one else noticed. As he bowed to kiss her hand, he found his voice at last. "It's a pleasure to meet you, Ms. Jackson." As he looked up, into her eyes, he said, "Mr. Santana has spoken of your charm and beauty…and I believe his comments were understated."

"Oh Christ," exclaimed Carter. "Not another goddamned Romeo."

Ball turned to Carter and said with a thin smile, "Not necessarily, Jeb. Perhaps someday you will learn to recognize the manners of a gentleman."

Adam and Santana jointly held the chair for Belinda and as Adam resumed his seat, he was consumed with emotion. It was all he could do to stop himself from pulling her into his arms. He had no idea that his first contact with Belinda would have such a devastating effect on him. Fortunately Santana had picked up the slack in the conversation and his momentary lapse seemed to have gone unnoticed. Santana looked at Ball and said, "We will be returning to the base in Mexico tomorrow afternoon. Will you need any assistance here in the next few days?"

Ball pursed his lips and said, "Possibly. The plans are in process. I expect to be able to answer your question before you leave."

Carter looked at Adam and asked with a smirk, "Tell me, Mr. Bentley, have you ever shed your 'gentlemanly' ways and gotten your hands dirty?"

Adam looked Carter squarely in the eye and replied, "I believe I have. What did you have in mind?"

Ball interjected, "I believe Jeb refers to any military or other activity where violence of one sort or another was involved."

Adam replied, "If you refer to capability with weapons, yes, I have had considerable experience with their use."

Carter, somewhat miffed by his employer's comment, dove back into the conversational fray. "Since you're not leaving until afternoon, maybe we should try you out on the range in the morning. How about that?"

Adam looked between Ball and Carter and said, "I'd be delighted, just name the time and place."

"Not to change the subject," said Santana, turning to Belinda, "but you are looking exceptionally beautiful this evening, my dear."

"Thank you, Miguel." She looked at Ball. "You are to be complimented, Sean, for gathering such a handsome, splendidly groomed entourage."

Ball showed little surprise at the compliment as he replied, "Thank you, Belinda. Perhaps a walk in the garden would be in order after our guests retire?"

The comment was lost on Adam, but Belinda's involuntary cringe indicated that it had deep meaning for her. Just then, two waiters entered and dinner was served. As Adam expected, the presentation was splendid and the food a gourmet's delight. Sea bass with a rich lobster sauce was accompanied by a variety of delicious squashes. Santana carried the conversation during dinner, paying particular attention to Belinda without ignoring his host and Adam. Carter seemed content with his miniscule input. Adam was careful to limit his eye contact with Belinda while his peripheral vision told him she looked at him only when he was the recipient of a question or comment. When the plates were cleared, Ball called for cappuccino to be served with a coffee-flavored pudding topped with hot brandy sauce. Belinda ate little dessert and announced shortly that she was tired and asked to be excused. She nodded to Adam, said she was glad to have met him and said goodnight to the others. She walked from the room with that special style and grace Adam had never witnessed in another woman.

The evening ended soon after Belinda's departure. Adam was invited to breakfast at seven with a tour of the grounds and range to follow. As he reflected upon the evening, two things stood out. The most important was his unexpectedly moving reaction to Belinda's presence. She literally hit him like a ton of bricks. The question was, had he affect her the same way? All he could think of was being with her alone, touching her, asking her again to believe in him as she once had. Would it ever happen? The other thing was the curious effect on Belinda from Ball's comment about 'a walk in the garden.' She seemed to retreat into her shell, never to return for the rest of the evening.

His thoughts turned to the formidable task before him. Tomorrow, after the tour and firing range, he had to talk his way into a sightseeing trip downtown to make contact with Mack and Leach or their people. That and finding time to scope out the security of the compound...all before an early afternoon flight. A difficult, if not impossible, undertaking.

He awoke at 4:30 a.m. after a troubled sleep. Belinda whirled through violent dreams in which he was repeatedly unmasked and executed by Carter, Ball or both. The dream that woke him with a start ended with Belinda, at Ball's insistence, shooting him several times in the chest. The smile on her lips as she fired again and again was indelibly etched in his mind.

He got up, dressed in a sweat suit and sneakers, and quietly let himself out of the room. As he walked toward the grand staircase, he spotted a large man seated at the apex of the hallways. He approached him casually and asked if there was an exercise area available. He was directed to the gym one floor below. Adam was impressed by the size and scope of the training facility. Along with the usual treadmills, bikes and free weights, there were a dozen or more machines to tone every part of the body. He began with stretching, followed by a run on a treadmill. The clock on the wall read 5:45 a.m. when he heard the door open. She wore a skin-hugging black training suit with her hair tied back off her face. Without makeup, her face was even more stunning. As she stepped onto the adjoining treadmill, her greeting was appropriate, not for a former lover, but for someone she had met at a dinner party the night before. He replied in kind, saying, "Good morning Ms. Jackson. You are certainly an early bird."

"As are you, Mr. Bentley, but please call me Belinda."

"Thank you, and my name is Bryce. Do you spend much time in the gym?"

"I try to put in an hour or two nearly every day. Are you an exercise nut?"

"I'm afraid so," he replied. "It sort of runs in the family. I was hoping to run outside, but the gentlemen upstairs recommended the gym. Are there any good trails or paths around this place?"

"Yes, but it's a little dangerous. The business requires very high security and there are people outside that are responsible for that security. They could mistake an innocent jogger for an enemy and take…extreme measures, if you take my meaning."

"I believe I do," said Adam as the time ran out on his treadmill program. As he stepped off, he said, "It's been a pleasure talking with you…Belinda. I hope to return to Columbia soon and look forward to seeing you again."

"That would be nice. Thank you and happy landings." As she said this she 'accidentally' dropped a Kleenex from her hand. He picked it up and as he made a motion to hand it to her, she said, "Would you mind dropping it in the basket over there?" She pointed to a trash container just behind Adam's machine.

He replied, "No problem. Have a great day." He stepped over and casually threw the Kleenex in the container. He walked directly to the door of the gym and returned to his room. After checking for any hidden cameras, Adam carefully unfolded the small wad of paper Belinda had enclosed in the Kleenex. There were three sheets of thin parchment containing extremely small print and diagrams. He read and memorized all of the material including detailed floor plans of the hacienda. He then took a tiny Phillips screwdriver and opened the case of his cell phone. Refolding the pages to fit the space, he inserted them and reassembled the phone. He quickly shaved, showered, refreshed his makeup and dressed in a denim shirt, jeans and lightweight hiking boots. At 6:55, he walked into the main floor dining room to mark the official beginning of the day.

Carter was dressed in fatigues and Santana in a navy-blue jumpsuit. They had a hearty breakfast and Carter suggested they wear jackets to ward off the 'below-the-equator summer cool.' Santana did most of the talking as they walked through a large concrete warehouse behind the main house. Locked steel doors shielded the company's product from prying eyes or light-fingered hands. A bunkhouse with a dozen beds, recreation room and kitchen provided living quarters for the workers/security force. Carter opened another locked steel door and gathered an Uzi, three Glock pistols and ammunition before relocking the arsenal. They left the warehouse and took a clearly defined path that wound around large rocks and brush to a clearing. A forty-foot-long shed roof protected ten firing positions that looked out over a range of 300 yards. Both paper targets and pop-up dummies were spaced intermittently through the range. Adam had spent considerable time with Carter on the Range at Fort Monmouth and would now modify his shooting style and let Carter outshoot him. He would shoot well enough to impress, but Adam Packard, the superlative marksman, would not show up today. They fired 100 rounds and Carter took the honors with Adam shooting even with Santana…still expert. They trudged back up the trail and arrived back at the hacienda just before nine. When Carter left, Adam turned to Santana and asked, "Any chance of taking a little tour of the city before lunch?"

Santana pursed his lips momentarily and said, "I see no reason why not. I must meet with Mr. Ball shortly and, assuming he places no great demands upon my time, I should be delighted to be your guide…you know, of course, that this is my home?"

"There's nothing like a home-town guide," said Adam. "I'll be ready to go at your convenience." At 10:30, Santana knocked on Adam's door and they walked out the front door where a black Suburban with a bodyguard and driver waited. Adam studied the road and terrain carefully as they descended to the city below. He noted the two manned guard houses, located one-third and two-thirds of the way up the mountain. Each had a heavy steel gate that would require a bulldozer or a tank to penetrate. To attack with any surprise, both would have to be breached with subterfuge rather than force. He turned to Santana and said, "Security looks pretty tight. Anyone would have quite a problem forcing their way into this compound."

"Correct. Mr. Ball has fortified well. To be successful, an attack would almost need to be made by air...helicopters or parachutists."

"What about necessary traffic, deliveries and such?" asked Adam.

"The turnoff at the lower gate is the inspection point for all traffic," Santana responded. "Trucks or vans are searched at that point and the all clear is signaled to the second gate and the house before the gate is opened."

"Mr. Ball is to be complemented on his thorough planning," said Adam. "It looks like he has little to fear from his enemies."

"That remains to be seen," said Santana with a strange look on his face. He did not elaborate. Paz de Rio lay like a small jewel in the mountains north of Bogota. The heart of the town was ancient with some newer, larger buildings along the resurrected riverfront. As they drove down the narrow streets of the old section, Adam spotted a Radio Shack incongruously nestled between two open markets. He asked Santana if they had time for a stop. He needed to have someone look at his cell phone, perhaps a new battery. The Suburban backed up and the man riding shotgun stepped out, opened Adam's door and accompanied him across to the store. Inside Adam asked if they serviced Nokia phones. A very dark man of indeterminate age replied in perfect English, "Yes, sir. Could it be that your battery is faulty?"

"I suspect that's the problem," said Adam, handing his phone over the counter.

"I will check it out. It will only take a moment." He turned and went through a curtain to the back room. Meanwhile, the bodyguard watched the street without missing any of the exchange between Adam and the clerk. The clerk returned in a few minutes and as he handed the cell phone back to Adam, said, "That was it, I replaced the battery. That will be $18.50 U.S."

Adam accepted the phone, pulled a $20 bill from his wallet and said, "Thank you, I don't need any change." The man smiled and gave a small bow as Adam turned and left the store. He pocketed the new satellite phone. They completed the tour in an hour, staying within the bulletproof shell and windows of the SUV. As they drove up the mountain and passed the check points, Adam thought how fortunate that Ball had placed so much reliance on securing the road…since the cavalry to rescue Belinda would be coming in another way.

*July 16th, 1999,
Hotel La Grande, Bogotá,
Colombia, 11:15 a.m....*

Leach finished reading the parchment papers with the aid of a magnifying glass, put them on the table, then turned to Mack Rogers. "By God, that woman is good. How Belinda gathered all this intelligence…being a captive and all, is beyond me. I wish we had a way of contacting her when we're ready to strike. Maybe, if Adam can get back, he can give her a message?"

"If we can carry out *her* plan, it won't be necessary," said Mack. "Adam feels that they are so hung up on the road or an air attack, that their security within the compound is not that tight. We just have to remember that they have some smart, tough people and the element of surprise is vital."

"So it looks like we're a 'go' for the 20th. What's going on with your advance team?" Leach asked.

"The agent in place has contacted Belinda's source and he has agreed to guide us on the scouting mission tomorrow night. I'm taking two of our best-conditioned men and we're bringing in equipment to make it easy for old-timers like yourself to scale the heights on Tuesday."

"You'd better bring some battleship anchor rope if it's going to support that fat ass of yours," replied Leach with a smirk. "I'll probably beat you to the top."

"This body may not be the speediest on the planet, but I can carry the load necessary to make it easy for guys like you," Mack said. "In fact, I'm headed for the gym to further enhance these bulging muscles. It wouldn't be a bad idea for you to get off the couch and get some exercise."

"Fear not, brave warrior, when the arrows and spears fly, you'll wish you had my compact physique, which will be difficult, if not impossible, to hit."

"Leach, you should weigh 300 pounds, you're so full of shit," was Mack's parting shot as he left the suite. After a hard workout, he showered, dressed and met with Middleton Oakes, Juan Juarez and Antonio Lopez in a small meeting room in the hotel. The two wiry Colombians had been chosen for their outstanding physical condition, combining strength with endurance…and they spoke English. Mack asked Oakes, "Are you sure the ladders will be available tomorrow?"

Oakes replied, "The shipping clerk said the shipment was delivered to American Airlines at 8:20 a.m. and they assured him it would be in Bogotá early this afternoon. Your willingness to pay a 33% premium really got their attention. However, I suspect the demand for rope ladders may not be at an all-time high."

"Good," said Mack, "we'll pick up the shipment at the airport and leave for Paz de Rio from there. I have arranged lodging near the mountain. I'd like to scout the area at a time of high activity, like around five-thirty to six in the afternoon. We'll carry some of the gear in and leave it in the mineshaft. This will cut down on the load we'll have to carry on Tuesday. Any questions?"

"Where shall we meet, Señor Rogers?" asked Juan.

"The truck is parked behind Rosita's Laundromat three blocks south of the hotel. We'll meet there at 1:30 and pick up the other supplies before heading for the airport. OK?"

"*Bueno*," said Juan as they rose to leave. When the two had closed the door, Oakes said, "The warehouse is six blocks east of the Embassy, 6378 LaConda Street. The explosives, gas, riot gear, weapons and ammunition are all there. Take what you want today and come back on the 20th for the balance. After you explore the mines, if you need anything else, let me know as soon as possible. Oh, by the way, I hope you're going to cover up that red hair and those freckles?"

"Yes to the last part and my sincere thanks for the rest. I hate to think of trying to carry out this mission without your help."

"I wish I could join you," said Oakes. "One of the embassy guys Ball killed was a close friend of mine, but for reasons I am not privy to, we can only be involved to a limited extent. I sincerely wish you good luck." Mack shook his hand and returned to the suite.

Late Saturday morning, Leach ordered up truck-driver-sized lunches with huge slabs of roast beef and all the trimmings. He told Mack that he better start with a full stomach, because who knew when he'd get the next meal. Mack downed every morsel…with relish. With Leach's condescending help, he dyed his hair black and covered his freckles with dark makeup. Leach said he looked like an Irish beggar with a face full of blackheads. He donned baggy old clothes that concealed the Browning automatic in his shoulder holster and slipped out of the hotel via the loading dock. He discarded his normal purposeful fast pace in favor of a slow, slouchy stroll that took over five minutes to traverse the three blocks to the truck.

Ah, and what a truck. The 1987 Chevy three-quarter-ton pickup was scarred, rusted, and generally looked like a piece of junk. The large topper didn't match the color of either the truck or the two odd-colored fenders. There was, however, under that inauspicious exterior, a heart of gold. A new 7.4 liter engine, 6-speed transmission and AWD undercarriage made it a veritable mountain goat. With all the refinements, a few rattles and squeaks were retained…purposely.

When Mack and his two henchmen drove off, the windows were open. The air conditioning worked perfectly, but who would expect such a truck to have working air? They picked up gear at the CIA warehouse and ladders at the airport before bumping and clattering over what the Colombians called a highway. Averaging a solid 42MPH, they arrived in Paz de Rio just after 5 p.m. Mack consulted a homemade map and relayed instructions to Juan, the driver. They drove past the intersection with the road leading up the mountain to Ball's compound and Mack commented on the two check points clearly visible in the late afternoon sun. They toured the city briefly before heading out of town where they turned off on a dirt road that circled the base of the mountain. A scattering of shacks graced the rutted road that led to a small settlement on the backside of the mountain. Dirt-poor buildings housed a gas station, used (junk) car lot, grocery store, bar & restaurant and a broken down hotel. Mack thought about bedbugs and God knows what else one might find in such a flea bag hotel. They parked the truck in back of the hotel and rented three rooms. The room was more than Mack expected...much worse. He had a few unkind thoughts toward his partner, Leach, living in luxury in Bogotá.

The three explorers gathered downstairs and washed down greasy tacos with beer. The atmosphere in the dingy, smoke-filled bar was surprisingly jovial considering the obvious poverty of its patrons.

Dusk was falling as they drove back into the hills to find their guide. Tupo Juanicouez was of Indian decent and they judged him to be somewhere between sixty and a hundred years old. His home was perched on top of the highest hill (other than the mountain) for miles around. Small, but clean, it was nestled in pines whose lower branches were missing...affording marvelous views in every direction. An easy place to defend, thought Mack. Tupo had no time for the drug lords and when asked to cooperate, had agreed eagerly. Mack expected to set out in the failing light, but the old man shook his head and said they would wait for complete darkness...the way it would be for the real thing. While they waited, he showed them drawings on stretched leather that were made by his grandfather nearly 100 years before. They depicted miners destroying the plants, trees and streams in their quest for silver. Cavernous holes in the mountainside were mine entrances. The rich vein of silver had run out before he was born, but he had explored all of the abandoned mines as a boy and heard many stories of the dreaded miners from his grandfather. The old man told so many stories, Mack felt he'd known him all his life.

At eleven they finally set out for the mountain. Tupo loaded a strange wooden rake-like device in the truck...to wipe out the tire marks. They left the 'two tire track' road and by moonlight, bumped uphill over hills and rocks, climbing steadily for what seemed like an eternity. Tupo, who had called every turn, finally said, "Stop over there, by those bushes." They left the truck and followed him. When he reached the brush, he carefully pushed the branches aside and motioned for them to enter. He turned on the lantern and revealed a long, musty smelling tunnel supported by ancient timbers. Tupo led them deeper into the mine and after about 150 feet, stopped at a mound of dirt. He shined the lantern up a shaft heading up into the depths of the mountain. They studied the walls and were dismayed by the rotting wood encasing the shaft. Mack asked "Is this the only way up? And how far up the mountain are we?"

"This is the only way and we are over half way up," replied Tupo. "This goes up fifty feet or so and then another shaft cuts into the mountain. There are four such vertical shafts before we come out on the mountainside. We will then be about 150 feet from the top."

"Why don't we just scale the mountain on the outside?" asked Mack.

"There are wide cliffs nearly 300 feet high that cannot be climbed. They have men watching the entire mountainside, except the cliffs."

"Okay, let's get some equipment in here and see what we have to do," said Mack heading back toward the entrance. They hauled in a ladder, rope, pulleys, climbing spikes, rope ladder and lights. Juan climbed the ladder and tested the wood on the sides of the shaft. They found two sides quite rotten, but the others were sound. With hand and foot spikes, he climbed to the top of the shaft and secured a heavy hook-eye and pulley to a crossbeam. He then attached a rope to the pulley and they hauled a rope ladder and other supplies to the second level. When all was secure, they brought additional supplies in and pulled them up. Over the next two hours they repeated the process until they were at the top level with all the equipment.

The exhausted troops descended the rope ladders and reached the truck at three a.m. Tupo insisted that they drive in their previous tire tracks and Antonio walked ahead in one of the tracks using a small flashlight sparingly to guide the truck. Tupo walked behind, sweeping away the tire tracks. This process took nearly an hour and by the time they delivered Tupo to his house, the first signs of dawn were breaking.

The trio fell into bed just before sunrise and paid little attention to their squalid surroundings as they slept like the dead until afternoon. They left the hotel at 2 p.m. and were back in Bogota in just over two hours. Mack reentered the hotel through the delivery entrance and soaked in a hot tub for half an hour. Leach suggested they burn the clothes Mack had worn, but expressed fear that the smoke might pollute the entire city. Well scrubbed, and somewhat less stiff and sore, Mack dressed in clean clothes and downed two Heinekens before tackling the steak Leach ordered from room service. He recited the adventure to Leach, between gulps and bites, and they agreed to hold the initial briefing with their troops that evening.

They met in the back of an old saloon, just off the main square of the old town at 7 p.m. on Sunday night. The six hired guns were given specific assignments and timing was established for each. Leach had made larger drawings of the buildings and layout for the men to commit to memory. They would meet again at 9 a.m. the next morning and each man was expected to recite every detail of his role, including the precise timing. Following that meeting, they would separate and make their way to Paz de Rio…and whatever fate awaited them.

XI

July 19th, 1999, Ranchero Grande, Paz de Rio, Colombia, 12:15 p.m....

As they drove through the second checkpoint, Adam turned to Santana and asked, "Have they beefed up security throughout the compound?"

Santana replied, "I have heard nothing about *additional* safety measures on the road, but they have installed guns on the roof to repel any assault by air. Mr. Ball feels that is the most likely point of attack. He is certain, however that we will...how do you say it? Beat them to the punch."

"Do we have a definite date to take on Dominguez?"

"Barring unforeseen circumstances, we will go on the 22nd, a day before Dominguez's earliest attack date," said Santana as he opened the door of the Suburban. "You will be in the same guest room. Get settled and I'll call you when I find out what has been planned for us."

Before leaving Mexico, Adam had called Mack and Leach. His satellite phone had been patched through the CIA office in Miami. He told them he'd be flying down to Colombia that morning and that he was included in the team that would attack Dominguez. Now he must gather as much intelligence as possible with their attack on Ball's complex scheduled for just 27 hours away. He had hoped to return a day earlier and possibly repeat the early morning meeting with Belinda in the gym, but he had no choice in the matter. He unpacked and steamed his suit in case he was invited to dinner. Santana knocked on his door as he was hanging clothes in the closet. Adam opened the door and Santana asked, "Are you prepared to attend a briefing for our upcoming *party*?"

"Certainly," replied Adam, "I'm looking forward to it." They ascended the grand staircase and joined a dozen or more men in a large room adjacent to the dining room. Santana motioned to a seat for Adam before joining Carter at a table in the front of the room. Small talk ceased when Sean Ball entered and sat between Carter and Santana.

Ball began, "I will conduct this briefing in both Spanish and English. Although most of you are conversant in both languages, there must be no misunderstanding of your duties in this mission." Ball then painstakingly explained his plan to unseat drug lord Dominguez. He requested and answered numerous questions. Adam's role was primarily backup, but clearly one in which he was expected to use his judgment rather than perform a specific task. When the briefing concluded an hour and a half later, Adam shook hands with Ball and Carter and was invited to dinner that evening. As he and Santana left the room, Adam asked, "Any chance of firing a few rounds at the range this afternoon?"

Santana replied, "Sounds like a good idea, I'll set it up. How about four o'clock?"

"Fine, that will give me an hour in the gym. I'll be ready for your knock or call." Adam changed into his workout clothes and put a tiny note in his pocket. Written in code, the note gave details of the attack and some instructions for Belinda.

He was running on the treadmill when the door opened and his heart leaped at the sight of her. She mounted the treadmill beside him and said in a cool, but friendly voice, "Good afternoon, Bryce. Welcome back."

Adam removed the note from his pocket and she palmed the note as they shook hands. Adam said, "Thank you. It's always a pleasure to spend time in such a magnificent place…with such intriguing people." While running at a similar pace, they chatted about neutral subjects for a half an hour before Adam took his leave. Belinda continued on the treadmill for another twenty minutes, wiped the sweat from her brow and walked to the lavatory. She closed the door on a toilet stall before opening and reading Adam's note. She committed it to memory, tore it in tiny pieces and flushed it down the toilet.

The sun, still fairly high in the sky, had lost its midday heat and the mountain air was cool and refreshing. A light breeze favored shooting and they fired hundreds of rounds in pistols and Mac 10 submachine guns. The Uzi was better at long range, but the Mac 10's big .45 caliber slugs cut up the target best at close range. When they completed the practice, Adam asked if he could take a short walk…if he stayed in the vicinity of the range. Santana gave a smiling acquiescence, with a warning to stay close and return on the same path they had taken to the range. When Santana and the range officer had disappeared down the path, Adam walked around the range, withdrew his cell phone and made a call. He was again patched through the CIA office in Miami to Bogota. Mack Rogers answered with a simple "Yes?"

"Things are stable here. B has the info on the plan. When you reach the range, take the center path to the Ranchero, the right path to the supply depot and living quarters. I saw no cameras, but they could be well hidden. What's your ETA at the range?"

"We're estimating 0300 hours with a completion time just after 0345. Any intelligence on guards?"

"Unfortunately, no. I suggest sending two or three of your stealthiest men out to scout and neutralize any outside security. I'll take care of the inside."

"Right," replied Mack. "I think we're set. Anything else I should know?"

"I think that's it…see you in the morning, buddy." Adam disconnected and put the phone away as he walked the path back to the Ranchero.

XII

July 20th, 1999,
Mountain Base, Paz de Rio,
Colombia, 0100 hours...

Juan drove the pickup with Tupo sharing the front seat and the other five men in the back. Tupo retained his calm demeanor in spite of the nearly impossible task facing him...driving the truck back to his house. Juan had spent nearly two hours giving a driving lesson that afternoon, but was not confident that his pupil was ready for the trip down the mountain. He turned to the old man and asked, "Are you sure you can drive the truck back?"

Tupo looked at him and Juan could just make out a look of disgust in the dim light from the dash. He grunted, "Young man think age robs all ability from good man. Worry not, truck will be returned."

Mack Rogers and Al Leach were already in the lowest mineshaft arranging the equipment for the big climb. Juan had ferried them up with the balance of the supplies before picking up the soldiers. The men had taken several different buses from Bogotá earlier in the day and rendezvoused at a safe house until after dark.

As they exited the back of the truck, Juan noted confident smiles on their faces. No strangers to combat, these were men he had fought alongside in many battles, serving in the Army against both rebels and drug lords. Many comrades fell before the blistering fire of mercenaries hired by drug kingpins, and to a man, they sought vengeance this day.

Rogers told Leach to douse the lights as they heard the men approach. Once all had entered the mineshaft and the blackout curtain secured against the opening, the lights were restored. Mack asked each man to locate and pack the equipment that he would employ in the attack. He then explained the trip up the rope ladders warning them to climb carefully to avoid sway in the ladder. He asked for any questions and hearing none, gave the order to begin the arduous climb. All reached the top level by 0205 hours.

Mack announced, "We are approximately fifteen minutes from the compound. That gives us thirty minutes before we mount the attack. Juan, I want you to pick two men to neutralize any sentries they may have outside. Be careful of cameras, trip wires or anything else that could give away our presence. They will leave at 0215 hours and we'll follow twenty minutes later. Everyone check your radio and remember to whisper, the throat mike will pick up the slightest sound. Remember, other than the sentries, the attack begins at exactly 0300 hours."

XIII

July 20th, 1999, Hacienda Grande, Paz de Rio, Colombia, 0245 hours...

Adam dressed in black and blackened his face and hands. He checked the 14-round magazine in his Glock and put two more magazines in his pockets. The gun was holstered and he left the room with a stiletto in his teeth and a small flashlight in his left hand. He advanced down the central hall and hugged the wall, keeping out of sight of the staircase sentry. When he was just around the corner, still out of sight, he tossed a small lighted cube toward the stairway. The guard reacted quickly and started toward the cube. Adam silently moved behind him, put a stranglehold on him and jabbed the stiletto into his head. The guard collapsed silently in his arms, then Adam dragged the body to a chair arranging it so it appeared the man had fallen asleep. He backtracked and unlocked the front door before heading for the alarm control center. He opened the door to the small room, turned on the light and removed a small electronic device from his pocket. He turned it on and scanned the alarm panel. With six clicks, he disabled the main alarm system and then proceeded to turn off the video surveillance except for the two guardhouses on the road.

He crept noiselessly up the stairs, not sure of the position of the second floor guard. He turned right and moved slowly down the wide hallway. Dim nightlights outlined his target at the hallway junction. He stepped into a recessed doorway and threw another cube back down the hall, the way he had come. The guard left his chair in a flash, but was wary enough to spot Adam in the doorway. They met wordlessly in the middle of the hall and after grappling briefly, Adam smashed the man's vertebrae with a killing chop to the neck. As before, he placed the body back in a chair. He removed the Smith & Wesson automatic from the guard's shoulder holster and headed further down the hallway. He fumbled a bit before successfully picking the deadbolt on the door at the end of the hall.

His felt his heart beating like a trip-hammer as he opened the door and Belinda, dressed in her workout clothes, leapt into his arms. She hugged him hard and then pushed him away as she whispered, "Did you get all three guards?"

As he handed her the guard's gun, he answered softly, "No, I took out the staircase guard and the guy right down this hallway. Where's the third one?"

"Down the hallway, left of the staircase, near Ball and Carter's rooms. Did you get the alarm?"

"Yes," he whispered. "Let's go get them."

Mack's two scouts reached the edge of the compound without being observed. There were three guards and fortunately for the attackers, two of them gave away their positions with the red glow of a cigarette. Coordinating their timing by radio, the scouts circled each of their targets, approached soundlessly and cut their throats before they could utter a sound. The third sentry, undiscovered at that point, heard a rustle and moved quickly toward them. As he crossed an open space, a bullet from a silenced pistol entered his forehead and the only sound was the thump as his body hit the ground. The three were dragged out of sight and after scouring the area thoroughly, the scouts radioed the all clear. They then took up their attack positions and waited for the appointed time.

At 0247 hours, two men laden with backpacks silently edged their way along the storehouse/barracks and stopped at a window. A steel rimmed six-inch suction cup was attached firmly to the glass and a glass cutter was employed to remove a perfect six-inch hole. A tight-fitting hose was inserted and the second man opened the valve on a large cylinder. They quickly took up positions covering the two exits with silenced automatic weapons at the ready. Of the thirteen men inside, only two made it to the door and they stumbled out and collapsed, holding their throats with both hands. No shots were fired. They radioed Juan to report that the warehouse was secured.

At precisely 0300 hours, Mack, Leach, Juan Juarez and Antonio Lopez stepped up to the front door. Mack grasped the door handle, swung the door open and stepped inside. With his silenced Mac 10 at the ready, he advanced into the semi-darkness, motioning the others to follow and spread out. They made their way to the main staircase. With his gun pointed at the figure in the chair, Mack cautiously approached and felt the man's neck. Finding no pulse, he motioned for Antonio to stay and guard this main intersection of the house while he and the others climbed the stairs. They were nearly at the top when they heard gunshots and several soft pops, reports of silenced weapons. Mack made a 'follow-me' signal and they moved cautiously toward the sound. With a pencil light, Mack flashed a prearranged signal to identify them. The signal was returned and they soon saw a figure lying on the floor and two crouching on either side of an open door. Mack moved to Adam's side and nodded to Belinda across the doorway. Adam whispered, "Carter's in there. I think I winged him, but it's too dangerous to rush him. Do you have a tear gas grenade?"

"Yes," replied Mack as he pulled his backpack around and removed four gas masks and two grenades. He tossed a mask to Belinda and gave one to Adam and Juan. When the masks were in place, he pulled the pin and threw the grenade well into the room. Carter responded instantly by firing at the grenade as it landed, hissing tear gas. Less than a minute later, Carter rose and, firing an Uzi, rushed the door. The Uzi was in his hand, still spitting bullets as his body hit the floor. They would later find eight bullets in his body, from three different weapons.

They immediately turned to the door of Sean Ball's room. With two on each side, Adam reached out and tried to open the door. When it did not open, Mack stepped up and fired a short burst from the Mac 10 and the door swung open. Since no shots followed from within the room, they burst in and searched the master suite. Juan discovered a hidden doorway in the back of a closet. Behind the door were stairs. After stationing Leach to cover the second floor, Adam led the group down the narrow stairway that turned at the first floor and led to the basement level. As they started down the second set of stairs, Adam asked Belinda, "Is there any way out of this level?"

She replied, "An elevator goes up two floors and to the roof, but somewhere down here, there's a tunnel to the warehouse. He could escape from there."

Mack said, "Juan, contact the guys watching the warehouse. Tell them that Ball may be heading for the warehouse through a tunnel. If they have any gas left, have them release it now. Tell them to be alert. If anything comes out of that warehouse, *shoot it.*" Juan flipped his radio transmitter button and relayed the message.

Adam held up his hand when they reached the door at the bottom of the steps and said, "Ball is slick. He may have left something behind. Keep your eyes open for booby traps...and let's not stay too close together. After we pass this door, Mack, you and Juan stay to the right. Belinda and I will stay left. Ready?"

Adam grasped the door knob and found it unlocked, so he pushed open the door hard and took a crouched shooting position just inside. He motioned for the others to follow and they moved forward one team at a time, pausing between advances to look and listen. The dim overhead lights cast grotesque shadows, but provided adequate light to see their way. They passed a large diesel generator with its exhaust piped through the wall at ceiling level. Storerooms for supplies of all kinds lined the left wall. Glass doors revealed the contents of each and frost on the glass indicated refrigerators or freezers. Adam and Belinda stopped short when the elevator appeared before them. Would Ball take the elevator back up or proceed to the warehouse? Adam made a quick decision, motioned to Rogers and when he was at his side, said, "You and Juan continue to search the basement and find the tunnel. Belinda and I will take the elevator and check the floors above. We also have to find Santana. Get some more people down here before you go into the tunnel...and wear your masks. If we find anything upstairs, we'll holler."

"We're on it. Be careful. You may want to check the roof, but I'd take some of my people with you. We haven't heard from anyone up there, but he must have someone guarding against an aerial attack."

"Right," replied Adam. "We'll check it out. Let's get to it." Belinda had pressed the elevator button and they stepped away from the door with weapons at the ready, but the elevator was empty. Adam pushed '1' and they exited the elevator cautiously after disabling its controls. Adam said to Belinda, "Let's check with the guard Mack left on this floor and then see about Miguel. He may be hiding under his bed, but we can't risk him sneaking up behind us." Adam flashed the identifying signal as they moved to the central hall. Belinda explained their plan to Antonio and she and Adam moved to each side of Santana's door. Adam tried the doorknob and, finding it locked, fired three quick rounds into the door before kicking it open. Santana yelled, "Don't shoot. I'm unarmed!" They quickly tied his hands and feet and moved back to the central hall. The three ran up the staircase and asked Leach if anyone had appeared from the roof access. He replied in the negative and was told to stay in place unless he heard gunfire from the roof. In that case he should radio Rogers to come to the roof. Adam had decided that, although the elevator went to the roof, they would be sitting ducks if someone were waiting as the doors opened. They climbed a metal stairway and reached a roof access panel. Adam raised it very slowly until he could peek out. Just as he did, they heard the sound of helicopter blades. Adam let the panel down and said, "We'll wait until the bird is almost down. People on the bird *and* the roof will be most distracted at that point, then we'll come out hard. Okay?"

"Okay," said Belinda as she relayed the message to Antonio. He nodded and they waited as the sound of the approaching helicopter grew louder.

When he judged the copter was close to landing, Adam threw open the access panel and leaped onto the roof, with Belinda and Antonio close behind. There were four people on the roof including Sean Ball. They were between the helicopter and Adam's party, looking away from the roof access. Unfortunately for him, one turned and was about to yell when Adam's bullet entered the center of his forehead. Belinda shot a second man as the third and Ball turned and reached for their weapons. Adam downed the third man as he was bringing his pistol to bear on Belinda. They hit the deck to avoid Ball's fire. The helicopter was now down and machine-gun fire from its cabin pinned down Adam, Belinda and Antonio. Ball reached the open side of the copter and was hit in the leg by one of Belinda's bullets just before he pulled himself into the machine. The helicopter roared off the roof, still emitting a steady stream of fire.

As it rose, Adam looked around and spotted a gun position behind him. He ran a zig-zag pattern to a 50mm machine gun and pulled the bolt to chamber a round. With bullets landing around him, he aimed the gun and pulled the trigger. Tracers guided his fire and his bullets found their target, hitting the engine. As the blades slowed, the helicopter began a free fall. It crashed about 300 feet below the summit and exploded in a huge ball of flame that cascaded down the mountainside.

While Antonio and Leach, who had just arrived on the roof, checked the vital signs of the three bandits, Adam returned to Belinda and found her looking down the mountain, a determined look on her bloody face. He took her head gently in his hands and said, "You've been hit. Do you have any wounds other than your face?"

"I don't think so," Belinda replied as she put her hand to her face and examined the blood on it. "I didn't even know I was bleeding."

After reporting Ball's fiery death to Rogers by radio, he took her arm and guided her to the elevator. When they reached her quarters, Adam carefully wiped her face with a cool washcloth. The wound was small, apparently a fragment of a bullet that had ricocheted off the roof. When he completed first aid, he took her in his arms and kissed her gently. She responded by throwing her arms around him, pressing her body to his and kissing him with such fervor that he was more convinced than ever that no other woman could share his life…and he must win back her love!

PART FIVE

July 20th, 1999,
Hotel La Grande, Bogotá,
Colombia, 6:45 p.m....

They had arrived at the hotel in the mid-morning. Adam asked for and received a luxurious, two-bedroom suite. After calling their families with the good news, the first order of business was a shower. Belinda gave a passing thought to inviting him to shower with her, but dismissed it when she suddenly felt unsure of herself. After that devastating evening with Ball, her confidence had been shattered. It returned full force with Adam's arrival and their joint efforts in the attack on Ball. Her love for him was not the question. The question lay within her. Would she have to learn to love herself again before she could return his love? She knew what he would expect when she walked out of the bedroom door...would she, could she, give that to him?

After her shower, she put on the thick, terrycloth robe and was about to leave the bedroom. She stopped suddenly, removed the robe, and dressed in her filthy workout suit. She wiped a tear from her eye and opened the door.

Adam, dressed in a robe, sat facing her bedroom door. His brow lifted slightly when he saw her, but he said nothing.

She went to him, took his hands and led him the sofa. They sat, facing each other. She held his hands firmly and said, "Adam, I don't quite know how to start..."

He placed a finger gently on her lips and said, "Let me begin by saying I love you. I have loved you from the first day I saw you. And in the time we've been apart, I have never stopped loving you. We can't change the past, but I need to tell you about Sela Pierce. When my memory finally came back, I realized that I had not been intimate with her...in any way. I asked her to admit that she had lied to you, but she not only refused, she blamed me for Jeffrey's paralysis and incarceration. That was when she wrote you and verified her lie while bad-mouthing me in every possible way. At that point, I foolishly gave up on convincing you of my innocence. But you *must* believe me, I had nothing to do with her."

"Oh, Adam, I never let myself think about it until I was held captive by Ball. I had time for a lot of soul-searching then, and finally realized that I never gave you a decent chance to explain and I...we...lost so much." Belinda contemplated for a time and with a tear in her eye, finally said, "I have something to tell you. Something that may cast a shadow on our relationship. Over the years, since we parted, I have dated few men...none for any length of time and none that mattered. I was practically a nun until Sean Ball kidnapped me." She paused and obviously found it hard to continue, but with downcast eyes said, "He drugged and raped me many times before I finally escaped, only to be recaptured. After that, I made a deal with him. I agreed to submit to him if he would stop forcing drugs upon me. They were cold submissions that only increased my hatred for him...until one night. I don't know if it was the wine or just giving in to my seemingly hopeless situation. Whatever the reason, I responded with passion that night. When it was over, I fell into the deepest depression of my life. I cried all night and my gravest regret was that I had betrayed *you*. You see, I never considered that I was ever untrue to you until that night. Can you possibly understand that?"

"Yes," replied Adam softly.

"I love you, but I don't feel worthy of you. Whatever you think of me, I must clear this problem within myself. That's why I am wearing my dirty clothes and not the robe I put on after my shower. I want you, but I'm afraid." Belinda put her face in her hands and cried softly.

Adam put his arms around her and said tenderly, "Belinda, you are the strongest woman I know. What you have endured would have destroyed anyone else. Of course, you have issues. Of course, you need time to sort out those issues. And, of course, I will be here for you, to help you, to rekindle our love. We will go as slowly as you need to go. Just let my love light your way."

She smiled through her tears and asked, "Can we lie down and just sleep in each others arms?" As they lay together, Belinda said, "After that night, Ball begged and pleaded with me for a repeat performance, but it never happened. Then you came into the dining room that night. You will never know what it meant to me... to *see you*. I literally arose from the dead."

Adam kissed her lightly. "If only I could have made it sooner. When I think of your suffering, I wish I could have given Ball the slow, painful death he deserved, but that wouldn't change what you went through."

"No, but now, I'm safe in your arms. If I have a nightmare, remind me of that."

They slept soundly for almost five hours. Belinda was the first to wake. She gazed at his face, and love and desire raged in her mind and body. She slipped from the bed, took another shower and donned the robe. When Adam stirred, she put her arms around him and kissed him hungrily. He responded and slipped his arms around her, under the robe, feeling her naked body. She thrust her hips against his as they lay side by side. She could feel his hardness pressing against her and with rising passion, took him in her hand. As she drew him to her, she suddenly stopped, pushed herself away and cried, "Oh, God, what is wrong with me? I am so sorry...I don't know what I want."

Adam, trying desperately to recover from the peak of desire, said in a shaky voice, "It's all right...just holding you is all I need. Everything will happen in good time."

"Oh, I hope so. And I hope you can be patient with me, until that time comes."

Adam heard this as a soulful plea for help. His response was to put his arms around her and whisper, "As long as it takes, I'm here to love you, any way you need or want." He got up, went to the bath and returned with a cold washcloth. He placed it over her eyes and said, "This will wash the red out and restore the beauty to those eyes. I'm going to throw on some clothes and go downstairs for a minute, then we'll find a drink and some grub. I'm starved." He returned with a sweat suit with 'Bogotá, Colombia" inscribed on the breast. He handed it to her and said, "This is the only thing available, but you'll look great in it."

Belinda found a smile. "Thanks, I love it."

They met in the hotel dining room at seven p.m. and ordered a drink to celebrate their victory. Before the glasses were empty, the liquor took effect. Leach said with the slightest of slurs, "Anybody remember *eating*? You know, you put food on a fork and aim it at the biggest hole in your face?"

"Barely," replied Mack. "We'd better order soon or we'll all be under the table. I wish Amy were here to celebrate with us."

Adam looked at Mack and said, "Hey, why don't you call her. Have her hop on a plane in the morning and we'll have a blast tomorrow night. We'll be busy with Oakes most of the day and when she gets in, we can do it up right."

"Great idea, Adam," said Belinda. "Amy truly deserves to be a part of the victory party."

"Done," said Mack, rising from his chair. "Order me the biggest T-bone on the menu, medium rare…I'll call her right now."

Mack returned to the table with a smug look. Amy would make reservations and be there for the party. The food arrived and put a serious dent in the small talk as the diners attacked their plates with cave-man ferocity.

When the dishes were cleared, Adam said, "Let's talk a bit about tomorrow. Although the CIA thoroughly, if unofficially, endorsed our mission, it may be prudent for us to omit details such as who shot or otherwise took care of whom. Other than that, I believe we should be forthright on what went down." No objection was voiced.

Back in their suite, Belinda was quiet as they watched the news on TV. At its conclusion, she asked Adam if he minded if they slept in separate bedrooms. The disappointed look on his face betrayed his feelings, but he readily agreed.

Sunshine lit the room as Belinda opened her eyes. Yellow rays etched a delicate pattern on the wall by her bed. When she got her bearings, her relationship with Adam leaped into her consciousness. What had seemed so difficult yesterday, took on a totally different look. She felt her confidence flowing back, like a river, flooding her with energy and vigor. In the bath, the mirror reflected not red, but bright, shiny eyes and the return of an eagerness to her face. She whistled in the shower, dressed in her new sweat suit and greeted Adam as though yesterday hadn't happened.

Middleton Oakes arrived with Travis Campbell at 9:30 a.m. They met in Mack and Leach's suite and after coffee was distributed, Oakes said, "You guys did a helluva job up there. I called the local gendarmes right after I got your radio message and they were most pleased. Nine dead bodies, two wounded and the rest tied up neatly with a ribbon and bow. These boys like that kind of takedown…when somebody else does their dirty work. I have been instructed to congratulate you on behalf of Director Rains. He wants to meet with you when you return to the states. Now for the really good news. I don't know if you realize it, but there's a substantial reward on Ball's head…half a million. Who should they make the check out to?"

Without hesitation, Adam spoke up, "Make half to McKinley and Amy Rogers and the other half to Alfred Leach."

"Hey, wait a minute, Adam," interjected Mack. "You've spent a small fortune on this project…and taken most of the risks. We can't take this money."

"Yes you can," countered Adam. "I can well afford the enterprise that took out Ball, but more importantly, rescued Belinda and brought us back together." As he said this he gave Belinda a warm smile.

"Hold on," said Leach. "I am hereby making an effort, if somewhat half-hearted, to force some or all of this dough on Adam. Failing that, I'd like to place half of my half in trust for Adam and Linda Rogers, for their education." Turning to Mack, he concluded with, "And I ain't takin' no for an answer."

"Enough," said Oakes with a smile. "When you finally decide who gets the money, let me know. Now, I'd like to debrief you on the details of this operation. Any objection to my turning on the tape recorder to ensure an accurate report?" Oakes received approval from the group and proceeded to interrogate each individual.

At noon, debriefing concluded, Adam and Belinda excused themselves and walked, hand-in-hand to a charming, old-world restaurant where they washed down portions of tender veal and exotic vegetables with a fine vintage wine. As they sipped the last of the wine, Adam said with the broad smile he'd worn ever since Belinda's greeting that morning, "I have an idea for this afternoon…let's go shopping. Your wardrobe needs work, to say the least, and I could use a few things."

Belinda smiled and said in a happy voice, "What a splendid idea. I hope you don't plan to spend all your money on me. I am not a poor waif you've taken off the street, you know."

"Would you, fair maiden, deny me the most pleasurable task that I have undertaken, in public that is, for these many years?" quipped Adam.

"When you put it that way, I would be a horrible fiend to deny you such pleasure. Lead on, oh mighty corruptor of fair maidens."

Adam failed to realize the difficulty he had brought upon himself. Absolutely everything this woman tried on gave her a look that should grace the cover of a magazine. He offered to buy everything. Belinda's cooler head prevailed, however and she limited the purchases to four outfits and some casual clothes. To her relief, Adam headed for the men's department when she began shopping for the more personal items. She picked up a sheer teddy that would leave no part of her body, or her intent, to the imagination. Her renewed confidence slipped away as she thought of presenting herself in that teddy. The flippant attitude and breezy sarcasm that had returned for a day suddenly seemed out of place. Was she able to be her old self only until she considered opening herself to Adam? Was the ice maiden back? And, just how long would his patience suffer her rejecting him in the bedroom? She put down the teddy and bought a pair of elegant, but opaque, silk pajamas.

She managed to put on her best smile when she rejoined Adam. It was nearly five o'clock when they returned to the hotel and dressed to welcome Amy and get on with the festivities.

Al Leach poured himself a second martini from the larger-than-life shaker and turned to the assembled warriors. "I propose a toast to end all toasts. Never have so few *Davids* taken on and defeated so many *Goliaths*. I am proud to be a member of this tough bunch that tamed a mountain and the giant perched on top."

"Hear, hear," shouted Mack Rogers as he put his arm around his wife, Amy. "And let us applaud our fearless leader and hero Adam, and the fabulous Belinda, who we welcome back to the fold after her horrible experience."

Amy said, "I'll drink to both toasts, but I'm dying to hear the gory details of this marvelous coup."

"It began with Adam infiltrating Ball's camp," said Mack. "Why don't you tell us the whole story, Adam?"

"If you insist." Adam told how, with the help of the CIA in Miami, he was hired as a pilot to run drugs into the United States from Ball's new base in Mexico and his entrée into Ball's kingdom, disguised as he had been taught by Belinda.

Mack related his and Leach's adventure in the mines and their attack on Ball's complex. Adam talked of Belinda's release and her part in neutralizing the interior guards and taking out Carter. He asked Belinda to tell the story from that point and she recalled their two-pronged attack, the fight on the roof and Adam's shooting down the helicopter.

Amy said, "Wow, that could be made into an action movie. What did you do with those people afterwards?"

"We didn't want to be identified," said Mack. "So we tied up anyone that was mobile, and made our exit back down through the mines. The local police were making their way up the road as we left the compound. Tupo met us at the base of the mountain with the truck. We drove back here in early morning light, cleaned up and then slept away the day."

Cocktails flowed, hors d'oeuvres stowed and stories told. By the time Amy's curiosity about the takedown and rescue was satisfied, the volume of the participants' voices had increased by many decibels. Adam, sensing the rapid decline in sobriety among the revelers, suggested they order dinner. Generous helpings of Chilean sea bass drenched in rich lobster sauce with all the trimmings had a sobering effect on the celebrants and the sound soon returned to near-normal levels.

Mack announced that he and Amy would spend Thursday touring the area and fly back on Friday. Adam, Belinda and Leach would leave the next morning. Adam convinced Mack, with Amy's reluctant approval, to accept half of the bounty for him and Amy, and a quarter for their children. They both hugged Leach, and to everyone's surprise, he returned Mack's hug without a smart remark.

Amy took Belinda aside. "We all felt, from the beginning, you and Adam were really made for each other. I never had a doubt that if you accepted Adam back, he would jump at the chance. Are you back together for good?"

The last remark struck a chord in Belinda. Had Amy's intuition recognized her difficulty in resurrecting her romance with Adam? She decided to level with her. "I certainly hope so. Just between us, Amy, I am having some problems being the person Adam knew before. He is the greatest, but I need some time to get my head straight. I hope to God he's willing to wait for that to happen."

Amy took Belinda's hand and said softly, "You know he will. Patience is one of the virtues of real love…like yours. I know you will be honest with him and he will help you put the horrible memories behind you." Amy gave her a hug as she said, "I know this will work and I will *always* be there for you."

Belinda returned the embrace and brushed away a tear. "Thank you, Amy, you'll never know how much that means to me. I promise to keep you informed, and maybe even cry on your shoulder now and then."

"I would be honored…anytime. What are your plans now?"

"We're flying back to Miami tomorrow. Dennis Rains is flying down for a meeting. He wants to debrief us in person. Then I…er…we fly home to Atlanta. My practice was left in the lurch." Belinda thought, 'The question of whether I still *have* any clients, perhaps should be whether I'm capable of *treating* them.' "I have to straighten that out before anything can happen with Adam. I know he needs to tend some fires at home, too…so…"

"Just don't let too much time go by…apart. When the right thing comes along, you have to grab it. And you and I need to keep in touch."

"Let's make a pact," Belinda said, "to talk at least once a week. If Friday rolls around and we haven't spoken, one of us must pick up the phone and find out what's happening. Is it a deal?"

Amy put out her hand. "Put 'er there, partner."

The party broke up at 9:30. With adrenaline flowing like water for over a week, particularly in the last two days, the normal letdown drained the energy from all of them.

Adam and Belinda, back in their suite, looked at each other in that special way reserved for lovers. She did not resist when he took her in his arms and she kissed him longingly, but still withheld the passion that lurked beneath the surface. His smile, before they retired to separate bedrooms, assured her that he was, indeed, a patient man.

Another sunny morning brought Belinda's mood of yesterday roaring back. They had breakfast with Mack and Amy in the hotel dining room before checking out and taking a limo to the airport with Leach. They all boarded American Airlines Flight # 916 at 10:17 a.m. and landed in Miami just after 2 a.m. Big-spender Leach, with $125,000 coming from the Ball reward, continued on to Newark in a first-class cabin.

Adam and Belinda were met by CIA agents Scheffer and Munsen. Abby gave Adam a long hug before meeting and hugging Belinda. Scheffer offered warm handshakes. They were met by a black Suburban and driven to the CIA headquarters downtown.

Rains greeted them enthusiastically when they arrived in the conference room. As soon as the five were seated, Rains began, "Great job, you two. An amazing feat to defeat Ball's legions with no casualties on your side. Splendid work."

Adam said simply, "Thank you."

Rains continued, "In cooperation with the Army and the local police, we were allowed to search Ball's complex immediately after you left. Although little data was in plain English, our code-crackers quickly solved Ball's code. It seems that JoAnn Cleveland, although confined to the mental institution, was able to communicate and transfer substantial funds to Ball. The message contained instructions to eliminate certain parties that had broken up the Right Brigade. You two were at the top of that list. The fact that he chose to kidnap rather than kill Colonel Jackson was undoubtedly for personal reasons. That list also contained the names of General Rayburn, Senator Hawthorne, Anita Warwick, James Young, Alfred Leach, and McKinley and Amy Rogers. Is this any surprise to you?"

"No," replied Belinda. "Those are all the people involved in the Right Brigade takedown. The question remains, is Ball's death the end of this vendetta…or will others take his place?"

"That's what I want to discuss with you. Ball had contracted with a terrorist group from Libya for the downing of Rayburn's plane. We believe we have enough information to...shall we say *neutralize* them?"

"I think we must plug the leak that allowed JoAnn to set this up," said Adam in a stern voice. "She probably knows about Ball's death, and what's to stop her from finding others to finish the task Ball started?"

"I have taken steps to prevent just that," said Rains. "I have sent a team of agents, with the cooperation of the FBI, to the hospital. Until further notice, she will have contact with no one that is not employed by either the FBI or us. We will absolutely cordon her off from the outside world. We also have put surveillance on her son, Jeffrey. We are limiting his contacts and monitoring his conversations. Hopefully this will end the threat, but I must warn you to be ever vigilant. I know you have significant resources and I suggest you employ some security...other than the electronic kind."

"Thank you, Director Rains," said Adam. "I hadn't planned on hiring personal protection, but I think you're absolutely right and I know just the person to head up such a detail."

As Adam and Belinda were being driven back to the airport, she said. "I bet I know who you have in mind to lead that security detail."

"Oh, and who might that be?"

"Leach, of course," she replied.

"Of course, the job fits him like a glove. I hope he won't think I'm giving him a handout when I make him an offer."

"That, my dear, depends on how you do it. As an industrial psychologist, I could be retained to prepare a *most* professional proposal that even the likes of Leach could not possibly refuse."

"Consider yourself hired. Now, I'd like to talk about us. After we check out your condo in Atlanta...have you thought about what comes next?"

"Yes, I have thought, and thought. I must admit, I have no definite answers. I have to do something about my practice. I'm not sure I want to slide back into my... *pre-Ball* routine."

"Would you like a suggestion?" asked Adam.

"Shoot. I'm open to any and all good ideas."

"I would like to stay with you, in your spare bedroom, until you clean up your business. Then we fly to Minnesota and I will introduce you to my life there. No commitments. I also have a spare bedroom. Meanwhile, I will romance you in the most formal and judicious manner."

Belinda was quiet for a moment. Finally, she said, "How could a girl refuse such an elegant offer? But can you spare the time?"

Adam looked into her eyes and said softly, "You are the most important project in my life, so I can and will spare whatever time it takes." He smiled. "It's settled then?"

"Yes, and thank you, for everything." As she said this, the CIA vehicle pulled up to the terminal. Belinda asked, "What time is our flight?"

Adam looked at his watch. "In just over 30 minutes, so we'll have to run for it. Our luggage is checked through, so all we have to do is check in. Are you ready?"

"You bet," said Belinda, her face reflecting the return of her competitive spirit. They raced through the terminal and were in their seats ten minutes before they closed the cabin door.

II

July 22nd, 1999, Atlanta, GA, 9:45 p.m....

They took a cab to Belinda's condo and tears came to her eyes as she walked through the front door. "I never thought I'd be so happy to see this place again," she said.

"I can understand that," said Adam. "I was here right after you disappeared. I went over the house with a fine-tooth comb. I found your message to the general on your computer."

She put her arms around him and asked softly, "It's over now, Adam, isn't it?"

"I believe so, but we can't let our guard down...not until we're sure all the people that were involved are put away...or dead. For now, my sweet, relax. In case you don't know it, you and I are by no means easy marks."

"I guess I can't disagree with that," Belinda said as she looked around the room. "God, this place is filthy. Some housecleaning is called for, but we'll just crash tonight and hit it hard in the morning. Maybe you'd like to volunteer for some of that while I attend to my other business?"

Adam bowed low and said, "Your every wish is my command, m'lady. May I ask for your car keys and the directions to the nearest market? I will slip away at dawn and fill the larder."

"Thanks for the reminder. Before bed, I will throw out some food that's been rotting in the refrigerator. Then, you may do some re-stocking. Are you adequate as a grocery boy?"

"Absolutely. While you're cleaning out the debris, I will take inventory."

The fragrant aroma of fresh coffee awakened Belinda's senses the next morning. She looked over at her clock radio, 6:30 a.m. She supposed Adam had just gotten up and would be leaving for the market. She put on a robe and following the scent, padded quietly to the kitchen. There he was, fully dressed in a sport shirt and khakis, unloading a grocery bag on the counter. Sensing her presence, he turned and smiled, "Good morning, darling. I trust you slept well?"

"The best, for a very long time. Your support had a lot to do with it. In fact, you have been so supportive, I have decided to lessen your load by assisting in some basic cleaning of these quarters. I will dress, we will eat and we will fall in for duty."

After the breakfast dishes were loaded in the dishwasher, Belinda filled a small pail with hot, soapy water and added a sponge. She said, as she handed it to Adam, "OK, barracks boy, what'll it be, kitchen or bathrooms?"

"I'll take the bathrooms, they're smaller," replied Adam.

"Good, just remember I still outrank you and my white glove inspections have been characterized as hard-ass."

"My nickname is Mr. Clean. Your gloves shall remain spotless after gliding over my immaculate surfaces. Now, I must get on with my task." By 11 a.m., the entire residence sparkled. Belinda was about to retire to her home office and begin listening to her messages when Adam said, "Let's call Leach first."

"Do you mind if I get on the line with you? I may be able to put in a comment or two to assure him he is really needed."

"It wouldn't hurt to lay a little feminine charm on him," said Adam as he checked his address book and moved to the speaker phone.

Leach answered after the second ring with "Yeah?"

"That's not a very friendly greeting, but it sounds like you," said Adam. "How are you, Al?"

"Hey, Adam," said Leach in a more upbeat voice. "I'm great, going to the Yankee game tomorrow and the Mets on Sunday. I never had it so good. What about you guys?"

"We're terrific," interjected Belinda, "but we miss you already."

"Belinda, my love, when are you gonna dump that bird and run off with me?" asked Leach.

"Well, you can hardly vie for my hand out there in New Jersey," said Belinda. "Maybe you need to be a little closer."

Adam cut in, "Al, I'd like to talk to you about doing something for me…us. In our meeting with our friend from Washington, he suggested that although the risk may be reduced, we should employ some serious security. When he said this, both Belinda and I immediately thought of you. We'd like you to consider hiring and managing a security force to take care of that little matter."

"You just want me to set something up?"

"No, we want you to set it up and run it, permanently. It would involve both my company and us personally," said Adam. "And I know you could learn to be a dedicated Twins and Vikings fan."

"Are you kidding? Me, move from the Big Apple out there to the sticks? You must want to pay me a lot of money or give me Belinda. Which is it?"

"Let's me see, which would I rather offer? I have to give that some serious thought." Adam paused and finally said, "I guess I'll opt for paying you an exorbitant salary…say a hundred grand?"

"Shit, you trying to give me a handout?"

"No, Al, we really believe you're the right man for the job," said Belinda, "and I'd really like having you around."

"You guys are really rotten, throwing money *and* Belinda at me… both of which I truly love. I'll give it some thought."

Adam replied, "Great, we'll be going up to Minnesota in a few days. Think it over. If you have any questions, you know my number. We really need you, Al."

"Don't give me any goddamn sob-story. I said I'd think it over. Bye."

Belinda laughed, "Typical Leach. Think he'll do it?"

"Yeah, under that tough façade lurks a true friend. Now, is there anything I can help you with to get the business under control?"

"Not right now. Let me listen to messages, return some calls and I'll keep your offer in mind as I organize this mess. I plan to talk to each of my clients, give them a name of a replacement, but ask them to keep me in the loop. Gives me the option to pick them up again after a brief hiatus."

"If they ask you to define *brief,* what will you tell them?"

Belinda reflected for a short time. "Probably three to six months.

If I can't determine what I want to do with my life in that time, it's unlikely I'd be much help to them."

"Well, go to it, babe. I'll put together a light lunch and be the man-servant here as long as you need me."

She kissed him affectionately on the forehead and turned to her task. Belinda had retired from active duty with the Army in 1994 as a full or 'bird' colonel. She received her Ph.D. in psychology a year later from Duke University. Her practice as an industrial psychologist had grown steadily over the next three years and she had begun to limit her client list to assure time to properly serve each client.

At four-thirty, Belinda shed her reading glasses and said loudly, "Adam?" He appeared in a minute and she said, "I just had an idea. It's Friday afternoon and I won't be able to make any contacts over the weekend, so why don't we run down and see my family?"

"Hey, I'd really like to meet them."

"Fine, I'll call them right away…and see if they're available for company."

After loading their luggage in Belinda's cherry-red Cadillac STS, they were on the road by eight o'clock the next morning. They made the 240-mile journey to Thomasville, a quaint southern town of 18,000, in just under five hours including a brief lunch break.

Melanie Jackson Ford was the first one out of the front door and she ran to the car and hugged Belinda with unbridled enthusiasm. The sisters cried with joy and were soon surrounded by her three children and their parents John and Mattie Jackson. Adam was given perfunctory hugs, but the center of attention was their long-lost daughter, sister and aunt. Belinda looked at her childhood home with teary eyes, turned to Adam following her up the walk, and squeezing his arm, told him, "I never expected to get back here. If it weren't for you, I never would have walked up this sidewalk again."

Her seven-year-old nephew Jason made a face. "Ugh, they're kissing."

The house was nearly a hundred years old with traditional white pillars supporting a balcony that stretched across the entire front of the house. Red brick walls with white shutters and trim, the brick virtually hidden by a forest of ivy. Dappled sunshine mottled the lawn as the breeze moved the leaves of huge trees dominating the large yard. The effect was that of a giant mirror ball spinning above. The house had been purchased by John Jackson's grandfather during the Great Depression and now housed its third generation of Jacksons.

The family settled in the expansive living room, furnished with priceless, but surprisingly comfortable antiques. Tea was served and the rest of the afternoon passed quickly as Belinda and Adam related their adventures leading up to and including Belinda's rescue and the demise of Ball's empire.

Melanie's husband Vinton arrived just after four o'clock. Although his manners were impeccable, he had the winning ways of an old shoe. He and Adam liked each other from the start.

Belinda expected a pleasant family dinner, but her mother had other plans. With a mere twenty-four-hour notice, the woman had put together a ball that would make Scarlett O'Hara proud.

Adam and Belinda were kept in the dark until her father looked at his watch and announced, "My, my, it's five o'clock already. Time to dress for dinner. Cocktails will be served promptly at six-thirty and I know you two will want to wash away the grime from that dusty road. Shall we be off?"

Adam's only choice was a navy blue suit, white shirt and silver tie, packed in case of Sunday church. Belinda had had neither the time nor materials for proper hair and makeup since they came together. When she went up to her bedroom, a hairdresser was waiting. Her auburn hair was cut and styled, her makeup applied with expertise and care. And then there was the dress. Belinda's body was voluptuous, but not to the extent of the nudes of classic painters. She could appear very sexy or prim and proper. The shimmering blue gown she wore this evening complemented her form while portraying a sense of elegance.

She literally took Adam's breath away. He took her hands in his as they met in the upstairs hallway, looked at her from head to toe and said for the first time in eight long years, "You are undoubtedly the most beautiful woman I have ever seen."

Belinda did a little curtsey as she replied, "Thank you, kind sir. May I say that you are more handsome than any man I have introduced to this family. Shall we make our grand entrance?" They walked arm-in-arm down the large curved staircase. As they looked up, a hush came over the family and assembled guests until one by one they began to clap their hands. By the time Adam and Belinda, totally stunned by the size of the crowd, reached the bottom of the stairs, it had become thunderous applause. Over fifty people, dressed to the hilt, greeted them and toasted Belinda repeatedly. Champagne, cocktails and dinner were followed by the ball. Music from the 40s through the 80s was played by a ten-piece band and sung beautifully by Melissa Ford. Adam danced with a number of eager dance partners as Belinda's dance card was full to overflowing…she was indeed the belle of the ball.

The party ended at midnight. Adam and Belinda, once again, slept in separate bedrooms. Sunday dawned bright and promised to provide more than adequate heat and humidity. With that in mind, a tour of the countryside began at 9 a.m. with a breakfast stop at ten and a return for the eleven-thirty service at the First Methodist Church. They took a late lunch in the Jackson air-conditioned sunroom.

Dr. Jackson proposed a toast. "To Adam Packard, a man among men. Without his brave intervention, our beloved Belinda would not be at this table today. I salute you and should you wish to become a part of this family, we would all be honored."

Belinda's scarlet blush was apparent to all. She looked at everyone, except Adam and at last blurted, "Thank you, Father, but Adam and I are…not ready to declare anything quite that permanent. We are sort of getting reacquainted."

The uncomfortable silence that followed was broken by Adam, who cleared his throat. "Thank you for those kind words, Dr. Jackson. As Belinda said, we are feeling our way at this point. I must say, however, that some day, nothing would please me more than to become part of this fine family." Belinda, barely recovered from the first one, blushed again. Tearful goodbyes were said and they were back on the road at two-thirty.

Monday and Tuesday passed rapidly as Belinda completed her contacts with her client base. Adam made reservations on Northwest Airlines for Wednesday morning.

III

July 28th, 1999, Minneapolis-St. Paul International Airport, 1:15 p.m....

Adam's family provided a joyful greeting at the airport and whisked them away to the family 'farm' in Afton. When they entered the big Suburban, everyone talked at once until Adam put up his hand and fairly shouted, "Hold it! We want to tell you everything that happened, but please, one question at a time." The story had been outlined by the time they disembarked from the truck and was completed over cocktails and a splendid, home-cooked dinner.

"How long can you two stay?" asked his mother.

"I'm not sure," replied Adam. "We'll spend the day tomorrow, then if you'll give us a ride over to Hudson to pick up my car, we'll drive to my house on Friday morning. I'm anxious to give Belinda a tour of the house and the business. We will play it by ear from there."

They spent an enjoyable family day on Thursday and picked up Adam's BMW on the way back from the boat. George and Catherine kept an upscale twenty-four-foot pontoon boat at the Hudson marina and they tooled down the scenic St. Croix River. The day was beautiful and they lunched at the Steamboat Inn at Prescott, Wisconsin. The restaurant looks across shimmering blue water at the bluffs of Minnesota and the point where the St. Croix flows into the great Mississippi.

Adam and Belinda set off for Adam's home in Edina at nine on Friday morning.

As they traveled west on I-494, he thought about the house. He'd lived there for six months before moving to the Sandells' for some minor remodeling and major redecorating. He shuddered involuntarily as he recalled that first night in the renovated house...the explosion, his hurried flight and all that was to come. Less than two months ago, but it seemed like a lifetime. He turned into his street and came upon the construction. Sandells' house had been transformed from a burned-out skeleton to a clean framework of new lumber. As they drove by, Adam pointed it out to Belinda and said, "That's the house I had been staying in for nearly a month. It was destroyed because the assassin believed that I was inside. I moved my things to my own house just three hours before the attack."

"This isn't easy for you, is it?" asked Belinda with concern.

"No, but I'll get through it. Having you with me is making a huge difference. I want to put the past behind and have you see the things I treasure in the best possible light."

As they pulled into Adam's driveway, Belinda took in the graceful yet solid architectural treatment of the large, but not imposing, house. Two huge pillars supported the entrance portico and its roof extended back to a large, flanged overhang on the house proper. The all-stone house was complemented by a high roof of hand-split shingles with four dormers breaking up the expanse. The three-car garage was set back, but attached to the rear portion of the house. The brick-paver circle driveway ran through the portico and back to the garage. Adam stopped under the portico, came around, took Belinda by the hand and said. "Your first entry shall be through the front door, so we'll do the grand tour first, and see to the luggage later."

"Adam, it's beautiful, and if the interior is half as impressive as the exterior, it is truly fit for a king…and perhaps a queen," she finished with a wink.

Adam had insisted that the decorating theme should not be frilly, but at the same time, not have the air of a men's club. The interior designer had accomplished the neutrality he sought with both fashion and flair. The foyer was large, two stories high, and featured a wide, flowing staircase to the second floor. The great room was straight back with the dining room and kitchen on the left and a library/study and master suite on the right. After exploring the main floor, they climbed the stairway hand in hand and Belinda marveled at the three complete bedroom suites and an unfurnished room suitable for a second office or craft sanctuary. They returned to the main floor and Adam opened the patio door to the stone terrace that curved around two wide steps to a large kidney-shaped swimming pool. The surrounding fence was of white wood lodged between stone pillars. Boulders formed a graduated wall at one end of the pool and water flowed through them before cascading into the pool. The backdrop of landscaping, evergreens and flowers gave a softening effect to the entire scene.

"I'm overwhelmed," exclaimed Belinda.

Adam didn't say a word as he led her back into the house and into the master suite. He went to the large built-in dresser, opened a drawer and took something out. He turned and opened his hand revealing a sparkling diamond ring. He said huskily, "You once wore this ring and I know we haven't discussed the future in any detail, but my dream is that you will want to wear it again and spend the rest of your life with me…here, in this house."

She took his face tenderly between her fingers and said, "There's nothing in the world I'd rather do. There are issues I have to deal with… and if I can do that, I can see myself living here, and loving it…and you." She put her arms around him as she found his lips with hers. They kissed hungrily, but the moment was one of deep love and affection and did not lead to the inviting king-size bed, a few steps away.

**July 30th, 1999,
Packard Electronics, Inc.,
Bloomington, MN,
10:10 a.m....**

Adam showed Belinda into his private office after a half-hour tour of the research lab, manufacturing facility and office. She had been formally introduced to more than a dozen people out of seventy-five employees of the firm, but everyone they passed welcomed Adam back with incredible warmth and friendship. She said, "It's a gorgeous office, Adam, but after seeing what you did with the house and the rest of this plant, I'm not surprised in the least. We've never really had a chance to measure each other's taste, but I have to say, yours is truly exceptional."

While holding a chair for her, Adam said, "Thank you. I've always felt compliments can be measured two ways, by volume, the number one receives, or by quality, the degree of taste or style displayed by the person offering the compliment. Needless to say, I value any compliment from you, *very* highly."

"I'm glad, because I have some other very positive observations," said Belinda. "The entire company is remarkable. The architectural touches and physical layout of the building, the decorating all seem to just...flow. The cleanliness of both the plant and employees are all outstanding. But do you know what impressed me the most?"

"No, but if I keep my mouth shut, I bet you'll enlighten me."

"And you would be correct, sir," said Belinda, ignoring the jibe. "The quality of your employees and their superb attitude is obvious. When you walked through each department, you were welcomed back as 'Adam', not 'Mr. Packard.' But more important, the *way* they greeted you...with a unique blend of friendship and respect. I have worked with companies large and small and have seldom seen relations as good as you seem to have here. Now if you can accept all that and your hat still fits, you're too good to be true."

"Now *I'm* impressed! Before you start erecting a statue of me, I have a confession to make. If I have a talent, it's the ability to pick people or firms that are the best in their field and bring them together to solve the problem at hand. The way you treat people makes all the difference. We respect employees, suppliers and customers alike and that, my dear, is the secret of our success."

Belinda clapped her hands vigorously. "Bravo! If you tire of electronics, I'll put you on the road giving seminars on running a better business."

Adam took a deep bow and said with a smile, "In spite of the success I've been fortunate enough to achieve, my life was still somehow empty...missing something I could never quite put my finger on. Now I realize it was you. I was always aware that I missed you, but never knew just how much. I guess I also missed the excitement and danger we faced when we battled the Right Brigade...and in the last two months. Maybe we'll have to open a detective agency and chase bad guys at some point..."

"All the time we've spent together, since we first met, we have never been *out* of danger. I have never discerned a bored look on your face, but now that I've been warned, I shall watch you carefully for any sign of discontent."

"The excitement you bring to me is all I need," said Adam, taking her hand. "I simply want to be with you...and live happily ever after."

"Let's just see what happens," said Belinda in a serious tone. "How about that tour you promised me?"

"In a moment," said Adam, leafing through his messages and selecting one. "This is from our proposed chief of security. I want to deal with this right away." Adam dialed the number on the message and after a pause, said, "Al, what are you up to?" He listened for a minute. "Okay, I'll send a first-class ticket overnight. We'll expect you on Monday. Are you good with that?" Another pause. "Great, see you at the airport." Adam looked up and said with a broad grin, "He's on board."

After arranging for Leach's flight, they drove through the Bloomington strip and took the River Drive up to Franklin Avenue, then drove into downtown Minneapolis. Adam parked in the garage at the IDS Center and they walked through the skyways connecting all the major downtown buildings. Back in the car, they drove through the University of Minnesota on the way to St. Paul. Adam drove by the State Capitol with its gleaming gold horses atop the building, guarding the base of the dome. They stopped at the Cathedral, the landmark Catholic Church of the area. From its vantage point on the hill, they viewed the downtown area and the Mississippi River. Lunch was at Forepaugh's, a restored Victorian mansion overlooking historic Irvine Park…a neighborhood of other restored Victorian mansions. They drove out scenic Shepard Road which wound along the river to Fort Snelling, where they viewed the stone walls of the round fortress built to withstand Indian attacks in the 1800s. Leaving the past, Adam pulled onto I-494 and drove past the airport to the largest shopping center in United States, the Mall of America. They parked and Adam pointed out the huge amusement center surrounded by four major stores and countless shops selling goods and vittles of every possible description.

He said nothing to Belinda, but throughout the tour, Adam kept an eye on the rearview mirror for a tail and was relieved when none appeared.

They arrived back at the house at 3:45 and sank gratefully into the deep cushions of the sofa in the great room.

Belinda sighed gratefully, "Adam, I really enjoyed the day. The Twin Cities are quite interesting. They seem to radiate the good points of the really big cities, with a small town flavor…how big are they?"

"The seven-county area has a population of over three million," said Adam, "And you're right, it does feel like a smaller place. Big in theater and the arts, too." At 5:30, Adam scrounged around in the freezer and came up with two thick filets and a package of frozen vegetables. He thawed the steaks in the microwave and dunked them in his special marinade. He put the vegetables on low heat before he mixed a shaker of Bombay martinis. As he handed a glass to Belinda, he said, "I thought about this day, over and over. I just about gave up on the belief it would ever happen, but here we are."

"I know. I tried to put you out of my mind, but it never worked. Now, when I see what you've built, and better understand the kind of man you are, I'm so proud of you. Every day we spend together, I become more comfortable…just being with you. Then, I realize that the comfort zone I'm creating is the very thing that is fueling my fears. I'd give anything to crawl into your bed and make love, but something gets in the way. I'm even starting to think about seeing someone. Know any good shrinks?"

"No, but I know someone who does. Are you serious about this?"

"I guess we should give it a bit more time. The 'physician, heal thyself' theory hasn't worked so far, but who knows, maybe tomorrow or the next day…"

Adam brought the steaks in from the grill and laid a plate before her. "Maybe a good meal will fuel some good vibes, and erase some fears. Shall we give it a go?"

Belinda agreed, and ate heartily, but the fears that she could not comprehend continued to plague her. She faced the fact that this night and those in the foreseeable future would be spent in a separate bedroom…separated from the man she loved…and couldn't love.

August 2nd, 1999,
Minneapolis-St. Paul
International Airport, 1:45
p.m....

Alfred Leach walked down the concourse in a dark blue, short-sleeved shirt, navy slacks and black sneakers. He rolled a carry-on with a briefcase hung over the handle. Adam thought Leach looked more like a drug dealer or hit-man than the newly appointed security chief of a multi-million-dollar corporation. Adam and Belinda greeted him warmly and Adam said, "We have to go down a flight to pick up your luggage."

"What luggage?" asked Leach. "It's all here. I'm not a goddamn fashion plate like you."

"That's true," said Adam, "but I would think you'd bring a bit more…you do plan on staying, don't you?"

"Sure, but since you were in such a freaking hurry." He turned to Belinda and said, "See how I clean up my language when you're around?" To Adam he continued, "I plan to set this thing up in a jiffy. When I'm satisfied the right people are in place, I'll go back and tie up the loose ends in Jersey. Okay by you?"

"Sounds like a plan," said Adam. "While you're setting up, you'll stay with us. We'll worry about something permanent later."

"You sure you got room?"

Belinda replied with a smile, "It'll be tight, but we'll squeeze you in."

When they drove up to the house, Leach gaped and said, "Yeah, you'll squeeze me in all right. This is the fanciest f…freaking house I've seen since Atlanta. Maybe I should be 'the man who came to dinner.' Stay here for the duration, ya' know."

"We'll see about that, Al. First we have to determine if you're housebroken," said Adam. When they had shown the house and settled

Leach in one of the upstairs bedrooms, they met for a drink in the kitchen eating area. Adam said, "We'll rent you a car first thing in the morning, then give you a tour of the area and the plant. After that, you tell me what you need."

"How's your arsenal?" asked Leach. "I didn't bring any heat and I feel a bit naked without it. I have a license as a private investigator in Jersey, but I'll have to apply for that and a gun permit here. We should do that tomorrow."

"Done, we'll go over to St. Paul and make that part of the tour. Do you have anything in mind about personnel...local or out of town?"

"Yeah, I want some of each. I want some guys that know the area. I'll look over what you've got. Then I want some spooks that can operate without you ever knowing they're there. I might go back to your pal, Colonel Corrigan. See if I can steal a couple or three of his jungle fighters."

Adam looked at Leach with respect as he said, "I'm impressed. You keep going like this, I may have to consider giving you a raise."

"Hell, all I've done so far is talk. Save the moola till you see some action, but you'll want to pay me what I'm worth...which is a shitload." They had a short cocktail hour before driving to Kincaid's Restaurant on Normandale Road, just South of I-494. Adam recommended the sautéed Norwegian salmon, and three servings thereof were downed with relish. The return of Leach's dry wit, with his 'Joisey' accent, was most welcome.

Tuesday morning dawned with a pink sky and the promise of both heat and humidity. Comments from both Leach and Belinda put Adam on the defensive regarding weather in the 'cool' northland. He brushed them off, promising all the coolness they could ever desire, come winter. The first order of business was renting a Buick LeSabre for Leach. Belinda then traipsed off in the BMW, with shopping as her objective. Adam and Leach visited the government office that handed out private investigator's credentials. They were pleased to learn that the process was simple and immediate. They verified Leach's current license in New Jersey and his lack of any criminal record. Adam later confided his surprise at the latter. The concealed weapon permit was included and Leach was free to 'carry' without further delay.

Adam drove him around the Cities, concentrating on somewhat different points of interest than the earlier tour with Belinda. After lunch at the Lincoln Dell, they repaired to Packard Electronics. Adam introduced Leach to the staff and granted him unlimited security clearance within the company. He was installed in a medium-sized, pleasant, but not luxurious office with a telephone, computer and fax machine.

Leach settled in his chair and swung his feet up on the desk. Adam said, "Now that you've assumed your normal working position, I will retreat to my office and tackle the pile that has accumulated. Swing by about five and we'll see what Belinda's been up to."

"I was hoping you'd finally get out of here and let me go to work," said Leach. "See you at 1700 hours, boss." Notwithstanding his casual, flippant demeanor, Leach was, in fact, well organized and highly productive.

As they drove home on Thursday night, he reported, "I have completed my initial survey and it calls for a force of eight. One supervisor, three security agents inside and four outside guys. If and when the threat is eliminated, we could cut two or three from that number. I have a dozen interviews lined up starting tomorrow and I'll have a budget on your desk by noon."

Adam looked at Leach in awe. "I knew you were good, but that's a helluva job in two and a half days."

"In the words of the immortal Al Jolson, 'You ain't seen nothing yet.' I plan to have this outfit operational in less than a week. To make 'em a crack squad, may take another week or so. Colonel Corrigan has three men that just finished their twenty-year hitches and haven't re-upped. He swears by all three. I have a Viet that was too young for the war, but his daddy taught him everything he knew…he's close to being a 'Ninja,' talks good English too. While we're on the subject of security, we ain't practicing much. I'm moving out tomorrow. Gonna rent a different car and only show up at your place during the dark of night. If anybody's been watching, we've been sitting targets. I want to vary both of your schedules, too."

"That's what you're here for. You name it, and we'll do it," replied Adam.

"Good, I'll lay out a schedule and we'll put it in place on Monday."

VI

August 6th, 1999, Adam Packard's House, Edina, MN, 5 p.m....

Belinda was somewhat disappointed when Al Leach bid her goodbye that morning. He had packed his meager belongings and left for God knows where. When he and Adam left, she sat in the kitchen, the morning sun casting intricate shadows from the grills that divided the windows. She sipped coffee, and thought of Adam. The time she played the 'ice maiden.' Their torrid affair. The fun, the wise-cracking…could they ever return to that? Then there was the battle in Colombia. The fighting side-by-side…and the time with her family. And now, here in his home. She smiled and her face lit up, far brighter than the sunlight. Her decision had been made…tonight would be the night!

Belinda had spent the better part of the last two days at the University of Minnesota Research Library poring over psychological profiles. Profiles that would shed light on her inability to fulfill normal sexual response with a man she believed she loved. There were several possibilities. The first dealt with Adam's alleged infidelity. Was it possible that, although she had consciously ruled him innocent, unconsciously she still found him guilty? This theory was quickly trashed. The second was, 'did she really love him?' She retraced her failed relationships and compared them to Adam. This also failed, she *did* love him. The last, and most likely scenario was centered on Sean Ball. Could it be the many episodes of rape and humiliation themselves, or was it that one night? The night she gave herself willingly, passionately.

Although it was painful, she forced herself to replay those dreadful days in her mind, over and over. The more she thought of the trauma she suffered, the more she realized that her response was not only justified, but probably normal. She had laid a ridiculous degree of blame on herself…even thinking herself a slut. A ray of sunshine penetrated her psyche when, at last, she realized that this black cloud *could* be chased away. Chased away only by looking it squarely in the face.

When Adam arrived at home that evening, she met him at the door, pulled him into her arms and pressed her body into his. As she raised her lips to his, she opened his mouth with her tongue and revealed her passion. His response was immediate, and without a word being spoken, they moved as one, to his bedroom. They made love with fierce hunger and lay panting and exhausted in its wake.

When Adam found his voice, he whispered, "Whew, you sure know how to greet a fella after a hard day."

"You've had that coming for a long time." She traced her finger gently along his jaw. "I plan to make up for the celibate life you have been living. Would you mind terribly if I moved my things into your bedroom?"

"Mind? I have hoped and prayed for that…more than you'll ever know. Maybe we should do it right now, while you're in the mood?"

"Don't worry, this was not an impulse, or a spur of the moment act. A great deal of study and thought led to this…seduction. And," she said with a most tantalizing smile, "I must say, it was wonderful."

They retired, in the same bed, for the first time since they were reunited. The wild abandon that had accompanied their earlier coupling was replaced by tender, caring love. Over the next two nights, Belinda was surprised how quickly she regained her confidence in bed with Adam. Sunday was a long day of strenuous exercise. Adam insisted that they take the bike trail from Cannon Falls to Red Wing and back. They loaded bikes in the SUV and drove south 35 miles to the blacktop trail, built on an abandoned railroad track. They rode to Red Wing and had lunch at the fabled St. James Hotel. When they emerged from the cool restaurant, the heat and humidity hit them like a furnace. They sweated for just over half of the way back when a link Adam's chain shattered, leaving him on foot. She insisted on taking turns pushing the wounded cycle, while the other rode. The shower they took together was to be the last intimacy their tired bodies would share before sleep overtook them.

Belinda eyes fluttered open. The clock read 5:45 a.m. She had a wonderful, devilish feeling and wondered if Adam were ready for what she had in mind. She smiled wickedly, punched Adam on the arm and said, "Hey sailor, I didn't work my way into your bed last night just to catch a few Zs. A girl likes to get a little ride once in a while. Whadda ya' say?"

Adam rolled over, opened one eye as if to see who was in bed with him, and said, "I must've been really drunk, I don't remember picking you up, babe…whatcher name?"

"Never mind, big boy, just roll over and see what I've got for you." The ensuing exercise left no doubt as to the recovery of their energy… or their old repartee.

Adam was delighted with the return of the 'old' Belinda. He saw her love come full-circle in a matter of days. On Tuesday, just four days after the 'seduction,' he made his move.

He arrived home early. He carried a package and when she rose to kiss him, he held it behind his back. She asked coyly, "What, pray tell, are you hiding?"

Adam smiled, shook his head. "It's a surprise. Please go into the study, sit patiently and I will join you in three minutes."

"My, aren't you the sly one. I love surprises, so I will go in and set my stopwatch."

Adam arrived as promised with two glasses and a bottle of red wine. He set the glasses on the desk, out of Belinda's view, and poured the wine. He turned and, showing her the bottle, said, "This is a very special bottle of French Bordeaux. My father brought it from Vietnam. It was originally owned by a French officer. It was confiscated when the French were ousted from the country, and presented to my father for saving the life of a Vietnamese colonel. It has been waiting all these years for this moment." He handed her a glass, "Now a toast to you…the love of my life!"

Belinda sipped, and as she tipped the glass, heard a slight tinkle from within. She drank deeply, but carefully and exposed the bright glow of a diamond. "Oh, Adam, is it my ring?"

"Yes." Adam slipped to one knee. "I asked you before and I ask you now, to marry me and spend the rest of your life in my care. I promise to treasure you as long as I live."

She took his face in her hands. "I said yes once before, but this has even more meaning. Love lost, and found again, flows like fine wine." She raised him up, took him in her arms and whispered, "The answer is yes. There is nothing in this world I want more than spending the rest of my life in your care…and in your arms."

The next morning at breakfast Adam asked, "Do you prefer a long engagement or should we be thinking about a date?"

"I thought you'd never ask. Since we are finally living in sin once more, there's no particular rush. I would like to start planning soon, however, to give whoever will be involved time to arrange schedules."

"Makes sense to me. Who do you have in mind, the list?"

"Well, our immediate families, for starters." Belinda mused. "Add Leach, Mack and Amy and you have the 'must attend' group. We work out from there."

"So, we clear a date with them as the first step?"

"Not so fast, sailor," said Belinda with a smile. "We also need to know what kind of wedding…and where. Are we talking big church wedding, justice of the peace, house, here or Georgia?"

"Why did I think this would be simple? Weddings are women things and you can have any kind you want. Do you want a big wedding?"

"Heavens no!" exclaimed Belinda. "My choice would be at this house or my parents place in Thomasville."

"I'm good with either one," Adam said thoughtfully. "The advantage in having it here is that I can work, be with you and we can maintain maximum security during the planning and wedding."

"Hmm, I hadn't thought of that, but I do agree with all three points. We probably will invite about the same number from each place, so that's not an issue…now what about the date?"

"As soon as possible, Minnesota weather, you know. Why don't you look into the time frame for what has to be done, and based on that, we'll set the date?"

"You got a deal. I'll get crankin' right quick."

Belinda, not short on organizational skills, put the necessary information together in two days and after clearing the date with Leach, called the Rogers' house in Georgia.

Amy answered the phone on the second ring. Belinda said, "I missed a couple of weekly-call commitments. Can you find it in your heart to forgive me?"

"Hey, Belinda," said Amy with obvious pleasure, "as long as you promise not to let it happen again, I forgive you. How *are* you?"

"We're great. Adam's on the line with me. Is that big redhead around?"

"Just got home," she held her hand over the phone as she yelled, "Hey, Mack, pick up the phone. There was a click and then they heard, "Rogers here" in his formal military voice.

"Relax big fella, it's a social call," said Adam and Belinda joined in with, "How are you, Mack?"

"Just great and it's wonderful to hear your voices. What's up?"

"We're planning a wedding," said Belinda. "And we'd like you two to be part of it…like the best man and matron of honor."

"Oh, Belinda," said Amy in a shaky voice, "you know we'd be delighted. Have you set a date?"

"We've set a tentative date, but it won't be cast in stone until it clears with some calendars. Yours first, then our families. How are you guys for the 18th of September, Saturday?"

Amy paused, obviously checking, and finally said, "No problem, we're good for that weekend. What about the kids?"

"They absolutely must come," said Adam. "We have plenty of room, you'll all stay at the house. Adam and Linda won't mind hanging around a swimming pool, will they?"

"Hardly, they'll love it. Will this be a formal affair?" asked Amy.

Adam looked quizzically at Belinda and said, "I don't know, we haven't discussed that part, but whatever Belinda decides, we'll do."

Belinda said, "I think we need to sleep on that, decide if it will be outside, consider the weather. For now, we simply need your agreement with the date."

"You have it," said Mack. "And we're really looking forward to helping you dive into the matrimonial morass. Misery loves company, you know."

Amy piped up with, "Shame on you, Mack."

"Methinks you've spent a bit too much time with our friend Leach, Mack," said Adam, "But, enough of this folderol and to the business at hand. We really appreciate your willingness to play a major part in our wedding. We will be in touch about the details." Belinda added, "I second all of that. See you soon."

The date was verified with both families and Belinda completed the guest list after consulting the experts on the subject…their mothers.

VII

August 13th, 1999, Plaza Hotel, New York City, NY, 10:20 a.m....

Dressed in one of the Plaza's thick white terrycloth robes, the man answered the telephone with a grunt. The caller responded with, "Well, and a pleasant good morning to you, too."

"Don't be a smart-ass, Ivan. What do you have for me?" the man said in a hoarse whisper.

"My news is mostly bad. You remember I said we should hit them right away? Well, they've brought Al Leach in and he's putting together some security that will certainly get in our way."

The man in the robe replied, "You know very well why I want to wait. I want the satisfaction of seeing their faces just before they meet their maker, all of them...at one time and in one place. Now, give me the details."

"I intercepted a cell phone call last night and they have set a wedding date for September 18th, at Packard's house," said Ivan. "As far as Leach is concerned, he's interviewed a half-dozen people in the office, and could have met some outside."

"What do you mean, *could have?*" whispered the man in New York. "Didn't you put a twenty-four-hour tail on him?"

"I did, but he's a sneaky bastard. He shook the tail on two occasions," said Ivan defensively.

"That must mean he's on to you. What have you got, a bunch of amateurs working for you?"

"No. I think Al Leach operates that way all the time...as if someone were following him. I've known a few birds like that, it's like a game with them. As far as my men are concerned, I've bounced a couple and put the fear of God into the rest. He'll not slip away again."

"Have you made all the people he's hired, checked them out completely?" asked the man in the robe.

"Only two, a couple of ex-cops. We have a sheet on them with home addresses, family, the works. If he's hired any others, he did it away from the office and they haven't shown their face to date."

"Have you bugged Packard's home and office?"

"I can't put a bug in either. He's a security guru," said Ivan. "I have no doubt they sweep both places every day. If they find a bug, it'll tip our hand. We're better off having less knowledge of them if it means their having *no* knowledge of us."

"Maybe, but we absolutely must know the timing for the wedding guests to arrive in Minneapolis and you need to identify his security people and nail down their method of operation."

"I know. The first part should be relatively easy. I've sent a woman down to Thomasville, Georgia. She'll con the woman's family into giving us all the details of the wedding. We should know in a few days. Getting a handle on the cagey Mr. Leach's grunts may be a little tougher, but I'll get it done."

"*See that you do!*" said the man in the robe as he slammed down the phone.

The meeting was held in the back room of Sgt. Preston's saloon, on the outer fringe of downtown Minneapolis. Six men sat at a round table. They were an odd lot; two were swarthy, tough guys, dressed in black. Two were dressed in suits, not flashy or expensive, but neat. The final pair looked like athletes in work-out garb. Ivan walked in, surveyed the group and asked, "Who's on Leach?"

A tall, handsome thirty-ish man in Nike wear, said, "Roxy and Sam. We'll relieve them and get on the house as soon as we leave here."

"Good," said Ivan. "I just got off the phone with the man from New York. He's pissed about our losing track of Leach. As I warned you… that *cannot* happen again. Now, I want all of you to scrutinize each and every person that goes in or out of Packard Electronics. Anybody that has the slightest look of a guard dog, get their picture. Afterward, we'll put a tail on each of them and see if they're part of Leach's team. We also have to spot and identify any outside guys. When you're watching either the house or the plant, keep an eye out for anybody that could be a *watcher*. This means you have to be doubly careful about being spotted yourselves. You must change your appearance, vehicles and location from which to watch. Leach is good and I can't imagine him hiring anybody that just fell off the turnip truck. Any questions?"

"Just one," said the Nike guy, apparently second in command. "Is the sky the limit on the budget here? If we're going to do this right… avoid being identified…we'll need many changes of clothing, wigs, vehicles, etc…it won't come cheap."

"No sweat, the man in New York is looking for results, not a bargain price," said Ivan. "If there's nothing else, you know your assignments. Just remember what I said here. *Mistakes are not acceptable.*"

August 15th, 1999, Packard Electronics, Inc., Bloomington, MN, 8:20 a.m....

Leach sat down and immediately slouched in the comfortable chair in front of Adam's desk. "We have a major problem, Boss."

"And what do you consider a major problem?" asked Adam in a light-hearted tone.

"I'm not kidding around here," said Leach in a very serious voice. "Someone has put us under twenty-four-hour surveillance...and they're very good."

"Damn," said Adam, now serious. "This thing just won't go away, will it? If they're good, how did you make them?"

"They're good, but my guys are better. The four outside people I have in place are like ghosts...you just never see them. They have a make on six different people and if there's any more they'll have 'em in a few more days. Do you think they're investing those kinds of resources to just *watch* us?"

"That's a very good question. Let's think it out, put ourselves in their shoes. First, we must assume they want to kill us." Leach nodded affirmatively, so Adam continued. "Second, they've had every opportunity. When we first arrived we were particularly vulnerable, so why didn't they do it then? Third, if you say they're good, they probably know you're setting up security, right?" Another nod from Leach. "So, what are they waiting for?"

"Now that your highly analytical mind has laid out a clear trail, I can only guess they're waiting for something specific, like an event, like maybe...a wedding?"

"I like that conclusion. Maybe the fact that Mack and Amy will be here…we'll all be together. They may even want to harm our families." Adam pursed his lips and concentrated. After a long pause, he said, "Suppose you can identify *all* of these perps. We can't just take them out…this isn't Colombia. Even if we could, would we be able to identify the source, the person or organization behind this?" The only way we can ever finalize this thing is to set a trap, let them tip their hand…and then do whatever we have to do. What do you think?"

"It's more dangerous, but I think you're right. If we don't nail the main man, this will just happen again and again until they get us." It was Leach's turn to furrow his brow in thought, and at last he said, "Every trap needs bait. Maybe to prevent a massacre at the wedding, we need to bring in the cheese they *really* want, earlier…give them a shot at all of us, the principals that is, a day or two before all the family and guests arrive."

"I like that," said Adam. "We have to contact Mack and Amy, warn them of the risk and make sure they're willing to be part of it. We have to think about their kids, too. If they come along, we'll have to take steps to protect them. I think we have to bring Rains in on this."

"I'm concerned he'll send people that could give away our position. Some CIA agents don't necessarily have all cylinders firing. Maybe you can convince Rains to keep 'em in the background, until the last minute. They could be the Cavalry…riding in only on *our* say-so."

"I think that can be arranged, but before we take any steps, I'd like to lay this all out for Belinda, and you should be there. How and where do you want to meet?"

"Why not at your house?" asked Leach. "You could invite me for dinner and we can hash it out. Sometimes new ideas pop up when you are explaining a plan to someone else. You and I will also have some time to think it over. Is tonight too soon?"

"No, I'll call Belinda and make arrangements. Shall we say six o'clock?"

"Delighted," said Leach as he rose and headed for the door.

They brought Belinda up to date on the situation and their morning's conversation. When they finished, she sighed. "I'm not altogether surprised. I went from a normal, if unexciting life to dreadful torture…

then to great joy. Perhaps it was just too good to be true."

Adam took her hand and gently said, "That joy is here to stay, Belinda. We will get through this, trust me."

Leach said, "Absolutely. I guarantee that my people are better and will defeat the bad guys as we have in the past. We're not only more stealthy, we're smarter…and smart always wins in the end."

Belinda gave them a thin smile. "Please forgive my pessimism. I'm really not that concerned for myself. I have great faith in our ability to win this. It's dragging the others into it that I fear. Not only Mack and Amy, but the families. How can we be sure they're safe?"

"Belinda, I promise you, if we can't work out a foolproof plan… one that you approve unconditionally, we will not set a trap, but will take out these people before the fact. Are you good with that, Al?"

"I'd have it no other way," said Leach. "If we're right in thinking they're waiting for the wedding, we have a month to get more dope on 'em and put together a plan. *And* an alternate plan."

"That certainly is fair," said Belinda. "And I know you won't take any unnecessary risks with the lives of the people we love. Now, if you'll follow me to the kitchen, I'll dish up a seafood salad guaranteed to satisfy your boyish appetites."

The next morning, Adam made two calls on a secure line from his office, one to CIA Director Dennis Rains and the other to Mack Rogers. He then wrote a long memo containing all of the details of the situation, their discussions and several possible scenarios regarding the solution. These were faxed over the secure line to Rains' office and to the Rogers' neighbor's home.

IX

August 19th, 1999, Cincinnati-No. KY International Airport, 12:15 p.m....

Earlier that morning, a complicated routing of three cars allowed them to rendezvous at the Radisson Hotel garage in St. Paul. Shortly thereafter, a silver Ford Expedition pulled out and headed for the Downtown St. Paul Airport, just across the river. The SUV pulled into a large hangar on the west side of the airport. Moments later a Lear Jet was towed from the same hangar, fired up and took off.

Flying at 42,000 feet at a ground speed of 580MPH, the Lear landed in Cincinnati at 11:10 a.m. EDT. The pilot taxied to the executive aviation terminal and two passengers deplaned and stepped directly into a stretch limousine that had pulled up to the side of the airplane. The limousine picked up another passenger at the terminal and drove to FBI Headquarters in downtown Cincinnati.

When they arrived at a comfortable conference room, Dennis Rains introduced Adam, Leach and Rogers to Harry Heiser, Deputy Director of the FBI in Washington and Atwood Moen, Agent-in-Charge in Cincinnati. Moen took their order for refreshments.

When Moen left the room, Adam began with, "I want to thank you both for arranging this meeting." Turning to Heiser, he continued, "I assume Director Rains has filled you in on the situation?"

"Yes, he sent your memo over on Friday. I have some background with your operation. I oversaw the FBI's role in your takedown in Atlanta. Dennis gave me the rest of the story on the way out here...and a most interesting tale it is."

Rains spoke up, "We owe you fellas big time for your efforts in Colombia. You know, Colonel Jackson received her early training at Langley. Then unfortunately, we lost her to the Army. We still think of her as one of ours and her rescue was quite a piece of work. Exacting a bit of revenge for the agents they killed in Bogotá was also very satisfying to the Company. That said, how can we help you finish this project?"

Adam replied, "You can help us two ways. First, this afternoon, we'd like to brainstorm possible solutions and come up with a viable plan. Second, based upon that plan, we may need support in carrying it out. We have a well-trained security force that we expect to carry the load, but look to you for backup."

"We have an excellent team in Minneapolis," said Heiser. "The Agent in Charge is Peter Groveland. I will see that he gives you complete cooperation."

"Thank you," said Adam. "Now to the issue at hand. Al Leach, Belinda... that is, Colonel Jackson and I have had a discussion, the synopsis of which was included in the report you received. Al and I have discussed it further and I'd like to have him outline our strategy for you."

Leach looked up with a furrowed brow. "We talked about a number of ways to handle these mutts and concluded that unless we can turn somebody, preferably the head man in Minneapolis, there's too much risk to use ourselves as bait. My people have a handle on most, if not all, of their surveillance people. We have pictures of them and in two cases, a set of prints." He tapped a folder on the table before him. "The first thing you can do for us is run these through your mill to identify them. If we get a hit, then we need to identify all known associates. We plan to study these birds a bit more, then choose the most likely to break. We pick him up and squeeze him...but you may not want to know about that." Leach gave his crooked smile. "We think the person behind this thing is not local, but hopefully will come in for the showdown...gloat a bit before doing his or her dirty deed. If we can identify and grab the top soldier, I think we can turn him and put a fox in the hen house, so to speak."

"Are you saying you'd trust the turncoat to carry this thing, all the way to the showdown?" asked Heiser.

Adam replied, "I believe we can be extremely persuasive. We will offer a substantial monetary reward along with the *promise* of unspeakable consequences should he fail to comply."

"You have an advantage over us in that. We must operate within the law. You must, of course, insulate us from any illegal acts," said Heiser.

"Absolutely," Adam replied. "We will not, under any circumstances, ask your people to be part of anything that's even close to breaking the law. I think Mr. Rains can vouch for that."

Rains nodded as he said, "I've worked with this group through some pretty gritty action and they always do it on their own. Our part has been supplying intelligence and some grunt work far from the action."

"I'm good with that," said Heiser, "but what if you fail to locate and turn the local leader?"

Adam said, "Then we abort the whole plan, postpone the wedding and go underground. We refuse to risk the lives of anyone unless we have a foolproof plan in place."

Mack Rogers, who had been silent through the whole discussion, asked, "While I wholeheartedly endorse the plan, I do wonder, Adam, how far you'll go before pulling the plug."

"We haven't gotten that far, but I'd say we need to have our guarantees no later than the end of the month. What do you think, Al?"

Leach paused for just a moment before responding, "I'm good with that. I think we can complete our surveillance in a week and arrange our little talk with someone right after that."

They discussed other details over lunch and the meeting concluded before 3 p.m. Rains and Heiser hurried away to their duties in Washington and Adam asked Moen if they could remain and get a later ride to the airport. He was agreeable and Adam turned to Mack, "Al and I want to talk this over with you privately, Mack. We want to be absolutely sure you and Amy understand the risks. Even though we believe in the plan and our ability to carry it out, something always can go wrong."

"I know that, but I have utmost faith in both the plan and the players. I am ready to commit to it. Amy hasn't heard the details, but when she does, I have no doubt she'll go for it. I do have a question about the kids, though. Would they still come up with us?"

Adam replied, "I think it best that they be on the plane with you, but they wouldn't stay at my house. We're thinking of inventing a cousin, in Minneapolis. They would stay at an FBI safe house until the action goes down…then we'll all get back together for the wedding."

"I like that idea," responded Mack. "Can you imagine your relief, and Belinda's, when this thing is finally over? If this threat hadn't appeared the way it did, your wedding would be tainted by the fear that somebody's still out there to get you. The 18th of September may turn out to be the happiest day of *all* of our lives."

August 27th, 1999,
Leach Safe House,
Minneapolis, MN,
10:20 a.m....

The tall handsome athlete lay on his stomach, his hands and feet trussed up behind him. His position was such that his back was bent the wrong way. Although not painful at first, the discomfort increased rapidly, until it became torturous. Leach looked down on him and asked, "What is your name?"

The man winced as he replied, "John Smith, what's yours?"

"Well, John, I think we should get something straight. You are not in a position to ask me any questions. You will learn shortly that smart-ass replies will earn you great pain. Now I'd like to begin by asking you a few civil questions. If you give me the right answers, you will not be harmed. If you refuse, you will suffer permanent damage to that fine body and handsome face. You've obviously worked with body builders…my friend Wong here is a talented body *breaker*. Now what will it be…cooperate early or after you have a broken bone or two?"

"Fuck you, I'm a stand-up guy," said 'John Smith.'

"Not any more," said Leach as he turned to Wong and nodded. Wong stepped up, took Smith's right foot in both hands and gave a sharp twist. The snap of the bone was like a pistol shot and Smith screamed in pain. When Smith's cries were reduced to sobs, Leach said, "Now that's an example. What you need to understand is that this initial break will heal and you will recover full use of that ankle. The next one will not. You will limp the rest of your life. Think about it carefully before you answer."

Smith hestitated, then shakily said, "Okay, what do you want to know?"

"Good decision," said Leach. "Before I ask you any questions, I'd like to tell you about my team. We have been stalking your little band for over two weeks. We have pictures of eight people, fingerprints on three and your name is Lance Stone from Grand Rapids, Michigan. Now, my first question is, have you seen any of my people…spying on you?"

"No," Stone allowed in a meek voice.

"Something else you should know. Adam Packard has very substantial resources and an unrelenting commitment to track down and *neutralize* any and all mutts intending to harm himself and/or his friends. Do you understand where this is going?"

Stone spit out, "You want info…and my cooperation."

"Ah, a very bright boy." Leach turned to Wong and said, "Release his bonds and see to his ankle. I believe we can treat one another as gentlemen now. Don't you agree, Mr. Stone?"

"I know when I'm out of my league. I'll do anything you ask," he replied in a resigned voice.

Stone was now seated in a chair, with Wong applying an ice pack to his broken ankle. Leach handed him a sheaf of photographs and asked, "Do these represent your entire team?"

He looked through the pictures and replied, "Yes, all but Ivan."

"Is Ivan the leader of your group?" asked Leach.

"Yes, he put the team together and runs it, but doesn't go out in the field."

"OK, now what's Ivan's last name and who is behind the whole thing? There must be someone pulling Ivan's strings," Leach queried.

"I don't know either, I've never heard Ivan's other name and all Ivan ever called the big boss was 'the man from New York.'"

"Do you have periodic meetings…that Ivan attends?"

"Yes, we have one on Monday…the 30th."

"Where and when is this meeting scheduled?" asked Leach.

"It's at the Lincoln Dell at 10 a.m., in the southwest corner of the restaurant."

"All right, Lance, here's what we're going to do. I assume you run or do some kind of exercise?" Stone nodded and Leach continued, "After you have given us complete information on the team and Ivan, we will take you, in our van, to the place you normally run. When no one is looking, we'll put you out on the path. You will then call Ivan on your cell phone and explain that you've taken a nasty fall and think you have broken your ankle. Let him take care of it from there. You will not say a word about this meeting and will carry on as if it had not happened. I don't have to spell out what will happen to you if you do *not* do exactly what we tell you."

"No, don't worry, I'll cooperate," said Stone as Leach pulled out a legal pad to record the whole story on Ivan and his henchmen.

On Monday morning, Leach's men identified Ivan in the restaurant as he met with his team. After the meeting he was followed and abducted as he exited his car in the parking lot of the Hotel Sofitel in Bloomington. Leach employed a slightly different approach to Ivan than he had with Stone. He offered to up the ante from what 'the man from New York' was paying, but promised a slow, painful death if he failed to cooperate. No bones were broken, but pain was inflicted. Leach convinced him that he could not possibly escape the clutches of Adam Packard's people and Ivan Rubin agreed to cooperate in every way. When he was asked the name of 'the man from New York,' he swore he did not know his identity, and Leach believed him. He said he had been contacted by a broker of covert operations and had only spoken to the man on the telephone…at the Plaza Hotel in New York. He volunteered the room number he used when making contact.

Leach made a call to a retired NYPD detective who had worked for him off and on as a private investigator. He then instructed Ivan to call the Plaza the next morning at precisely 9:30 a.m. CDT. He was to report that all was well, that the Rogers family would arrive in Minneapolis on September 14th and that he had a good safe house to take them to whenever the man scheduled the final takedown. Before he released Ivan, Leach introduced one of his men, Mark Mason, an ex-sergeant from Colonel Cochrane's outfit as the replacement for Stone, who he understood was indisposed.

At 10:35 EDT, Tuesday, August 31st, a man knocked on the door of suite 14A and simultaneously inserted a pass key and entered the living room of the suite. After a quick search of all the rooms, he called a number in Minneapolis on his cell phone, and said, "There's nobody in the suite, Al, but there's what looks like a fax machine hooked up to the phone."

"Can you check the occupancy of that suite for the last month or so?" asked Leach.

"Yeah, there's an assistant manager here owes me…if you know what I mean. I'll call you back."

Leach received a return call within ten minutes. The detective reported, "Suite 14A's been rented for six weeks to a Mrs. Gloria Headley. That name ring any bells with you?"

"No," replied Leach. He gave the caller an address for him to mail his bill and hung up. Leach then called his mole, Mason at Ivan Rubin's headquarters and received verification that Rubin had talked to the man at the appointed time. Mason reported that the man said he would travel to Minneapolis on the 14th, and would contact Rubin when he arrived.

Leach walked into Adam's office later that morning and reported the events that had transpired in New York. Adam said, "You say the suite was rented to a Gloria Headley? I have no idea who that could be, do you?" Leach shook his head. "As far as the phone calls, the 'fax' machine was undoubtedly a call forwarding device. If I had my hands on it, I probably could tell where the calls were forwarded to, but that would tip our hand. I don't think we should pursue the New York lead any further, unless we get some new information."

"I agree, but it was worth a shot," said Leach. "Mason is working out well as the new man on Ivan's team. He's getting to know the other members and he said Ivan the Terrible is acting as if nothing has happened. Our Mr. Stone is still on the payroll, doing odd jobs around their safe house. His disability apparently hasn't interfered with his banging the solitary female member of the team."

"That's good news," said Adam with a chuckle. "I talked with Groveland this morning and he's arranged to care for the Rogers children when they arrive. An FBI 'couple' will meet them at the airport, drop Mack and Amy off at the house and then take the kids for a day or so. That said, we need to talk about the exact way we're going to be *taken*."

"Since we are so damn good, it has to be a helluva scheme. The five of us can't just walk into an ambush…particularly since I have this hotshot team protecting us."

"My thought exactly," said Adam. "Perhaps we should let them kidnap the women, then we get taken…following the ransom instructions. The problem is, it really doesn't address the issue of 'where is your security force?'…unless you call them off for some reason."

"Yeah, if I could dream up a good reason…" Leach was silent for a time, the wheels obviously turning rapidly in his head. "Hey, what if their guys captured ours…except it would *really* be the other way around."

"Brilliant idea," exclaimed Adam. "We can go out and capture their team first, then introduce your men to the big boss as Rubin's team. We can use Stone and Mason to reveal the location of Rubin's troops. We have to be careful that the man from New York doesn't want to eliminate his own team…particularly Mason."

"I think we can work around that. We probably have to devise a smoke screen…some way to throw *my* team off guard, so it would be plausible for *their* team to capture us. Maybe, as far as the other side knows, they turn one of our guys?"

"It just keeps getting better," Adam responded with a smile. "How about Mason? That puts all the good guys back on the same side."

"I think we have a plan," said Leach. "I'd like to be there when you give Belinda the details…see her face."

"Let's do it at dinner tonight. You and I can work on the script this afternoon and we'll lay out the action blow by blow at cocktail time."

"Terrific. Let's be sure to ask for her input. Remember Colombia, the lady is no slouch when it comes to working out battle plans," said Leach with respect.

"I'd have it no other way," Adam replied. "All right, let's talk about who, where and when…"

That evening, Belinda greeted Leach with a hug and a kiss on the cheek, stepped back and said, "Al, you look wonderful. Clandestine operations must agree with you. You almost look like the cat that swallowed the canary. Do you plan to share whatever's making you look so smug?"

"Oh, babe of my dreams, you look right through this simple sucker. I could never hide anything from those see-all eyes," confessed Leach.

"I must interpret that as a positive reply…you will bare your soul to me this night, correct?" asked Belinda.

"I am your slave," Leach implored with the dramatic reach of a Shakespearian actor.

Belinda clapped her hands and said, "In that case, take your unworthy self to the bar and mix drinks. You may also prepare one for yourself."

Leach said, "As you command, oh mighty mistress," and took himself to the bar to obey her order. As they sipped their drinks, Adam opened the discussion of the plan they had crafted. The two of them took turns and frequently asked and received Belinda's sage comments. Adam took notes on the additions and changes they agreed upon.

When the story was complete, Belinda said, "I'm really impressed. When you promised to give me veto rights on the plan, I rather thought I would be forced to exercise those rights. Unless something unexpected comes up, this cannot fail…and I heartily endorse the plan. Do you intend to share it with Mack and Amy?"

"Yes, I'll make the changes we talked about and fax an encrypted version to them in the morning," said Adam. "I'm anxious to hear their opinions on it."

A return, encrypted fax arrived late the next day with nothing but enthusiastic approval for the plan. Nothing remained but to execute that plan.

XI

September 14th, 1999,
Adam Packard's Home,
Edina, MN, 12:30 p.m....

A non-descript gray Dodge minivan pulled into the circle drive and stopped under the portico. Four adults and two highly excited children emerged and were welcomed enthusiastically. Adam and Belinda exchanged emotional greetings with Amy and Mack and their children, Adam and Linda. After the hugs and kisses, Amy motioned to the other couple and said, "This is my cousin, Laura and her husband, Frank Nelson." Turning back, she continued, "Meet our dear friends Adam Packard and Belinda Jackson…soon to be Belinda Packard." After the handshaking, Amy said, "They have children close to the ages of Adam and Linda. We thought it would be fun for them to spend a day or two together, then come back here for the wedding." The men unloaded the luggage and Belinda took them all on a quick tour of the house before the 'Nelsons' and the children drove off.

The Rogerses were installed in a bedroom suite, unpacked and were downstairs shaking hands with Leach in less than thirty minutes. Belinda laid out fresh pumpernickel bread, lathered it with horseradish sauce, then heaped on a generous pile of pastrami. A plate of crispy Kosher dills completed the absolute favorite lunch of both Mack and Leach. Meanwhile, Adam raided his arsenal for some firepower for both Mack and Amy. As he handed a .40 caliber Smith and Wesson automatic to Mack, he said, "The plan is all set. The only variables are the timing and any changes requested by 'the man from New York.' We have not heard from Rubin, which means he hasn't heard from the *man*. We're in a holding pattern until the phone rings…so let's enjoy some lunch."

Although the conversation was light and friendly, the tension they all felt was like a heavy blanket weighing on each of them. The conversation stopped abruptly when the phone rang. Adam picked it up and pressed the speaker button on the phone.

An unfamiliar voice said, "The man's in town. He's taking a cab to the house and should be here in about a half an hour. If he buys the plan, I'll give you one beep on your beeper, then two when we take off." Adam deactivated the speaker and hung up the phone.

Mack asked, "What's the ETA for them to 'capture the bad guys' and return to the base?"

"One of our teams will hit Ivan Rubin's safe house, containing four bogies," Adam responded. "Simultaneously, another team will pick up the other three from their stakeouts. It should all come down within fifteen minutes. Mason will see that they each get an injection of a strong sedative that will put them out for over four hours. That way, none of them can blow our cover…rat on Rubin to the *man*."

The nervous tension that accompanies waiting…and disappears with action…continued to build, even though every person in the room had substantial experience with violent action. The single beep came forty minutes later…the double beep followed in just ten minutes.

Lance Stone hobbled up to the front door of Rubin's safe house, an unimposing bungalow on 44th and Beard in South Minneapolis. He was down to one crutch and hoped to be in a walking cast within two weeks. He walked through the front porch and inserted a key in the front door. As he stepped into the living room, one of Rubin's 'bad guys' came out from behind the door with a .357 magnum Smith & Wesson revolver in his hand. "I heard you limpin' up the walk, Lance baby, but we can't be too careful."

"That's right, Ace," said Stone, "You just never know when the wrong guy is going to come through that door. Where's Roxy?"

"Aw, she's takin' a nap in the back bedroom. Maybe you'd like join her, huh?" said Ace with a nasty leer.

"Maybe I will," said Stone as he limped toward the back of the house. He poked his head into the kitchen where two other men were playing gin rummy, then walked down the hall to the bedroom. He opened the door softly, listened carefully and heard her even breathing.

He went over to the bed, thinking, 'Honey, I hate to do this to you, but it must be done.' He withdrew a hypodermic needle from his pocket, straddled the sleeping girl and plunged the needle into her arm as he put his other hand over her mouth. She struggled to no avail in his strong grip and soon lapsed back into an unconscious state. He rearranged her body into a relaxed position and left the room.

He refilled the syringe and went back into the tiny living room where Ace was watching TV. He walked up behind him and made some small talk. Ace responded, but his eyes never left the TV screen. Stone withdrew his pistol and brought it down hard on his comrade's head. Ace slumped in his chair and never felt the strong sedative flowing into his arm. Stone propped him up and headed back into the kitchen. He walked past the two card players, opened the back door and stood for a time on the small back porch, looking out over the back yard. He came back in, drew his Browning 9MM automatic and said, "Okay, boys, hands in the air." As he said this, two men entered the room behind him. The card players were bound and gagged before being sedated like the others.

Stone said, "The girl's in the bedroom and the other one is in the living room. They've both had the shot, but should be bound and gagged." While the other two men attended to that task, Stone dialed Rubin's number on his cell phone and said, "All secure at the nest, Ivan. Four down with no problems."

The sign on the side of the van parked in the driveway across from Adam's house read, 'Rover's Landscaping.' One of Rubin's henchmen, dressed in tan coveralls, was trimming bushes. He looked up when another man, in a suit, pulled into the driveway and walked over to him. The man in the suit, with one hand in his pocket, said something to the gardener and they walked over and climbed in the van. After a few moments, the van pulled out leaving the man in the suit's car in the driveway.

As another Rubin team member walked his Labrador retriever past Packard Electronics, he was approached by a security guard who came out a side door. After a short conversation, the two men and the dog disappeared into the plant.

A van with dark-tinted windows was parked on a side street adjacent to Packard Electronics. A man walked down the street toward the van, carrying a long narrow package. Another man walked casually from the other direction and on the other side of the street. When they had each reached a point even with the van, the man with the package stepped up onto the lawn of a house, removed the paper and took a prone firing position, aimed at the van, with what looked like a bazooka. The other man pulled a cell phone from his pocket and put it to his ear. The door of the van opened almost immediately and the occupant of the van accompanied the two pedestrians to the front door of Packard Electronics and disappeared within.

The Rover's Landscaping van pulled into the underground parking garage of Packard Electronics ten minutes later. Leach's team, the good guys, had now replaced Rubin's team, the bad guys, for the final showdown.

XII

September 14th, 1999,
The Leach Safe House,
Minneapolis, MN, 3:45 p.m....

Rubin hung up the phone and turned to 'the man from New York,' saying, "That's the last of them. All of Leach's men are now under our control."

"Good, then we are ready to bring the targets to our final rendezvous, correct?" queried the man.

"That's right. Our team is on their way to the Packard home as we speak. To assure that Leach will not be tipped off by trying to contact any of the men we have captured, our inside man, Mason, is calling him to verify the security assignment for tonight. My hope is that they will go out to dinner...and it's very likely they'll want to celebrate their reunion. Since we have the Leach team's vehicles, we can follow without arousing their suspicions. Taking them *outside* of Packard's home environment will be far easier than having to raid the house. Your long wait for revenge is a matter of hours away," said Rubin smugly.

According to plan, Adam and company left their house in Adam's BMW at 6:15 p.m. They drove to Giorgio's on France Avenue. Adam dropped the party at the front door before parking the BMW. As the time for the confrontation with the man behind the scheme to kill them drew near, each of the proposed victims dealt with their own fears and concerns. Although they faced incalculable danger, to a casual observer they were a happy group enjoying a friendly dinner. Food was the last thing on their minds, but they managed to put away a good share of excellent Italian cuisine. They exited Giorgio's at 8:10 and as they stepped from the restaurant, five armed men hustled them into Leach's Chevy Suburbans.

They drove down the alley behind Leach's safe house at Vincent and West 60th. Both vehicles parked in the space in front of the detached double garage. The group of ten then marched to the back door and down a narrow stairway. The basement was just that…unfinished, musty and with cobwebs that would have done a Halloween party proud.

Five chairs were lined up on a large plastic sheet with a makeshift desk and chair facing them. Adam, Belinda, Amy, Mack and Leach, blindfolded with their hands tied behind them, were placed unceremoniously in the chairs. The five 'captors' stood silently behind them. After several minutes, Adam said, "We've apparently been invited to a party. When do the festivities begin?"

"Soon enough, so relax and enjoy the peace and quiet…while you can," replied an ominous voice, which Leach recognized as Mason's. They heard footsteps on the stairs, first a normal tread, then the heavy step of a large person, finally the sound of a person landing on just one foot.

They heard a wheeze from what must have been the heavy person as he said in a booming voice Adam recognized instantly. "Well, I finally have you all together…for a special reunion or, if you prefer, a day of reckoning. I want you to know how I have longed for this day. To finally pay back the people who ruined my life! Before I have the pleasure of ending *your* lives, I want you to know that JoAnn Cleveland was not behind the plot to kill General Rayburn. Nor was she behind Ball's aborted attempts to kill you." The man motioned to the men at the back of the room and the five blindfolds were simultaneously removed. "I was the power behind *all* of it!" They blinked at the harsh light and recognized a grossly inflated version of an old nemesis, *Gordon Foote.*

Always a huge man at 6' 7" and well over 250 pounds, he now looked to be approaching 400 pounds with jowls that reached almost to his shoulders. The gruff voice continued. "During my years in prison, I spent a great deal of time considering how I would take your lives and I devised a perfect plan. By utilizing a hatred scale, I will start with the one I have the least hatred for and gradually work up to the top…that would be Adam Packard. Since I have two pistols, each with fourteen rounds, I will put five bullets in each of you until Packard…you get eight. So you can appreciate the suffering I endured at your hands, you will each receive painful but non-lethal wounds until the last one, between the eyes. Doesn't that sound like a jolly party?"

"It sounds like the plan of a very sick man," said Belinda. "You need help…the kind JoAnn is receiving. Put down the guns, Gordon, and I promise you will not be harmed…you'll receive the help you need."

Foote stood, waving the pistols, "What, and miss the chance of a lifetime? They say revenge is sweet, but no one will ever know how sweet this is for me."

"I have a question, Gordon," said Adam. "If you were behind all this, tell us how you arranged the General's death."

"Ha, you thought you had that figured out…Rains is chasing a terrorist group from Libya. You ferreted out Johansen, but the person that worked that caper is still in place, deep in the bowels of the CIA."

"Since we're letting it all hang out here, you mind telling who it is?" asked Adam.

Foote hesitated momentarily and then said, "It gives me great pleasure to rub your nose in it by revealing that the *real* mole in the CIA is my sister. My dear baby sister is Dennis Rains' very own executive assistant. She knows everything that goes on, including who the renegade agents are and how to get to them. The whole thing was a CIA operation. How do you like them apples*?"*

"So everything we did…with Rains…you knew about. I'm surprised you weren't successful before this," said Adam incredulously.

"I didn't underestimate you after the Right Brigade affair," said Foote. "I simply *over*estimated the capability of the people I sent against you. I am, however, very happy that you survived…so you could meet your maker in this miserable place, by my hand! Now since I have almost nothing against her, I will start with the lovely Mrs. Rogers. Where would you like the first bullet, dear?"

Foote began raising the gun and said, "How about a kneecap for starters?"

Adam whipped his Glock from behind his back and fired. The report of the 9MM weapon was deafening in the closed space. Foote dropped the weapon, blood streaming from his hand. As he started to raise the gun in his other hand. Adam shouted, "Drop it…now!" Foote paid no heed and three ear-splitting shots rang out. One from Adam's gun, hitting Foote's forearm, and two to the head from a gun behind them. Foote's lifeless body slumped to the floor.

Adam turned and demanded, "Who fired those shots?"

Ivan Rubin, with a smoking gun in his hand, admitted, "I did. I couldn't take the chance, I was afraid he was going to kill you."

"We agreed that I was the only one shooting from our side of the table," said Adam in an angry voice. "Are you sure you didn't have another agenda?"

"No, I've been 100% on your side since my meeting with Leach. Besides, there is no way I could let that sick bastard live to seek *another* revenge."

While Leach supervised the wrapping of Foote's body in the plastic tarp, Belinda put her hand on Adam's shoulder and said, "Adam, it's probably better this way. The monster Gordon Foote had become deserved no less than what he got." After a pause, she continued, "How are you going to handle the details…the body? Will the FBI clean it up?"

"I'm calling Rains, right now. He has to nail the sister and get her to rat out the CIA mutts that did in Rayburn. Then I'll tell him about our little problem with Foote. I'm more than a little pissed at the Company and I'm going to dump this in his lap."

Belinda's thoughts turned to her lifelong friend and mentor, Arthur Rayburn. His life had been sacrificed in the war against the Right Brigade, Ball and the others. Was the victory worth the cost? Someday, perhaps she'd know the answer to that question. She was jolted back to reality as Amy took her arm and asked, "Are you all right, Belinda?"

She gave her friend a wan smile, took her in her arms and said, "Oh, Amy, I was thinking about General Rayburn…what a tragic loss. He meant so much to so many people. I suppose we should be happy that this is finally over, but we have *all* paid such a heavy price."

"No one has paid the price you have, Belinda. But now, it's time to put it all behind us," said Amy with a consoling tone and a smile, "and turn our thoughts to a certain event that transpires in just four days."

"Easier said than done, but you're right, we need to buck up. For starters, let's get out of this horrid basement."

When they reached the kitchen, Adam was switching off his cell phone. "I reached Rains at home and told him the whole story. He's sending agents to pick up Catherine *Foote* Cartwright at once. He's also working on a cover story with the FBI…to explain Foote's death. Let's go back to the house and we'll sort out the particulars…over a stiff drink."

"Great idea," inserted Leach. "I'll send some of the boys over to the safe house and have them wait for our instructions. What about Rubin and Stone?"

"Send 'em home for the night. Tell them to come to the office at ten tomorrow morning with all their records. We'll settle up with them then."

"Done, you go ahead. I'll have the boys drop me off after we look in at Rubin's fortress." After he arrived, Leach had a short phone conversation with Adam. He then instructed his men to gather any weapons, untie Rubin's crew, and when they came to, tell them they would be paid off the next day and were free to go back to where they came from.

It was after ten o'clock when the five comrades-in-arms gathered at the round table in the great room of Adam's house. To varying degrees, all had been shaken by the chaotic climax they witnessed. The tension was broken by Mack. "Man, that was some party you threw, Al. I don't know if we want to attend any more of your little get-togethers."

Leach replied with uncharacteristic seriousness, "I agree, Mack. Maybe I'm getting too damn old for this kind of crap."

"I think we all could use a little peace and quiet," said Amy. "But I'm curious, "What are you planning to do with Rubin's people?"

"Well," said Adam, "they really haven't committed any crime. The best thing to do is pay them off and send them on their way." He turned to Leach. "We may want to work with Stone. I'm impressed with how he handled himself. Maybe we should consider hiring him."

"It's a thought. I'll check him out, see if he fits anyplace," said Leach as he raised his bottle of Heineken. "I'd like propose a toast to *everyone* at this table. We have schemed, plotted and fought side by side, and for my part, I have never served with a better outfit."

"I'll second that," said Mack with his bigger-than-life grin. "I think the next four days are going to be damn special. Here's a special toast to Adam and Belinda."

"They need our support, poor darlings," teased Amy. "Two unattractive people that don't know where their next meal is coming from, having to live in this hovel, our hearts go out to you."

"Enough," demanded Belinda. "I truly love each of you and I want to say, coming from Al, that was probably the biggest compliment any of us have ever received. Now, before we break an arm patting ourselves on the back, I suggest we hit the sack...like the 6th of June, 1944, it really has been *the longest day*."

Breakfast was an event. The tensions of the previous day melted away and the bright sunshine erased the terrors of the night. Amy and Belinda assisted Chef Packard as he constructed another omelet *extraordinaire*. Mack manned the toaster and Leach squeezed oranges. All of these elements came together at precisely 8 a.m. and the patter was as bright as the sun streaming in the windows.

Adam's BMW was retrieved by Leach's crew, and he and Leach left for the office at nine o'clock. An hour later, Belinda drove Amy and Mack to the FBI safe house to pick up the children.

Ivan Rubin and Lance Stone were shown into Adam's office just after ten o'clock. Adam addressed Rubin with, "I am prepared to make the final payment owed by Gordon Foote plus the bonus Mr. Leach discussed with you. I assume you came prepared to submit an accounting of your income and expenses related to this project?"

"Yes, I believe you'll find everything in order," Rubin replied as he passed a file folder to Adam.

Adam opened and studied the file for a moment, hit the intercom button on his phone and said, "Marsha, would you please come in and copy a file for me?" He turned to Rubin and continued, "To save time, I'd like my associate Mr. Leach to go over your file at the same time. By the way, I plan to give you the benefit of the doubt regarding your claim, but you should know that I will be gathering *all* of Mr. Foote's records and if they don't agree...I will, of course hold you accountable. Is that understood?"

"Mr. Packard, since I have had the opportunity to work with you and your associates," he cast a furtive glance at Leach, "I have developed a healthy respect for your capabilities. There is no way I would *consider* cheating you."

"That's good to hear," said Adam. The phone rang and Adam answered. His assistant informed him that Dennis Rains was on the line. He said, "I'll take it out there," turned to his guests and said, "If you'll excuse me, I have an important call. I'll be right back."

The tone of Rains' voice clearly indicated his mood, one of success. "Adam, I know it's been a long, long road, but you can finally hang up your musket and powder horn. When Catherine learned that Foote had given her up, she fell apart. The fact that he betrayed her seemed to bother her more than his death. We also have the two renegade agents and although they haven't talked, she gave me enough to nail 'em without a confession."

"That's terrific news, for all of us. Did somebody pick up a package last night?" asked Adam.

"Yes, it went according to plan."

"I have one final favor to ask," said Adam. "I want to get my hands on all of Foote's records. Correspondence, telephone, and particularly, financial records. Any problem?"

"These things are always a problem, but one I can handle, and I do owe you. I should be able to assemble the info in a few days," Rains said.

"Thank you. By the way, will we see you on Saturday?"

"Of course, I wouldn't miss your wedding for anything. You two are very special people. If I ever run into an unsolvable problem, I'll come to you for help."

"I appreciate those kind words." Adam responded. "For the moment, Belinda and I plan to take a stab at living a normal, comfortable life. If we should get bored, we'll let you know. See you Saturday."

Adam returned to his office and with a smile said, "Good news, everything is taken care of out east. Now, let's have a look at the damage." Leach was already poring over the information provided by Rubin. Adam studied the expense reports and after a few minutes said, "This looks reasonable. Are you in agreement, Al?"

"No problem," replied a suddenly magnanimous Leach, who had little problem spending Adam's money. "We'd like to have a little chat with you, Lance. Who knows, we might be able to use your services around here someplace."

Stone spoke for the first time since his arrival, "I'm cool with that."

Adam asked Rubin, "One last thing. Do we have any ongoing problem or threat from any of your people?"

"Absolutely not. First, they hold your ability and toughness in high esteem. Second, I will make it very clear that any action against you or your people will be considered an act against me. They know I can gather dangerous forces to repay any such acts."

"Good," said Adam as he wrote some names and numbers on a sheet of paper. "Al, would you please take Mr. Stone to your office for an interview?" He handed the paper to Leach and continued, "On your way, would you be good enough to hand this to Bill Strong and ask him to bring the checks back to me?"

"Sure," replied Leach. "Mr. Stone, come with me."

When the financial details were completed, Adam stood and said, "Mr. Rubin, if we should ever need services such as you render, how can I contact you?"

Ivan Rubin reached into his suit coat pocket and produced an embossed calling card. "You can reach me anytime of the day or night on my satellite cell phone. I would consider it an honor to serve you." With this, he gave a slight bow and left the office.

At noon, Adam called Leach's office and said, "Al, take care of any last minute details with Rubin's entourage. I'm off to see about a wedding."

XIII

September 18th, 1999, Adam Packard's Home, Edina, MN, 4:00 p.m....

A huge tent stood in back of the 100 chairs set for the wedding ceremony. It had a wooden floor and was set with tables of white linen, boasting silver and elegant glassware. Blown-glass centerpieces were filled with roses of several colors and the bandstand was flanked by lavish floral displays.

A rose-covered trellis marked the entrance and a winding stone path had been laid, just for the occasion, leading to the outdoor wedding chapel. The guests began arriving at 5:30, the organ struck up its first chord at six and by 6:15, the chairs were nearly full.

At precisely six-thirty, the processional began. Belinda's sister, Melanie, was followed by Adam's sister, Judy and finally, matron of honor Amy Rogers. All were resplendent in orchid dresses. Adam, Mack, Leach and Vint Ford, Belinda's brother-in-law, waited patiently at the altar. Adam, with his white shirt, vest and tie, was not only handsome but looked very much 'in place' in his well-tailored black tuxedo. The others wore tuxes with black ties and appeared quite comfortable in such attire...all but Leach, that is. He constantly ran a nervous finger between his starched collar and his neck.

There was a hush over the audience as the notes of "The Wedding March" reverberated over the yard. As Belinda, dressed in a magnificent white gown, was accompanied down the aisle by her mother and father, the intakes of breath and sighs were rampant. Her beauty radiated with an ethereal glow. Her lips were parted in a smile as she nodded to guests on both sides of the aisle. Her parents gave her a parting kiss as they turned her over to a smiling Adam. He took both her hands in his and looked deeply and lovingly into her eyes for several moments before turning to the altar and the waiting pastor.

The traditional words were recited until it was time for them to declare their vows. When the pastor said, "Do you, Belinda, take Adam to be your lawfully wedded husband, to have and to hold…"

Belinda looked at Adam with a tear in her eye, took the microphone and said, "Dear Adam, I do. I take you to be my husband, my lover and my hero…and I pledge my unconditional love to you, now and forevermore."

When it was Adam's turn, he cleared his throat, obviously touched by her words. At last he responded, "*I do*. Belinda, I have loved you from the very first day we met. I pledge to love you, keep you and honor you…with all my heart and soul…forever."

Without waiting for the pastor's instruction, they embraced and kissed with significantly more passion than was normally displayed at the altar.

The love that glowed from the two of them was so intense that tears were in the eyes of virtually every person in attendance. When the pastor smilingly said, "It gives me great pleasure to introduce, Adam and Belinda Packard," the sniffling turned to thunderous applause.

The reception was joyful, elegant and in the eyes of a few, a bit too long. At the insistence of Adam's father, George, the dinner was catered by the Lake Elmo Inn and drew raves from the now very happy throng. The speeches, kicked off by best man Mack Rogers went on and on. The newlyweds were relieved when Mack announced the start of the dance …shutting down the seemingly endless parade of *would be* poets and comedians.

Adam and Belinda took to the floor and danced to the CD of George Straight's "Cross My Heart." Parents and the wedding party joined them and Vic Tedesco's eight piece band rocked the neighborhood until well after midnight.

When Belinda finally asked Adam to help her out of her gown, she leaned against him and said, "this was the *best* day of my life. I never thought it would happen. Adam, thank you. Thank you for loving me, thank you for rescuing me and thank you for just being *you*." She put her arms around him and whispered in his ear, "Now I'd like to prove just how much I appreciate your heroic deeds…and you!"

Adam swept her up and carried her to their bed. "My dear, there is nothing on this earth I would rather do…than accept your graditude."

ABOUT THE AUTHOR

An avid reader of all kinds of fiction, Milt Klohn cut his author's teeth in the fields of banking and politics. He grew up in the Groveland Park neighborhood of St Paul, MN, and spent two years in the Army as a Sergeant in the Signal Corps. Returning to civilian life, he did a stint as an interior designer before embarking on a long career in banking. Along with lengthy service on health care boards, he conducted intensive lobbying of community banking issues at the state and national level. Four children and seven grandchildren later, he now lives with his wife, Dorothy in Lake Elmo, MN.